10

True Confessions

True Confessions

Rachel Gibson

First published in 2001
by AVON BOOKS
An imprint of HARPERCOLLINS PUBLISHERS, USA

First published in Great Britain in 2007
by LITTLE BLACK DRESS
An imprint of HEADLINE PUBLISHING GROUP

1

Cataloguing in Publication Data is available from the British Library

ISBN 978 0 7553 3738 5

Typeset in Transit511BT by Avon DataSet Ltd,
Bidford-on-Avon, Warwickshire

Printed and bound in Great Britain by
Clays Ltd, St Ives plc

Headline's policy is to use papers that are natural, renewable and recyclable
products and made from wood grown in sustainable forests. The logging and
manufacturing processes are expected to conform to the environmental
regulations of the country of origin.

HEADLINE PUBLISHING GROUP
An Hachette Livre UK Company
338 Euston Road
London NW1 3BH

www.littleblackdressbooks.co.uk
www.headline.co.uk

This book is dedicated
with much appreciation
to the big Kahuna
for his exhaustive hours of research.

Face of God Photographed in Clouds

There were two universal truths in Gospel, Idaho. First, God had done His best work when He'd created the Sawtooth Wilderness Area. And except for the unfortunate incident of '95, Gospel had always been heaven on earth.

Second – a truth just as adamantly believed as the first – every sin known to heaven and earth was California's fault. California got the blame for everything, from the hole in the ozone to the marijuana plant found growing in the Widow Fairfield's tomato garden. After all, her teenage grandson had visited relatives in L.A. just last fall.

There was a third truth – although it was viewed more as an absolute fact – come every summer, fools from the flatlands were bound to get lost amid the granite peaks of the Sawtooth Mountains.

This summer, the number of lost hikers rescued was already up to three. If the count stayed at three, plus one more fracture and two more cases of altitude sickness, then Stanley Caldwell would win the Missing Flatlander Betting Pool. But everyone knew Stanley was an optimistic fool. No one, not even his wife – who'd put her money on eight missing, seven fractures, and had thrown in a few cases of poison oak for excitement – expected Stanley to win the kitty.

Almost everyone in town played the pool, each trying to outdo the other and win the sizable pot. The betting pool gave the people of Gospel something to think about besides cattle, sheep, and logging. It gave them something to talk about besides tree-hugging environmentalists, and something to speculate over besides the possible paternity of Rita McCall's brand-new baby boy. After all, though Rita and Roy had been divorced going on three years now, that alone didn't put him out of the running. But mostly, the pool was a harmless way for the locals to pass the hot summer months while they pulled in tourist money and waited for the relative calm of winter.

Around the beer case at the M & S Market, conversation centered around fly-fishing versus live-bait fishing, bow hunting versus 'real' hunting, and, of course, the twelve-point buck the owner of the market, Stanley, had shot back in '79. The huge varnished antlers hung behind the battered cash register, where they'd been on display for more than twenty years.

Over at the Sandman on Lakeview Street, Ada Dover still talked about the time Clint Eastwood had stayed in her motel. He'd been real nice and he'd actually spoken to her, too.

'You have a nice place,' he'd said, sounding just like Dirty Harry; then he'd asked for the location of the ice machine and for some extra towels. She'd about died right behind the check-in counter. There was some speculation on whether or not his daughter with Frances Fisher had been conceived in room nine.

The citizens of Gospel lived and breathed the latest gossip. At the Curl Up and Dye Hair Studio, the favorite topic of conversation was always the sheriff of Pearl County,

Dylan Taber, usually because the owner herself, Dixie Howe, dropped his name while chatting over a shampoo and set. She'd cast her line in his direction and planned to reel him in like a prize trout.

Of course, Paris Fernwood was angling *her* bait in Dylan's direction, too, but Dixie wasn't worried. Paris worked for her daddy at the Cozy Corner Café, and Dixie didn't consider a woman who served coffee and eggs serious competition for a businesswoman like herself.

There were other women vying for Dylan's attention as well. There was a divorced mother of three over in the next county, and probably others Dixie didn't know about. But she wasn't worried about them, either. Dylan had lived for a time in L.A., and he'd naturally appreciate someone with flash and cosmopolitan polish. In Gospel, there wasn't anyone with more flash than Dixie Howe.

With a Virginia Slims cigarette clamped between two fingers, the light catching on her bloodred nails, Dixie settled back in one of the two black vinyl salon chairs and waited for her two o'clock cut and color.

A thin stream of smoke curled from her lips as she thought of her favorite subject. It wasn't just that Dylan was about the only eligible man over the age of twenty-five and under fifty within seventy miles. No, he had a way of looking at a woman. A way of tilting his head back a fraction and gazing through those deep green eyes of his that made her tingle in all the right places. And when his lips slid into a slow, easy smile, all those tingling places just pooled and melted.

Dylan had never set foot inside the Curl Up and Dye, choosing instead to drive all the way to Sun Valley to get his hair cut. Dixie didn't take it personally. Some men were just peculiar about walking into a classy studio like hers for a custom design. But she'd love to run her fingers through his thick hair. Love to run her hands and mouth over all of him. Once she got the sheriff into bed, she was sure he wouldn't want to leave. She'd been told she was the best lay this side of the Continental Divide. She believed it, and it was time she made a believer out of him. It was time Dylan used his big, hard body for something other than breaking up fights at the Buckhorn Bar.

There was only one potential little storm cloud in Dixie's plans for the future, and that was Dylan's seven-year-old son. The kid didn't like Dixie. Kids usually didn't. Maybe because she generally thought they were a pain in the ass. But she'd really tried with Adam Taber. She'd bought him a pack of gum once. He'd thanked her, shoved about ten sticks in his mouth, then ignored her. Which would have been just dandy if he hadn't plopped his skinny butt on the couch between her and his daddy.

Dixie wasn't worried about Adam, either. She had a new plan. This morning she'd heard from Dylan's secretary, Hazel, that he'd bought a puppy for his son. Dixie figured that after she closed the shop for the day, she'd go home and squeeze her biggest assets into a skimpy halter. She'd swing by with a big, juicy bone for the new dog. That finally ought to get the kid's attention. Just like her double D's ought to finally get his daddy's attention. If Dylan didn't notice and take advantage of what she offered him, then he was just plain queer.

Of course, she knew he wasn't. Back in high school, Dylan Taber had been a wild man, tearing up the streets of Gospel in his black Dodge Ram, one hand on the wheel, the other on some lucky girl's thigh. Most, but not all, of the time, that lucky girl had been Dixie's older sister, Kim. Dylan and Kim had what Dixie would call a real fire-and-ice relationship. It was either hot or cold. Nothing in between. And when it was hot, it heated up Kim's bedroom like an inferno. Back then, Dixie's mother spent most of her time at one of the local bars, and Kim had taken full advantage of her absence – not that her mother would have noticed if she had been home. Before she'd become born-again, Lilly Howe had spent most of her time drinking, drunk, or passed out.

Dixie might have been only eleven at the time, but she'd known what the sounds coming from the other side of the bedroom wall meant. The choppy breaths, deep throaty moans, and sighs of pleasure. At eleven, she'd known enough about sex to figure out what her sister was doing. But it wasn't until several years later that she could appreciate how long they'd made those springs squeak.

Dylan was thirty-seven, the sheriff of Pearl County, and he had a son to raise. He was respectable, but Dixie would bet her last bottle of blond hair dye that beneath the uniform, he was as wild as ever. Dylan Taber was a big man in the community now, and the rumor around town was that he was big where it counted, too. It was time she found out for herself.

While Dixie schemed, the object of her fantasies pulled his black Stetson low on his forehead and stepped off the warped porch of the sheriff's office. Heat rose in waves from the black asphalt and the hoods of vehicles parked up and down Main Street. The smell of it filled his nostrils.

'The hikers were last sighted about halfway up Mount Regan,' Dylan informed his second-in-command, Deputy Lewis Plummer, as they moved to the sheriff's brown-and-white Blazer. 'Doc Leslie is already on her way up there, and I've radioed Parker to meet us at the base camp with the horses.'

'A trek into the wilderness just isn't how I wanted to spend my day,' Lewis complained. 'It's too damn hot.'

Usually, Dylan didn't mind helping in the search for missing backpackers. It got him out of the office and away from the paperwork he hated. But he'd been kept awake most of the night by Adam's puppy, and he wasn't looking forward to a nine-thousand-foot climb. He walked to the driver's side of the Blazer and shoved a hand inside the pocket of his tan pants. He pulled out the 'cool' rock Adam had given him that morning and stuck it in his breast pocket. It wasn't even noon yet, and his cotton uniform was already stuck to his back. Shit.

'What in the hell is that?'

Dylan glanced across the top of the Chevy at Lewis, then turned his attention to the silver sports car driving toward him.

'He must have taken a wrong turn before he hit Sun Valley,' Lewis guessed. 'Must be lost.'

In Gospel, where the color of a man's neck favored the color red and where pickup trucks and power rigs ruled the roads, a Porsche was about as inconspicuous as a gay rights parade marching toward the pearly gates.

'If he's lost, someone will tell him,' Dylan said as he shoved his hand into his pant pocket once more and found his keys. 'Sooner or later,' he added. In the resort town of Sun Valley, a Porsche wasn't that rare a sight, but in the wilderness area, it was damn unusual. A lot of the roads in Gospel weren't even paved. And some of those that weren't had potholes the size of basketballs. If that little car took a wrong turn, it was bound to lose an oil pan or an axle.

The car rolled slowly past, its tinted windows concealing whoever was inside. Dylan dropped his gaze to the iridescent vanity license plate with the seven blue letters spelling out MZBHAVN. If that wasn't bad enough, splashed across the top of the plate like a neon kick-me sign was the word 'California' painted in red. Dylan hoped like hell the car pulled an illegal U and headed right back out of town.

Instead, the Porsche pulled into a space in front of the

Blazer and the engine died. The driver's door swung open. One turquoise silver-toed Tony Lama hit the pavement and a slender bare arm reached out to grasp the top of the doorframe. Glimmers of light caught on a thin gold watch wrapped around a slim wrist. Then MZBHAVN stood, looking for all the world like she was stepping out of one of those women's glamour magazines that gave beauty tips.

'Holy shit,' Lewis uttered.

Like her watch, sunlight shimmered like gold in her straight blond hair. From a side part, her glossy hair fell to her shoulders without so much as one unruly wave or curl. The ends so blunt they might have been cut with a carpenter's level. A pair of black cat's-eye sunglasses covered her eyes, but couldn't conceal the arch of her blond brows or her smooth, creamy complexion.

The car door shut, and Dylan watched MZBHAVN walk toward him. There was absolutely no overlooking those full lips. Her dewy red mouth drew his attention like a bee to the brightest flower in the garden, and he wondered if she'd had fat injected into her lips.

The last time Dylan had seen his son's mother, Julie, she'd had that done, and her lips had just sort of lain there on her face when she talked. Real spooky.

Even if he hadn't seen the woman's California plates, and if she were dressed in a potato sack, he'd know she was big-city. It was all in the way she moved, straight forward, with purpose, and in a hurry. Big-city women were always in such a hurry. She looked like she belonged strolling down Rodeo Drive instead of in the Idaho wilderness. A stretchy white tank top covered the full curves of her breasts and a pair of equally tight jeans bonded to her like she was a seal-a-meal.

'Excuse me,' she said as she came to stand by the hood of the Blazer. 'I was hoping you might be able to help me.' Her voice was as smooth as the rest of her, but impatient as hell.

'Are you lost, ma'am?' Lewis asked.

She blew out a breath through those deep red lips that on closer inspection appeared to be completely natural. 'I'm looking for Timberline Road.'

Dylan touched the brim of his hat with the tip of his forefinger and pushed the Stetson to his hairline. 'Are you a friend of Shelly Aberdeen's?'

'No.'

'Well, now, there isn't anything out on Timberline but Paul and Shelly Aberdeen's place.' He took his mirrored sunglasses from his breast pocket and slipped them up the bridge of his nose. Then he folded his arms over his chest, rested his weight on one foot, and lowered his gaze down the slim column of her throat to her full, rounded breasts and smiled. Very nice.

'Are you sure?' she asked.

Was he sure? Paul and Shelly had lived in that same house since they'd first got married, about eighteen years ago. He chuckled and raised his gaze to her face once more. 'Fairly sure. I was just out there this morning, ma'am.'

'I was told Number Two Timberline was on Timberline Road.'

'Are *you* sure about that?' Lewis asked as he glanced across the light bar at Dylan.

'Yes,' the woman answered. 'I picked up the key from the realtor in Sun Valley, and that's the address he gave me.'

Just the mention of that house conjured up some wild memories in people's minds. Dylan had heard the house finally sold to a real estate property manager, and apparently the company had found a sucker.

'Are you sure you want Number Two Timberline?' Lewis clarified, turning his attention to the woman in front of him. 'That's the old Donnelly place.'

'That's right. I leased it for the next six months.'

Dylan pulled his hat back down his forehead. 'No one's lived there for a while.'

'Really? The realtor never told me that. How long has it been empty?'

Lewis Plummer was a true gentleman, and one of the few people in town who didn't outright lie to flatlanders. Lewis had also been born and raised in Gospel, where prevarication was considered an art form. He shrugged. 'A year or two.'

'Oh, a year or two isn't too bad if the property has been maintained.'

Maintained, hell. The last time Dylan had been in the Donnelly house, thick dust covered everything – even the bloodstain on the living room floor. MZBHAVN was in for a rude shock.

'Do I just follow this road?' She turned and pointed down Main Street where it curved along the natural outline of Gospel Lake. Her fingernails had that two-tone French manicure that Dylan had always thought was kind of sexy.

'That's right,' he answered. From behind his mirrored glasses, he slid his gaze to the natural curves of her slim hips and thighs, down her long legs to her feet. One corner of his mouth turned up, and he fought to keep from laughing outright at the peacocks painted on her silver-toed boots. He'd never seen anything like them this side of a rodeo queen. 'Keep driving about four miles until you come to a big white house with petunias in the window boxes and a swing set in the yard.'

'I love petunias.'

'Uh-huh. Turn left at the house with the petunias. The Donnelly place is right across the street. You can't miss it.'

'I was told the house was gray and brown. Is that right?'

'Yeah, that's how I'd describe it. What do you think, Lewis?'

'Yep. It's brown and gray, all right.'

'Great. Thanks for your help.' She turned to leave, but Dylan's next question stopped her.

'You're welcome, Ms –?'

She stared at him for a prolonged moment before she answered, 'Spencer.'

'Welcome to Gospel, Ms Spencer. I'm Sheriff Taber and this is Deputy Plummer.' She said nothing and he asked, 'What are you planning to do out there on Timberline Road?' Dylan figured everyone had a right to privacy, but he also figured he had the right to ask.

'Nothing.'

'You lease a house for six months and you plan to do nothing?'

'That's right. Gospel seemed like a nice place to vacation.'

Dylan had a doubt or two about her statement. Women who drove fancy sports cars and wore designer jeans vacationed in 'nice' places with room service and pool boys, like Club Med, not in the wilderness of Idaho. Hell, the closest thing Gospel had to a spa was the Petermans' hot tub.

'Did the realtor mention old Sheriff Donnelly?' Lewis asked.

'Who?' Her brows scrunched together and dipped below the bridge of her sunglasses. She tapped an impatient hand three times on her thigh before she said, 'Well, thank you, gentlemen, for your help.' Then she turned on her fancy boots and marched back to her sports car.

'Do you believe her?' Lewis wanted to know.

'That she's here on vacation?' Dylan shrugged. He didn't care what she did as long as she stayed out of trouble.

'She doesn't look like a backpacker.'

Dylan's gaze settled on her behind in those tight jeans. 'Nope.' The thing about trouble was, it always had a way of showing itself sooner or later. No reason to go looking for it when he had better things to do.

'Makes you wonder why a woman like her leased that old house,' Lewis said as Ms Spencer opened her car door and climbed inside. 'I haven't seen anything like her in a long time. Maybe never.'

'You don't get out of Pearl County enough.' Dylan slid behind the wheel of the Blazer and shut the door. He shoved the key in the ignition and watched the Porsche drive away.

'Did you get a load of those Tony Lamas?' Lewis asked as he got into the passenger seat.

'Couldn't miss those boots.' Once Lewis shut his door, Dylan put the vehicle into drive and pulled away from the curb. 'She won't last six minutes, let alone six months.'

'Do you want to bet?'

'Even you aren't that big a sucker, Lewis.' Dylan cranked the wheel and headed out of town. 'She's going to take one look at the old Donnelly place and keep right on driving.'

'Maybe, but I got a ten in my wallet that says she lasts a week.'

Dylan thought of MZBHAVN strolling toward him, all smooth and shiny and expensive. 'You're on, my friend.'

Bloodthirsty Bats Attack Unsuspecting Woman

Hope Spencer shut the car door behind her, folded her arms beneath her breasts, and leaned her behind against her silver Porsche. White-hot sun beat down from an endless blue sky, immediately baking her bare shoulders and the part in her hair. Not so much as a hint of a breeze touched her face or penetrated the cotton-and-Lycra tank sticking to her skin. The steady buzz of insects joined the whine of a my-man-done-me-wrong country song drifting from the lone house across the gravel road.

Hope's gaze narrowed and her Ray-Bans slid down the bridge of her nose. Number Two Timberline was brown and gray, all right. Brown where the gray paint had peeled away.

The house looked like something out of *Psycho* and absolutely nothing like the 'summer home' she'd been led to expect. True, the 'grounds' had been recently mowed. A twenty-foot perimeter around the house and a trail to the beach had been chopped down and cleared of waist-high weeds and wildflowers. From where she stood, the lake appeared a mix of light and dark greens. Sun collided with shadow and bounced off ripples as if bits of tinfoil floated on the surface. An aluminum fishing boat was tied to the sandy shore, rocking with the swell of gentle waves.

Hope pushed up her sunglasses and turned her attention to the rugged Sawtooth Mountains practically in her backyard. The view looked just like the postcards her employer had given her of the area. America the beautiful. Thick, towering pines and granite peaks reached straight up and touched the endless sky. She supposed the scented breeze and all that mountain majesty inspired awe in most people. Like God shedding His grace. Like a religious experience.

Hope trusted religious experiences about as much as she trusted Bigfoot sightings. In her line of work, she knew too much to trust tales of hairy wild men, weeping statues, or strychnine-drinking zealots. She didn't believe anyone who saw Sasquatch running through the forest or who claimed they'd found the face of Jesus on a tortilla.

Hell, one of her most successful articles, 'Lost Ark of the Covenant Found in the Bermuda Triangle,' had developed a huge religious following and spawned two equally successful stories: 'Garden of Eden Found in Bermuda Triangle' and 'Elvis Found Living in Garden of Eden in Bermuda Triangle.'

Elvis and the triangle were always a big hit with her readers.

But mostly when Hope looked at the immense mountains and wide-open space before her, she just felt small. Insignificant. Alone. The kind of alone she thought she had overcome. The kind that threatened to reach out of the dry mountain air and choke her if she let it. The only thing keeping her from feeling like the last person on the planet was the irritating tweak of steel guitar pouring from the neighbor's radio.

Hope grabbed her Bally bag from inside the car and

headed across the lumpy dirt path to the front door. Caution tempered each step of her Tony Lamas. She'd done her research. Snakes resided in this part of the country. Rattlesnakes.

The realtor had assured her that rattlesnakes stayed in the mountains, which she figured put Number Two Timberline smack-dab in Rattlesnake Central. She wondered if Walter had done this purposefully to get back at her for the trouble she'd caused him and the paper lately.

A fine layer of dust covered the porch, and the old steps creaked a bit beneath her feet, but to her immense relief, the wood felt solid. If she fell through the porch, no one would miss her for three days. Not until her deadline passed would anyone even think to look for her, and maybe not even then.

Neither her CEO and publisher nor her editor, Walter Boucher, was very happy with her at the moment. This 'working vacation' had been their idea. She hadn't produced anything good for months, and they'd strongly urged her to take in some new scenery. Somewhere that would inspire Bigfoot stories and alien articles. And, of course, there was that whole Micky the Magical Leprechaun fiasco. They were still ticked off about that one.

Hope stuck her key into the doorknob, then pushed the door open. She didn't know what she'd been expecting, but nothing happened. No knife-wielding psycho dressed up like his mother, no ghosts, no wild animals to freak her out. Nothing. Just the smell of stale air and dust, and the sun behind her spilling into the entry and lighting up the room to her right. Hope found a switch just inside the front door and flipped it on. The chandelier overhead buzzed once, then cast shimmers of light into the remaining shadows.

She shoved her sunglasses into her bag, left the door open just in case, and made her way further inside the house. To her left, the dining room was filled with heavy sideboards and an ornate china hutch. Both could benefit from a dose of lemon oil and Windex. A long table took up most of the space, and an issue of *Hunter's Digest* and a block of wood had been shoved under one leg. A fine layer of dust covered everything.

While the dining room gave off the impression of neglected elegance, the living room, to her right, resembled a hunting lodge. Overstuffed leather and wood furnishings, a televison with rabbit-ear antennae, a bearskin hanging over the rock fireplace. On the hearth stood a stuffed bobcat, teeth and claws bared. The coffee and end tables were constructed of antlers and topped with glass. And on the walls, more antlers, and dozens of impressive animal heads with huge racks were nailed above the wainscoting. Hemingway would have loved it, but Hope thought it looked like an accident waiting for a victim. She could imagine walking through this room at night and impaling herself.

Her bootheels echoed in the empty house as she made her way to the kitchen. Except for the past three years, Hope had always lived with someone. Her parents, college roommates, and then her ex-husband. Now she lived alone, and while she much preferred it, for the first time in a long time, she wished she had a big strapping man walking in front of her, shielding her from the unknown. A man she could curl into and hide behind. A man the size of the sheriff she'd met earlier. Hope was five-seven, and the sheriff had easily been half a foot taller – all broad shoulders, hard muscles, and zero body fat.

She stepped into the kitchen and turned on the light. Gold. The linoleum, the countertops, and the appliances – everything except the wrought-iron pots-and-pans rack hanging above the stove. She pulled open the oven door and discovered a dead mouse lying prostrate on the broiler pan. She let go, the door slammed shut, and she again thought of the sheriff and of how sometimes men did have their uses.

Before he'd reached for his sunglasses, Sheriff Taber's deep green eyes had studied her from a face more suited for the silver screen than the wilderness of Idaho.

He wasn't pretty-boy handsome. Pretty boys lost their looks in middle age, and there was no way anyone would ever mistake the sheriff for a boy. He was all man, a towering hunk with a smile that could easily turn a no into a yes, make a weak woman stand a bit straighter, stick her chest out a bit farther, and want to flip her hair. Hope didn't consider herself a weak woman, but even she had to admit that she'd checked her posture several times during the course of their short conversation.

She didn't know what she'd expected the law enforcement to look like in this part of the world. Maybe like the pencil-thin deputy, or maybe like Andy Griffith. A 'gee, shucks' country bumpkin. But behind those green eyes and that easy smile was an obvious intelligence that could never be mistaken for a hayseed.

Hope made her way back through the living room to the stairs leading to the second floor. She flipped the switch at the bottom of the step, but nothing happened. Either the light didn't work or the bulb was burned out. She stood for a moment gazing up into the deep shadows of the second floor; then she forced herself to walk up the darkened stairs, her heart pounding in her ears.

Sunlight spilled into the hall from four of the five open doors, and a faint smell of something slightly familiar from the edges of her childhood, like a long-forgotten memory, penetrated the hot air. Hope walked to the first room and peered inside. The heavy drapes were shut against the light from outside, but she could make out the shape of the bed and the dressers covered with drop cloths. She could see the outline of an old wardrobe, the doors thrown open. The smell intensified, bringing with it the recognition of ammonia and the faint memory of the summer of '75 – the one and only time she'd attended Girl Scout camp.

Hope reached for the light switch next to the door. There were spots on the floors and drop cloths like dried mud, and she recognized them for what they were a split second before she heard the telling squeak, the sharp, scratchy nails, and the flutter of wings from within the wardrobe.

Two shadows swept toward her, and just like she was ten again, standing in the doorway of her cabin at Camp Piney Mountain, she opened her mouth and screamed. But unlike that time twenty-five years ago, she spun around on the heels of her boots and ran like hell. This time she didn't wait for the slap of bat wings against her cheeks or the tangle of bat claws in her hair.

She flew down the stairs, past the wall of antlers, and out the front door. She was still screaming when she jumped off the porch, her feet in motion even before she landed. Her heart pounded faster than her boots, and she didn't stop until she was safely hidden on the far side of her car. Her chest ached as she crouched on her knees in the dirt, sucking hot air into her lungs.

'OhmyGod-ohmyGod-ohmyGod,' she wheezed and placed her hand on her throat. She saw spots in front of her eyes, and beneath her fingers she felt her pulse pounding at warp speed. If she didn't slow it down, she would pass out, or have a heart attack, or burst something vital in her head. She didn't want to die. Not in the dirt. Not in the wilderness of Idaho.

Hope took a deep breath and stuck her head between

her knees. She was going to kill that realtor. Just as soon as she caught her breath, she was going to jump in her car, drive to Sun Valley and mow him down. She thought of the realtor's face, and she heard laughter – real laughter – for the first time.

Hope lifted her gaze and glanced to her left at two young boys doubled over. Both were shirtless. Both wore blue nylon shorts and brown cowboy boots. One pointed at her while the other held himself as if he were trying not to wet his pants. They were having a real good time at her expense. She didn't care. She could practically feel an aneurism bursting in her head and was way beyond feeling remotely humiliated.

'You-you-you,' the one pointing at her stuttered before he collapsed in the road, laughing so hard his bony shoulders shook.

Hope raised herself enough to peer over the rear of her car toward the house. 'Did you see bats fly out after me?' she asked above their high-pitched laughter.

The boy holding himself shook his head.

'Are you sure?' She stood, then dusted off the knees of her jeans.

'Yep.' He giggled and finally dropped his hands to his sides. 'Just saw you fly out.'

She reached for her sunglasses in the purse that was no longer on her shoulder. She placed a hand on her brow to shield her eyes and looked across the dirt yard. No Bally bag. No sunglasses. No car keys. She'd obviously dropped the purse inside. Probably upstairs. By the bat room.

'Do you boys want to earn a few bucks?'

At the offer of money, the boy on the ground jumped to his feet, although he couldn't quite control his laughter. 'How much?' he managed.

'Five dollars.'

'Five dollars!' the boy who'd been holding himself gasped. 'To share or apiece?'

'Apiece.'

'Wally, we could get a bunch more darts for our guns.'

For the first time, Hope noticed the neon-orange pistols and matching rubber darts stuck in the waistbands of both boys' shorts.

'Yeah, and candy, too,' Wally added.

'What do we gotta do?'

'Go in that house and get my purse.'

Their smiles fell. 'In the Donnelly house?'

'It's haunted.'

Hope studied the faces before her. The boy named Wally had copper-red hair and was covered with freckles. The other kid looked at her from big green eyes and a face framed by short dark curls. He had a missing front tooth, and the new one was growing in a bit crooked. 'Ghosts live in there,' he said.

'I didn't see any ghosts,' Hope assured them and turned her gaze to the front door, still standing wide open. 'Just bats. Are you afraid of bats? I'd understand if you are.'

'I'm not. Are you, Adam?'

'Nope. My grandma had bats in her barn last year. They don't hurt you.' There was a pause before Adam asked his friend, 'Are you scared of ghosts?'

'Are you?'

'I'm not if you're not.'

'Well, I'm not if you're not. And besides, we got these babies.'

Hope turned her attention back to the boys and watched them load their plastic guns with rubber darts. Personally, Hope would prefer a legion of ghosts to one lone bat.

She glanced from one boy to the other. 'How old are you two?'

'Seven.'

'Eight.'

'You are not.'

'Almost. I'll be eight in a couple of months.'

'What are you going to do with those toy guns?' she asked.

'Protection,' Adam answered as he licked the suction end of the dart.

'Wait, I don't think that's a very good idea,' she said, but neither boy listened as they took off across the yard. She followed them to the foot of the porch. She'd never really been around children, and it occurred to her that maybe she ought to get permission from their parents before she sent them into a bat-infested house. 'Maybe I should talk to your mothers first before you go inside.'

'My mom won't care,' Wally said over his shoulder as the two climbed the steps. ''Sides, she's talkin' on the phone with Aunt Genevieve. Probably be a couple hours before she's off.'

'Can't call my dad. He's workin' on the mountain today,' Adam added.

The bats were probably long gone and her bag was probably just inside the door, Hope reasoned. The boys probably wouldn't get attacked and die of rabies. 'If you get scared, you run back out. Don't worry about the purse.'

They paused in the open doorway and looked back at her. Wally whispered something about ghosts, which prompted a short-lived punching match. Then he asked, 'What does your purse look like?'

'Bone leather with burgundy alligator accents.'

'Huh?'

'White and reddish brown.'

She folded her arms and watched the boys – guns raised – slowly move into the house. Lifting a hand, she once again shaded her eyes from the piercing sun and saw them move first to the left and then cross the hall into the living room. They were gone maybe half a minute before they ran back out, Hope's purse in Adam's free hand.

'Where was it?' she asked.

'In the big room with the antlers.' He handed her the bag and she reached inside for her sunglasses. She slipped them on, then slid two five-dollar bills from her wallet.

'Thank you very much.' In Hope's line of work, she'd slipped money to doormen, doctors, and dwarfs. But this was a first. She'd never paid little kids for a favor. 'You are the bravest guys I know,' she said as she handed them the money. Their eyes lit up and their smiles turned mercenary.

'If you need us to do anything else, we will,' Wally assured her as he stuck his pistol into the waistband of his shorts.

The dinner rush had hardly slowed by the time Sheriff Dylan Taber entered the Cozy Corner Café. The tint on the windows let a person see out, but from the street, they looked like silver foil wrap. If the sun hit them just right, they could burn a hole through your corneas.

On the jukebox next to the front door, Loretta Lynn sang about her Kentucky roots while Jerome Fernwood called out a pickup order from behind the grill.

The smell of fried chicken gravy and coffee assaulted Dylan's senses and made his stomach growl. He tried to keep fast-food nights at his house to a minimum, but tonight he was tired and covered with dust and the last thing he wanted was to cook dinner. Not even hot dogs and macaroni and cheese, Adam's favorite.

Finally off duty, he wanted to eat, take a long shower, and fall into bed. The shower was easily managed, but bed would have to wait for several more hours. Adam had a T-ball game in forty-five minutes, which always wound him up tight as a ball of string. Between the excitement of the game, the new puppy, and the 'cool box' Adam had bought that afternoon for his special rock collection, Dylan doubted his son would nod off before eleven.

When he'd checked in with Adam earlier, his son had told him a strange tale of bats and ghosts and a woman in 'bird boots' paying him five bucks to find her purse. If Dylan hadn't already met the woman in question, he probably wouldn't have believed Adam's story. Adam had a tendency to make up a lot of stories, but not even Adam could have made up those boots.

'Hey, there, Dylan,' Paris Fernwood called out as she rushed from behind the counter, her arms filled with plates of food.

'Hey, Paris,' he returned and reached for his black Stetson. He took it off and ran his fingers through his hair. As he moved toward a vacant stool, he exchanged 'heys' with several locals.

'What can I get for you, Sheriff?' Iona Osborn asked from behind the counter.

'The usual.' He took a seat on the red vinyl stool and placed his hat on his knee.

Iona grabbed a hidden pencil from the ten-gallon pile of wispy gray hair on her head and wrote down his order. Then she clipped it to the stainless-steel ticket wheel. 'Two fries and two cheeseburgers to go,' she yelled, even though the cook stood just on the other side of the half wall. 'One with everything, one plain with mayo only,' she added.

Without missing a turn of his spatula or looking up to see who'd placed the order, Jerome said, 'I'll get that right out to you, Sheriff.'

'I'd appreciate it.'

Iona reached for a big gray tub and began to clear the counter of dirty plates and glasses. 'So did ya find that flatlander?'

Dylan didn't even bother asking how the waitress knew police business. In Gospel, everyone just knew. Not only did Iona have the distinction of having the biggest hair in town, she was also the biggest gossip, which in Gospel was quite an accomplishment.

'We found him on the lower east face of Mount Regan. He saw all that snow and decided to do a little skiing,' he said and hooked the heel of one boot on the stool's metal rung. 'In his shorts and tennis shoes.'

Iona dumped the last glass in the gray tub, then reached for a washcloth. 'Flatlanders,' she scoffed and wiped down the counter. 'Most of 'em traipse off into the wilderness without so much as a first-aid kit.' She worked at a ketchup spot and got to the important question. 'Well, did he bust anything? Melba's bet on a heap of fractures this year.'

He knew about the Flatlander Pool, of course. He didn't play, but he figured it was all pretty harmless. 'Broke his right ankle and tore some ligaments in his knee,' he answered. 'Has quite a case of exposure, too.'

'Right ankle, you say? I bet on a sprained right ankle. Don't suppose I could claim a break as a sprain, though.'

'No, I don't suppose you can,' he said and tossed his hat on the cleaned counter.

The front door to the diner opened, setting off the cowbell tied to the knob. Loretta sang her last note, a plate broke somewhere in the rear, and Iona leaned across the counter and spoke in a loud whisper. 'She's back!'

Dylan glanced over his shoulder, and there, standing by the jukebox, looking as fresh as a peach, was MZBHAVN herself. She'd changed out of her tight jeans and into a little summer dress with little straps. She'd pulled her hair up in the back and put away her boots in favor of flat sandals that crisscrossed over her feet.

'She was in here around noon,' Iona said beneath her breath. 'Ordered a chef's salad, dressing on the side, asking all sorts of questions.'

'What kind of questions?' He turned and watched Ms Spencer walk right past him, eyes forward, as if she didn't notice the attention she attracted. Through the thick odor of grease and the evening's blue plate special, he could swear he almost smelled the scent of peaches on her skin. The hem of her dress flirted with the backs of her thighs as she moved to a booth in the back. She slid across the worn red vinyl to the corner and reached for a menu. A lock of her blond hair fell across her cheek, and she raised a hand and swept it behind her ear.

'She wanted to know if everything in her salad was fresh and she asked about available men.'

'Available men?' Hunger curled deep in the pit of Dylan's belly, and he wasn't positive it had anything to do with food this time.

'Yeah, available *young* men to clean out the Donnelly house. At least that's what she *says*.'

He turned back to Iona. 'And you don't believe her?'

The waitress's lips pursed with disapproval. 'I called Ada over at the motel, and sure enough, the woman checked in there. I guess she made a long-distance call from the lobby. Ada says she made a big stink, yelling and cursing and carrying on about weeds and dirt, and I guess the place is full of bat— you know what, but she didn't say "you know what." Ada says she has a foul mouth and a bad temper. Ada also said the woman started right away asking about available men, even before the ink was dry on her paperwork. She isn't wearing a wedding ring. So she's probably divorced, and she told us if we knew anyone interested in helping her that she's staying at the Sandman Motel for a few days. Sounds to me like she's lookin' to start things up out there again.'

Which Dylan figured was one of the dumbest things he'd heard in a while, but it didn't surprise him. Even after five years, people in town still loved to talk about Sheriff Donnelly and the things he'd done in that old house. The unsavory details of the sheriff's personal life had been the biggest shock to hit town since the earthquake of '83. 'Sounds like she just needs help cleaning up bat droppings. Nothing wrong with that.'

Iona shoved the tub below the counter, then folded her arms across her ample bosom. 'She's from California,' the waitress said, as if no further explanation was needed. She gave one anyway. 'Ada said that when the woman was in the motel, her jeans were real tight. She didn't have a detectable panty line, so we figured she's obviously wearing thong underwear, and the only reason a woman would ever wear something that uncomfortable is to show off for men. Everyone knows those California women play fast and loose.'

Dylan looked over his shoulder and watched Paris take the blonde woman's order. Ms Spencer pointed to several different places on the menu, and by Paris's pained expression, she was obviously one of those pain-in-the-ass 'on the side' girls. Ms Spencer looked like trouble, all right, but not the kind Iona meant. Dylan unhooked his bootheel and stood. 'I guess I better go ask her about those panties,' he said. 'Can't have a woman walking around in a thong and me not knowing about it.'

'Sheriff, you're bad.' Iona giggled like a teenager as he walked away, across the red-and-white linoleum, to the booth in the back.

When Ms Spencer didn't look up, he said, 'Hello, there, heard you've had a real rough day.'

She gazed up at him then. Looked at him through the clearest blue eyes he'd ever seen. Blue the color of Sawtooth Lake. So clear he could see the bottom.

'You heard about my problem?'

'I heard about your bats.'

'I guess good news travels fast.'

She didn't ask if he'd like to sit, and he didn't wait for an invitation. He slid into the seat across from her. 'My son is one of the boys you paid to retrieve your purse.'

Her gaze moved over his face and she said, 'Then Adam must belong to you.'

'Yes, ma'am.' He settled back in the bench seat and folded his arms across his chest. Her expression gave nothing away. Purposely smooth, this woman was in control.

'I hope you don't mind that I hired your son.'

'I don't mind, but I think you overpaid those boys just to get your purse for you.' He made her nervous, which didn't really tell him anything. His badge made most people nervous. Could mean she had unpaid parking tickets and nothing more. It could also mean she was hiding something, but as long as she stayed out of trouble, she could keep her secrets. Hell, he understood about secrets. He had a big one of his own. 'I also hear you're looking to hire young men to help you clean out that house.'

'I didn't specify age. Frankly, I'd welcome your great-grandfather if he'd kill those damn bats for me.'

Dylan stretched his legs and his foot bumped hers. He'd crossed the boundary of her personal space, and as he suspected she would, she immediately drew her feet back and sat a bit straighter. He didn't even try to hide his smile. 'Bats won't hurt you, Ms Spencer.'

'I'll just take your word for that, Sheriff,' she said, then glanced up as Paris set a glass of iced tea and a small plate of sliced lemons on the table.

'They don't get any fresher than that.' Paris's thick brows lowered over her brown eyes. 'I just sliced them.'

The corners of Ms Spencer's lips turned up in a very insincere smile. 'Thank you.'

Dylan had grown up with Paris. Played Red Rover and kickball with her in grade school, been in most of her classes in junior high, and listened to her valedictorian speech on graduation night. He'd have to say he knew her pretty well. She was usually pretty easygoing, but somehow, MZBHAVN had managed to irritate the hell of Paris.

'Ms Spencer here is our newest citizen,' he said. 'Appears she's going to be staying out at the Donnelly place.'

'So I've heard.'

Growing up, he'd always felt a little sorry for Paris, and he'd always gone out of his way to treat her nice. She had beautiful long hair that she usually wore in a braid. Shy, she didn't talk much, and while a man could appreciate that sometimes in a woman, she also had the misfortune of being built like her father, Jerome, tall, big-boned, with man-hands. A guy could overlook a lot of physical imperfections in a woman. A big nose and linebacker shoulders were one thing, but wide hands and beefy fingers were something a man really couldn't overlook. They ranked up there with a moustache. A guy just couldn't get himself excited about kissing a girl with facial hair, and there was absolutely no way he ever wanted to look down and see man-hands reaching for his Johnson.

'Can I get you something while you wait, Dylan?' she asked.

'Nothing, thanks, honey. I'm sure my burgers are just about up.' And it probably didn't help that Paris's mother was only slightly more feminine than her father.

Paris smiled and threaded her fingers in front of her stomach. 'How did you like that raspberry cobbler I dropped off the other day?'

Dylan hated any sort of fruit with little seeds that got stuck in his teeth. Adam had taken one look at it, declared it looked 'all bloody,' and they'd thrown it out. 'Adam and I ate it with ice cream,' he lied to make her happy.

'Tomorrow's my day off and I'm making up some Amish cakes. I'll bring one by.'

'That's real sweet of you, Paris.'

Her eyes lit. 'I'm getting ready for the fair next month.'

'You planning on winning a few blue ribbons this year?'

'Of course.'

'Paris here,' he said, focussing his gaze on Ms Spencer, 'wins more blue ribbons than any other woman in the county.'

Ms Spencer raised the glass of tea to her lips. 'Oh, how thrilling for you,' she murmured before she took a drink.

Paris's brows lowered again. 'My next order is up,' she said and turned on her heel.

Dylan tilted his head to one side and chuckled. 'You've been in town less than twenty-four hours, and I see you're already making friends.'

'This town hasn't exactly sent out the Welcome Wagon.' She set the glass on the table and licked a corner of her lips. 'Of course, it may have come but I wasn't home. I was standing in the lobby of the Sandman Motel, getting abused by a woman in sponge rollers.'

'Ada Dover? What'd she do?'

Ms Spencer leaned back and relaxed a little. 'She practically needed my entire family history just to rent me a room. She wanted to know if I'd been convicted of any crime, and when I asked her if she wanted a urine sample, she told me I might not be so ornery if my jeans weren't so tight.'

Dylan remembered those jeans. They'd been tight, all right, but there were several women in town whose Wranglers were downright painful to look at. 'It's probably not personal. Ada takes her job too serious sometimes. Like she's renting out rooms at the White House.'

'Hopefully I'll be out of there by tomorrow afternoon.'

His gaze lowered to her full lips, and for a brief moment he allowed himself to wonder if she would taste as good as she looked. He wondered what it would be like to eat the lip gloss from her mouth and bury his nose in her hair. 'You still planning on staying for the whole six months?'

'Of course.'

He still had his doubts about her lasting more than a few days, but if she planned to stay, he figured he should let her know exactly what she was in for. 'Then let me give you some advice that I'm sure you don't want, and I'm equally sure you won't take.' He raised his gaze and put an end to his mind's wanderings before he embarrassed himself. 'This isn't California. People here don't care if you're from Westwood or South Central. They don't care if you own a Mercedes or an old Buick, and they don't care about where you shop. If you want to see a movie, you have to drive to Sun Valley, and unless you have a satellite dish, you get four television stations.

'We have two grocery stores, three gas stations, and two restaurants. You're sitting in one. The other is down the street, but I would advise you not to eat at the Spuds and Suds. They were shut down twice last year on account of health violations. We have two different churches and a large Four-H Club.

'Gospel also has five bars and five gun-and-tackle stores. Now, that should tell you something.'

She reached for her tea and raised it to her lips. 'What, that I've moved to a town of alcoholic, guntoting, sheep-loving Four-H'ers?'

'Oh, boy,' he said as he shook his head. 'That's what I was afraid of. You're going to be a pain in the ass, aren't you?'

'Me?' She set the glass back down and innocently placed a hand on her chest. 'I swear to God, you aren't even going to know I'm in town.'

'Somehow, I doubt that.' He rose from the booth and looked down at her. 'If you need help with the Donnelly house, ask the Aberdeen boys. They're about to turn eighteen and not doing anything this summer. They live right across the street from you out there on Timberline, but ask before noon or they'll already be out on the lake.'

Hope gazed up at the man towering over her, at his deep green eyes and the lock of brown hair that fell in an arc over his forehead. The light from the windows picked out streaks of gold that Hope would bet her Porsche were put there by the sun and not a beautician's brush. Too bad he had no sense of humor, but she supposed when a man looked like the sheriff, humor wasn't essential. 'Thank you.'

He smiled, and for the first time, she noticed that while he certainly could have been cast in a big-budget Western, his teeth weren't movie-star straight. They were white enough, yes, but they were a little bit crowded on the bottom. 'And good luck, Ms Spencer,' he drawled.

She supposed he meant she needed luck finding someone to take care of her bat problem and she hoped she didn't need luck. He headed toward the front of the diner and her gaze followed.

His tan shirt fit flat against his back and was tucked inside tan pants with a brown stripe running down the side of each leg. Those pants should have looked like a fashion nightmare, but on him they seemed to accentuate his tight glutes and long legs. He had a revolver strapped to his hip, a pair of handcuffs, and a variety of leather pouches and cases hooked to his service belt.

Even with all that leather and hardware, he managed to move with the easy grace of a man who was in no great hurry to be anywhere other than where he happened to be. He exuded the confidence and authority of a man who could take care of himself and the little woman in his life. A testosterone cocktail that some women might find irresistible. Not Hope.

She watched him reach for the cowboy hat on the counter with the same fluid motion he used to comb his fingers through his hair. He shoved the hat on his head and spoke to the older waitress near the cash register. The woman with the big hair giggled like a girl, and Hope glanced away. There had been a time in her life when she, too, might have melted just a bit beneath his slightly imperfect smile. Not any more.

She looked back one last time at the sheriff and watched the rude waitress with the long braid hand him a paper sack. The journalist side of her brain churned with questions. She'd noticed the absence of a wedding ring on the man's finger, not that that meant a damn thing, but by the conversation he'd had with the waitress, Hope would guess he wasn't married. She would also hazard a rather obvious guess that the waitress had a thing for the good sheriff. Hope wondered if they were involved, but she doubted it. From just the few moments she'd witnessed them, any feeling beyond friendship seemed to be completely one-sided and rather pathetic. If the waitress had been nicer to Hope, she might have felt sorry for her. But the waitress wasn't nice, and Hope had problems of her own.

Demonic Car Alarm
Hypnotizes Community

The hard chair in her motel room put Hope's behind to sleep. She stood, stretched her arms over her head, and yawned. Her eyes, fixed on the blank screen of her laptop, blurred and she rubbed them with the heels of her hands. Nothing. For three hours she'd sat in that chair, straining her gritty eyes, racking her tired brain for something to fill up the screen. Anything. Yet the screen remained empty. She didn't have one idea. She hadn't written one sentence. Not even one *bad* sentence she could expand into something better.

Hope dropped her hands and turned from the laptop. She flopped on the bed and stared up at the ceiling. If she were at home, she was sure she'd be scrubbing her spotless bathroom, ironing her T-shirts, or flipping her mattress. If she had her nail kit, she'd be giving herself a manicure. She'd gotten so good at it, she sometimes wondered if she should just give up writing and do nails for a living.

Giving herself manicures was only one of the many time-wasting contrivances she performed to avoid the reality of an empty screen.

One of the many time-consuming tricks she used to avoid the reality of her life. The painful reality that she had no one. No one to talk to when the nights got lonely. No one to hold her hand and tell her she was okay.

Her mother had died in the fall, and her father had remarried by spring. He'd moved to Sun City, Arizona, with his new wife to be near her family. He called. Hope called. It wasn't the same. Her only sibling, Evan, was stationed in Germany. She wrote. He wrote. That wasn't the same, either.

She'd had a husband once. For seven years she'd lived a beautiful life in a beautiful house in Brentwood, gone to lavish parties, and played a mean game of tennis. Her husband, Blaine, had been a brilliant plastic surgeon, handsome and funny, and she'd loved him desperately. She'd been secure and happy, and the last night they'd spent together, he'd made love to her as if she were the wife of his heart.

The next day, he'd had her served with divorce papers. He'd told her he was awfully sorry, but he'd fallen in love with her best friend, Jill Ellis. The two hadn't wanted to hurt Hope, but what could they do? They were in love, and, of course, Jill was five months pregnant, giving him the one thing Hope could not.

Hope no longer had a husband; had no friends, no children.

She had her career, though, and while that wasn't how she'd necessarily envisioned her life, it hadn't been so bad. At least until she'd hit the wall blocking her.

For three years she'd turned her back on her past, refusing to acknowledge the depth of her pain even to herself. She'd ignored the ruins of her life and buried herself in her work. First as a freelance writer for magazines such as *Woman's World* and *Cosmopolitan*, and she'd also done some freelance reporting for the *Star* and *The National Enquirer*. She'd done that for a year, but she hadn't really enjoyed sneaking around prying into the lives of celebrities, and besides, she'd done it for the wrong reasons anyway.

She'd quit gossip completely to take a job as a staff writer for *The Weekly News of the Universe*, one of those black-and-white tabloids that claimed Elvis was alive and well and living on Mars. No more rumor or scandal. Now she made up fictional stories. Under the pen name Madilyn Wright, she was the most popular writer at the paper, and she loved it.

That is, until two months ago, when it seemed she'd hit an invisible wall. She couldn't ignore it, couldn't go through it, and couldn't see to go around it. She was stuck. She couldn't seem to hide from it or get lost in the bizarre stories she made up in her head. She hadn't been able to write a decent sentence for a while now. Hope figured a psychiatrist could tell her what was wrong with her, but she also figured she already knew.

Her editor had become extremely anxious and had suggested Hope take a break. Not because he was a hell of a guy, but because she made him look good. She also made the paper a lot of money, and they wanted their most popular reporter back, churning out the strange and unusual.

Walter had even gone so far as to choose her vacation destiny, and the paper had paid the six months' lease on the house. Walter told her he'd picked Gospel, Idaho, because of the fresh air. That was what he'd said, but he hadn't been fooling anyone. He'd picked Gospel because it looked like the sort of place where Bigfoot hung out. Where people were routinely abducted by aliens, and where weird cults danced naked beneath a full moon.

Hope sat up on the edge of the bed and sighed. She'd agreed to Walter's plan because she recognized that her life had become stagnant, a rut she no longer enjoyed living in. She needed a new routine. She'd needed to get out of L.A. for a while. Take a break and, of course, put the entire Micky the Magical Leprechaun fiasco behind her. She needed to clear her head of that whole trial.

Without much enthusiasm, she rose, changed into a pair of flannel shorts and a Planet Hollywood T-shirt, then returned to her seat in front of the laptop. With her fingers poised above the keyboard, she stared at the blinking cursor. Silence surrounded her, heavy and complete, and before she knew it, she'd lowered her gaze to the ugly sculpted carpet beneath her feet. It was without a doubt the grossest carpet she'd ever seen, and she spent fifteen minutes trying to determine if the colors were supposed to run like that, or if a previous guest had dropped some pizza.

Just when she concluded that the carpeting was *supposed* to look splotched with deep red, she caught herself procrastinating and forced her attention back to the screen.

She stared like a hypnotized cobra, counting each blink of the cursor. She counted two hundred and forty-seven flashes when a shriek split the still night and propelled Hope to her feet.

'For the love of God,' she gasped, her heart lodging in her throat. Then she realized it was her Viper alarm and dug into the bottom of her purse for the transmitter hooked to her key ring. She shoved her feet into her sandals, then ran outside and wove her way through the small parking lot filled with pickups, minivans, and dusty SUVs with kayaks strapped to the tops.

The manager of the Sandman stood by the hood of Hope's Porsche. The sponge rollers were still in her hair, and a deep scowl narrowed her eyes as she watched Hope approach. Fellow guests looked out their windows or stood in the doorways of their rooms. Dusk had settled over

Gospel, painting deep shadows across the rugged land-
scape. The town appeared laid-back and relaxed, except for
the six tones of the Viper piercing the calm. Hope pointed
the transmitter at her car and disengaged the alarm.

'Did you see anyone trying to break into my car?' she
asked as she came to stand in front of Ada Dover.

'I didn't see anything.' Ada placed her hands on her hips
and tipped her head back to look up at Hope. 'But I about
choked on a chicken bone when that thing went off.'

'Someone probably touched the door handle or the
windows.'

'I thought it was the alarm going off down at the M and
S Market, so I called Stanley and told him someone was
breakin' into his store and to get down there huckuty buck.'

'Oh, great,' Hope groaned.

'But he says he doesn't have an alarm. Just the signs and
such so people think he does.'

Hope didn't know Stanley, but she doubted his lack of
security was something he wanted spread around town.

'I was just about to call the sheriff's Dispatch,' Ada
continued, 'but decided to find out where all the racket was
coming from first.'

The last thing Hope needed was to have the sheriff
dragged to the Sandman, not after she'd assured him he
wouldn't even know she was in town. 'But you didn't call,
right?' In L.A., no one called the police for a car alarm. On
any given day, chances were good one was going off in a
parking lot somewhere. Chances were just as good the
police were driving by and not even bothering to stop.
Didn't these people know anything?

'No, and I'm glad I didn't. I'd have felt real stupid. As it
is, I just about died on that chicken bone.'

Hope stared at the shorter woman in front of her; night
was rapidly falling and she couldn't see much more than the

outline of rollers on her head. The cool air raised the hairs on Hope's arms, and she knew she should feel a little bit bad that her Viper had caused Ada Dover to choke, but honestly, what kind of idiot chewed on a chicken bone? 'I'm sorry you almost died,' she said, even though she sincerely doubted the woman had been close to death. She glanced over her shoulder and was relieved to find that the motel guests had gone back inside and had shut their curtains.

'That thing isn't going to go off again, is it?'

'No,' Hope answered and returned her attention to the motel manager.

'Good, 'cause I can't have that thing screeching and waking up the other guests all night. These people pay good money for a quiet night's rest, and we just can't have that sort of ruckus.'

'I promise it won't go off,' Hope said, her thumb itching to engage the Viper. She turned to leave, with Ada Dover's parting shot trailing after her:

'If it does, you'll have to leave, huckuty buck.'

The woman had Hope over a barrel and she knew it. She would have loved to tell her to kiss her huckuty buck, whatever the hell that meant, but there was only one other hotel in town and Hope was sure it was as full as the Sandman. So she kept her mouth shut as she walked to her room and shut the door behind her. She tossed her keys into her purse and returned to her seat in front of her laptop.

Entwining her fingers on top of her head, she scooted down in her chair. The night before, she'd stayed at the Doubletree in Salt Lake City. She clearly remembered waking that morning in the nice, normal hotel, but at some point she must have driven into the twilight zone where women ate chicken bones.

A slow smile curved her mouth, her hands dropped to the keyboard, and she wrote:

INSANE WOMAN CHOKES TO DEATH
ON CHICKEN BONE

During a ritualistic ceremony, bizarre chicken worshiper Dodie Adams . . .

The next morning, Hope rose early, took a quick shower, and dressed in jeans and a black tank top. While her hair dried, she pulled on her boots, then plugged the telephone line into the side of her laptop and fired off her chicken-bone story. It wasn't Bigfoot, but it was good enough to print in next week's edition. Most important, she was writing again. That she had Ada Dover to thank didn't escape her, and the irony made her smile.

After she pulled her hair back in a ponytail, she drove three blocks to the M & S Market. She'd slept a total of four hours but felt better than she had in a long time. She was working again, and it felt good. She didn't even want to contemplate the possibility that it might have been a fluke, and tonight she might again face hours of a blank computer screen.

The first thing she noticed when she entered the M & S was the antlers behind the front counter. They were huge and mounted on a lacquered plaque. The second thing was the mingling scent of raw meat and cardboard. From somewhere in the back, she heard a radio tuned to a country station and the heavy whacks of what sounded like a cleaver hitting a butcher's block. Other than herself and the unseen person in back, the store appeared empty.

Hope found a blue plastic basket next to the cash register and hung it from her arm. She made a quick scan of the newspaper-and-magazine rack. *The National Enquirer,* the *Globe*, and Hope's biggest competition, the *Weekly World News*, were all stuck beside *The Weekly News of the*

Universe. She would have no byline this issue, but her chicken-bone story would appear next week. Before leaving the hotel, she'd received an e-mail from her editor, and he was rushing to put it into production.

The hardwood floor creaked beneath her feet as she made her way through the cereal and crackers aisles toward the refrigeration section.

She opened the door to the glass case and placed a pint of low-fat milk in her basket. Next, she read the sugar content on the back of an orange juice bottle. It contained more corn syrup than actual fruit juice, and she put it back. She reached for a bottle of grape-kiwi, decided at the last moment she wasn't in the mood, and grabbed cranapple instead.

'I'd have gone with the grape-kiwi,' drawled a now familiar voice from behind her.

Startled, Hope turned and the glass door slammed. Her basket swung and bumped her hip.

'Of course, grape-kiwi might be a bit wild for this time of morning,' the sheriff said. He wasn't wearing his black Stetson today. He'd replaced it with a battered straw cowboy hat that had a band made of snakeskin. A shadow from the brim fell across his face. 'You're up pretty early.'

'I've got a lot to do today, Sheriff Taber.'

He opened the glass door and forced her to take a few steps back. 'Dylan,' he said as he grabbed two pint-size cartons of chocolate milk and shoved them beneath one arm. He looked very little like the lawman of the previous day. His blue T-shirt was old and slightly wrinkled and tucked into a pair of Levi's so faded that only the seams gave a hint of the original color.

The glass door fogged except where it pressed against the back of his broad shoulders and his behind. His back pocket was torn and an edge of his wallet poked out. He bent and picked up what looked like two small Styrofoam containers of ice cream. 'Did you find someone to help you today?' he asked as he straightened.

'Not yet. I thought I'd call my neighbors like you suggested, but I wanted to wait in case they are still in bed.'

'They're up.' He moved aside and the glass door closed behind him. 'Here.' With his free hand, he held out a bottle of passion fruit. 'This is my favorite.'

She reached for it, but he didn't let go. Instead, he stepped closer until he stood just a few inches from her. 'Do you like passion fruit, Ms Spencer?'

Her finger brushed his thumb, and she looked up from their hands to his deep green eyes gazing at her from beneath the brim of his battered straw hat. She wasn't a silly country girl who got all flattered and tongue-tied over a sexy-as-hell cowboy in a pair of jeans worn thin in interesting places. 'It might be a bit early in the day for passion fruit, Sheriff.'

'Dylan,' he corrected her as a slow, easy smile curved his lips. 'And, honey, it's never too early for passion fruit.'

It was the word 'honey' that got to her. It just slid inside and warmed the pit of her stomach before she could do a thing about it. She'd heard him use the same endearment with the waitress, too, and she'd thought she was immune. She wasn't. She tried to think up a witty comeback and couldn't. He'd invaded her personal space, but she didn't know what to do about it. She was saved by the approach of his son.

'Dad, did ya get the night crawlers?' Adam asked.

Dylan dropped his hand from the bottle and took a step back. His gaze lingered on Hope for a moment longer; then he directed his attention to his son. 'Right here, buddy,' he said and held up the two Styrofoam cups.

'Those are worms?' Hope glanced from what she'd assumed were little ice-cream cups to his face.

'Yes, ma'am.'

'But they were' – she pointed to the glass case – 'next to the milk.'

'Not right next,' he assured her. He took the chocolate milk from beneath his arm and gestured toward Hope. 'Adam, say hello to Ms Spencer.'

'Hi. Do you need me to scare any more bats?'

She shook her head as she gazed from one to the other.

'What kind of doughnuts did you get for breakfast?' Dylan asked his son. 'Powdered sugar?'

'Nope, chocolate.'

'Well, I guess I can choke down a few chocolate.'

'We're going fishing for Dolly Varden,' Adam informed her.

Obviously they thought worms in the milk-and-juice case was perfectly normal. 'Dolly who?'

Deep laughter rumbled within Dylan's chest as if he were extremely amused. 'Trout,' he answered. 'Come on, son. Let's go catch some Dolly who.'

Adam laughed, a younger, childlike version of his father.

'City girls,' Dylan scoffed as he walked away.

'Yeah,' Adam added, the squeak of his rubber-soled sneakers keeping perfect time with the heavier tread of his father's worn boots.

Really, who were they to laugh at her? Hope wondered as she watched them move toward the front counter. She wasn't the crazy one who thought worms belonged next to milk. She was normal. She set the bottle of juice in her basket and made her way to the housewares aisle. Across rows of Comet and boxes of dog food, she watched a large man with a potbelly, a handlebar mustache, and a blood-smeared apron approach from the back. As he rang up Dylan's purchases, Hope moved up and down the aisles and dumped two pairs of pink rubber gloves, half a gallon of pine cleaner, and a can of Raid into her basket. In the small produce department, she smelled the peaches for freshness.

'See you around, Ms Spencer.'

She glanced up from her peaches to where Dylan stood holding the door open for Adam. He looked over at her, one corner of his mouth curved up, and then he was gone.

'Are you ready to be rung up?' the big man behind the counter asked. ''Cause if you're gonna be a while yet, I've got some meat to wrap in the back.'

'I'm ready.' She placed the peaches in a produce baggie and walked to the counter.

'Are you the woman with the car alarm?'

Hope set the basket on the counter, next to a display of cigarettes and lighters. 'Yes,' she answered warily.

'Ada called me last night when that thing went off,' he said, his big fingers pecking out the keys on the cash register.

'I'm sorry she disturbed you.'

'She nearly choked to death on a chicken bone, you know.'

Apparently Hope was the only one who found that odd.

He checked the price sticker on the Raid, then rang it up. 'Are you going to be in town long?'

'Six months.'

'Oh, yeah?' He looked up. 'Are you a tree hugger?'

'No.'

'I didn't think so.' He reached beneath the counter and pulled out a paper sack. 'You don't look like no tree hugger.'

Hope didn't know if he was complimenting her or not, so she kept quiet.

'I hear you're staying at the Donnelly place.'

'Yes, I am.'

'What are you going to do out there?'

That was the second time in two days she'd been asked that question. 'Spend a relaxing summer.'

'My wife, Melba, was over at Dixie's getting her hair kinked when Ada called from the Sandman saying you need some available men.'

'To clean the bats out of the house I leased,' she clarified. He subtotaled her purchases and she pulled a twenty from her wallet.

He looked at her closely and must have decided she was harmless, because he shook his head and smiled. 'Yeah, that's what Ada said.' He took her money, then counted out the change to her. 'Too bad. I have a nephew working the mine up near Challis, and he sure could use an available woman. 'Course, you don't look like the kind of woman who'd be interested in Alvin.'

He'd piqued her curiosity and she asked, 'What kind of woman is that?'

'A woman not in her right mind.' The ends of his mustache curled on his cheeks beneath his eyes.

'Thank you.'

'You're welcome. My name's Stanley Caldwell. Me and my wife Melba own this store, and if there's something you need in the way of a special order, just let me know.'

'I will.' She took the paper sack. 'Do you know where I can get a cappuccino?'

'Yep. Sun Valley.'

She'd never wanted a cappuccino bad enough to drive an hour for it. She thanked him anyway and left the market. Her Porsche was parked by the front doors and she dropped the sack on the passenger seat. As she pulled from the parking lot, she slipped a CD in the player, pumped up the volume, and sang along with Sheryl Crow. 'Run baby run baby run,' she sang as she drove down the main street of Gospel and continued around the lake to Timberline Road. It was just after eight when she pulled into the driveway of the house she'd leased. It looked just as bad as it had the day before.

She wasn't about to step foot inside until it was bat-free. Instead, she walked across the road and knocked on her neighbor's door. A woman with red, curly hair and freckles, and wearing a blue chintz robe, answered. Hope introduced herself through the screen.

'Dylan said you might be coming by.' She held the door open and Hope entered a living room decorated with a profusion of tole painting. It was everywhere, on pieces of driftwood, old saw blades, and metal milk jugs. 'I'm Shelly Aberdeen.' She wore big bunny slippers and could not have stood much over five feet.

'Did Sheriff Taber mention my problem with bats?'

'Yeah, he did. I was just about to wake up the boys. Why don't you have a seat and I'll tell them what you need.'

She disappeared down a hall and Hope sat in a swivel chair next to the stone fireplace. From the rear of the house she heard a door open.

'Are you the one driving a Porsche?' Shelly called out.

'Yes.'

Silence and then, 'Do you know Pamela Anderson or Carmen Electra?'

'Ahh, no.'

More silence and then Shelly reappeared. 'Well, that's a real disappointment to the boys, but they'll help you out anyway.'

Hope rose. 'How much do they usually make an hour? I don't even know what the minimum wage is any more.'

'Just pay them what you think is fair, then come back by around noon and I'll make you lunch.'

Hope didn't know what to think of the offer, other than it made her uncomfortable.

'I'll make crab-stuffed pitas and we'll get to know each other.'

That was the part that made Hope uncomfortable. Shelly

would naturally ask what Hope did for a living, and Hope didn't talk about it with people she didn't know. She didn't want to talk about her personal life, either. Yet deep in a buried part of her soul, she wanted it so much she could feel it like a bubble working to get free. And that scared her. 'I wouldn't want to put you to any trouble,' she said.

'No trouble. Unless you say no and hurt my feelings.'

Hope looked into Shelly's big brown eyes, and what could she say except, 'Okay, I'll be here.'

The Aberdeen twins, Andrew and Thomas, were tall and blond, and, except for the color of their eyes and the slight difference in the shape of their foreheads, looked exactly alike. A wad of tobacco bulged out their bottom lips in identical spots, and they both stood with their left shoulders higher than the right. They were quiet and well mannered and looked at each other first before they answered a question.

Hope had them search the house for bats while she sat on her front porch. She heard thumping and yelling from the second floor, and about forty minutes later, Thomas came out with the news that they'd found five bats altogether. Two in one bedroom and three in the attic. He spit a stream of tobacco into a Coke can he held in his hand and assured her the bats were no longer a problem. She didn't ask how. She didn't care to know.

Once the problem of the bats was solved, she put the boys to work cleaning and vacuuming the upstairs while she started in the kitchen. She cleaned the stove, tossed out the dead mouse, then washed out the oven and refrigerator. The pantry was empty except for a layer of dust, and she cleaned the dishes and pots and pans with soap she found beneath the sink. The windows could wait for another day.

By eleven thirty, the first floor of the house was close to

finished. There was a dark brown stain on the hardwood floor in front of the hearth, and no amount of scrubbing got it up. At noon, she gave the twins the task of taking down the wall of antlers and storing them in a shed out back. Then she headed across the street.

Shelly Aberdeen saw her coming and opened the front door before she had a chance to knock. 'Let's eat before the twins decide to come home for lunch. They eat like every meal is their last.'

Shelly had dressed for the day in a Garth Brooks T-shirt, tight Wranglers with a belt buckle the size of a saucer, and snakeskin boots. Hope had been in town only a day, but she'd already noticed that snakeskin was a fashion must-have in Gospel.

'How are the boys working out?' Shelly asked over her shoulder as Hope followed her into a small dining room off the kitchen.

'They're doing a good job. They're very polite and didn't even complain when I asked them to clean up the bat droppings.'

'Shoot, why would they complain about that? Those two have been tossing cow patties at each other since they could walk. Last summer they worked slaughtering cows over at Wilson Packing.' She poured Hope a glass of iced tea. 'I'm glad to hear they're minding themselves. They're going to be eighteen in about a week and think they know it all.' She handed the glass to Hope. 'How's the inside of the house look?'

Hope took a drink and let the cool tea wash the dust from her throat. 'Better than the outside. Lots of cobwebs and there was a dead mouse in the oven. The good news is that the electricity and the plumbing work.'

'They should,' Shelly said as she set two plates loaded with pita sandwiches on the table covered in a white-and-blue checked cloth. 'The realtor who bought the place this past fall had the whole place plumbed and wired. Couldn't get the bloodstain up, though.'

'Bloodstain.'

'Hiram Donnelly killed himself with his hunting rifle right in front of the fireplace. Blood went everywhere. You might have noticed the stain on the floor.'

Yes, she'd noticed that stain, but she'd assumed someone had skinned some unfortunate animal in the front room. The fact that it was a human bloodstain was kind of freaky. 'Why'd he kill himself?'

Shelly shrugged as she sat across from Hope. 'He was caught embezzling money from the county to pay for kinky sex.'

'Was he a judge?'

'No, he was our sheriff.'

Hope placed her napkin on her lap, then reached for her pita. Her curiosity piqued more than she wanted her neighbor to know, she asked as if she were inquiring about the weather, 'How kinky?'

'Bondage and domination, mostly, but he was into a lot of other weird stuff, too. A year after his wife died, he started getting hooked up with women through the Internet. I think it started out innocent enough. Just a lonely guy looking for some female company. But toward the end, he got real kinky and didn't care if the women were single or married, their age, or how much it cost him. He was out of control and got careless.'

Hope bit into her pita and tried to recall if she'd read anything about a sheriff embezzling money to pay for his sexual addiction. She didn't think so, because if she had, she would have remembered. 'When did all this happen?'

'He killed himself about five years ago, but like I said, it started about a year before that. No one in town knew it, either, not until the FBI was about to arrest him and he shot himself.'

'How out of control did he get?'

Shelly glanced away, clearly uncomfortable talking about the details. 'Use your imagination,' she said, then changed the subject. 'What brings you to Gospel?'

Hope knew when to push and when to back off. She tucked away the information and let it go for now. 'It seemed like a nice area,' she answered, then, just as neatly as Shelly, turned the subject away from herself. 'How long have you lived here?'

'My family moved here when I was about six. My husband, Paul, was born in this house. I graduated from Gospel High School with most of the people around here.' Shelly counted them off as if Hope naturally knew whom she was talking about. 'Paul and me, Lon Wilson and Angie Bright, Bart and Annie Turner, Paris Fernwood, Jenny Richards. Kim Howe and Dylan, but that was back when Dylan still lived at the Double T with his folks. His mom, sister, and brother-in-law still run the place. And, of course, Kim ran off with a trucker right after graduation and lives somewhere in the Midwest. I can't remember what happened to Jenny.' Shelly took a bite of her sandwich, then asked, 'You married?'

'No.' Hope's neighbor looked at her as if she thought Hope might elaborate. She didn't. If she mentioned the word 'divorce,' other questions would follow, and there was no way Hope would share that ugly and clichéd part of her life with anyone. Especially not a stranger. She reached for her tea and as she took a long drink, she tried to remember the last time she'd had lunch with someone, other than for business. She wasn't positive, but thought it probably had been right after her divorce. As was usual for a lot of married couples, her friends had been *their* friends, and whether they'd stopped calling or she stopped calling them didn't matter. The end result was the same. Their lives had changed and they'd drifted apart. 'Where did you live before you moved to Gospel?' she asked.

'Outside Rock Springs, Wyoming. So it wasn't much of a shock moving here. Not like I imagine it is for you.'

That was so true it made Hope chuckle. 'Well, I don't think I'm very popular at the Sandman.'

'Don't worry about Ada Dover. She thinks she's running the Ritz.' Without much of a pause, she asked, 'What do you do for a living?'

'I'm a freelance writer.' Which was partly true. In the past, she'd certainly done freelance under a lot of different pseudonyms, and if she wanted, she could again. For now, she liked writing bizarre fictional articles. Although she had to admit that she was intrigued by the bizarre history of Number Two Timberline and the sheriff who'd lived there.

'What do you write?'

Hope was asked that question a lot, and she usually fudged. Not that she was ashamed of what she did, but in her experience, people had one of three reactions. One, they were condescending, which Hope didn't appreciate but could handle. Two, they wanted to tell her about the time they'd been abducted and had an alien probe stuck up their anus. Or three, if they weren't crazy themselves, they knew someone who was. And they always wanted her to do an article on their great-aunt so-and-so who was possessed by the spirit of her dead dog.

Hope never knew when she'd run into one of these crazy people, could never tell from appearances. They were like peanut M&M's; they had a normal-looking shell but were hiding a nut inside. Hope wrote fiction and wasn't interested in real nuts.

'I write whatever interests me.' Then she did what she

did best: She added a lie into the mix of truths and half-truths. 'Right now, I'm interested in the flora and fauna of the Northwest, and I'm writing an article for a Northwest magazine.'

'Wow, a writer! That must be a really fun job.'

Fun? Hope took another bite of her sandwich and thought about Shelly's remark for a moment. 'Sometimes it *is* fun,' she said after she swallowed. 'Sometimes it's so cool I can't believe I'm doing it.'

'A couple of summers ago, we had a guy who was here writing some sort of backpacking guide. Before that, a lady wrote about bicycling trails in the Northwest. Last summer, there was someone else in the area writing about something. I can't remember what that was, though.' Shelly took a drink of her tea. 'What have you written that I might have read?'

'Let's see . . . about two years ago, I did a piece for *Cosmo* on hysterectomies.'

'I don't read *Cosmo*.'

'*Redbook*?'

'No. Have you written anything for *People*?'

'I submitted an outline once.' Hope set down her sandwich and wiped her mouth with her napkin. 'But I got a form rejection.'

'The *Enquirer*?'

Not recently, but at one time, not only had she written for them, she'd also been their 'inside source' on who had had their faces lifted and their breasts enlarged. 'No, I don't like to write articles about real people,' she said. At least not any more. She much preferred to make up stories about a fifty-pound locust.

'Hmm . . . Paul subscribes to *Guns and Ammo*. I don't suppose you ever wrote an article about elk hunting?'

Hope looked across the table at her neighbor, at the

laughter creasing the corners of Shelly's eyes, and she relaxed a bit.

'No, I don't really go in for the violent stuff, but when I was first starting out, I did write several articles for *True Crime* magazine. I needed publishing credits, so I wrote a few stories about a serial-killing hooker who got caught when traces of her victims' blood were found on her stilettos.'

'Oh, yeah? My mother-in-law reads those like the Bible and swears they're true.' Shelly leaned across the table and whispered, 'She's crazy. Last year for my birthday, she paid the first installment toward a Ronco food dehydrator, then had me billed for the rest.'

'You're kidding!'

'Nope. I had to pay over a hundred bucks for that thing, and I've never used it.' She did a one-shoulder shrug. 'But I guess it wasn't as bad as the pig cookie jar she got for my sister-in-law. You lift the lid and it squeals like Ned Beatty in *Deliverance*.'

Hope leaned back in her chair and chuckled.

'Do you have a man in your life?'

Oh, Shelly was good. Real good. Trying to get Hope to relax, soften her up before she sneaked in a few personal questions. But Hope was better.

'Not right now,' she answered.

'There are a few available men in town. Some of them still have their own teeth and most of them have a job. Stay away from anyone with the last name Gropp. They look normal, but none of them are right in the head.'

'That's okay,' Hope assured her. 'I'm not looking for a man.'

Lizard Tastes Just Like Chicken!

Hope rinsed her plate, then washed her hands with Lemon Joy. When she turned off the water, the sound of Shelly's bootheels and the low hum of a motorboat out on the lake filled the silence.

'Sounds like Paul and the boys are back,' Shelly said as she walked across the kitchen.

Hope reached for a towel and dried her hands. She glanced out the back screen door into the shaded yard but couldn't see anything. 'I better get back across the street.'

'Stay a minute and meet my husband.' Shelly stuck her head into the refrigerator, looking for something. She was nosy, but Hope could appreciate her style. She'd invite Hope to lunch to pump her for info, nonchalantly slipping in personal questions between amusing stories, bits of gossip, and bites of crab. 'Are you staying in the Donnelly house tonight?'

Out of habit, Hope hung the towel over her shoulder. 'That's the plan. My things are supposed to be delivered later today.' She leaned her behind against the counter and folded her arms beneath her breasts. 'But the way my luck is running, my stuff is probably lost in transit. Probably fell off the truck in Vegas.'

The screen door opened, then slammed. 'Gotta piss so bad my back teeth are floatin',' Adam Taber said as he ran through the kitchen.

'Where's Wally?' Shelly called after him.

'At the boat,' he answered, then was gone.

'Hey, there, Adam.' A deeper voice spoke from just outside the door. 'You know better than to go into somebody's house without knocking.'

Only that morning, Hope had heard the same voice ask if she liked passion fruit. She straightened and dropped her arms to her sides.

'Why should he knock when his daddy never does?' Shelly asked.

Dylan raised one hand above his head and rapped his knuckles against the wooden frame. 'Knock, knock,' he drawled. 'Can I come in?'

'No,' Shelly replied and shut the refrigerator door. 'You smell like fish guts.'

He came in anyway and walked toward Shelly. From across the kitchen, his broad back and shoulders filled Hope's vision. He wasn't wearing the battered hat he'd worn that morning, and his short hair stuck to the back of his neck. He advanced on Shelly, his hands out in front of him as if he meant to touch her.

'Stay away, Dylan Taber, and I mean it!'

He chuckled, three deep 'huh-huh-huhs,' then asked, 'What are you going to do?'

'I'll beat you up like I did in the fifth grade.'

'Come on, now, you didn't beat me up. You kicked me in the bean bags, Shelly. It's not right kicking a guy in the bean bags.'

'You touch me,' she warned, 'and I'll tell Dixie Howe you love the way she looked in that sequined tube top she wore to the T-ball game last night.'

He dropped his hands. 'There you go. Hitting below the belt again.'

'Paul, get in here,' Shelly called out. 'We have company.'

'Dylan's not company.'

'I'm not talking about Dylan. Hope Spencer from across the street is here.'

Dylan shot a glance over his shoulder and slowly turned to look at her. His brows rose up his forehead, and the kitchen light above his head picked out the gold in his brown hair.

'So,' Paul Aberdeen began as he and Wally entered the house, 'you're our new neighbor. Welcome to Gospel. I'd shake your hand, but I've been gutting fish.'

Hope offered him a smile. 'Thank you.'

Paul was big and blond and his fair complexion had been burned red except for a white strip at his hairline. He gave Hope a quick up-and-down with his eyes before turning to Dylan and shaking his head. 'I'll see your five and raise you ten.' He opened the refrigerator and stuck his head inside. 'Would you like a beer, Hope?'

'No, thank you.' Although she couldn't imagine why, she had a feeling that they were betting on her.

'Dylan?'

'Yep.' The word was barely out of his mouth before a Budweiser was lobbed at him. He caught it in midair and popped the top.

'Remember me?' Wally asked as he came to stand before her. Like his father, he'd been burned by the sun, but that was where the resemblance ended. He was clearly his mother's child.

'Of course,' she said. 'You rescued my purse.'

'Yep.' He nodded and looked at his mother. 'Where's Adam?'

Shelly pointed in the direction of the bathroom and

Wally went out of the kitchen. 'Hope's writing an article for a Northwest magazine,' she informed the men.

'What kinda article?' Paul closed the refrigerator door and hung one arm around his wife's neck.

'Hope is into flora and fauna.'

Dyan raised the Bud to his mouth and watched her over the top of the can.

'I'm working on a nature article. I want to get some pictures of native wildlife and indigenous vegetation.'

Dylan lowered the beer as one brow lifted slightly. 'At first glance, I'd never take you for a nature lover.'

'You don't know me.'

'True.' He moved to the sink and set the can on the counter, next to her elbow.

'If you want to see nature,' Paul said, 'you might want to camp out at the falls. Now that's some beautiful country.'

Dylan stood so close his arm bumped hers as he turned the water on. Her pulse picked up a beat or two, but she stood perfectly still and refused to let him know he made her nervous. 'I might do that,' she said.

He glanced at her out of the corner of his eye. 'Have you ever camped out somewhere other than a motel room?'

Well, there had been that one summer at Girl Scout camp. 'Sure, I camp all the time. I love to commune with nature.'

He chuckled and reached for the lemon dish soap. His T-shirt brushed her bare shoulder. 'Careful,' he whispered next to her ear, 'your nose is growing.'

Heat radiated from his big body and she slid a few steps down the counter and walked around him. Okay, so he did make her a little nervous. He was just too big, too masculine, and too good-looking, and he probably knew it, too. And she suspected he was *trying* to make her nervous.

'Remember that writer last summer?' Shelly asked. 'What was he writing about? I can't remember.'

'He said he was a survivalist,' Dylan answered.

Paul scoffed. 'Yeah, but he had his pack filled with ready-to-eat army rations.'

'You should write something like that, Hope,' Shelly suggested. 'All kinds of stuff is written by men, mostly Grizzly Adams he-man stuff. You could go on one of those survivalist treks. It might be interesting to read something like that from the point of view of a woman like you.'

He-man stuff? Survivalist trek? 'Like me?'

Shelly made a palms-up gesture as if nothing needed to be said.

Paul said it anyway. 'An indoor woman. If you went on one of those survivalist treks, you could write about eating wild onion and snakes.'

Her disgust must have shown on her face, because Paul quickly added, 'Hell, it tastes just like chicken.'

'That's true,' Shelly interjected.

'Maybe catch yourself a fat lizard,' the comedian at the sink added.

They were all crazy. All of them, and it was on the tip of her tongue to confess, *It's a lie, people. Get real. I write Bigfoot and alien-baby stories. I* don't *eat reptiles!*

The water from the faucet shut off and Dylan moved behind her. She felt him slide the thick towel from her bare shoulder. 'I think I'll just stick with *writing* about what I see around here.' She turned and glanced up at him. 'I don't think I can eat wild flora and poor, helpless fauna, anyway.'

He dried his hands and the leather band of his wristwatch. 'Now, that is a shame.' He looked up from his watch and added, 'There's nothing quite like shooting helpless fauna and cooking it up with some wild flora.'

Shelly and Paul thought he was a real hoot, but Hope really didn't see what was so funny. She got that twilight-zone feeling again. Like she'd been dropped onto an alien planet. Like she was living one of her own stories.

The sun beat down on Dylan's straw cowboy hat as he pulled the cord on his old lawn mower. The engine sputtered, then died. Sweat dampened his armpits and spine, and he reached for his hat and tossed it on the front steps.

Sundays in June were for fishing or napping in a hammock with a hat pulled down over a man's eyes. Not for pushing a lawn mower around. Unfortunately, his grass was up past his ankles and the shrubs by his front door were so out of control a person had to fight to find the doorbell. Which didn't bother him much, since everyone always came to the back door anyway. But his mother and sister had been down the week before and had bitched so much about it he'd started to feel kind of trashy. Like Marty Wiggins across town, who parked his old truck in the front yard and let his kid run around with gunk stuck to his face.

Dylan pulled his T-shirt over his head and rubbed a trickle of sweat from his bare chest and belly. He thought about giving the mower a good kick, but he figured all he'd get out of it was a broken foot. He glanced from the mower to his son standing on the porch near the biggest shrub, a pair of small grass clippers in his hands. Adam's puppy, Mandy, lay near his feet.

'Don't cut more than I showed you.' Dylan ran his fingers though his damp hair, pushing it from his forehead.

'I won't.'

Dylan would never let Adam out of the house without making sure he was clean, his hair and teeth were brushed, and his clothes matched. A few shrubs didn't make a guy trashy, for God's sake. 'And don't cut off your fingers. I'm not any good at sewing stuff back on.'

'I won't.'

He tossed the T-shirt next to his hat and pulled the cord again. This time the engine sputtered to life. The sound cut through the lazy quiet and sent Mandy jumping off the porch and running around the side of the house.

The grass was so thick in patches he had to lower the handle and raise the front wheels off the ground to keep the engine from stalling. Lawn clippings sprayed from the side, and when he got close to his dirt driveway, clouds of dust filled the air and little rocks peppered the ground like buckshot.

On his fifth pass, he ran over something that felt an awful lot like a big stick. He glanced to the left as chunks of tan plastic flew across the deep green grass.

Dylan cut the engine and stared down at the dismembered body of an X-Men action figure. The closer he studied it, the more it reminded him of the time, about ten years ago, when he'd just made homicide detective for the Los Angeles Police Department. He'd responded to an A.M. call on Skid Row, expecting to see a murdered transient. Instead, a bunch of beat cops stood around scratching their heads and staring at a torso sitting on a bench at a bus stop, no head or arms or legs, just the torso wearing a blue shirt, a tie, and a Brooks Brothers jacket. But seeing a torso in an expensive jacket on Skid Row wasn't even the strangest part of the murder. Whoever had killed the man had also cut off his private organs. Dylan could understand getting rid of identifiable parts, but a guy's jewels? That was plain cold-blooded. In the three years he'd remained in L.A., the case had never been solved, but he'd always figured the perpetrator had to be a woman.

'What was that?' Adam asked as he pointed to the mangled figure on the grass.

'I think it was your Wolverine.'

'His head's chopped off.'

'Yep. How many times have I told you not to leave your toys around?'

'I didn't. Wally did.'

There was probably a fifty-fifty chance that what Adam said was the truth. 'Doesn't matter. You're responsible for your own stuff. Now pick up the pieces and throw them away.'

'Oh, man!' Adam complained as he scooped up the bits of plastic. 'He was my favorite.'

Dylan watched his son stomp off before he restarted the mower. There were a lot of images he carried in his head that he would prefer to forget. The images still haunted him from time to time, but at least he no longer *lived* them. The biggest crime to hit Gospel since he'd been sheriff was the murder of Jeanne Bond by husband Hank. And while it had been unfortunate, it was one case in the past five years. Not one in the past five hours.

Dylan pushed the mower to the backyard and cut the grass around Adam's swing set. His decision to move back to Gospel had almost been as easy as leaving. He'd left at the age of nineteen and attended a year and a half at UCLA before quitting to join the police academy. He'd been a twenty-one-year-old kid with ideas of catching the bad guys. Making the world safer. He'd turned in his badge ten years later, tired of the bad guys winning. He'd left Gospel a naive country boy with cowshit on his boots. He'd returned a lot older and a whole lot wiser. He'd returned with a much better appreciation for small towns and small-town people. Sure, everyone in Gospel owned a gun, but they weren't shooting each other over the color of a bandanna.

The weird thing of it was, Dylan hadn't even really realized he was tired of dealing with all the homicidal crazies until the day two-year-old Trevor Pearson had been kidnapped from his front yard and later found dead in a

Dumpster. Dylan could always distance himself from other abuse cases, but Trevor was different. Finding that baby had changed him.

He'd gone home that night to his house in Chatsworth, taken one look at Adam sitting in his high chair with his little Tommy cup in one hand and Cheerios in the other, and decided right then and there he'd had enough. He was taking his son and going someplace where Adam could play. Where he could go outside and be a kid. Where his house didn't have an alarm system.

Of course, Adam's mama hadn't been too happy about his decision. Julie had made it real clear she wasn't leaving. He didn't blame her, but he'd made it just as clear he wasn't staying. They'd argued about Adam, even though there was never really any question that he would go with Dylan. Julie wasn't a great mother, but he didn't blame her for that, either. She'd never known her own mother and didn't seem to have the instincts everyone just assumed females possessed. She loved Adam, but she simply didn't know what to *do* with him.

And Adam hadn't exactly been an easy baby. He'd been premature and colicky, making the first few months of his life hell for everyone. If he wasn't crying, he was projectile vomiting, and instead of smelling like a sweet, powdery baby, he mostly smelled like an old French fry.

It was Dylan who'd walked the floors with Adam at three in the morning, rubbing his back and singing him old honky-tonk songs. As a result, when Adam got old enough to reach out, he reached for his father.

In the end, leaving Julie had been real easy. Maybe too easy, confirming what he'd secretly suspected. He'd stayed with her for Adam. His decision hadn't been as easy for Julie, but she'd done what was best for all of them. She'd signed custody over to Dylan, making only one demand:

that Adam spend the first two weeks in July with her.

Dylan had come home with his year-old son, and he'd never regretted his decision. As far as he knew, Julie didn't have any regrets, either. She now had the life she'd worked so hard for, the life she'd always dreamed of having. When he'd talked to her the week before to confirm her plans with Adam, she'd sounded happier than ever. She had what she wanted, and so did he. He had his son he loved more than anything on the face of the earth. A little boy who made him laugh even as he made him scratch his head. Adam was normal and happy. He loved his dog, and had an obsession with rocks. He collected them everywhere he went, as if they were gold. He had shoe boxes full of them under his bed. He gave them out only to grown-ups he liked, or to the girls at his school he wanted to impress.

With the sun beating down on his bare back and shoulders, Dylan mowed the lawn below his deck and across his yard to the fenced pasture. Dylan and Adam's horses, Atomic and Tinkerbell, stood beneath the shade of several pines, dozing, indifferent to the sound of the engine. When he was through, he pushed the mower to the weathered barn to the left of the pasture and stored it beside his John Deere.

He filled the trough with fresh water and then turned the hose on himself. Bent at the waist, he let the cold water run over his head, the back of his neck, and down the sides of his face until he felt his brain freeze. He straightened and shook like a dog, sending a spray of water in all directions. Droplets slid down his spine and chest and were absorbed in the waistband of the soft Levi's hung low on his hips. He rinsed grass clippings from his boots, then reached for the spigot and turned it off. He thought of standing in Paul and Shelly's kitchen earlier that day, washing his hands and listening to Ms Hope Spencer.

'Flora and fauna,' he scoffed. Who in the hell ever used words like 'flora and fauna'? And he'd bet his left gonad that her idea of communing with *nature* was to open the sunroof of her car as she tootled down Santa Monica Boulevard.

He wondered if she ever smiled, really smiled with her blue eyes shining, full lips tilting up. He wondered what it would take to put a smile like that on her face. Another place and another time, he would have liked to try.

She was too perfect. Her clothes, her make-up, her everything. She was the kind of woman his hands just itched to mess up real good, but for a lot of reasons, that kind of itch could get him into trouble. Especially with a woman like her. A writer spelled out big trouble in neon letters for him and Adam.

It wasn't uncommon for writers to spend time in the wilderness area, working on travel guides or backpacking articles. Only MZBHAVN didn't look like she spent much time in the great outdoors. He didn't know the real reason for her move to Gospel, but he had a few doubts about her story. It was best if he just stayed away from her. Best if he didn't even think about her, because when he did, it reminded him of exactly how long it had been since he'd made love to someone besides himself.

He walked around the side of the house to the front porch and reached for his shirt. Adam was making a mess out of the shrubs again, but Dylan couldn't work up enough energy to care. He pulled his T-shirt over his damp hair and shoved his arms through the holes. The shrubs could wait for another day.

'Are you about done?' he asked as he tucked the ends of the old cotton shirt into his jeans. 'I think it's about time we cooked those trout we caught today.'

Adam put down the shears and dug into his pocket. 'I found a pretty rock. Do ya wanna see?'

'Sure.'

Adam jumped off the porch as a Dodge truck turned into their dirt drive.

'Don't be rude,' Dylan warned as he watched Paris Fernwood pull the truck to a stop. She got out and walked toward them with a cake in her hands.

'I don't like her,' Adam whispered and shoved his rock back inside his pocket.

'Be nice anyway.' He looked up and smiled at Paris. 'What have you got there?'

'I told you I'd bring you an Amish cake.'

'Well, now, isn't that sweet?' He nudged his son. 'Don't you think that's sweet?'

Adam's idea of being 'nice' was to purse his lips and not say a word. He didn't like women paying attention to his father. Not one little bit. Dylan didn't exactly know why, but he figured that it more than likely had something to do with Adam holding onto a fantasy that his mama would someday come and live with them.

Dylan picked up his cowboy hat and brushed his hair back with his fingers. 'I'd invite you in, but I'm afraid you've come at a bad time,' he said and pushed the hat down low on his forehead. 'Adam and I are busy cutting back these shrubs.' He reached for a pair of hedge trimmers and whacked off some foliage. 'Adam, why don't you take that cake from Paris and run it in the house.' Dylan had to nudge him a few more times before he did what he was told.

'I really can't stay anyway,' she said and turned her head to watch Adam walk away. Her braid fell over her shoulder. She'd woven daisies into her fine brown hair.

'Paris, you put flowers in your hair. I like a girl with flowers in her hair.'

She patted the braid and blushed. 'Just a few.'

'Well, you look real pretty,' he said, which she took for an invitation to chat for a good half hour. By the time she left, Dylan had whacked the hell out of one shrub and had started on another.

That night, as he and Adam ate dinner, Adam looked up from his plate and said, 'If you weren't so nice to all those girls, they wouldn't come around here.'

'All those girls? Who you talking about?'

'Paris and Miss Chevas and' – he held out his hands as if he were holding up watermelons – 'you know who.'

'Yeah, I know who.' Dylan bit into his corn bread and watched Adam pick a bone from his fish. 'Miss Chevas? You mean your teacher from kindergarten?'

'Yep. She liked you.'

'Get out of town.'

'She did, Dad!'

'Well, I don't think she did.' Dylan pushed his plate aside and looked into his son's big green eyes. Even if what Adam said was true, Dylan wasn't looking for a wife. And ultimately, that was what all the single women within a hundred miles wanted. 'You've got to quit being so ornery to the ladies. You've got to be nicer.'

'Why?'

'' 'Cause it's a rule, that's why.'

'Even the ugly ones?'

'Especially the ugly ones. Remember when I told you that you can't ever hit a girl, not even if she kicks you in the shins? Well, this is like that. Men have to be polite to ladies even if they don't like them. It's one of those unwritten laws I've told you about.'

Adam rolled his eyes. 'What time is it?'

Dylan glanced at his watch. 'It's almost eight. Put your plate in the sink. Then you can go turn on the TV.' Dylan gathered the other dishes on the table and rinsed them in the sink. He washed the heavy oak table, scooted in the four matching chairs, then set Paris's cake in the middle.

Living in the same town with Paris was like belonging to the dessert-of-the-week club. He really wished she'd quit bringing him food, but he just didn't know how to tell her. He knew of her marital intentions, of course. Hell, he was the best prospect in Pearl County, but compared to the other contenders, that wasn't exactly a compliment. Then there was Dixie Howe. He didn't know if she was interested in marriage or just sex. Either was out of the question. Just the thought of it shriveled him.

Even if there was a woman he wanted to bring home for the night, he couldn't. He had a young son, and he didn't believe in exposing children to that sort of thing. He couldn't park his car outside a lady's house for very long without the whole town knowing about it, talking about it behind his back, and speculating on a wedding date. Not only did he want to avoid being the object of rumor for Adam's sake, he was the sheriff, an elected official, and couldn't afford that kind of gossip. Especially not after Sheriff Donnelly had been caught with his pants down.

Dylan tossed the dishcloth into the sink and moved to the entry to the living room. He leaned a shoulder against the wall as the theme music for Adam's favorite television show, *Heaven on Earth*, filled the room. Fluffy clouds, blue sky, and the beautiful face of Adam's mother filled the screen. Golden springy curls waved about her face as if she really were the angel she played. America's sweetheart, Juliette Bancroft, rolled her eyes toward heaven and a light appeared above her head.

The Julie he knew was nothing like the angel she portrayed. When she'd lived with him, she hadn't been so soft-spoken, and as far as he could remember, she'd never spent one hour in church. Heck, her hair was really brown, the color of their son's.

'Come sit by me, Dad.'

Dylan pushed away from the doorway and sat next to Adam. Just like he always did, Adam scrambled onto Dylan's lap and laid his head on Dylan's shoulder. And as always, Dylan wondered if Adam really understood that what happened on television wasn't real. That his mother wasn't really an angel who spread goodness and saved souls. They'd talked about it many times, and Adam had always shrugged and said he knew. Dylan wasn't so sure. 'Remember what we talked about last week?' he asked.

'Yep, Mom's not a real angel. She just acts like one.'

'Your mom's an actress.'

'I know,' Adam answered, distracted by the opening scene.

Dylan held Adam close and kissed the top of his head. 'I love you, buddy.'

'Love you, too, Dad.'

Hope stared out the window of Number Two Timberline, at the crescent moon hanging at the top of the Sawtooth Mountains like an ornament placed atop a Christmas tree. Its pale light spilled across Gospel Lake. Stars crammed the inky-black night, one almost on top of the other, and Hope was sure she'd never seen so many stars in her life. Like the night before, she was once again struck by the utter silence that surrounded her. No cars, no sirens, no helicopters buzzing overhead. Not even the bark of a neighbor's dog to drive her nutty.

Her focus changed to her own wavy reflection in the glass and the light splashing across the porch and into the dirt yard. Gospel, Idaho, had to be the loneliest place on the planet.

She let the heavy green drape fall back into place. She'd accomplished a lot since that first day. The downstairs of

Number Two Timberline was clean, and she'd taken the bearskin from the wall and placed it over the bloodstain on the floor. She'd unpacked some of the boxes that had arrived with her things and cleaned the bedroom across from the bat room. She'd added her own personal touches, and hung her clothes in the closet. There was a lot more to do, but it was past time she got to work.

She moved into the dining room and booted up her laptop as well as her other computer, which also had arrived that afternoon. She placed a throw pillow on the hard chair, then sat at the long table. After the previous night's chicken-bone story, she figured her muse was back. With her fingers resting lightly on the keyboard, she closed her eyes and cleared her mind, freeing the clutter.

Half an hour later, she jumped to her feet. 'Shit,' she swore as she grabbed a bottle of Windex and a soft cloth. When another hour passed and cleaning the house hadn't uncovered her muse, she dragged out her fingernail kit. She chose a polish to fit her mood and painted her nails a deep blood red.

Blood red. She glanced over her shoulder to the fireplace in the other room. She didn't write true-crime stories. She didn't write about real people or the secrets and demons that drove them.

Hope rose and blew on her nails as she walked into the living room. With her toe, she pushed aside the bearskin and gazed down at the dark brown stain on the hardwood floor. She wondered what had been so horrible that the old sheriff had felt the only way out was a bullet through his head.

Shelly had mentioned something about kinky sex. People didn't kill themselves because they liked to be spanked, and Hope wondered just how kinky things had gotten in this house and how much the people in town knew about it.

Woman Parties at Her Own Wake

The Buckhorn Bar was the oldest surviving establishment in Gospel. Rebuilt after the fire of '32, and erected several years before Our Savior Jesus Christ Church, it also held within its rough-timbered walls a devout following. Wednesday nights were 'twofer' nights until ten, and there weren't many in the Buckhorn congregation who could pass up two beers for two bucks.

Perhaps the Buckhorn was so popular with the locals because, like them, it never pretended to be something it wasn't. The Buckhorn was simply a place to tip back a few, play some pool in the back room, or two-step to Vince Gill. During the summer months, the regulars put up with the tourists the best they could, but no one was blamed if a flatlander had to be forcefully removed from a favorite stool.

The choice of music pouring from the new juke was country, strictly country, and loud enough to drown out the rattle of the swamp cooler. Last year, some smart-ass had sneaked into the bar after hours and switched George Jones with Barry Manilow. Barry had no more sung half of 'I Write the Songs' before Hayden Dean picked up a barstool and put the old juke out of its misery. Now the stools were nailed to the floor.

The owner of the Buckhorn, Burley Morton, had never had a real keen eye for decor, but he did kind of like the way the new juke blinked to the sound of steel guitars and coordinated with the big Coors light behind the bar. Except for the poolroom in the back, walking into the Buckhorn was like walking into a dimly lit cave. The denizens who called it their second home liked it that way.

Hope stood in the entrance, giving her eyes a moment to adjust. Although she could see little beyond shadows and glowing neon bar signs, the place reminded her of the bar in Las Vegas where she'd first met her inspiration for Micky the Magical Leprechaun, Myron Lambardo. It smelled strongly of beer, decades of cigarette smoke, and rough timber. That probably should have warned her to turn and run, but she was a bit desperate these days. She shoved her headphones into her fanny pack and took a few steps to the right so a big cowboy could squeeze past. Her shoulder came into contact with a large bulletin board, and she lifted her gaze to a flyer pinned to the cork. It was a sign-up sheet, inviting people to participate in the:

ANNUAL FOURTH OF JULY
ROCKY MOUNTAIN OYSTER-EATING CONTEST
AND TOILET TOSS

Of course she'd heard of an oyster feed. When she was growing up, her family had often hosted seafood barbecues. A toilet toss? That was a new one, but, considering what she knew of the town, not all that surprising. In the five days she'd been in Gospel, she'd discovered some pretty strange things. Like the number of guns on open display. It seemed there was some rule that if you owned a truck, you had to have at least two rifles in the rear window. If you wore a belt, it had to have a buckle the size of your head, and if you had a pair of antlers, they must be nailed to your house, your barn, or your truck. The prevailing bumper-sticker sentiment could be summed up in one sentence: If you're not a cowboy, eat shit and die.

Hope glanced at her sports watch and figured she had an hour before it turned dark outside. She hadn't planned on coming into the Buckhorn at all, but she'd been jogging past and thought she should check it out. She hadn't been able to write a decent article since the chicken-bone story. Walter had e-mailed her this morning and wanted something big. Preferably something to do with Bigfoot, or aliens, or Elvis. He was losing patience with her, and she hoped she might find a Bigfoot Elvis impersonator hiding inside the Buckhorn.

Once Hope's eyes had adjusted to the light, she made her way to a vacant booth along the far side of the building. She was very aware of the stares that followed her, as if the people had never seen a pair of black spandex jogging shorts and midriff sports bra. She'd pulled her hair back into a ponytail, and she wore very little make-up.

She ordered a Corona, settled for a Bud Lite, and listened to the pool game in the rear. Over the whining of steel guitars from the jukebox, she could hear the couple in the booth behind her discuss something about flatlanders. The longer she eavesdropped, the more she gathered there was some sort of betting pool going on. It seemed that with the latest accident, Otis Winkler was now ahead with three cases of poison oak, two torn ankle ligaments, a broken thumb, and a cracked rib.

Hope listened carefully, then begged a pencil from the waitress. As she poured her beer into a red plastic cup, she grabbed a napkin and began to write:

ALIEN SABOTEURS HIDE WITHIN
THE HIGH MOUNTAINS OF IDAHO

In a sleepy town somewhat reminiscent of that television classic, Mayberry, aliens trick unsuspecting tourists . . .

Dylan hit the door of the Buckhorn Bar with the heel of his hand, sending it crashing against the wall. He was absolutely not in the mood for this shit. Two of his deputies were dealing with a nasty two-car accident south of Banner Summit, another was on vacation, and Lewis was still half an hour away. That left it up to Dylan to strap his duty belt over his Levi's, pin his star to the pocket of his plaid shirt, and come deal with the idiots at the Buckhorn.

The combined sounds of fists hitting flesh, shouts of bets being placed, and Conway Twitty's 'Hello Darlin' ' filled the bar.

Dylan pushed his way through the spectators and barely missed a roundhouse punch intended for Emmett Barnes.

Someone pulled the plug on Conway and flipped on the lights just as the other contender, Hayden Dean, delivered a blow to Emmett's jaw that connected and sent him staggering into the crowd. Dylan wasn't surprised to see Emmett involved. On a good day, Emmett was a mean son of a bitch with a little man's complex, and this didn't look like a good day. He stood five-seven in his custom-made boots and was built like a pit bull. Add alcohol into the mix, and Emmett was just one big beer muscle waiting to be flexed.

Dylan signaled to the owner of the bar, who grabbed Hayden in a big bear hug. Burley Morton hadn't come by his nickname because he'd been born small.

Dylan stepped in front of Emmett and put a restraining hand on the man's chest. 'Fight's over,' he said.

'Get out of my way, Sheriff!' Emmett hollered, his eyes glazed with anger. 'I'm not through kicking Hayden's bony ass.'

'Why don't you just calm down?'

Instead, Emmett smashed his fist just beneath Dylan's left eye. The impact rocked Dylan's head back, knocked his hat off, and shot needles of pain through his head. He blocked the next shot with his forearm and punched Emmett in the belly. The air whooshed from the other man's lungs, doubling him over, and Dylan took full advantage of his position and slammed an uppercut to Emmett's face that sent him to the ground. Without giving Emmett a chance to recover, he rolled him onto his stomach and cuffed him behind his back. 'Now, you just lie there and exercise your right to be silent,' he said as he patted down Emmett's pockets and found them empty.

He stood, placed his booted foot in the middle of Emmett's back, and threw a second set of cuffs to Burley, who had no problem slapping them on the much skinnier Hayden.

'Okay,' Dylan addressed the suddenly silent crowd, 'what happened here?' He raised his hand to his cheekbone and winced.

Several people talked at once.

'Emmett bought her a round.'

'She said something to him and he started hassling her.'

'That's when Hayden stepped in.'

Emmett squirmed and Dylan pressed his bootheel into his spine until he quit moving. 'Who?' He looked at his fingertips. He wasn't bleeding, but he'd have a brilliant shiner in the morning.

Everyone in the bar pointed to a booth several feet away. 'Her.' And there, standing on top of the table, frozen to the wall like a deer caught in a headlight, was Ms Hope

Spencer. Her eyes were huge, her top small, and there was beer spilled everywhere. She clutched a fistful of napkins to her chest.

'Get up, and I'll hogtie you,' he told Emmett, stepping over him. He knew from past experience with Emmett that once he was down, the threat of getting his hands and feet shackled together usually subdued him.

Dylan walked toward Hope and held out his hand. 'Why don't you hop on down from there, ma'am?' She took three hesitant steps to the edge of the table and shoved the napkins into a fanny pack she had strapped around her hips. She placed her palms on his shoulders, and his hands reached up and curved around her bare waist. As he looked into her blue eyes glassy with fright, his thumbs just naturally brushed her soft skin and pressed into her flat stomach. He lifted her from the table and slowly set her on her feet before him.

'Are you all right?' he asked. His gaze lowered from her face to his hands resting on her waist. The heat of her bare skin warmed his palms, and he kept them there, right there against that soft, soft skin. She smelled of beer, and of the Buckhorn, and of flowers, too. Lust rolled through his belly and curled his fingers, and he finally dropped his hands to his sides.

'I thought he was going to hit me,' she said, tightening her grasp on his shoulders. 'Last year I took self-defense classes, and I thought I could take care of myself. But I froze. I'm not the Terminator.' Her breathing was shallow, and with each little gasp, her breasts rose in that little top.

He looked into her face, absent of cosmetics and color, her normal cool facade gone. 'You don't look like the Terminator.'

She shook her head and it didn't appear like she was going to get over her panic any time soon. 'That was my nickname in class. I was very fierce.'

'Are you going to pass out?'

'No.'

'You sure?'

'Yes.'

'Why don't you go ahead and take a deep breath anyway?'

She did as he asked and he watched her suck in several even breaths. She probably wasn't aware that she held onto him, but he was very aware of the weight of her touch. He felt it all over, warming him as if they were more than strangers. As if the most natural thing in the world would be for him to lower his mouth to hers and kiss her until he made her eyes a bit more glassy, her breathing a lot more choppy. Dylan reached for her hands and removed them.

'You feeling better?' he asked, figuring it had been way too long since he'd been with a woman if a touch on his shoulders got him hot.

She nodded.

'Why don't you tell me what happened?'

'I was just sitting there, minding my own business, and the shorter guy walked up and put another round on my table. I told him no thank you, but he sat down anyway.' A frown settled between her brows, but she didn't offer further explanation.

'And?' Dylan prompted.

'And I tried to be nice, but he wouldn't get the hint. So I figured I needed to make it really clear that I wasn't in the mood for company. You know, so that there was no misunderstanding.'

Not that it mattered, but out of curiosity, Dylan asked, 'What did you say to him?'

Her frown spread to the corners of her mouth. 'I think I said, "Please remove your carcass from my booth." '

'I guess he didn't take that very well.'

'No. Then he got really mad when I suggested to him that he had a drinking problem and should enter rehab.'

'And?'

'I think that's when he said I should fuck myself.'

'And?'

'And I said I'd rather fuck myself than a short man with a little penis.'

Dylan's head suddenly ached like a bitch and his eye began to hurt a lot more. 'Uh-huh.'

'That's when he reached across the table and tried to grab me. I screamed and that skinnier guy grabbed the short guy and pulled him out of the booth. If it weren't for him, I don't know what would have happened.'

Dylan knew. Emmett probably would have smacked her around before someone put a stop to it. Dylan was going to hogtie him just for the fun of it.

'So he didn't touch you?'

'No.'

'Threaten you with anything like a knife or a broken bottle?'

'No.'

Lewis Plummer finally entered the bar and moved through the crowd toward Dylan. 'Did someone take a poke at you?'

'Yep. Go ahead and Mirandize Emmett Barnes, then charge him with aggravated assault and aggravated battery on a police officer. I didn't find anything on him, but just to be sure, why don't you frisk him again?'

'What about Hayden?'

Dylan returned his gaze to Hope. 'Did you see who swung first?'

'The short guy.'

'Hayden can go home.'

'Are you going to come into the station?' Lewis asked.

'No. Adam is at home with a sitter, so I'll do the paperwork in the morning.'

'See ya in the morning, then.' Lewis held up his hand in an abbreviated wave.

Dylan watched his deputy pull Emmett to his feet, then turned to look into Hope's face. She was still a bit pale and her eyes still a bit glazed, but she didn't appear too upset by her experience at the Buckhorn. 'Do you want to go to the station and make a statement tonight, or would you prefer to come in tomorrow morning?'

'I just want to go home.'

Someone plugged the juke back in, the lights were once again turned low, and Deputy Plummer escorted Emmett Barnes from the bar. It was ten o'clock, two hours before closing time. Just enough time for those still around to polish off a few more beers.

'Are you okay to drive?' he asked Hope as Conway Twitty once again poured from the juke.

She glanced down at herself, and Dylan glanced, too. At her tight spandex shorts and sports bra. Light from a Coors sign flashed from across the bar and lit up her flat stomach. 'I jogged here,' she said.

Dylan forced his gaze from the blue light shining on her belly button. 'Let me get my cuffs from Burley and I'll take you home.'

'Thank you, Sheriff.'

'Dylan,' he reminded her.

'Dylan.' Then it happened. For the first time since she'd driven her little sports car into town, she smiled at him. Her full lips curved upward and she flashed him the straightest teeth he'd seen since leaving L.A. He figured relief from her ordeal must have warmed her up. Most women tended to get real weepy or *real* grateful after an ordeal.

From behind, someone placed a caressing hand around

Dylan's arm, and he looked over his shoulder and down into the shadows hiding Dixie Howe's eyes. 'Here's your hat, Dylan.'

'Thanks, Dixie.' He brushed his hair back and replaced his hat.

'You're not leaving, are you?'

'Afraid so.'

'Can't you stay for a game of pool? I heard you tell Lewis that Adam is home with a sitter.'

'Not tonight.' He tried to pull his arm from her grasp, but her grip tightened. She pressed one big breast into his arm, and he knew her well enough to know it wasn't an accident. He'd known Dixie most of his life. He'd dated her sister, and he'd remembered her as a scrawny kid. Life hadn't been real kind to either Howe sister, and he felt bad about that, about the way they'd grown up, but he felt nothing more. 'I have to take Ms Spencer home.'

Dixie cast a quick glance in Hope's direction, then once again focused her attention on Dylan. 'You remember my offer the other night?'

Of course he remembered. There hadn't been many times in his life when a woman had walked up to him at a T-ball game and blatantly offered oral sex.

'Any time.' She finally released her grasp and Dylan pulled free.

'Good night, Dixie,' he said and moved to the bar before she could grab hold again. Hope followed beside him, and while he quickly retrieved his handcuffs from Hayden's wrists, he had to listen to her express her appreciation to Hayden for his 'heroic intervention.'

As far as Dylan was concerned, she laid it on too thick and gushed too much. She had the poor fool blushing and stammering about how it had been his pleasure to get his nose broken for her. Hope had been in town for five days, he'd run into her three times, and she hadn't smiled at him until five minutes ago. He guessed he now knew what it took to make her smile. It took getting hit in the face.

As they left the bar, a cool breeze loosened tendrils of blond hair from Hope's ponytail and blew them across her smooth cheeks. His gaze lowered from her face to her arms and the very distinct points in the front of her top. Dylan's chest got tight, his left eye throbbed, and he looked away.

He helped her into the sheriff's Blazer, and on the short drive to Timberline Road, he wondered what kind of woman dressed in spandex, walked into a redneck bar, and provoked a man like Emmett.

Someone who thought she was a badass. The Terminator.

'Who was that woman in the bar?' she asked, breaking the silence.

'There were several women in the bar. Which one do you mean?'

'Blonde. Big hair. Big breasts.'

His brows lifted and he winced. 'Dixie Howe,' he answered and gingerly touched his cheekbone just beneath his eye.

'Is she your girlfriend?'

'No.' Damn, his face had started to swell. 'Why do you want to know?'

'Just curious.'

He looked over at her, the light from the switch panel illuminating half her face. Her ponytail was a bit ragged. She smelled strongly of beer. 'Curious if I have a girlfriend?'

'No, curious about what she offered you.'

He turned the Blazer onto Timberline Road and said, 'Now, that would be telling.'

'I bet I can guess.'

He laughed and pulled the Chevy into her dark drive. 'Maybe she just wanted to talk.'

'Yeah, maybe through the bone phone?'

He slammed on the brakes, and if the vehicle hadn't already been slowing, he would have put her through the windshield. 'What?'

She put her hands on the dash to stop herself. 'Maybe she wants to talk through—'

'Jesus H. I heard you the first time.' He stared at her and suddenly it all made perfect sense. Her glassy eyes, easy smiles, and the stench of beer he'd assumed had spilled *on* her. Relief hadn't warmed her up to him at all. 'How many beers did you drink?'

'Hmm? Well, usually I'm not much of a drinker, but it was twofer night.'

'How many?'

'I must have had four.'

'In how many hours?'

'Two.' She reached for the door handle and was out of the car before he'd even shut off the engine. 'I probably should have eaten dinner before I had anything to drink,' she continued as she walked across the dirt yard.

Dylan tossed his hat on the passenger seat and followed. The house was completely dark. No light spilled into the yard from the porch or windows. The full moon provided the only illumination, and it shone on Hope's hair, turning it gold. She stopped at the top of the steps and stared at her front door.

'Where is your key?' he asked as he came to stand behind her.

'I wasn't going to be gone long, so I didn't leave any lights on.' She fished around in her fanny pack and said, 'This is kind of spooky.'

Dylan unhooked the MAG-LITE from his duty belt and shined it on the front door. It was slightly ajar. 'Did you leave your door open?'

She looked up, and with the keys in her palm said, 'No, I always lock it when I leave.'

'It's still locked, so you probably just didn't pull it shut all the way.' He stepped back and trained the light on the windows and the front of the house. Nothing was broken. 'Stay here. I'll be back in a minute.' He walked around the house and shined the flashlight on the windows. He checked the back door, but it was locked and there didn't appear to be anything out of the ordinary. 'Yeah, I think you just didn't shut the door tight,' he said after he'd once again moved to stand beside her.

'Yeah, maybe.' She quickly stepped behind him. 'You first.'

He'd already planned on checking out the house for her, but what he hadn't planned on was her hooking her hand around the back of his belt and urging him forward like a human shield. Now, there were times in Dylan's life when he hadn't minded women using his body, but they'd always been naked at the time. He didn't know how he felt about being used as a target so Hope could run like hell if anything hit him first.

Her knuckles poked the small of his back and urged him forward. He entered the house and flipped on the lights. 'Anything out of place?'

She raised up on her toes and her breasts pressed into his back as she looked over his shoulder. 'I don't think so,' she said right next to his left ear.

Her breath warmed the side of his neck and turned his blood hot. 'Jesus.'

She dropped to her heels and her knuckles once again urged him forward. She steered him toward the dining room and he turned on the light. The room had been buffed and polished and on the long table sat a closed laptop, a printer, a scanner, and a fax machine. Stacks of books and magazines and newspapers sat next to a computer. Things Dylan imagined a writer would need, but to write *what* was still the question.

'Everything okay in here?'

This time she leaned to the right and peeked around his shoulder. 'Yes.' Her knuckles poked his spine again and they headed to the kitchen. Like the dining room, it, too, was spotless. The pots and pans hanging on the rack had been polished, the floor buffed, and the windows cleaned. All the furniture had been placed in the house recently.

One of the last times he'd been standing in the kitchen, the FBI had been here, too. They'd swarmed the place shortly after Hiram killed himself, and they'd taken most everything that hadn't been nailed down. Dylan wondered what Hope would think if he told her that when they'd found Hiram dead, they'd also found red crotchless panties and a bullwhip hanging from that rack. The significance of those items became clear only after viewing the photographs and videotapes Hiram Donnelly had made of himself.

The thud of Dylan's bootheels and the squeak of Hope's running shoes directly behind him were the only sounds on their way to the back door. For her peace of mind, he checked it again; then they moved into the living room. When he turned on the lights, she did that raising-on-her-toes thing and pressed into his back again. Pure fire shot straight to his groin and he went from semi to stiff in less than a second. He wondered what she would do if he slid one hand around her waist, and stuck his tongue down her throat. His blood throbbed in his veins and he wondered if she'd melt into him. If she'd let him touch her breasts and feel between her legs. If he took her hand and pressed her palm into his erection.

'Everything looks good from here,' she said and dropped to her heels. 'Let's go upstairs.'

He knew he should step away, put his hands in the air, and leave the area, but he couldn't quite force himself to do what he knew he should. Not yet. 'You stay down here.'

'Don't you think I should go with you?'

He looked over his shoulder and into her upturned face a few inches from his own. His gaze slid over her smooth forehead and perfect blond brows to her big, slightly out-of-focus blue eyes. He studied the bow of her top lip, and he said, just above her mouth, 'Do you want me to check out your bed?'

'Yes,' she said and he about popped a vessel. 'And then look behind the shower curtain in the bathroom. I don't want to take a shower and get stabbed by Norman Bates.'

'Jesus, stay here.' His head spinning, he removed her hand from the back of his belt and walked away. 'You should definitely stay here.'

He moved upstairs and quickly checked for intruders. He couldn't say why, but he was glad to see that she hadn't chosen the master bedroom. Glad she wasn't sleeping in the same room where old Hiram had been tied up and spanked. Perhaps if he hadn't seen the videos, hadn't seen the faces of teenage girls, he wouldn't see the taint of it now.

When Dylan came to the room she'd chosen for her bedroom, he stopped in his tracks. The way she'd decorated, it was obvious the woman lived alone. Everything was covered in white lace and purple flowers, like she slept in some sort of overrun garden. He seriously doubted the realtor who rented the property had placed that stuff in the house.

He shut the door before he started picturing her naked, on the white downy comforter, her hair all tousled, her lips parted and wet from his kiss, and her legs all tangled with his. He walked down the hall to the bathroom and looked behind the shower curtain as she'd asked. He turned to the mirror above the sink and stared at the deep red splotch beneath his left eye. The center was already beginning to turn blue. He touched it and carefully pulled down his bottom lid to look at his eyeball.

While he had absolutely no problem imagining Hope naked, any kind of involvement was out of the question. She was beautiful and the way she filled out spandex had to be a sin, but there were a lot of beautiful women in the world. Women who didn't threaten the life he'd made and the security of his son.

He knew little about Hope, other than she had a rare talent for pissing people off and, in all likelihood, had lied about why she'd moved to Gospel. Ms Hope Spencer was a mystery he had no intention of solving. If she kept her nose clean, she could keep her secrets from him and everyone else. Just as he intended to keep his – especially from her.

He'd seen another side of Hope tonight. She was more relaxed, less uptight, more approachable. Softer. Drunk. And in all honesty, he had to say he preferred the drunk. His attraction to her was purely physical and turned his thoughts to hot, sweaty things that were never going to happen. The way his body reacted to her didn't worry him. It made him uncomfortable, yes, but it didn't mean he was going to do anything about it.

Dylan moved out into the hall. He'd bet by morning, everyone in town would know he'd given Hope a ride home. They'd likely start placing bets on how long he'd stayed. Dylan had to be very careful where he parked his truck, which was probably the reason that he hadn't parked it in a long time.

Growing up, he'd had a wild reputation. A reputation he'd deserved, but he was the sheriff now. An elected official. The father of a young son, and he could no longer afford negative gossip or speculation about his sex life. He had his own past to live down, as well as that of the former sheriff. Sometimes he wondered if the citizens of Gospel were all watching, waiting for *him* to mess up.

When he returned downstairs, he found Hope in the kitchen, wrapping a towel around a bag of ice.

Her back was to him; he let his gaze slide down her spine to the curve of her sweet spandex-covered butt. Maybe Iona was right. Maybe MZBHAVN wore thong undies.

She turned and smiled at him again and he felt it tighten his chest. 'How's your eye?'

It was obviously past time for him to go home. 'It hurts like a bitch.'

She handed him the towel, and he figured since she'd gone to such trouble for him, he could stay a minute or two. 'I thought this might help.'

Dylan leaned his behind against the counter and crossed one foot over the other. 'You've really cleaned the place up. It looks nice.'

She shrugged her bare shoulders. 'It took me a few days to get rid of all the dust and dirt.'

He raised the towel to the corner of his eye. 'And bats.'

'And bats.' She nodded.

'Shelly told me about the bloodstain. Did you know the late Sheriff Donnelly?'

'Sure. I was one of his deputies.'

'Then you know why he killed himself?'

'Yep.'

When he didn't elaborate, she prompted, 'Well . . . why?'

He figured that anything he told her, she could probably find out if she dug deep enough. 'He had a fondness for kinky sex. Real dominance-and-submission stuff. He liked women to dress up in red lace and stilettos, and he'd videotape himself getting his droopy butt flogged.'

'Weird, but nothing to kill yourself over.'

'You didn't know Hiram.' The old sheriff had been a real hard-assed lawman. 'Are you thinking of writing an article about him?'

'I'm thinking about it.' She drew her brows together. 'I usually don't like to write about real people, but yeah. Maybe. How do you feel about helping me get the police report?'

'Can't help you with that. The FBI was in charge of the case. We got wind of it about the same time Hiram did. By the time anyone got here, he was already dead.'

She sighed. 'So I'll have to send an FOIA request to the Feds, and that could take a few weeks or several months.'

She obviously knew the system. 'Call and pester them,' he advised. Despite her statement of not usually writing about real people, he wouldn't mind if her attention was distracted by the old story. That way, she wouldn't be snooping around and looking to report a new one. The late sheriff was still a favorite topic in the country, and if the people in town found out she was writing a story about Hiram, they'd form a line and talk her into a coma. 'You might ask around. Get information from people who knew Hiram.'

'I don't think people will talk to me. They haven't been exactly friendly.'

'Give them another chance. They'll probably help you out.'

'What about you?'

'I'll do what I can,' he volunteered, then figured it was time he changed the subject completely. 'Tell me something, is there a Mr Spencer?'

Hope cocked her head to one side and studied the tall cowboy standing in her kitchen. His left eye had begun to swell a bit and a shadow of beard darkened his chin and jaw.

He kind of had a glow about him, and she wondered if it was the trick of the light or the Budweiser. She felt good and free, and she was old enough to recognize she'd had more than her share to drink. She was buzzed, all right, but not the kind of drunk that made the room spin or her stomach heave. The kind that made everything okay. Like in a dream, where all her problems receded into the background, and where a big, strong man saved the day, broke up fights, and checked out her spooky house for her. The kind that had a handsome cowboy standing in her kitchen and offering to help her with a story she just might write. None of it seemed quite real. 'There is,' she finally answered. 'But he's someone else's Mr Spencer these days.'

'How long were you married?'

The answer to that question was easy. 'Seven years.'

'Long time.' He lifted the towel from the corner of his eye. 'What happened?'

She leaned a shoulder into the refrigerator and thought about the next answer, which wasn't so easy. 'He found someone he liked better.'

'Younger?'

She was drunk, but not that drunk. 'No, not younger. It's not even very interesting. Just the old cliché about a doctor having an affair with his nurse,' she lied, because lying was so much easier than the truth.

His lips curved into a one-sided smile she found slightly irresistible. 'She couldn't be prettier than you.'

Okay, more than slightly irresistible. 'Actually, she has big teeth.'

The other side of his lips slid up and his whole face smiled. 'I hate that in a woman.'

The more he talked, the more she liked him. 'And a shelf butt,' she added.

'Hate that, too.'

'The last time I saw her, she got herself some big ol' breasts to match.'

He didn't say anything. Just continued to smile.

'Oh, yeah, I forgot about your girlfriend from the Buckhorn.'

'I told you, Dixie isn't my girlfriend, but I can pretty much vouch that she isn't filled with bags of saline.'

'How do you know?'

'Because her older sister, Kim, *was* my girlfriend in high school. They're built about the same.'

'Is Kim the girl who ran off with a trucker right after graduation?'

His brow furrowed and he pressed the towel over his eyes. 'How do you know about that?'

'Shelly told me.'

'Yeah, that figures.'

'If she was your girlfriend, why'd she run off with a trucker?'

'Because,' he said as he set the towel on the counter and straightened, 'Kim was a girl with marriage on her mind, and I had plans that didn't include hanging crepe paper in the grange hall and saying "I do." '

'What plans?'

'Getting as far away from this town as I could get.' He shrugged. 'Seeing the rest of the world.'

'But you're back.'

'Yeah, I guess I didn't like what I saw.'

'I've been wondering about something since I first came here.' She looked into his deep green eyes surrounded by thick lashes, the left one starting to swell a bit more. 'What's it like to have several women in this town in love with you?'

He shook his head and took a few steps forward. 'Honey, you've got that all wrong,' he said and stopped directly in front of her. 'I just happen to be single and have a job. That makes me a prime target for women who want to get married. That's all.'

No, that wasn't all. He was also a six-three cowboy with hard muscles and a slightly imperfect smile that only made him more perfect. His hair was always a bit messed from his tendency to comb it with his fingers, and she'd noticed as she'd followed him around earlier that he had a very nice behind. But more than his physical perfection was the way he had of looking at and talking to a woman, of focusing all that male attention directly on her. Of casually calling every woman in town 'honey,' yet making it sound personal.

'Did the ice help your eye?' she asked.

'No, got any other ideas?'

'I might have a frozen steak.'

'I don't think so.'

Hope pressed a finger to her lips, then lightly touched his bruise. 'How's that?'

He shook his head and his gaze slid to her mouth. 'I'm afraid that didn't get the job done.'

She placed her hands on his chest, rose to the balls of her feet, and softly kissed the corner of his eye. 'Is that better?'

The word 'no' whispered across her cheek and Hope's senses completely scattered, only to regroup and concentrate on where she touched him. Her cheek and hands tingled and the sensation spread like fire through the rest of her body. She froze, knowing she should push him away, yet unable to move from the warmth of his big, solid body. Standing and feeling him so close was like coming in from the cold. Like holding your frozen hands close to the fire.

'Dylan,' she uttered, and he responded by turning his head and covering her mouth with his. The kiss never got the chance to start slow and sweet. The instant their lips touched, it became an openmouthed tongue thruster. He placed his hands on the sides of her face and, with her back against the refrigerator, he held her to him. His slick tongue stroked hers while he created a light suction within her mouth. He tasted very good, like something elusive that she couldn't quite catch. Like something she hadn't had in a long time, but until that moment hadn't even realized she desperately missed.

She ran her hands over his chest, felt his hard muscles bunch and flex beneath his shirt. She moaned deep in her throat, and her palm closed over the star pinned to his breast pocket. He kissed the way he did everything else. He gave every inch of her mouth his full attention. She breathed the air from his lungs and drew in the scent of him through her nose. It went straight to her head like pure oxygen. He made her light-headed and dizzy and gasping for more.

Hope slid her free hand down his chest to his flat belly. He sucked in his breath and her fingers curled in the cotton plaid of his shirt. She pulled it from the waistband of his jeans, but Dylan grabbed her wrists and pinned them to the refrigerator while he made love to her mouth. His tongue slid in and out, hot and slick. Her mouth clung to his. She wanted more. She wanted it all. All the hot touches and fiery hunger that had been missing from her life for so long. She wanted to feel him beneath her greedy hands and fought to free them. But when he finally let go, he ended the kiss and stepped backward, out of her reach.

His breath was ragged; his eyes ate her up. He wanted her. He wanted her as much as she wanted him. Her lids felt heavy, weighted as she stared at him, her body aching, responding to all that potent want and need staring right back at her. Yet he turned and walked away.

He moved to the doorway of the kitchen and he stopped. 'Hope?'

She looked at the back of his wide shoulders and the brown-and-gold hair on the back of his head. She opened her mouth, but no sounds came out.

'Stay away from the Buckhorn,' he said, and then he was gone.

Satan Photographed in Wilderness Town

At nine o'clock the next morning, Hope finished the rough draft of her alien story. She thought the intro might be a bit vague, and she'd waited until the third 'graph to make her transition, but she thought the article was shaping up nicely.

She'd created a wilderness town populated by ship-wrecked aliens who disguised themselves to pass for normal, everyday, small-town weirdies. In reality they passed the time while waiting for their mother ship by tricking tourists and profiting off them in their betting pool.

She'd been working on the article since dawn, when she woke with the outline already written in her aching head. She'd downed several Tylenol with a coffee chaser and hadn't bathed yet. Her hair was wound on top of her head and held in place with two Bic pens. She still wore her cow pajamas and a pair of slouch socks. She figured she smelled bad, but she knew better than to stop when she was on a roll. While she worked, she never answered the telephone, and only a raging house fire could have forced her to open the front door.

She'd e-mailed Walter the idea for her new article. He'd

loved it, but wanted pictures to accompany the story. *Believable* pictures. Which meant Hope would have to drag out her Minolta and snap a few photos of the wilderness area. Later, she would scan them into her computer and superimpose the likenesses of aliens dressed up as local townspeople. It would take time, but it wasn't impossible. And certainly not as hard as when she'd morphed Micky the Magical Leprechaun into a reasonable likeness of Prince Charles.

At around nine thirty, Hope finally took a break. When the phone rang, she picked up the receiver. The call was from Hazel Avery, of the sheriff's office, wanting to know when she planned to come in and fill out a victim's report. Hope looked down at herself and told the woman to give her an hour.

It wasn't that she'd forgotten she needed to go to the sheriff's office. It was more in the neighborhood of something she *wished* to forget. She wished she could forget the entire night, starting from the moment she'd stepped foot inside the Buckhorn to the moment Dylan Taber had walked out her door.

Hope hit SAVE on her keyboard and made a backup copy of the alien story. Well, maybe not forget the entire evening, but she definitely should have left the bar after she'd heard about the Flatlander Pool and before Emmett Barnes had plopped his sorry behind in her booth. Her troubles had started as soon as she'd looked up from the napkins she'd been scribbling on and seen his I-know-you-want-me grin.

No, she amended to herself, they'd started the minute she'd begun ordering twofers. If it hadn't been for her excitement over the alien story, she would have paid more attention to how the alcohol was affecting her. If it hadn't been for the beer buzz, she probably could have handled

Emmett. She certainly would have kept her comment about small men and small penises to herself.

Hope peeled off her clothes and stepped into the shower. If it hadn't been for the boozy glow, she definitely would have kept her hands and mouth off the sheriff.

She let the hot water run over her and didn't know which encounter had been worse, the one with Emmett or Dylan. One had been scary. The other, humiliating. She'd been wrong about Dylan. He hadn't wanted her the way she'd wanted him. He hadn't wanted to crawl all over her. He'd wanted to walk away, and that was exactly what he'd done. With the taste of him still on her lips, she'd watched him walk out the door.

Stay out of the Buckhorn, he'd said. No words of regret. No 'Gee, I hate to leave.' No lame excuse. Nothing.

Hope washed her hair, then stepped out of the shower. It had been a long time since a man had made her skin tingle. A long time since she'd let a man close enough for her to feel the warm pull of him low in the pit of her stomach. A long time since she'd wanted to feel a big, warm body next to hers.

Hope didn't believe in sex without love. She'd been there and done that in college. She was thirty-five now and knew there was no such thing as meaningless sex. If sex were meaningless, it wouldn't leave you hurt and hollow in the morning. And there was nothing more sad or more lonely than the morning after a one-night stand. Nothing more delusional than a woman telling herself it didn't matter.

But sex with love required a relationship. A relationship took effort. It took trust, and while she could tell herself it was time to try again, she could never quite place herself in the position to let anyone close. Intellectually, she knew that most men didn't cheat and create children with their wives' best friends but knowing it in her head and knowing it in her heart were two totally different things.

Shutting off the dark commentator in her soul was next to impossible. The critic that looked out from her eyes and saw the flaws hidden deep within her body.

Since the onset of puberty, Hope had suffered from endometriosis, and in the spring of her junior year in college, the symptoms became so severe she was left with little choice but surgery. At the age of twenty-one, Hope had a total hysterectomy, which left her free of debilitating pain. Free to enjoy her life. Free to enjoy relationships with men. It also left her unable to have children of her own, but the loss of her ability to procreate hadn't devastated her. She'd always figured that when the time was right, she'd adopt a child who needed her. The absence of a uterus hadn't ever made her feel as if she were less female than any other woman.

Until the day her husband had served her with divorce papers and she'd learned that he'd fathered a child with someone else. That news had knocked her flat and leveled her self-confidence. Now she wasn't sure of anything, least of all where she fit in the world.

Hope dried her body and brushed the tangles from her hair. Three years ago she'd thought she'd handled her life so well. She'd thought she'd picked herself up. She'd restarted her career, taken half of Blaine's money and his beloved Porsche. But she hadn't handled anything. She'd just avoided looking at it. She hadn't picked herself up, she'd just been operating from a flat position so no one could knock her on her ass again.

Last night she'd let herself feel passion again. Let it heat her blood and tease her skin.

She walked into her bedroom and opened her closet doors. Well, maybe 'let' was the wrong word. Much too passive. Once he'd kissed her, there had been no *letting*. No thought of letting, just doing. Once she'd felt the press of his lips and the feel of his hard chest beneath her hands, desire had taken control. For the first time in years, she hadn't run from it. She'd stood within the warmth of it, feeling it heat her up with the subtlety of a blowtorch. At some point she would have stopped. She would have. Of course she would have, but he'd stopped her, making it seem like the easiest thing he'd ever done. Then, without a backward glance, he'd walked out of her house, and right now, Dylan was the last person in the world she wanted to see. Maybe she'd be ready to face him tomorrow. Or next week.

In such a small town, the only way to avoid him would be to lock herself in her house, but she wasn't going to do that for two very good reasons. First, she wanted his help in getting old police files, and second, she wasn't about to give him a reason to think that she gave last night a second thought.

As Hope searched her closet, she told herself she wasn't looking for the perfect outfit to make the sheriff eat his heart out. She settled on what she would describe as a collision of city girl meets country girl. She dressed in a short turquoise sarong skirt, a turquoise silk halter, and her Tony Lama peacock-blue boots.

By the time she left for the sheriff's office, her make up looked perfectly natural, her hair volumized and the ends flipped slightly as if she hadn't had to curl and spray them into submission.

The Pearl County sheriff's office sat on the corner of Mercy and Main, and except for the shop advertising 'CLICK AND SHOOT – Photos In An Hour,' the building took up the entire city block. The outside of the sandstone building was pocked with age, and metal bars covered the windows in back. A new parking lot had been poured on the east side of the structure and the inside was thoroughly modernized. It smelled of new paint and carpet, and sunshine spilled through the wide windows.

A female deputy, wearing a beige blouse with a gold-star patch sewn above her left breast, looked up from her computer terminal as Hope approached the information desk. She directed Hope through a set of double glass doors with a huge gold star in the middle and the words 'Sheriff Dylan Taber' beneath. Inside the office was yet another woman, dressed like the first one. Her salt-and-pepper perm was too tight, and the nameplate proclaiming her to be Hazel Avery rested beside a plastic Jesus. Her desk sat in the middle of the room and squarely in front of a hallway. Hope wondered if, like Saint Peter, she was protecting the hall from heathen passage.

'You must be Hope Spencer,' Hazel said matter-of-factly as Hope moved toward her. 'Ada told me about your boots.'

Hoped looked down at her feet. 'I picked them up in a Western-wear store in Malibu.'

'Uh-huh.' Hazel clipped a ballpoint pen to a manila folder, then stood. 'Come with me, please.'

Hope followed Hazel down the hall to the first room on the left. Directly across the hall was the sheriff's office. The solid wooden door stood half open, and Dylan's name was painted in black and etched in gold. A surprising flutter settled in the pit of Hope's stomach, and she kept her gaze pinned on the two creases sewn into the back of Hazel's starched shirt.

Once inside the room, the woman gave Hope instructions on how to fill out the victim's complaint, and told her to describe the events as best as she could. Hope sat at a cleared desk and studied the form before her. There were certain 'events' of the previous night that were a bit hazy. Others that she wished she could forget.

'If you have any questions, I'll answer them for you.' Then Hazel added just before she left, 'So don't bother the sheriff with any more of your flirty skirt.'

Flirty skirt? Hope wondered if flirty skirt was related to huckuty buck, or if her clothing had just been insulted. She shook her head and took a seat. What exactly did Hazel think she was going to do anyway?

She filled out her name, address, and the date, and with her head bent over the folder in front of her, she raised her gaze to the half-open door across the hall and was provided with a view of half a chrome-and-black desk, half a telephone, and half a computer terminal. Her attention focused on the big hands with long fingers pecking at the keyboard. The same big hands that had wrapped around her wrists and pinned them on either side of her head. She glimpsed beige cuffs and just a sliver of his black leather watchband. He reached for a pen, rested his forearm on the desk, and, in a cramped, awkward fashion, scribbled something down.

Dylan was left-handed. He picked up the telephone receiver and tap-tap-tapped the desk with the pen. She could hear the muffled timbre of his voice and the pleasure in his deep chuckle.

Hope turned her attention to the form in front of her and concentrated on everything that had happened inside the Buckhorn. She remembered walking in, ordering beer, and eavesdropping. She'd been so excited about the idea for a new article that the time had flown. Emmett Barnes had insisted on buying her drinks and wouldn't take no for an answer. He got obnoxious. She got mouthy. Then the fight broke out, and she'd jumped on top of the table to get out of the way. The next thing she remembered was Dylan storming into the bar like the wrath of God and getting punched in the face. She remembered him hitting Emmett with a quick one-two and dropping him to the ground. Then he'd walked to her and helped her down from the table.

Her gaze returned to the room across the hall and the

tapping pen. He'd touched her bare stomach with those fingers. He'd touched her and asked if she was okay, and for the first time in a long time, she'd remembered what it was like to feel protected by a man. But it hadn't been real. She'd been drunk, and he'd been doing his job.

With a flourish, Hope signed the bottom of her statement and left the room. She handed Hazel the folder and watched her skim it.

'Lord help us,' Hazel said and flipped it close. 'If the prosecutor needs anything else, he'll be in touch.'

Hope glanced at the empty hallway one last time before leaving. Without looking back, she walked past the information desk and out the front door. But as she moved down the sidewalk and around to the parking lot, she felt somehow let down. She'd anticipated . . . what? Friendly conversation? A repeat of last night? Something.

A door on the side of the building opened and she glanced over her shoulder. Dylan stood at the top of the steps, his gaze directed at the duty belt he buckled at his waist. Without taking her eyes from him, Hope shoved her car key into the lock and watched Dylan walk down the concrete steps, his long legs closing the distance between them. He clipped some sort of microphone to the epaulet on his right shoulder. His full attention returned to adjusting his belt and he didn't notice her. She couldn't see his face for the shadow created by his black Stetson, but he appeared much as he had the first time she'd seen him. His tan dress shirt with the permanent creases sewn up his flat abdomen and chest. Star on one pocket, name badge on the other. Those tan trousers with the brown stripes up the sides. Hope had never been a sucker for a man in uniform, but she had to admit, Dylan made it look good. Then again, he made Levi's look good, too.

Her stomach did that weird little flutter thing again, and

she reminded herself that she'd forgotten to eat. She'd been working and hadn't eaten breakfast. Plus, she'd drunk about a pot of coffee. Hope opened the car door and he must have heard that, because he finally glanced up.

He paused by the left front fender of her car and looked at her from beneath the brim of his hat. The corner of one eye was swollen and black-and-blue. 'Hey, there, how are you feeling today?' he asked.

'I'm fine, but you don't look so good.'

'You should see Emmett.'

'Pretty bad?'

'He got what he deserved.' Dylan walked toward her, moving close until only the car door separated them. The man didn't seem to know the rules of personal space. 'I'm surprised to see you before noon,' he said.

Hope looked into his green eyes staring at her. Being the focus of his intent gaze was a little disconcerting, and she wrapped her hands around the top of the doorframe. 'Why, because I'm working?'

'No, because of your hangover.'

'I wasn't that drunk.' When he simply kept staring at her, she confessed with a shrug, 'Well, maybe a little, but I have to be worshiping at the porcelain shrine before I get a hangover.'

'Lucky you.' With the tip of his index finger, he pushed back his Stetson. 'What are you busy working on today? Your flora-and-fauna article for that Northwest magazine?'

'Actually, this afternoon I'm going to take pictures of the area.'

His gaze slid to the front of her shirt, framed in the car window. 'Dressed like that?'

'I thought I'd change.'

He placed his hands beside hers on the doorframe and slowly raised his eyes back up to her face. 'Where are you going to take your pictures?'

'I'm not real sure. Why?'

' 'Cause I don't want to get another call like last night.'

'Are you saying last night was my fault?'

'No. I'm saying you have a talent for trouble, and maybe you should just stay close to home for a while.' His hands brushed the outsides of hers and she felt his touch clear to her elbows.

She stood a little straighter and tried to ignore the sensation. 'Maybe you shouldn't think you can tell me what to do.'

'And maybe you should do something about that smart mouth.' He leaned closer. 'I've never said this to a woman, and it's just an opinion.' He paused, and she thought he might kiss her, but he didn't. 'Maybe you should consider becoming an alcoholic. You're a lot nicer when you're loaded.'

'Thank you, Sheriff. But in the future, when I want your opinion, I'll ask you for it.'

'Really?' A slow, evil smile curved his mouth. 'Honey, are you going to ask me on the bone phone, or should I make other plans?'

Hope felt her brows pinch together. That phrase was not only offensive but juvenile. She hadn't heard it since college, when she and her friends used it to refer to oral sex. She opened her mouth to tell him to grow up, to tell him real men didn't talk to women like that; then she recalled in perfect detail their conversation last night about the busty blonde in the Buckhorn.

She made a long, mental groan and quickly climbed into her car. 'You should make other plans,' she said and tried to shut the car door.

Dylan easily held it open. 'Just in case, do you want my number?'

She gave one hard tug and he finally let go. Without a

word, she fired up the Porsche and shoved it into reverse. She already had his number and it was 666.

Hope pulled the Porsche into the parking lot behind the Gospel Public Library. She hadn't written anything nonfiction in a while, but the first place she always liked to start was with old newspaper articles. It wouldn't hurt to check and see what the library had stored on the late Sheriff Donnelly. Shelly had seemed hesitant to talk about Hiram, and Hope didn't know anyone else in town – except Dylan. There was no way she'd ask him for anything. Not now. She didn't want to be within a mile, let alone speaking distance, of him. Not after he'd told her she should become an alcoholic. And especially not after the way she'd humiliated herself the night before. Her cheeks still burned when she remembered what she'd said, which had always been her biggest problem with booze and why she rarely got tanked. She thought she was funny when she wasn't.

If she wanted information, she would have to rely mostly on FBI files. It could take a while for them to comply, and she wasn't even sure she wanted to write an unsolicited article. That was a lot of work for no guarantee, and even if she did decide to write it, she didn't know what angle she would use – if she would slant it more toward a publication like *Time* or *People*. But the more she discovered about the old sheriff, the more intrigued she became. How had he gotten caught? And exactly how much money had he embezzled? Last night Dylan had mentioned something about videos. Had they been circulated through town? What was on them, and who'd seen them?

The Gospel Public Library building was about the size of two double-wide trailers stuck end to end, and the compact windows let in very little natural light. The inside was crammed with shelves and tables, and the front desk was piled with books. Regina Cladis stood behind the desk, her white hair a perfect dome on her round head. She studied several Goose Bumps books held close to her face, then shoved her Coke-bottle glasses down her nose and turned her head to study the covers out of the corner of one eye.

'Wash your hands before you open these,' she admonished three boys as she pushed her glasses back up her nose. 'I don't want any more black fingerprints on the pages.'

Hope waited until the boys had left with their books before she approached the desk. She looked into the librarian's enormous, slightly out-of-focus brown eyes and noticed Regina's irises were huge and cloudy. Hope figured the woman had to be legally blind, at the very least. 'Hello,' she began. 'I need some information, and I was hoping you could help me.'

'Depends. I can't check out library materials to anyone who hasn't resided in Pearl County for less than six months.'

Hope had been expecting that. 'I don't want to check out library materials. I'm interested in reading local news reports from five years ago.'

'What specifically are you interested in reading?'

Hope wasn't certain how the town would react to an outsider poking into its business, so she took a deep breath and just jumped right in. 'Anything associated with the late Sheriff Donnelly.'

Regina blinked, shoved her glasses down her nose, then turned her head and looked at Hope out of the corner of her eye. 'Are you the California woman living in Minnie's old house?'

Such intense scrutiny was more than a little unnerving, and Hope had to force herself not to back away. 'Minnie?'

'Minnie Donnelly. She was married to that no-good Hiram for twenty-five years before the good Lord called her home.'

'How did Mrs Donnelly die?'

'The cancer. Uterine. Some say that's what sent Hiram over the edge, but if you ask me, he was always a pervert. In the third grade he tried to touch my heinie.'

Hope guessed she no longer had to wonder if people would talk to her.

Regina pushed her glasses back up. 'What do you want with the news reports?'

'I'm thinking of writing an article about the old sheriff.'

'Have you ever published anything?'

'Quite a few of my articles have appeared in magazines,' Hope answered, which was the truth, but it had been a long time since she'd had anything appear in more mainstream publications.

Regina smiled and her eyes got even bigger. 'I'm a writer, too. Mostly poetry. Maybe you could look it over for me.'

Hope groaned inwardly. 'I don't know anything about poetry.'

'Oh, that's okay. I also wrote a short story about my cat, Jinks. He can sing along with Tom Jones to "What's New, Pussycat?" '

Hope's silent groan turned into a throat cramp. 'You don't say.'

'It's true, he really can.' Regina turned to a file cabinet behind her. She took a key from a rubber bungee cord around her wrist and, feeling for the lock, opened a file drawer. 'Let's see,' she said as she pushed her glasses to the top of her head. 'That would have been August of '95.' She stuck her face into the drawer and studied several small white boxes at close range. Then she straightened and handed Hope two rolls of microfilm. 'The projector is over there,' she said, pointing to a far wall. 'Copies are ten cents apiece. Will you need help with the projector?'

Hope shook her head, then realized Regina probably

couldn't see her. 'No, thank you. I've had lots of experience with these things.'

It took Hope a little under an hour to copy the newspaper articles. Because of the grainy projector screen, she didn't take the time to read them. She skimmed mostly, and from what little she saw, it seemed the late sheriff had been involved in several fetish clubs he'd found via the Internet. Over the course of a few years, he'd embezzled seventy thousand dollars to meet with other members. He'd met with them in San Francisco, Portland, and Seattle, and toward the end, his taste in girls had gotten younger and more expensive. In the last year of his life, he'd become so careless he'd paid for a few of them to come to his house. What Hope found most surprising was that for all his recklessness, no one in town knew a thing until his death. Or did they?

One name that drew her attention to the fuzzy screen every time it appeared was Dylan's. He was always quoted as saying, 'The FBI is investigating the case. I have no information at this time.' Luckily for the reporters, the other deputies hadn't been so tight-lipped.

When Hope finished, she gathered her Xerox copies and returned the microfilm. It was just after noon by the time she drove to Timberline Road, but she hadn't been home two minutes when the doorbell rang. It was her neighbor, Shelly, and she had something on her mind.

'You know,' Shelly began, 'I haven't had a neighbor for a long time now, and I guess I was hoping that we could be friends.'

Hope looked at Shelly standing there on the porch, her head cocked to one side, a few stray sunbeams turning her hair copper. She had no idea why her neighbour was so upset. 'We are,' she said, although she didn't think one lunch automatically made people friends.

'Then why did Dylan have to tell me about what happened to you at the Buckhorn?'

'I haven't had time to tell you,' Hope answered, even as she wondered if Shelly was really seeking friendship or just wanted information about what had taken place the night before. 'When did you talk to Dylan?'

'This morning when he dropped Adam off. He has quite a shiner. Emmett Barnes is a scary guy and you could have been really hurt.'

'I know, but a man named Hayden Dean stepped in. If it weren't for him, Emmett would have hit me.'

'Probably, but those Deans aren't much better, believe me.'

'Really? I was going to try and find out where Hayden lives so I could see how he's feeling today.'

Shelly shook her head. 'Stay away from those people. I think Hayden is his own first cousin.' One red brow lifted. 'If you know what I mean.'

Hope smiled, no longer caring if Shelly wanted friendship or information. It had been so long since she'd stood around gossiping with another woman, she'd forgotten how much she missed it. 'Do you want to come in? I think I might have a diet Pepsi.'

'Diet? Do I look like I need a diet?' asked the neighbor who looked like she'd had to lie down to get her Wranglers zipped up. 'I don't diet.'

'I might have some tea.'

'No, thanks. Wally and Adam and I were just headed down to the lake for a late picnic. Why don't you join us?'

Hope had a million and one things to do. Finish her alien story, take photographs of the area, have them developed at the one-hour photo place in town, scan them into her computer, then transpose some aliens into pictures. She had to read over the articles she'd xeroxed at the library, and she had to decide if there was a story in there somewhere. One that hadn't been told before.

Her eyes felt scratchy, her brain mushy. A few hours lying on the beach, emptying her head, and chatting about anything but work sounded like heaven. 'Okay,' she said. 'Give me ten minutes.' As soon as Shelly left, Hope ran upstairs and peeled out of her clothes. She washed her face and shaved her legs. Her blue-and-green tie-dyed one-piece was cut high on her hips, and she liked it because it made her legs look long. She grabbed an old picnic basket she found in the pantry and checked for petrified rodents. It was clean and she tossed in a few diet Pepsis, grapes, crackers, bleu cheese, and her Minolta camera and case. With a beach towel over one shoulder, a pair of Japanese flip-flops on her feet, and her sunglasses covering her eyes, she headed to the lake.

Adam and Wally were already in the water, while Shelly relaxed beneath the shade of ponderosa pines. She sat on the beach in a chaise longue, drinking a Shasta Cola and chowing on barbecued potato chips. She wore a Hawaiian print halter with a matching swimming skirt.

'We brought extra sandwiches if you're hungry,' Shelly offered as Hope sat in the chaise next to her neighbor.

'What kind of sandwiches?'

'Peanut butter and jelly, or ham and cheese.'

'Ham and cheese sounds good.' Hope sat, straddling the lounge chair. The metal frame warmed the insides of her thighs as she placed her picnic basket between her knees. 'I brought some fruit and some cheese and crackers,' she added as she opened the basket.

'Is it squirt cheese?'

'No, bleu.' Hope spread the cheese on a cracker, plopped a grape on top, then bit into it.

'Ahh. . . . no, thanks.'

Hope glanced at Shelly, who was watching her as if she were eating entrails. 'It's really good,' she said and popped the last of the cracker into her mouth.

'I'll just take your word for that.'

'No way. I ate your cooking, now you have to eat mine.' Hope fixed Shelly a cracker and handed it to her.

'This is your idea of cooking?' She looked doubtful, but she took it anyway.

'It is these days.'

Shelly bit into it, chewed carefully, then declared, 'Hey, this is better than I thought.'

'Better than squirt cheese?'

'Yeah, except for bacon flavor.' Shelly motioned for Hope's basket and they swapped.

'You can eat anything in there but the peanut butter and grape jelly,' Shelly told her as Hope pawed through the items. 'It's Adam's and he's real picky about his jelly. It has to be real smooth, no seeds or anything. Dylan has to make his sandwich special for him.'

Hope chose a ham and cheese made with the kind of soft white bread she hadn't had since she was a kid, and greasy potato chips. 'Where is Adam's mother?' she asked as if she weren't dying to know.

'Most of the time she lives in L.A.,' Shelly answered as she plopped a grape on top of a mound of bleu cheese. 'But when she has a visitation with Adam, they stay somewhere in Montana.'

'That's unusual.' Hope popped the top to a can of orange Shasta and raised it to her lips. 'Usually it's the father who has visitation.'

Shelly shrugged. 'Dylan's a good daddy, and when Adam needs female influence, he goes and stays with his grandma and aunt at the Double T. And, of course, a lot of the time he stays here with me and Wally when Dylan is working.'

Shelly bit into the cracker, then asked, 'Do you have children?'

'No. No children.' Hope waited for either the puzzled frown to wrinkle Shelly's brow or the oh-you-poor-thing look to cross her face. Neither happened.

'This stuff is addicting,' Shelly said while fixing herself another cracker.

Hope relaxed in the chaise and ate her lunch. She watched Wally and Adam stare intently down, hands poised over the surface of the lake. The meal was greasy and fattening and she polished it off with three Oreo cookies and a piece of licorice. When they traded the baskets back, all that was left in Hope's basket were a few pitiful grapes still on the vine, the two diet Pepsis, and her camera. She removed the Minolta from its case and pointed it at the two boys diving to catch minnows with their hands. Hope wasn't a great photographer, but she knew enough to get the shots she needed. She focused the lens and snapped.

'Are you taking pictures for your flora-and-fauna article?'

Suddenly Hope didn't feel so comfortable lying to Shelly. 'Yeah,' she said, which wasn't a *real* lie. She was taking pictures of the area for her alien article. She took several more photos; then the boys ran up the beach toward them and grabbed some towels.

Adam dug into the pocket of his swimming trunks and handed Shelly several small rocks. He told her she could have the most special one.

'Take a picture of me, Hope,' Wally urged as he flexed his pencil-thin arms.

'No, me.' Adam pushed Wally out of the way and posed like a bodybuilder.

'I'll take a picture of each of you and give them to you when I get them developed.' She took several photos before the boys grabbed their peanut butter sandwiches and sodas and took off to find more 'cool rocks' on the lake's shore.

'When are you going to finish your article?' Shelly asked.

Hope opened her mouth to rattle off a fictitious deadline, but stopped. They'd shared picnic baskets. She'd drunk Shelly's orange soda and eaten her Oreos, and she didn't feel like lying any more. Shelly hadn't judged Hope when she'd discovered that Hope didn't have any children. Maybe she wouldn't judge her profession or want to relate Elvis sightings. 'Well, if you won't spread it around, I'll tell you who I really write for.'

Shelly sat up a bit straighter and leaned toward Hope. 'I can keep a secret.'

'I really write for *The Weekly News of the Universe*. I lied about the Northwest magazine article.'

'You did? Why?'

'Because people assume all sorts of things about tabloid writers. Like we're sleazy and write gossip.'

'And you don't?'

'No. I write stories about Bigfoot and aliens and people living beneath the ocean in the Bermuda Triangle.'

'Hmm . . . that black-and-white tabloid they always sell next to the *Enquirer*?'

Hope waited for a boat to speed past before she snapped a picture of the clear green lake. 'Yes.'

'The one with Bat Boy on the cover?'

'Bat Boy,' Hope scoffed as she focused her camera on the distant shore. She made the trees the focal point and blurred the beach in the foreground. A perfect spot for fuzzy aliens to picnic. 'That's *Weekly World News*. They can't write their way out of a paper sack. Those people have absolutely no imagination.' As far as she was concerned, Bat Boy was one of the stupider stories she'd read from the competition.

'Oh! Giant ants attack New York?'

'Bingo.'

'Oh, my God! Did you write that?'

Hope lowered the camera and looked at her neighbor. 'No, but my stories are feature articles, and once in a while I write a sort of point-counterpoint advice column under the pseudonyms Lacy Harte and Frank Rhodes.'

'You're Lacy Harte?'

'I'm both Lacy and Frank.'

'You're kidding! I always thought those two were separate people. I mean, they're just so rude to each other.'

'At first I kind of felt schizophrenic, but I like it now. I also write features under the name Madilyn Wright.'

'What have you written that I might have read?'

Hope put the camera back inside its case, then stretched out in her chair and lifted her face to the sun. 'Last year, my series of Bermuda Triangle articles turned out to be real popular. I followed those up with the Micky the Magical Leprechaun features.'

'Oh, my God! I read some of those Micky the Magical Leprechaun stories. That was you?'

'Yep.'

'My mother-in-law buys those magazines and she gives them to me when she's through.'

As far as Hope could tell, only 'mothers-in-law' bought tabloids. Everyone read them, but she'd never met anyone who'd confessed to actually buying one. Kind of like trying to find anyone to admit they'd voted for Nixon.

Yet subscriptions alone to *The Weekly News of the Universe* were around ten million worldwide. There were a lot of closet readers, and they weren't all mothers-in-law.

'I really liked it when Micky transformed himself into RuPaul.'

That story had been the last of the leprechaun features and the beginning of her trouble. 'He hated that particular story.' When he'd read it, he threatened to sue Hope, her editor, and the president and CEO of the paper.

'Micky the Leprechaun is a real person?'

'He's not a leprechaun, he's a dwarf. His real name is Myron Lambardo, but he's also known as Myron the Masher. I met him in Vegas while I was there researching an article on Elvis impersonators. At that time, he worked in a little dive of a bar, wrestling women in a plastic kiddie pool filled with mud.' She'd paid him to let her photograph him, and she'd made sure he'd signed a release for the photos. 'At first he really liked the stories. He made the most of his fifteen minutes of fame and managed to get a few higher-profile wrestling matches as Micky. He used to call and leave messages on my business line, telling me how much he liked them. Then I did the RuPaul feature and he thought it made him look gay. He said I exploited and humiliated him, as if women pinning him in the mud was so much more dignified.

'When Myron discovered that he'd signed away his rights,' Hope continued, 'he started calling and threatening me. He wanted me to morph him into someone macho like Arnold Schwarzenegger. When I didn't respond to his threats, he found out where I lived and showed up at my door. He harassed me and wouldn't leave me alone, and I had to take him to court and get a restraining order against him.'

Shelly swung her legs over the side of her chaise. 'You're being stalked by Micky the Leprechaun?'

'Myron Lambardo.'

'Has he hurt you?'

'No, he just threatens to "tombstone" me.'

'But you're bigger than him.'

'Yeah, but he's one buff little dude. He wrestles for a living.'

Shelly's eyes got big and she raised a hand to her mouth. Hope thought she might have shocked her neighbor speechless, until Shelly burst into hysterical laughter.

Wally and Adam turned and looked at Shelly as if she were nuts. 'What's so funny, Mom?' Wally called out.

Shelly shook her head and the boys switched their attention to Hope, as if she had the answer.

Hope shrugged. What could she say? Some people were just plain nuts. Sometimes she wondered if she was the only sane person in an insane world.

Boy Grows Potatoes in His Ears

Water sprayed across Dylan's gray T-shirt, turning it black in spots. 'Hey,' he said as he poured shampoo on Adam's head. 'Get your fingers out of the spout.'

'I can do it myself, Dad,' Adam complained, sitting in the empty bathtub, the water running down the open drain.

'I know you can.' Sometimes Adam forgot to scrub his whole head, and Dylan liked to make sure at least once a week that all of Adam's hair got clean. 'What's in here?' Dylan asked. 'A gravel pit?'

'Nope. Wally and me got into a sand fight at his house.'

Like he'd done since the very first time he'd bathed his son as a newborn, Dylan shaped Adam's short hair into a point on top of his head, then leaned him back and rinsed out the shampoo. 'I'm surprised Shelly didn't beat on your behind.'

'Hope was there,' Adam said as he shut his eyes and relaxed. 'Shelly never whacks ya in front of company.'

'Hope went down to the beach with you?'

'Yeah.' Adam raised his hands to his face and cleared the water from his eyes.

'In a swimsuit?'

'Yeah. It was blue and green.'

'One piece or two?'

'One.'

It was on the tip of his tongue to ask how she'd looked, but he guessed he knew anyway. Hope Spencer would look good in a garbage bag. 'What did you all do?'

'Hope took some pictures, and then after a while she helped me and Adam build a sand castle. Only it got all wrecked when a beetle flew on her arm.'

Dylan raised Adam to a sitting position, then, using his hands, squeegeed the water from Adam's head. 'Did she scream?'

Adam laughed. 'Yep, and jumped around, too.'

Dylan would have liked to see Hope jump around in her swimsuit. He shoved the rubber plug into the drain and poured banana-scented bubble bath into the running water. 'There's the soap and washcloth,' he said, pointing to the soap dish. 'Scrub yourself real good.' He set a plastic basket filled with a mask, snorkel, and various action figures on the edge of the tub. 'Don't forget your parts. And,' he added over his shoulder as he stood and walked toward the bathroom door, 'clean your ears. There's enough dirt in there to grow potatoes.'

He moved down the short hall to the kitchen and the stack of dinner dishes waiting for him. He reached into the refrigerator, took out a bottle of Bud, and shut the door with his hip. He twisted off the cap, placed it between his thumb and middle finger, and snapped. The cap sailed under the kitchen table instead of into the garbage can and hit Adam's dog. The puppy lifted her head, then went back to sleep.

Dylan raised the bottle to his mouth and eyed the dishes stacked in the sink. Sometimes he thought it would be so much easier if he just got married. If he just found someone who could put up with him and be a good mama to Adam.

Someone who wouldn't mind taking her turn doing the dishes, and who would be home when he needed to take off on an emergency. Someone to talk to late at night. Someone to run the tips of her fingers across his belly.

But Dylan knew from experience that there was nothing worse than living with a woman for the wrong reasons. Nothing worse than living in a house with a woman he couldn't love for the long haul. Lying next to her in bed. Having sex with her because it was available, but no longer making love.

He'd done that with Julie. If it hadn't been for a broken condom, their relationship probably wouldn't have survived a year. Except for the fact that they'd both been raised on a ranch and both had hated it, they'd had nothing in common. If it hadn't been for Adam, the relationship wouldn't have lasted as long as it had. He loved his son and felt truly blessed to have him. They were buddies, but raising a child on his own wasn't easy. On him or on Adam, and he wouldn't have chosen it. He wouldn't have chosen the sole responsibility of raising his son to be a good boy and a decent man.

He wouldn't have chosen to see the pain and confusion in his son's eyes when they talked about why Adam's mama didn't live with them and why they didn't live with her.

Every July when Dylan took Adam to the airport to meet Julie, he always had to answer the same question: 'Why can't you come with Mommy and me?' And every year Dylan had to dance around the truth. He didn't want to spend time with Julie, but, more important, he didn't want Adam to get the idea in his head about their living as a family. Adam already had some weird notion that once his mother wasn't on television any more, she'd move to Gospel and live with them. But even if Julie's show was canceled tomorrow, Adam's dream would never come true.

Every year Adam would still go visit her, and every year

Dylan would camp out at the Double T for the two weeks that Adam was gone, looking over the books, helping out where he could, and irritating the hell out of his brother-in-law, Lyle. Lyle was a good cattleman and pretty good at the business, too, but even though Dylan had no interest in running the place himself, half the ranch was still his, and it would someday belong to Adam.

Dylan spent the first two weeks of every July going over the price of seed and feed and doing one of a million things that needed doing. But mostly he did it to avoid his empty house.

The water in the bathroom shut off, and Dylan set his beer on the counter. He rinsed the plates in the sink, and as he placed them in the dishwasher, his thoughts turned from his troubles with Adam to his problem with Hope Spencer.

Hope Spencer was a beautiful woman, and there was no denying that he liked the way she filled out her clothes. Even though he would probably never tell her, he liked that she was sort of sassy and smart-mouthed. He liked the smile she brought to his lips, even when he didn't know why he was smiling.

Kissing her had been a huge mistake. He'd known it even as he'd lowered his mouth to hers. She'd tasted all smooth and boozy. Like a swallow of expensive whiskey, she'd warmed him clear down to the very pit of his belly. The touch of her hands had squeezed his insides until he could hardly breathe. The look in her blue eyes, the passion shining back at him, had nearly sent him to his knees. Sent him there begging her to let him touch her naked skin and kiss between her thighs where she was warm and slick. If he'd had a condom in his wallet, he wasn't so sure he would have stopped. He wasn't so sure he wouldn't have had sex with her right there, in the kitchen, against the refrigerator.

Dylan closed his eyes and pressed a palm to the front of

his Levi's. He wasn't so sure he wouldn't have stripped off those Lycra shorts and buried himself deep within her. His tongue in her mouth, his hands on her breasts, and his penis inside where she was hot. Moving with her until her moist walls contracted and squeezed around him.

Beneath his hand, he was hard and he ached, and he didn't know what to do about it. Well, yes, he did know. He could do nothing or he could take care of business himself. Dylan reached for his cold beer.

Kissing her had been like being struck by lightning. It had raised his hair and burned his insides, but what really worried him about last night was that once he kissed her, he hadn't given another thought to her profession. She was a writer, and he just happened to be hiding the biggest story since the fall of Jim and Tammy Faye Baker. America's angel and PTL sweetheart, Juliette Bancroft, had an illegitimate son.

Something that was so important, he'd forgotten the second his tongue had swept the inside of her mouth. He was afraid the only thing that had stopped him was the thought of bringing another unplanned child into the world. No way in hell did he want another child under those circumstances.

Dylan looked out the window above the sink. In the dirt driveway, the setting sun cast long shadows on his Ford truck, parked next to the sheriff's Blazer. He wondered what Hope was doing over on Timberline. He wondered if she was watching TV or getting ready for bed. Adam had mentioned something about her taking pictures. Maybe she really was writing an article for an outdoors magazine. Maybe she hadn't been lying about that. Yeah, maybe, but that still made her a writer.

He could always run a check on her. He could run an NCIC and see if she had a criminal past. He could also run her license plates through his computer to find out anything he might want to know about MZBHAVN, but he wasn't going to do that. Not only was it against police ethics, it was against Dylan's. Unless she broke the law, she had a right to her privacy. She had a right to have all the people mind their own business.

Dylan understood privacy. Unfortunately, in Gospel, he seemed to be the only one.

Hope waited until Monday afternoon to drive to the M & S Market to buy a copy of *The Weekly News of the Universe*. She grabbed a blue plastic shopping basket and reached for a copy. The headline for her chicken-bone article appeared beneath the picture of a crazed-looking chicken in the bottom left corner of the paper. Her gaze lifted to the At-a-Glance box and she flipped to page fourteen. Dang, she'd been stuck behind 'Tinsel Town Gossip.' At least the feature was a full page with a photograph of fairly normal-looking women dancing around chickens, and the cutline: 'Bizarre cult eats the bones of chickens.' As she walked to the produce section, she flipped to the middle of the magazine. Clive Freeman's alien cow-mutilation article had been given the center spread.

Good, alien features were still hot. She'd sent off her own alien article the day before, complete with the slightly blurred shore of Gospel Lake and a few fuzzy aliens she'd retrieved from her CD-ROM library. She'd lined them up behind a rustic-looking table, and beneath the photograph she'd written the cutline, 'Aliens place bets on unsuspecting tourist in Northwest wilderness area.' She was extremely happy with the way the feature had come together and was already working on a follow-up article.

She'd also read the newspaper articles she'd photo-copied at the library, and she'd thought there was an interesting story to be told. Not about the salaciousness of it all, although there was plenty of that, but of a man whose personal and public lives were so diametrically opposed. How his personal choices had slowly consumed him until he'd become morally bankrupt in the end.

Hope slid the paper into her basket and picked through the sorriest bunch of avocados she'd ever seen. She'd been invited to the Aberdeen boys' eighteenth-birthday barbecue that night, and afterward she planned to ask Shelly a few questions about Hiram Donnelly.

The cantaloupe weren't much better than the avocados, but the lettuce was decent. Shelly had told her they were serving hot dogs, hamburgers, and the boys' favorite – Rocky Mountain oysters. Hope was taking a salad with sweet dressing, which was wonderful with seafood. She couldn't remember the last time she'd made her famous salad. Well, actually, when she thought hard enough, she could remember, but it had been a long time ago and was a sad commentary on her social life. Funny, she thought as she picked up a few household items, how moving to such a small town had emphasized the empty holes in her life. Funny how a few lunches with a woman she hardly knew, and an invitation to barbecue with her neighbors had left her wanting to get out more.

She thought about taking a bottle of wine to loosen Shelly's tongue, but Dylan and Adam had been invited, and she didn't want the sheriff to think she was a big boozer. She didn't know why she cared, and she didn't know what to think of the man who glanced at her from beneath the brim of his hat and stopped her heart. It was probably best not to think of him at all.

Hope took her place in line behind a couple decked out in REI and holding bottled water. Behind the counter, Stanley Caldwell rang up the purchases while his wife, Melba, bagged.

When it was Hope's turn, she set her basket on the counter.

'How're things out at the Donnelly place?' Stanley asked.

'They're good. How are you, Mr Caldwell?'

'I've got a bit of lower back pain, but I'm doing okay.' He took the avocados out of the basket and rang them up. 'I hear you're a writer.'

Hope raised her gaze from the basket to Stanley's face. 'Where did you hear that?'

'Regina Cladis,' he answered as he handed his wife the avocados to bag. 'She says you're writing a story about Hiram Donnelly.'

She glanced at Melba, then looked back at Stanley. 'That's right. Did you know him?'

'Of course we knew him. He was the sheriff,' Melba replied. 'His wife was a good Christian woman who never knew sin.'

'At least that's what she told everyone,' Stanley scoffed, ringing up the cantaloupe. 'Makes you wonder, though.'

'Makes you wonder what, Mr Caldwell?' Hope asked. Melba took the melon and placed it in the bag.

'Well, I don't think just because a man's wife dies, he goes so far off the deep end that he wakes up one morning and suddenly wants to put on leather underwear and get his hairy backside paddled.'

Melba shoved one hand on her hip. 'Are you saying Minnie was like Hiram? For the love of Pete, her daddy was a preacher.'

'Yep, and you know how they are.' He handed Melba Hope's copy of *The Weekly News of the Universe*.

Melba's brows lowered and then a light seemed to dawn in her eyes. 'Well, that's true.' She shrugged and glanced at the tabloid in her hand. 'There's a really good story in there about an eighty-pound woman giving birth to a twenty-pound baby.'

Finally, a person who admitted to reading a tabloid.

'And another good one,' Stanley added, 'is that article on aliens doing all those cow mutilations in New Mexico. Sure glad we don't have alien shenanigans going on around here.'

Oh, you're about to, Hope thought and wondered if they'd recognize themselves in her alien story. 'Did you read about the cult of women who eat chicken bones? One of them choked to death and they tried to revive her in a ritualistic chicken ceremony.'

'Didn't get to that one yet.' Stanley laughed and shook his head. 'Who makes that stuff up?'

Hope laughed, too. 'Someone with a creative imagination.'

'Or,' Melba said as Stanley hit TOTAL on the cash register, 'someone who's crazy.'

Hope recognized the music pouring from the boom box as country; other than that, she didn't have a clue. She'd dressed casually in a khaki skirt, white tank top, and flat sandals. She'd put her hair into a ponytail and pulled it through the back of her Gap baseball cap.

The early-evening sun cut a blinding trail across the lake as Hope stepped through the Aberdeens' back door. In her hands she carried her paper plate, half filled with the salad she'd brought and one of Shelly's deviled eggs.

A dozen teenage boys and girls ate at one of the two picnic tables sitting in the partial shade of the backyard. The smoke billowing from the big Weber barbecue enveloped the two men manning the grill. Only their lower halves were visible from behind. One wore his Wranglers at the crack of a flat butt; the other wore Levi's riding low on his hips. A breeze cleared the wafting smoke as both men stared down at the burning hamburgers, hot dogs, and Rocky Mountain oysters. Wally and Adam stood behind them with empty plates.

Paul turned at the waist and plopped a black weenie in each boy's bun.

'It's burned, Dad,' Wally complained.

'Put lots of ketchup on it,' Paul advised. 'You'll never know the difference.'

'I told him not to put so much charcoal in that barbecue,' Shelly whispered out of the side of her mouth as she and Hope made their way toward the grill. The breeze waned and the men were once again clouded with smoke.

From behind, all that appeared were two male butts and a glimpse of one green T-shirt, the other white. Hope didn't need to see their faces. After following Dylan around her house the night he'd brought her home from the Buckhorn, she easily recognized the width of his back beneath his white T-shirt, the pockets of his Levi's, and the worn denim hugging his hard buns.

Dylan looked over his shoulder at their approach, and the smoke curled beneath the brim of his beat-up straw hat. 'What are you ladies up for?' he asked.

'Which are burned the worst?' Shelly wanted to know.

'The hot dogs are pretty crispy, burgers are extra well done, but the oysters aren't too bad.'

'Keep those oysters away from me.' Shelly frowned. 'Burger, I guess.'

Dylan flipped a patty into a bun and handed it to Shelly.

'Paul is gonna give us all cancer,' she grumbled as she walked away.

Dylan turned his attention to Hope, and through the smoke, his green eyes stared into hers. 'What about you, Miz Behavin'?'

'I'll risk cancer and take a dog,' she told him.

'One black weenie.' He plopped a sizzling frank into a bun and set it on her plate. 'Paul says to put lots of ketchup on it.'

'Yeah, sorry,' Paul added.

'Actually, this is just right,' she assured the cook. 'I like black weenies. I don't eat raw meat.'

Dylan chucked, but he didn't say anything.

'Are you gonna try an oyster?' Paul asked her.

'Are they well done?'

'Sure are. How many do you want?'

'Just one.'

'I don't think that's a good idea,' Dylan told her while Paul placed a small breaded oyster next to her burned weenie. 'Have you ever eaten one of those before?' he asked.

'Sure.' She'd eaten seafood cooked all sorts of ways. 'Lots of times,' she added, then carried her plate across the yard and sat at the table with Shelly and the two little boys. At the other table, the teenagers were all in a deep philosophical discussion about who was the 'baddest badass,' Freddy Kruger or Chucky. The twins had finished eating and now had identical knots of Copenhagen bulging their bottom lips. The girls sitting next to them didn't seem to mind. In fact, their lips bulged, too.

'Look at them,' Shelly said and shook her head. 'Those boys were so cute when they were babies. I used to dress them alike. They had little sailor suits that were just so adorable. Now they're grown and they have nasty man habits.' As if on cue, Andrew spit a stream of tobacco into a Solo cup.

Hope quickly looked at Shelly. 'Are you feeling nostalgic today?'

'Old.' Her eyes got sad. 'I miss the way they used to smell. They don't smell like little boys any more.'

'I do, Mom,' Wally said from Shelly's other side.

'That's right.' She put her arm around her son and squeezed. 'You're my little stinkweed.'

Sitting across the table from Wally, Adam lifted his eyes

from the black hot dog on his plate. 'You can smell me if you want, Shelly.'

'Now, why would anyone want to smell you?' Dylan asked as he set a can of Coke on the table and swung one leg, then the other, over the bench seat and sat next to his son. 'You always smell like your dirty dog.' The tip of his boot touched Hope's bare toe and she slid her foot back.

'That's 'cause she likes to kiss my face.' He laid his head against Dylan's shoulder.

Dylan looked down at Adam and the brim of his hat cast a woven shadow across his nose and one cheek. 'Probably because you taste just like a pork chop.'

'Uh-uh, Dad.'

Hope bit into her crispy hot dog and studied Dylan's profile, looking for similarities with his son. Adam's hair was darker, his mouth and nose were different, but his eyes – his eyes were his father's.

Shelly pointed to Dylan's Coke. 'Aren't you going to eat anything?'

He looked up and the shadow moved to cover the top half of his face, drawing attention to his mouth. Hope watched his lips as he spoke. 'I choked down a few weenies before they got incinerated.'

Paul placed a plate heavy with food on the table and sat on the other side of Wally. 'I guess Hope is the only woman who appreciates my cooking.'

Actually, the hot dog was even a bit too burned for her. She liked them black, not crunchy, but she didn't say so. Instead, she took a bite. 'Mmmm.' One corner of Dylan's mouth lifted in a dubious smile, and when she swallowed, it felt like the crispy hot dog got stuck in her chest.

Shelly pointed to her husband's plate. 'Eat some of Hope's salad. You need to get healthy if you're going to win the toilet toss this year.'

'You going to enter that again?' Dylan asked.

'Yep, first prize is a big-screen TV.'

'That's right, and I want that TV,' Shelly said. 'So, starting tomorrow, I'm putting Paul on those steroids they feed cattle. He needs to be strong like a bull.'

'What if I wind up hung like a bull?' Paul wanted to know.

'Actually, those steroids will mess with your sex drive and can shrink your who-hah,' Dylan informed everyone.

'What's a who-hah, Dad?'

'I'll tell you later.'

Hope took another bite of her crunchy hot dog and lowered her gaze to her plate. With complete certainty, she could honestly swear that she'd never been surrounded by dinner companions who chewed tobacco, discussed slicing and dicing body parts, and talked about shrinking who-hahs.

While Hope ate her salad, she listened to Shelly and Paul plan their strategy for winning the toilet toss, which involved last-minute weight training and vitamin consumption. Again the tip of Dylan's boot touched her toe, and she drew her foot back with the other. She glanced up, but his attention was focused on Adam and Wally, who'd left to skip rocks across the lake.

'Stay where I can see you,' Shelly called after them.

Hope sprinkled a little salt on her oyster and reached for a plastic knife. She wasn't so sure she wanted it any more.

'Are you really going to eat that?' Dylan asked from across the table.

'What?' She raised her gaze as far as his hand wrapped around the Coke can. A bead of condensation slid down the red aluminum and disappeared behind his knuckle.

He lifted one finger from the can and pointed at her plate. 'That's not a real oyster, you know.'

'What is it, fake?'

'You could say that.'

This time she raised her gaze as far as the white T-shirt stretched across his broad chest. 'Like some packed crab is really whitefish?'

'No, honey. Like Rocky Mountain oysters are really balls.'

There it was again. *Honey* and the way he said it sort of poured over her like honey, too. 'Balls of what?'

'Jesus, I knew you didn't have a clue. Balls as in testicles.'

She finally looked up into his face, behind the shadow cast by his hat, and into his eyes. 'Sure they are. And next you're going to tell me that my hot dog is really a who-hah.'

His brows rose up his forehead and laugh lines appeared in the corners of his eyes. 'You don't believe me?'

'Of course not. That's repulsive.' She speared the oyster and lifted it to her lips.

'If you think so, you better not put that in your mouth.'

She gave it a slight sniff, then turned to Shelly, who was in a heated discussion about where she and Paul would place the big-screen television. 'Shelly, what is this?'

'What?'

'This.' She shook her fork.

'A Rocky Mountain oyster.'

'Is it a shellfish?'

'No, it's a testicle.'

'Oh, my God!' She dropped the fork as if it had suddenly zapped her. 'Whose?'

Dylan burst out laughing. 'Not mine.'

'They came from the Rocking C. I bought 'em during castration season,' Shelly told her.

'You *bought* them? Oh, my God!'

'Well,' Shelly answered as if Hope were the crazy one, 'they don't just give away free oysters, you know.'

'No, I don't know. I'm from California. We eat *real* food. We don't eat cow balls.'

'Steer.'

'Whatever!'

'They taste just like chicken,' Dylan informed her.

'You said the same thing about lizard!' She felt as if she'd been drop-kicked into an episode of *The Beverly Hillbillies*. Next they would probably break out the roasted squirrel.

'I was kidding about the lizard.'

'Dylan's right,' Paul added from down the table. 'Rocky Mountain oysters taste like chicken – crunchier, though. Like a gizzard.'

'That's what I hear,' Shelly said. 'Of course, I've never eaten one.'

Finally, some sanity. Hope raised her hands to the sides of her face. Her stomach was suddenly queasy, but she was saved from further culinary description by the twins.

'Mom, we're heading downtown,' Thomas informed his mother.

'What's going on downtown?'

'Probably nothin'. We'll probably end up playing pool over at Zack's.'

'If you drink and drive, I'll take your car away,' Paul warned.

'And be home by midnight,' Shelly added, which set off a debate on whether the twins were old enough now to do away with a curfew altogether.

While the Aberdeens argued, Hope carried her plate into the house and dumped it into the garbage can beneath the kitchen sink. She tossed her hat onto the counter and placed the plastic wrap on the salad she'd brought. She glanced out the window into the back yard and watched the teenagers move from the yard toward their cars. A few of them still wore braces on their teeth. Some suffered from teen acne. They looked so normal, but they weren't. They chewed tobacco and ate testicles. In her wildest imagination, she could not have made up something like that. But even if she had, no one would have believed it. Walter would have told her the story was too far-fetched, even for a tabloid that specialized in the far-fetched.

The back-door screen opened and Hope looked over her shoulder. Dylan walked toward her carrying several paper plates. She slid to the corner of the counter, and he dumped them in the garbage.

'Paul is a good guy,' he said, 'but he can't cook worth a damn. You didn't have to eat that hot dog.'

'It wasn't the hot dog I minded.' Hope reached for a mayonnaise lid and screwed it on the jar. 'How can you all eat testicles?' When he didn't answer right away, she turned her head and looked at him. He stood beside her, one hip shoved into the counter, his arms folded across his chest, his attention pinned to her behind.

He slowly raised his gaze to her face, past her mouth to her eyes. He shrugged and just smiled at having been caught staring at her butt. 'To tell you the truth, I never could work up an appetite for Rocky Mountain oysters.'

She imitated his casual poise. Arms folded beneath her breasts, hip resting against the counter. Outside, she heard snatches of conversation, engines racing, and the crunch of gravel beneath tires. Inside, it all receded to the peripheral of her brain, and she found herself completely focused on him. The sound of his voice, the exact color of his eyes, and the way he pushed his hat up his forehead.

'Personally,' he said, 'I never felt right about chewing on some steer's left nut.'

'How many have you eaten?'

'One.'

She looked at his mouth. She'd kissed a man who'd

confessed to eating a 'steer's left nut.' She should have been repulsed.

As if he'd read her mind, he said, 'I brushed my teeth for about an hour afterward, and I flossed real good.'

She couldn't have prevented her smile even if she'd thought to. 'I've always been a sucker for a guy with good oral hygiene.'

He reached for her hand and his warm fingers closed around hers. She tried to ignore the hot tingle warming her skin and spreading to her wrist. 'And I've always been a sucker for a sucker, especially if she's wearing a short skirt.'

She glanced down at herself, at the hem of her skirt resting about an inch, no more than two, above her knees.

'Did you know that when you bent over to set your plate on the table, I could almost see the color of your underwear?'

No way was her skirt *that* short. She looked back up into his face. 'You'd have to stand on your head to see the color of my underwear.'

'Actually, if I tilt my head just a little . . .' he confessed with an evil glint in his eyes as he brushed his thumb across her palm.

It was just her hand, nothing sexual about that, but for some unexplainable reason, the simple touch felt much more intimate. There was nothing to get excited about, she told herself even as her pulse leaped. No, nothing. 'That's kind of pathetic, Dylan. The last guy who tried to guess the color of my underwear was Jimmy Jaramillo. That was in fourth grade.'

'Now, I'm sure you're wrong about that. I'm sure there are a lot of guys standing around guessing the color of your underwear.'

'Just you and Jimmy.'

'No, me and Jimmy are the only ones who have told you what we were up to.'

'You're obviously bored. It sounds like you need a girlfriend.'

'Nah, a girlfriend is the last thing I need.'

'Why is that?'

He turned her hand over and studied each of her red fingernails. 'Why is what?'

'Why is a girlfriend the last thing you need?'

He shrugged. 'A lot of reasons. I don't have time. I don't want a serious relationship right now, and I'm not very good at it anyway. Adam keeps me really busy.' He turned her hand back over and stared at her palm. 'But I do miss having a woman around sometimes.'

She bet she knew what he missed. She missed it, too. Ever since the night he'd stood in her kitchen and kissed her, she'd thought about how much she missed it.

'I really miss feeling the weight of a woman's hand in mine as I walk down the street.'

That wasn't exactly what she'd been thinking. He looked at her, and in an instant, she recognized the emptiness and longing gazing back at her. Dylan Taber, the very eligible and extremely handsome sheriff of Pearl County, the man who drove women crazy with his easy smiles and causal endearments, was lonely. Just like her.

Incredible but true, and something deep inside Hope swelled and answered the yearning in his green eyes. His lids lowered a fraction, and he stared at her lips. Her breath caught in her throat, and her chest got tight. She raised her face as he slowly lowered his mouth toward hers.

The back door was thrown open hard enough to hit the wall. The moment shattered, Hope and Dylan jumped apart as Paul and Shelly raced into the kitchen. Paul held Shelly's hand above her head as blood ran down her arm and dripped from her elbow.

'Shelly cut her hand with my hunting knife,' Paul yelled

before anyone had the chance to ask. He grabbed a towel off the counter and wrapped it around her hand.

'That's dirty,' Shelly protested calmly. 'Hope, behind you in the third drawer down are the clean towels.'

'What happened?' Dylan asked Paul.

'I put my knife in a bucket of soapy water she had out there for the kids to put their dirty dishes in. Before I could tell her, she stuck her hand in it.'

Under the circumstances, Hope didn't think she could have remained as composed as Shelly. In fact, she was sure she'd be screaming her head off. She pulled a towel from the drawer and handed it over. 'Is it deep?'

'She'll need stitches for sure,' Paul answered. His breathing was shallow, and he was clearly more panicked than his wife. 'I'm going to run her to the clinic.'

'I'll drive you,' Dylan offered. 'We'll get there quicker.'

'What about the little boys?' Paul wanted to know.

'I'll watch them,' Hope volunteered.

Dylan turned to her. 'I don't think that's a good idea. I'll call someone.'

'I can handle two small boys,' she assured him, slightly offended that he didn't think her capable.

'Are you sure?' Dylan asked.

'Sure.'

How hard could it be?

Man Hypnotizes Chickens to Lay More Eggs

'Bloody finger one block awaaay . . .' Beneath a makeshift tent of blankets, safety pins, and kitchen chairs, Hope shined the flashlight under her chin and stared at the two young faces across from her. She opened her mouth and continued her scary story in her scariest voice. 'I ran and hid behind my bed, but still I heard, "Bloody finger one house awaaay . . ."' She slid her hand under a pile of sleeping bags and rapped her knuckles against the hardwood floor. 'Bloody finger at your door . . .' Adam's eyes got wide and Wally chewed on his lower lip. '. . . knock . . . knock . . . knock.' She reached out her hand. 'I opened the door . . . and there was a kid standing there.' She paused for dramatic effect, then continued. 'He had a bloody paper cut, and he needed a Band-Aid.'

For several long moments the boys stared at her within the darkness of the blanket tent. Then they looked at each other and snorted.

Adam shook his head. 'That was really lame.'

'It wasn't even scary,' Wally added.

'You guys were scared,' she said. 'I saw you.'

'Wally was, but I wasn't.'

Wally punched Adam on the shoulder. 'No way.'

'Come on, guys,' Hope complained as the two started punching each other in the arms. 'You'll knock down the tent again, and next time I won't put it back up.' The two had spent most of the evening in a wrestling tangle, and while they seemed to really enjoy slamming and pounding on each other, it drove Hope crazy. Made her contemplate that bottle of zinfandel she had in her refrigerator. One glass probably wouldn't hurt, but Adam's daddy already thought she couldn't handle two little boys. Probably wouldn't look good if he came to pick up his son and Hope was knocking back vino.

'You two tell each other stories while I clean up,' she said as she crawled out of the tent. She stood and stretched her arms over her head. Growing up, she and her brother had wrestled, and he'd tickled her until she'd wet her pants, but geez, never like Adam and Wally. Those two were in constant motion.

She picked up the half-empty cans of Pepsi from the coffee table, a bowl of popcorn kernels, and walked into the kitchen.

She'd heard from Dylan about forty-five minutes ago, calling to tell her that they'd transferred Shelly to the hospital in Sun Valley. The wound in her hand had been severe enough to require surgery to repair some of the damage. He'd also said that the twins were on their way to the hospital, and that as soon as they arrived, he would leave to pick up the two boys.

Hope set the bowl on the counter, then dumped out the cans of Pepsi and tossed them in the recycling bin. The drive from Sun Valley would take Dylan at least an hour, so she figured he'd arrive at her door anywhere from fifteen minutes to an hour and a half, depending on the Aberdeen twins.

'Hey,' came a muffled cry from the other room, 'get off my head, butt-munch.'

'You're the butt-muncher.'

She closed her eyes and lifted her hands to the sides of her face. She was going to ignore them for a few minutes; maybe they'd work out all their energy and just pass out. Instead, they giggled, which she'd learned was not a good sign.

She walked into the living room and stood quietly outside the tent made of blankets.

'That was bad, Wally,' Adam said.

'I've got another one. Quick, pull my finger.'

She thought for sure no one would be so stupid as to follow that command. She was wrong, and the room was filled with rude noises and more giggles. Hope made a vow to herself right then and there: If she ever decided to adopt a child, she would adopt a girl. No boys. No way.

She turned on the television and watched the ten o'clock news out of Boise. To her vast relief and utter surprise, the commotion within the tent quieted, and halfway through the weather report, Adam crawled out and informed her that Wally had fallen asleep.

'Do you want to sit with me or color something?' she asked him.

'Color, I guess.'

Hope gave him a box of colored pencils she used to correct her articles after she printed them out to proofread. She placed pieces of copy paper on the coffee table and he got busy.

'What are you going to draw?'

'My dog.'

Hope sat next to him on the hard floor. The antler legs of

the table provided very little room beneath, and she was forced to sit Indian-style.

'What are you going to draw?' he asked.

'You.' She reached for the green pencil and drew a boy with big green eyes and brown hair sticking up on his head. She wasn't much of an artist, and when she was through, the drawing looked nothing like Adam.

He looked at it and laughed. 'That's not me.'

'Sure it is.' She added a few freckles and pointed to the missing front tooth in her picture. 'See?'

'Okay, I'll draw you.' He grabbed a clean sheet of paper and a yellow pencil.

'Get my good side.' She presented him her profile.

'My mom's got yellow hair, too. But it used to be brown.'

Her interest thoroughly piqued, Hope carefully asked, 'Where does your mom live?'

He glanced up at her, then back down at his drawing. 'Most of the time in California, but when I see her, we go to my grandpa's house.'

'Where's that?'

He shrugged. 'Montana.'

Hope felt a little bad pumping the kid for information, but not bad enough to stop. 'Do you get to see her very often?'

'Yep. She's on the TV.'

On the TV? 'You mean her picture is on your TV?'

'Yep.'

One more question and then she promised to stop. 'Where does your mom work?'

'I'm not supposed to talk about that.'

Really? Hope immediately wondered what Dylan's ex-wife did that was so bad Adam couldn't talk about it. Hooker or stripper came to mind. 'Hey,' she said and pointed to the drawing of her. 'My nose isn't that big!'

Adam nodded and laughed. 'It is now.'

'Fine.' She grabbed another piece of paper and drew Adam with big ears and crossed eyes. 'Look at you,' she said, and the race was on to draw the goofiest face. When they finished, Adam won with his picture of Hope picking her nose with 'wolverine claws.'

'What do I get?' he asked.

'What do you mean, "What do I get"?'

'I won. I get something.'

'Hmm . . . I have some microwave popcorn.'

'No way.' He looked around and pointed at the stuffed bobcat on the hearth. 'What about that?'

'I can't let you have that. It's not mine.'

He pointed to the bearskin rug. 'That?'

'Nope.' Hope rose to her feet and walked into the dining room. The only thing she could think to give him was a small crystal hummingbird she'd bought to hang in the window by her computer. 'How about this?'

'What's it do?'

'When you hold it up to the light,' she explained as she handed it to him, 'it shoots really cool prisms around the room. It works best in sunlight.' His hair was a little too long and fell in his eyes as he studied the bird. She wondered what it would feel like beneath her fingers, or what he'd do if she pushed it from his eyes.

'It's pretty, huh?'

'I thought so,' she said and gave in to her curiosity. She raised her hand and combed his hair off his forehead. Warmed by his scalp, the baby-fine strands slid through her fingers.

Maybe one little boy wouldn't be so bad to have around the house, she thought as she dropped her hand to her side. 'What do you think?'

Adam's shoulder itched and he scratched it. The bird was

kinda girly, but okay, he guessed. 'It's all right.' He shrugged and walked back into the living room, watching his bare toes as he moved to the tent. He looked over at Hope. 'Tell me when my dad gets here,' he said and crawled inside next to Wally. He lay down on a sleeping bag they'd found in a closet upstairs and stared up at the blankets arching over his head. He wished he were at home. He wished his dad would hurry.

He held up the bird Hope had given him, then lowered it real close to his eyes. Light from the living room filtered in through the blankets and if he squinted really hard, he could see it through the hummingbird. He thought about Hope, and about her drawing pictures with him even when his dad wasn't around. She'd given him a present, too. And she hadn't brought it to his house just so she could see his dad. Not like those other girls.

Maybe Hope was like Shelly. Shelly wasn't like the others. She didn't come over and pretend she liked Adam so she could talk to his dad.

He rolled onto his side and shoved the little bird into his shorts pocket. Maybe he'd find Hope a cool rock. He liked it when she took pictures of him and Wally, and he liked those blue boots she wore sometimes. She'd built the tent out of blankets, and she was funny when she ran from bats. He liked the way her hair shone.

Like an angel. Like his mom. Adam knew his mother wasn't a *real* angel. He knew she lived in California and sometimes in Montana with his grandfather, but never in heaven. He knew she didn't sit around on clouds and pray a lot, because she didn't even pray at dinnertime. He knew his mom couldn't live with them 'cause she had to be on television. He knew he couldn't tell all his friends about his mother because then people would come and bug her during their special time in Montana. The only friend who

138

knew about his mom was Wally, and he couldn't tell anyone, either.

Adam tried to keep his eyes open, but the left one kept shutting. He thought maybe he'd close them both for just a few minutes, give them a rest before his dad came.

He knew his mom was an actress and that was her job. He knew some of the stuff she did wasn't for real, like she couldn't fly and she couldn't come into the room and be invisible if she wanted. But he figured some of the stuff she did on her show had to be real, and he wished he could meet those kids she'd saved when their house caught fire last week. She'd saved their cat, too. And his mom knew Santa Claus. She'd saved Santa when he'd drunk too much and got hit by a bus. She'd told him that he had to live for all the kids in the world who loved him, and Adam wished he could go to the North Pole and meet Santa. He and Wally had talked about that. Since his mom had saved Santa, for Christmas Adam would ask for something big, like the go-cart his dad said he couldn't have until he turned ten.

Adam yawned and shoved his hand beneath his cheek. He wished his mom could come live with him and his dad. Maybe if he were really good and wanted it really a lot, she would.

Dylan knocked on Hope's door and waited for her to answer. It was half past eleven, and he'd left the hospital as soon as the twins arrived, leaving them to take care of their father as much as their mother. Dylan had never seen Paul so upset. He'd never seen him so emotional before, but when they'd wheeled Shelly away, her husband had started bawling. Paul blamed himself and was acting as if he'd plunged the knife in her heart. He'd said he just couldn't stand to see her hurt.

Sure, Shelly's cut was bad, but it was nowhere near life-threatening. As he'd sat with his friend, instead of being repulsed by Paul's blubbering, he found himself a bit jealous instead. He'd never loved a woman like that. Not the kind that could make him cry like a girl, especially after nineteen years of marriage. He wondered why he'd never found a woman he could love that much. He wondered if he ever would.

Now, lust. Lust was different. He'd had a real lust-on since the morning MZBHAVN had pulled into town. And during the drive home, he'd thought of little else but standing in Shelly's kitchen, studying the soft skin of Hope's hand and the lines on her palm. And during that long drive from Sun Valley, he'd thought about the night he'd brought her home from the Buckhorn, too. He remembered the way she'd touched him, and like watching a movie stuck in slow motion, he recalled every detail. The moist texture of her mouth, the caress of her hands sliding down his chest, the heavy ache between his legs.

The front door swung open and there she stood before him, backlit by the chandelier in the entry. After so many hours with Wally and Adam, he expected Hope to resemble a crazed Medusa. She didn't. Her hair was down and a little messy, but she looked warm and drowsy, like she'd just gotten out of bed.

'Did I wake you?' he asked.

'No, I was lying down on the couch watching the end of Leno.' She stepped back and he entered the house.

She smelled all warm and drowsy, too, he thought. 'The boys give you trouble?'

'They're asleep.' She led him to the living room, and he let his gaze travel from the top of her hair, down her straight back, over the nice curve of her behind, to the backs of her smooth thighs. Her feet were bare. 'We found some sleeping bags and kind of camped out.'

The tent made out of blankets shocked him. He supposed he would have been less surprised if they'd constructed a beauty parlor.

'They played haunted house upstairs for a while, and then when they got bored with that, we told scary stories down here.'

He moved his gaze from the tent to Hope. 'They weren't too much for you?'

'Well, they did wrestle almost constantly. Everything they picked up turned into some sort of sword or knife or gun, and the pulling-finger thing was a bit disturbing.' She cocked her head and looked up at him through the corners of her eyes. 'I only thought about hitting the sauce once or twice.'

His attention was drawn to her smile, to her pink lips, and he wondered if she'd taste all sleepy, too. If she'd taste all warm and willing, as if he'd just woken her in the middle of the night to make love.

'Adam's a nice little guy. You're lucky to have him.' She brushed her hair behind her ears. 'How's Shelly?'

He opened his mouth to ask 'Who?' but caught himself. Pushing aside the opening in the tent, he looked in on Wally and Adam. 'She cut herself pretty bad. The doctors had to repair some tendons, but she'll be okay. She should be home by morning.' The boys lay on top of more blankets and sleeping bags and were curled up like hibernating bears.

'That's good news, I guess.'

'I think she's doing better than Paul. He was carrying on like he'd killed her.' Dylan dropped the edge of the blanket and looked over at Hope. 'I wasn't around when Shelly had her boys, but she said that Paul was pacing and crying when they were born, too.'

'Didn't you pace and cry when your wife had Adam?'

He didn't correct her about Julie not being his wife. 'I didn't have time. I barely got Julie to the hospital before he was born.'

'Short labor?'

'Long drive. We were visiting her father.' He moved toward her and glanced at the drawings on the coffee table. 'Adam was born in the hospital there.'

'Adam mentioned her tonight.'

Dylan glanced up. 'Julie? What did he say?'

'Just that she lives in California and has blond hair that used to be brown.'

It was definitely time to change the subject. 'You all recovered from your encounter with Rocky Mountain oysters?'

'I'll answer your question if you answer one of mine.'

'What do you want to know?'

'What your ex-wife does for a living.'

He looked her right in the eye and lied, 'She's a waitress.'

'Oh.' A wrinkle appeared between Hope's brows as she sat on the arm of the couch.

'Now tell me if you're recovered from the oysters.'

'Barely. If someone had told me that there were people who actually ate those things, I wouldn't have believed them. It's just too bizarre.'

At least when she talked about it now, she wasn't screeching and pale and looking like she was about to vomit. In fact, a smile threatened the corners of her lips. Dylan liked her smile. He liked the sound of her laughter, too, feminine and sort of breathy. He liked it so much, he opened his mouth and told her the second biggest secret he knew. The secret so embarrassing *no one* in his family talked about it. Not even at Thanksgiving, when they all got together and got hammered. 'If you think that's bizarre, then you should meet my cousin, Frank. He can hypnotize chickens.'

Hope's brows rose and she looked at him like he was crazy. 'How?'

Dylan raised his right hand. 'He holds them down and makes them concentrate on his finger.'

She laughed. 'You're full of it.'

If his mother found out he'd spilled the beans about Cousin Frank, she'd kill him. She didn't want anyone to know those kind of genes warped their DNA, but hearing Hope's laughter just might be worth getting killed for. 'I swear it's true.'

She shook her head and her hair fell forward and brushed her right cheek. 'Why would anyone hypnotize a chicken?'

' 'Cause he can, I guess.'

'What does he hypnotize them to do? Go up on stage and act like people?'

He chuckled and moved toward her. 'They just lie there, looking dead.' He pushed her shiny hair behind her ear, and the backs of his knuckles brushed her smooth cheek. 'My aunt, Kay, seriously thinks he's gifted.'

'You are seriously demented.'

Her hair tangling around his fingers was cool to the touch, and very soft. 'You don't believe me?'

'No.'

The brief contact twisted his belly into a knot, and he lowered his hand. 'I told you the truth about the Rocky Mountain oysters.'

'You also told me you ate a lizard.'

'No, I never said I ate lizard.'

'You let me think you did.'

'Yeah, but that's not a lie.'

'Maybe not technically, but you wanted me to believe something about you that wasn't true.'

His gaze slid from her cheek to the bow of her top lip. 'Well, then, I guess that makes us even.'

'You think I lie to you?'

He looked into her clear blue eyes, gone all wide and innocent. 'Since the day you drove into town.'

She drew her brows together. 'You could always do a check on me.'

'I could, but I don't check a person's background unless they give me a reason. It's against department policy.' He paused before he asked, 'Do I have a reason?'

'No.'

'Break any laws recently?'

'Not that I'm aware of.'

'No warrants for indecent exposure?'

'No.'

'Sexual harassment?'

She laughed. 'Not recently.'

He looked her over from head to toe, then back up again. 'That's a shame.'

She tucked in her chin and regarded him out of the corner of her eye. 'Are you flirting with me, Sheriff Taber?'

'Honey, if you have to ask, then I must be getting old.'

'How old are you?'

'Almost thirty-eight.'

Her lips became a seductive smile that warmed his chest. 'You look pretty good for such an old guy.'

'Ms Spencer, are you flirting with me?'

'Maybe.' A wrinkle appeared between her pale brows. 'It's been a long time since I've flirted with anyone, but I think so.' The wrinkle smoothed. 'I guess you got lucky.'

Lucky. He didn't know if he should run like hell or push her down on the couch and show her lucky. He took a step back. 'Did you send in a request for Hiram Donnelly's old files?' he asked, again changing the subject and putting a distance between them.

She stared at him for a few moments as if she didn't

follow the sudden shift in conversation. 'Ah, yeah,' she finally said. 'Last week.'

'Good. Let me know if you need help making sense out of them.' She stood and he took another step back. 'I better get the boys home and put them to bed.'

'Their shoes are upstairs. I'll get them.' Hope moved toward the stairs and felt very much like she had the night in her kitchen when he'd kissed her. After one touch, he couldn't get away from her fast enough, and like that night, she didn't know what she'd done.

When she got to the top of the stairs, she headed down the hall and went into a room on her right. Maybe she shouldn't have admitted that she hadn't flirted for a long time.

Maybe she'd scared him.

Beside the bed in the spare room at the end of the hall, she found Wally's cowboy boots and one of Adam's blue sneakers. As she crawled on the floor looking for the other shoe, she wondered if she gave off some sort of desperate vibe that freaked him out. By admitting she hadn't flirted in a while, maybe he thought there was something wrong with her, and maybe he was right to do that. She'd met Dylan just over a week ago. She really didn't *know* him, but when he looked at her or smiled at her or talked to her, her chest got tight. And when he touched her, she didn't think at all.

She walked into the closet and looked around. As she rummaged though the camping gear inside, she heard the heavy tread of Dylan's bootheels enter the room. She found the sneaker next to some extra sleeping bags, and when she came back out of the closet, Dylan stood in front of the window, over six feet of hard man, looking out across the lake.

'I've never seen the view from over here.' His shoulders filled the window, and the weak sixty-watt bulb overhead picked out the buried layers of gold in his hair and emphasized the stark white of his T-shirt tucked inside his Levi's.

Hope set the shoe by the others next to the bed, then moved to stand beside him. She really couldn't see out the window, but she really wasn't dying to, either. She still felt no awe for the beauty around her, but she had to admit that there was a certain stillness to it all. A sort of tranquility that couldn't be found in the most expensive resort or bought at the trendiest spa.

'You can't see it from here, but there's my house,' he said, pointing to the left and sliding over so she could see. 'Right over there beyond that biggest ponderosa. And see that bright star at about sixty degrees north?' When she didn't move, he wrapped an arm around her waist and pulled her to stand in front of him. With her back pressed against the solid wall of his chest, and one hand resting on her hip, he pointed to the stars. 'Look directly below to that pale spot. That's Devil's Chin rock. Right below that is the Double T Ranch. That's where I grew up. My mother and my sister still live there. If my mother had her way, I'd live there, too.'

He smelled faintly of musk and cologne, and the scent of cool night air clung to his skin. She looked out into the night, but there was nothing to see. The window faced the empty lake, and not so much as a sliver of light from her porch or the Aberdeens' yard penetrated the darkness. Instead of watching where Dylan pointed, she watched his reflection. 'I take it you don't want to live there.'

'No. I grew up herding cows and baling hay. It's a hard life. One you better love. I don't, but maybe Adam will someday.' He was silent for a moment, staring off into the distance as if he could see something that she could not. 'I couldn't wait to get out of this town. I left shortly after graduating high school.'

'But you came back.'

'Yeah. Sometimes you have to wander around until you find where you really belong. And sometimes it's right where you started. I had to get really miserable before I wanted to come home.'

'Where were you living that you were so miserable?'

Within the window's reflection, his gaze met hers and he smiled. 'First I lived in Canoga Park, and then I moved to Chatsworth.'

'You lived in L.A.?'

'For about twelve years.' His grasp on her hip tightened a fraction. 'I was a homicide detective with the Los Angeles Police Department.'

'I lived in Brentwood.'

'I probably could have guessed that,' he said and slid his hand from her side to her stomach.

'But I grew up in Northridge,' she added. She took deep, even breaths and thought about whether she should step away from his embrace or remove his hand. She felt like a teenager again, uncertain while every cell in her body tingled with life. But unlike that innocent time long ago, she knew where the feelings heating her up like a grow light would lead. What she didn't know was if she wanted to go there with him, or if he wanted to take her.

'You moved a little farther uptown than me.'

The heat from his palm seeped though the cotton of her tank top and warmed her abdomen from the inside out. With a little effort, she controlled her impulse to turn within his arms and touch him the way he touched her. 'Blaine already had a lot of money when I married him.'

'That was your husband, Blaine? Was he gay?'

'No.'

'You really married some guy named Blaine?'

'Yeah, what's wrong with that?'

He shook his head. 'A guy named Blaine can't be any good at buttering the muffin.'

'That's ridiculous. He could butter the muffin just fine.'

'Exactly. I said any *good*.'

'He is a very smart man,' she said, then wondered why she was bothering to defend her ex-husband.

'Uh-huh. What does he do?'

'He's a plastic surgeon.'

Through the glass, his green-eyed gaze shifted to her breasts.

'No, those are mine.'

He lifted his gaze and smiled, unrepentant. 'I'd hate to think they weren't.' He settled her into his chest and said, 'Something like that just might blow all my fantasies about you.'

She stilled. 'What fantasies?'

He buried his nose in her hair and looked at her reflection in the glass. 'I don't think I should tell you.'

'Why? Am I tied up?'

She felt his smile. 'In a few.'

A few?

Creases appeared in the corners of his eyes. 'Do you have a problem with that?'

Did she? She probably should. 'What, with the fact that you fantasize about me, or that I'm tied up?'

'Either.'

But she didn't. No problem at all. Just the opposite. It raised her temperature another notch and threatened to lower her lids. The heat in her abdomen spread between her thighs, and she squeezed her legs together. 'Did I enjoy myself?'

His thumb fanned her abdomen and brushed the underwire of her bra. 'Of course. I treated you real good.'

As if he'd actually touched her, her breasts grew heavy,

and beneath the thin cotton of her top and the thin nylon of her bra, her nipples tightened into hard, sensitive points.

'Do you want to hear how good?'

With her breath stuck in the back of her throat, she nodded.

Through the window glass, he watched her as he lowered his face and lightly ran the tip of his tongue down the shell of her ear. 'You liked it when I did this,' he whispered, then gently sucked her lobe. His breath warmed her cheek and a shiver tickled her spine. With his free hand, Dylan pushed her hair aside and slid his mouth to the side of her throat. 'And this.' He placed warm kisses on her neck, and she watched his face settle into the crook of her neck, felt him gently suck her flesh into his hot mouth, but before he left a mark, he moved on, and slowly he slipped the straps of her tank top and bra from her shoulder and down her arm.

'You're so soft,' he said and pulled her even tighter against his chest. 'Even softer than you look.' His hand on her stomach curled, bunching her shirt in his fist. The hard length of his erection pressed into her behind and she went all liquid inside. Lust pooled hot and wet and wanting between her legs. The thought of them naked, making love, almost had her turning around and hooking her legs around his waist. For a moment she allowed herself a fantasy of her own, one in which she stripped off his clothes and ran her hands all over him, but with what remained of the little sanity she still possessed, she reminded herself that she hadn't known him long enough to actually get naked.

'I don't think sex is a good idea,' she said just above a whisper.

His gaze lifted to hers in the window. 'Who said anything about sex?' he asked and kissed a warm trail to the end of her shoulder. 'We're just messin' around a little bit.'

'In front of the window?'

'Honey, there's no one out there for miles.' He tugged the bottom of her tank top out of her skirt and got back to business. 'If I make love to you, it won't be with two little boys right downstairs. I'll come prepared, and I'll make sure I have all night to touch you the way I want.'

She'd completely forgotten about the two boys asleep downstairs. 'Maybe we should stop.'

He slipped his hand under her shirt and his hot palm caressed her bare skin. 'Do you want me to stop?'

She looked up at him and her forehead brushed his rough chin. 'No.'

'Then keep your ears open for little feet coming up the stairs.' With his mouth poised above hers, he asked, 'How do you feel?'

'Fine,' she responded without thinking about her answer first. She shook her head when she realized that probably wasn't what he was asking. She raised her hand to cup his rough cheek. 'I feel like I should probably ask you to leave.' She kissed the corner of his mouth and bristly jaw. 'But I don't really want you to go. I want you to stay, but I know you shouldn't.' She buried her face in his neck and breathed in the scent of his skin. 'Mostly you make me feel confused and lonely.'

His fingers fanned her bare stomach, his thumb brushed the bottom swell of her breast, and she had to remind herself to breathe. 'With my hand up your shirt, how could I make you feel lonely?'

'Because you remind me of things I didn't even know I missed until I drove into this town.' She kissed his throat, then added, 'Like the sound of a man's boots on my floor and the feeling of a rough, scratchy cheek beneath my palm. The warm, solid pleasure of your chest against my back. Feeling safe.' And sex. He made her realize how much she missed being sexually intimate with a man, being desired and consumed and tangled up in sweaty sheets and raw lust. 'And sometimes when I look into your eyes, I think that maybe you're lonely, too.'

He was silent for a moment, watching her. Then he asked, 'Do you know what I see when I look at you?'

Beneath her lips, his pulse pounded and she shook her head.

'I see someone who reminds me exactly how long it's been since I've touched and smelled a woman's sweet skin.' Again he pressed his erection into her behind, and she felt the heat of him through the worn denim. It spread down the backs of her legs and curled her bare toes against the cool hardwood floor. 'When I look at you, I forget exactly why I'm living like a priest.'

She looked up into his face and her skepticism must have shown.

He pulled back. 'You don't think I'm living like a priest?'

'I've seen the way some of the women in this town treat you.'

'Yeah, but I don't have problems with control around them. They don't tempt me. Not like you do.' With her head tilted up, her neck arched, Dylan softly kissed her lips. 'They don't tempt me into fantasies about hot, down and dirty, no-holds-barred sex. They don't make me ache to touch their soft skin like I want to touch yours. All over, with my hands and mouth. Hope, I want to kiss your breasts and little belly button and between your things. I know I should stay away. Being around you makes it worse, but I can't make myself stay away. I have no control over wanting you.'

She knew the feeling. He gently pressed his mouth to hers and settled into a kiss so slow and sweet, and in such opposition to the blood she felt speeding through his veins, that she slid her hand from his cheek to the back of his head and forced deeper contact. For a man who said he had no control, he seemed to be doing just fine. She licked the tip of his slick tongue, and the kiss eased into a gentle mating of their mouths, a deep intimacy that teased much more than it satisfied. A maddening chase and follow. A slick advance and retreat of hot tongues and mouths.

Then, as if she'd suddenly lit a fire within him, the kiss turned greedy and he devoured her, sucking the breath from her lungs. In an instant, she was consumed, and she thought she rather liked the feeling of giving up control over something she couldn't control anyway.

Beneath her shirt, his hand moved upward to gently cup her breast, and everything got so hot and dizzy she gave up thinking about anything except his palm and his thumb brushing her nipple through the sheer nylon of her bra.

Dylan groaned deep in his chest and pulled his mouth from hers. His lust-filled eyes searched hers, and as Hope watched his profile, he slowly lifted her shirt up over her breasts, then completely stilled. She held her breath, watching him and waiting for his reaction.

'Look at you,' he said and turned her attention to the reflection in the window, of Dylan standing behind her, his big hands bunching the bottom of her tank top. His gaze pinned to her white bra, the material so sheer she might as well have been naked. Her breasts and her tight, puckered nipples straining against the thin nylon.

'You're beautiful,' he breathed and met her gaze in the glass.

She pressed her arms against her sides and kept her tank top up around her armpits. Then she placed her palms on the outsides of his hands and moved them to cover her breasts. He gently squeezed and a hot flush spread across her flesh. She tried to turn, but his grasp tightened. 'If you move, we're goners,' he said.

'I want to touch you, Dylan.'

'Tonight, I touch you.'

Her eyes closed and her lips parted. It had been a long time since she'd felt so good. Her back arched and her hands fell to her sides.

'Hope, open your eyes. Look at me. Look at me touching you.'

She did. She saw her shirt pulled up, the right straps of her bra and tank top shoved to her elbow. Dylan's palms cupped the weight of her breasts from behind, the dark pink tips poking out between his widespread fingers. She looked at her reflection, at the desire shining from her eyes.

Dylan squeezed his fingers together and pinched her nipples between them. Her knees buckled and he held her tight against his chest. 'If we were alone in the house,' he said in a whisper, 'I'd put my mouth right here.' He kissed the top of her head and the side of her face. 'Then I'd work my way down.' He reached for the bottom of her shirt and pulled it back down to her waist. 'But we're not alone, and leaving you isn't going to get any easier.'

He was right. Of course he was right. They couldn't make love while two little boys slept downstairs. That would be wrong. She supposed locking the bedroom door would be wrong, too.

He took a step back and placed his hands on her shoulders.

'Do you need help with Adam and Wally?' she asked.

'Honey, do us both a favor and stay up here until you see my taillights heading toward town.' His hands dropped from her shoulders and he backed away toward the bed. 'I'm afraid I used up all my willpower pulling that tank top down over your breasts. Leaving that see-through bra on you was just about the hardest thing I've ever done, and I can't take much more.' He picked up Wally's and Adam's shoes and looked at her one last time before he left the room.

Hope moved to her bedroom in the front of the house, and from the window she watched him start the sheriff's Blazer. He came back into the house and made two trips, carrying each boy one at a time. When he pulled out of her driveway, she thought she saw him glance up at her. But it was dark and she wasn't sure.

She looked at her reflection in the glass. At her weighted lids and puffy lips. She wasn't really sure who was looking back. The woman looked like her, but she wasn't behaving like Hope Spencer.

She walked from her bedroom and headed downstairs. She knew better than to want the sheriff the way she did. She didn't believe in meaningless sex. She knew better . . . but she just seemed to forget or not to care. When Dylan was around, she just didn't feel so lonely any more.

Dylan Taber made her feel like a desirable woman again. The sound of his deep voice and the touch of his strong hands twisted her insides into hot little knots, and she liked the feeling. She liked it a lot. No man since her divorce had looked at her and made her feel like that. Like a whole woman. She supposed it was because she hadn't given any man a chance, but it wasn't as if she were consciously giving Dylan the chance now. She just didn't have any control. The combination of Dylan's easy charm and hot touches was very hard to resist.

She wondered if she should even try.

Man Spontaneously Combusts

The next morning, Hope sipped coffee and stared blurry-eyed at her monitor. She scrolled through her e-mail and opened a letter from her editor, Walter. He loved the alien story and wanted more, which was perfect, since she already had an idea for an article on alien wilderness guides. At the end of the e-mail, he warned her that Myron Lambardo had contacted the paper and wanted to know where she was living. He'd obviously discovered she wasn't living in her condo, which also meant that he'd violated the restraining order.

Hope decided to do nothing about it for now. She wasn't worried. No way could Myron find her. He wouldn't even think to look in the wilderness of Idaho.

She set her cup on the table and got busy. Her fingers tapped furiously for half a page, then stilled. The image of Dylan standing behind her, his hands cupping her breasts, entered into her head and stopped her cold. She tried to push aside the memory and get her mind back to work, but she couldn't. He was there and he was staying, blocking her creative flow.

There was only one thing to do. Wait it out. She opened

a small vanity case and reached for a bottle of fingernail polish remover and a bag of cotton balls. She conditioned and cut her cuticles and painted her nails mauve because she was in a mauve mood. Not really bright and cheery, but not dark, either. In between and kind of uncertain. Like her life.

While she painted, she carefully looked over the information she'd gathered on Hiram Donnelly. As far as she could tell, the old sheriff had been into dominance and submission. During the day he'd been a control freak, but at night he'd liked to be dominated. From the information she'd read, outside of what was considered normal sexual behavior, d and s wasn't all that unusual a fetish. In fact, powerful men and women were the staple crop behind every successful dominatrix.

She also read reports and academic theories on why certain men were attracted to being dominated, but writing an article on the psychology and pathology of fetishes wasn't what she wanted. She was much more interested in the man who'd managed to get himself elected sheriff of a conservative town for over twenty years, while secretly fantasizing about sexual deviance that finally consumed him.

When Hope's nails were dry, she called across the street and checked up on Shelly. Paul told her Shelly was asleep but that she might be awake in a few hours, so to come over around noon. Since it was only ten Hope had hours to kill and painted her toenails, too. She thought about the aliens in her feature and the many possibilities for future stories. She thought about whether she should query magazines before she wrote her piece on Hiram Donnelly or just write it first. But mostly she thought about Dylan and what he'd said about living like a priest. She just couldn't imagine a guy like him on the wagon.

She thought about how he looked at her, the desire in his

eyes and in the rough texture of his voice that wrapped her up and warmed her all over. She'd tried to attach meaning to every smile, every word, every touch. She liked to think he cared about her a little, but she didn't know. And the fact was, except for liking him personally and craving him physically, she didn't know how *she* felt. Beyond loneliness and their undeniable attraction to one another, she couldn't say they had anything in common. She didn't even know if she would see him today or tomorrow or not again until next week.

Did she want more? Did he?

She thought about Dylan's ex-wife, too. If the woman was really a waitress, she wondered why Adam couldn't talk about what she did for a living.

Except maybe . . . she was a topless waitress. One of those women who worked in gentlemen's clubs. That would explain why Dylan might not want his son mentioning his mother's profession to anyone. Small towns could be closed-minded about that sort of thing.

At noon, Hope knocked on her neighbor's door, and Paul showed her into the living room, where Shelly sat in a recliner wearing her blue chintz robe. Her hair stuck up on her head like red springs and one hand was bandaged, so that just the tips of her fingers stuck out. Hopped up on painkillers and lack of sleep, Shelly was a bit rummy and feeling very sorry for herself. She didn't want Hope's offer of lunch, but she took one look at Hope's fingernails and decided she'd have a manicure instead.

While Paul retreated to his bedroom for a nap, Hope ran back to her house and grabbed her vanity case. When she returned, she sat on a stool next to Shelly's recliner and carefully conditioned and cut the cuticles on all ten fingers. While she gingerly filed the nails into perfect crescent moons, she listened to Shelly talk about last night's drama.

The house was unusually quiet and she wondered where Wally and Adam were.

'How were the little boys last night?' Shelly finally got around to asking. She set the vanity case on her lap and pawed through the rows of fingernail polish with her good hand.

'Pretty good, but they like to hit each other a lot,' Hope answered. She gently blew dust from Shelly's fingers, then added, 'And pass gas.'

'Yeah, boys'll do that.' Shelly pulled out a bottle of Hot Pants Pink and handed it to Hope. 'I like this. It looks like something a hooker would wear.'

It didn't, but Hope didn't want to argue. 'Where are Wally and Adam?'

'Dylan hired one of the Raney girls to watch them over at his house today. He thought I could use the rest.'

'That was nice of him.' Hope took out a bottle of clear polish. 'I imagine he's really tired, too,' she said as she gave Shelly's nails a base coat.

'Nah, he probably didn't get home too late.'

Hope knew better and concentrated on the thumb of Shelly's bad hand.

'Or did he?'

'Did he what?'

'Get home late. Paul said the twins got to the hospital around ten thirty. So Dylan must have pulled up to your house about an hour after that. After grabbing the boys, he probably got home around eleven forty-five.'

He might have made it home by then, too, if he hadn't stayed and kissed her neck and her mouth, and if he hadn't decided he wanted to touch her stomach and pull up her shirt. Hope kept her gaze averted and said on an indifferent sigh, 'That sounds about right.' She screwed on the cap of the clear polish, then shook the bottle of Hot Pants Pink.

'What happened?'

'Nothing.'

'Then why do you look like something did?'

Hope finally glanced up. 'I don't.'

'Yes, you do. This Percodan has me feeling kind of funky, but I'm not totally out of it.' Shelly's red brows lowered on her forehead. 'And besides, I saw you two jump apart when Paul and I came into the kitchen. I stabbed my hand, not my eyes. What were the two of you doing?'

'Talking.'

'Yeah, right. I think he likes you.'

Hope shrugged and painted the fingernails on Shelly's good hand. 'I think Dylan likes women – period.'

'Yeah, he does. Always has, even in grade school, but he talks to you a little bit different than he talks to anyone else.'

'How?'

'When he talks to you, he watches your mouth.'

Hope bit her lip to keep from smiling. She hadn't noticed Dylan watching her. Well, maybe once or twice.

'So what's up with the two of you?'

The last time Hope had spoken of her love life to a friend, her friend had used it to steal her husband. She knew that Shelly was different, and besides, nothing she could tell Shelly could come back to hurt her anyway. She didn't love Dylan, and he didn't love her.

'Nothing really,' she answered, which was basically the truth.

'It sure didn't look like nothing. Did he try his cheap moves on you?'

'Moves?'

'Yeah. In the eighth grade, he used to pretend to have an itchy pit so he could hook his arm around a girl and make it look like he was just scratching himself.'

Hope laughed. 'No itchy pit.'

'I should probably warn you away from Dylan.'

'Why, what's wrong with him?'

'Nothing. He just has it in his head that he can't get involved with a woman right now. He says he has to wait until Adam is older, but the way he looks at you . . . well, I haven't seen him stare after a woman in a very long time. Not since he used to watch Kimberly Howe run the hundred.' Shelly paused to blow on her nails and carefully offered Hope her injured hand. 'You've got to admit, he's better-looking than most of those sissy boys you see pasted up on billboards, and it's not every man who can look that good in a pair of jeans.'

That was true.

'Paul has a flat butt.'

Hope had noticed that, too. 'If Dylan's so great, why aren't you married to him?'

Shelly's nose wrinkled as if something smelly had entered the room. 'Sure, looking at Dylan is like looking at a work of art, but just 'cause you can appreciate the beauty of it doesn't mean you want it in your living room.' She shook her head, then added, 'I knew I wanted Paul Aberdeen the first time I laid eyes on him in the first grade. It took me ten years to hook him, but even if Paul were gone tomorrow, I'd never be interested in Dylan that way. We've known each other too long, and the way he does things drives me crazy.'

'Like what?'

'He only does laundry when everything in the house is dirty.'

Since Hope was the same way, she didn't think there was anything unusual about it.

'He puts his boots on the coffee table, and if he and Adam have a green vegetable for dinner, it's a miracle. Dylan thinks if you eat a banana or an apple every other week, you don't need vegetables.'

Hope finished painting Shelly's nails and sat back and waited for them to dry. 'Adam looks healthy and happy.'

'Healthy at least.' Shelly studied her injured hand. 'He's leaving this Friday to visit his mother. He's always a little weird when he comes back.'

'Weird how?'

'A little withdrawn and has a real bad case of the poor pitifuls. He thinks if his mama and daddy would just spend some time together, they could all live happily ever after.' Shelly shrugged. 'I suppose that's normal, though.'

'How long is he usually gone?'

'Two weeks; then it takes him an entire month to settle back into his routine. I've never met Adam's mama, but she must be extremely indulgent with him, because when he comes back, he sleeps in too late and just lies around like a slug.'

Hope was dying to ask Shelly to tell her everything she knew about Dylan's ex, but she didn't want Shelly to know she was interested. Even if Hope had been able to share her feelings, it was too soon and too new to talk about the confusing tangle of emotions tugging at her whenever Dylan happened to smile her way.

Hope missed sitting around chatting with other women, talking about men and life and sex. She missed the kind of connection it took time to develop. A deep connection with someone who understood the inequalities perpetrated against females and the injustice of running into your high school sweetheart on a bad hair day. She missed discussing burning issues like health care, world peace, the shoe sale at Neiman's, and whether or not size mattered.

She wanted that again. She wanted to talk about her confusion, her feelings, and her life. She wanted to tell Shelly why it was hard for her to talk about herself, why it was hard for her to trust a friend.

'What story are you working on for your magazine?' Shelly asked through a yawn.

The opportunity to open up passed, and Hope reached for Shelly's good hand. 'Aliens masquerading as humans in a wilderness town,' she said as she applied the second coat of polish. 'They play tricks on tourists.'

Shelly's eyes perked up. 'You're writing about Gospel?'

'A town similar to Gospel.'

'Oh, my God! Can I be an alien?'

Hope looked at her new friend, her red hair sticking up, her eyes wide and glassy, and really regretted that she couldn't use Shelly. She would have made a good alien. 'Sorry, but ever since Myron, I don't use real people any more.'

'Bummer.'

As Hope gently blew on the tips of Shelly's fingers, she glanced up into her drugged gaze. Now probably wasn't the best time to ask Shelly about the Donnellys. Not when she was high and her tongue was loosened by drugs, but maybe just a few simple questions wouldn't hurt. If Shelly was uncomfortable about discussing her old neighbors, Hope wouldn't press the issue. 'How well did you know Minnie Donnelly?' she asked.

'Why?'

Since it was no secret and half the town knew anyway, she confessed, 'I'm writing an article about what happened with Hiram.'

Shelly blinked and apprehension narrowed her gaze. 'For *The Weekly News of the Universe*?'

'No. I'm going to send out queries to more mainstream publications.' She told Shelly about her ideas, and once she explained that she wasn't interested in writing a salacious article about kinky sex, Shelly relaxed and opened up.

'Hiram could be a real son of a bitch, and I didn't like him very much. Still, I'd hate to see his sex life exploited for the sake of selling magazines,' Shelly said. 'There was more to his life than what he became. More than hookers and sex clubs and pornography. Ask anyone in town, and they'll all have a different story to tell about him. They'll also tell you that he treated everyone the same.' Shelly talked about Minnie and about how she'd been the real control freak. 'Everyone thought she was a saint, but I lived across the street from her, and I know she ruled that house with an iron fist. I could hear her yelling and hollering all the time. No wonder her kids left and never came back. No wonder that after she died, Hiram felt lost without someone to beat up on him.'

Hope carefully reached for Shelly's injured hand and applied a top coat to her nails. 'You sound like you feel sorry for him.'

'Hell, no. He was too big a pervert for me to feel sorry for him. Toward the end, he was hiring girls just shy of their eighteenth birthday. I don't feel sorry and I don't understand, but I can look at the situation and see how it happened. Out from underneath Minnie's thumb, he just spiraled out of control.'

'You told me several weeks ago that Hiram got careless toward the end and brought girls home. Did you ever see anything suspicious?'

'No.' Shelly lifted her bandaged hand and looked at her nails. 'When are you going to write the article?'

Hope didn't believe her but she let it drop. 'I'm waiting for the FBI report. Once I look it over, I'll figure out where to start,' she answered. But first she needed to finish the story she was getting paid to write, and in order to do that, she had to think about aliens and not a certain smooth-talking cowboy. 'I'd hoped you could show me those waterfalls you and Paul told me about. I wanted to take some pictures of them for my next alien article.' Hope shrugged. 'But I can wait until you're feeling better.'

'Ask Dylan to take you. He knows where they are, but ask before Friday, because he always takes time off when Adam is away.' Shelly settled back into her chair. 'He stays up at the Double T, helping out his mama and brother-in-law. If you don't ask him before he leaves, chances are you won't see him for a couple of weeks.'

Two weeks. For two weeks she wouldn't have to worry about seeing Dylan or think about the slow touch of his hands or his hungry mouth on hers. Two weeks would give her the time she needed to clear her mind and concentrate on her work. Which was the reason she'd come to Gospel in the first place. Now that her career was finally back on track, she needed to focus and push ahead. But suddenly work wasn't enough and two weeks sounded like a very long time.

Wednesday night, Dylan folded the last of Adam's laundry and packed it in his suitcase. Adam stared at him through his huge green eyes, his mouth a straight line of apprehension. About this time every year, Adam's excitement waned and gave way to anxiety.

'You aren't going to cry this year, are you?' Dylan asked his son.

'No. I'm bigger now.'

'Good, 'cause you make your mom feel real bad when you do that.' Every year Adam promised not to cry, and every year he held out until it was time to let go of Dylan's hand. 'Tomorrow, after your haircut, we need to go to Hansen's Emporium and buy you new skivvies,' he said and set the suitcase on top of the dresser.

'And a new snorkel, too. I accidentally broke mine.'

Dylan ordered Adam's dog off the bed before he tucked

his son between his sheets. He didn't know why the snorkel was suddenly important, but Adam probably had his reasons. 'Put it on your list.' He brushed the soft hair from Adam's brow and asked, 'Did you find your mama a special rock yet?'

'Yep, it's white.'

Dylan bent and kissed Adam's smooth forehead. 'Dream good dreams.'

'Dad?' Dylan knew what Adam would ask by the tone of his voice. He asked every year. 'Come with me this time.'

'You know I can't. Who's going to stay here and take care of your dog?'

'She can come with us. You, me, Mom, and Mandy. It'll be fun.'

Dylan moved to the bedroom door and turned off the light. 'No, Adam,' he said and watched his son turn on his side, turning his back on him.

Dylan hated July. Absolutely hated it. He hated coming home and not stepping over the toys he'd told Adam to put away. He hated the quiet of his house and the emptiness of Adam's room. He hated eating dinner alone.

Several floorboards creaked as Dylan walked down the short hall and into his dark bedroom. Through the slats of open blinds, moonlight spilled across the end of his bed and dresser and climbed up the wall. Slices of light slashed across his chest as he pulled his shirt over his head. He tossed it toward an old wing chair and missed. Tomorrow he would take Adam to buy new underwear; the day after, he'd drive him to the airport in Sun Valley and watch him board a private plane with Julie. He'd watch her take him away.

He hated that most of all. He hated the parting glance Adam always threw over his shoulder, one last plea in his watery eyes as if Dylan had the power to grant what he wanted most.

But he couldn't, and staying a few days or the whole two weeks wouldn't give Adam what he really wanted. A mom and dad who lived together. A mother who was more like the woman he watched on television every week than the woman he met once a year. An angel who cared for him like she cared for the homeless, or elderly, or the orphans she'd saved last week. A mother he could talk about to his friends.

Dylan sat on the end of his bed and pulled off his boots. Neither he nor Julie had intended to keep Adam separate from her life for so long. They'd never intended to make her a subject he couldn't share. They'd never intended to keep him a secret no one knew about. It had just happened, and now they didn't know what to do about it.

Adam had been only two when Julie had landed the starring role on *Heaven on Earth*. Dylan and Adam had already been living in Gospel, far from the spotlight Julie craved. With her beautiful face, translucent skin, and shrewd press releases, the public had instantly fallen in love with her. In a matter of months, her life had risen from struggling nobody actress to heavenly angel. Suddenly she was a frequent guest on mainstream talk shows and a paragon of Christian programming. Everyone believed the angel was beautiful inside and out. America wanted a symbol of good, and they found it in Juliette Bancroft.

Those first few summers she'd spent with Adam, she'd taken him to her father's small ranch because she'd needed a break from her life, a place where she could focus on him. The home where she'd been raised provided that for her, as well as a nice setting for Adam to get to know the few relatives who still lived in the area.

Now, five years later, she took him there because she had little choice. How could she suddenly tell the world that she had a son she saw only once a year? How would that look? How would that play on the talk shows, and what about the

Christian right who endorsed her show? What would that do to her heavenly image?

More important to Dylan, how would the tabloid papers treat the news that not only did Juliette Bancroft have a child she didn't raise and rarely saw, but she hadn't been married to her son's father, either? What would that do to Adam? What would that do to his and Adam's quiet life together?

Adam was seven now. Old enough to see that his life was different from that of other kids his age. Old enough to wonder why he couldn't brag about his mother. Old enough to be hurt by the truth, but keeping it from him longer would only hurt him more. He'd have to be told soon. Adam Taber was the illegitimate son of America's angel. Dylan just hoped Adam would understand, but he wouldn't be told tonight. Not tomorrow, either.

Dylan pulled off his socks and threw them by his shirt. Within the slice of moonlight spilling through the window, he stripped naked and scratched his chest. Having Hope in town made him realize he needed to talk to Adam soon. Perhaps as soon as Adam returned home. He had a few weeks to figure it out. While he helped out at the Double T, he'd have time to clear his head and think about what he would say, but it wasn't like he hadn't already practiced his speech in his head a million times before.

He pulled back the plaid comforter and slid into his bed. The sheets were clean and cool and he stuck his hand under his head and stared up at the ceiling. He'd leave out the part about him not loving Julie the way a man should love a woman and both of them knowing it would never have lasted anyway. Adam didn't need to know that he was the only reason they'd tried to make it work for as long as they had. All his son needed to know was that he was loved by both his parents. And he needed to be told by someone who loved him – soon.

*

When Dylan got off work Thursday, he took Adam to the Curl Up and Dye to get his hair cut. While buzzing the back of Adam's neck, Dixie promised to 'drop by sometime next week.' Dylan didn't bother telling her he wouldn't be home.

After the Curl Up and Dye, they stopped at Hansen's Emporium to grab some underwear. Adam chose briefs with X-Men on the behind. The store was filled with a few tourists buying souvenirs, and one or two locals who'd moved inside the air-conditioned store to get out of the relentless heat.

Dylan stood in the toy aisle helping Adam choose a snorkel and ignoring everything around him – until Hope Spencer walked in. As if she reached across the store and placed her fingers under his chin, he lifted his gaze the second she strolled inside. Over a display of Magic Bubbles, he watched her move with that big-city, don't-mess-with-me stride of hers, keeping her gaze straight ahead. She didn't look around, and she didn't notice him watching her as she grabbed two rolls of film and headed for a display of cow-pie candy. Using two fingers, she picked up the candy and read the ingredients.

She'd been out jogging again and her hair was up. Several fine strands fell from her ponytail and she'd pushed them behind her ears. They curled and stuck to the sides of her throat. He knew how she tasted there. Right there where her neck met her shoulder, she was soft and sweet. He knew the smooth creaminess of her skin and the weight of her breasts in his hands. He knew the curve of her behind against his groin. He couldn't stop the hunger or the wanting any more than he could stop himself from going to her. He left Adam by the rubber spiders and superballs and walked up behind Hope.

'That's not real cowshit,' he said and figured he probably

hadn't uttered something so impressive since the sixth grade, when he'd tried to dazzle Nancy Burk by telling her she wasn't as ugly as her sister.

Hope put down the candy and turned to face him. A smile flirted with the corners of her lips and he felt it low in his belly. 'I'd already figured that out, but it wouldn't have surprised me if it was.'

He let his gaze rest a few irresistible moments on her mouth before he looked away, over the top of her head to a mounted salmon in the fishing section. He was afraid she could read the hunger in his eyes and know what he wanted, that he wanted to reach out and fold her against him. Maybe bury his nose in her hair. Although after Monday night, she probably had some idea.

'Are you going to the Fourth of July celebration next weekend?' she asked. 'Are you entered in the toilet toss?'

'No. I'm afraid I'll miss the excitement.' His gaze traveled across a rainbow of folded T-shirts and ended up back on Hope, on her smooth hair and shiny ponytail. 'I won't be in town.'

She was silent for a moment and then she said, 'Shelly mentioned you'd be gone for a few weeks.'

He looked into her blue eyes, saw the disappointment there, and almost gave in to his urge. He almost reached for her, right there in Hansen's Emporium. 'Yes, that's right.'

'I need to take pictures of some waterfalls Shelly told me about, and I thought maybe you could take me. But if you won't be in town . . .' She shrugged. 'I guess I can wait until Shelly feels up to a hike.'

'Are these pictures for the article you're writing on the Northwest?'

She lowered her gaze to his chest. 'Yes.'

He didn't even want to think about what he would do if he ever found himself alone with her. Completely alone.

Just the two of them. No, that was a lie. He *did* want to think about what it would be like to make love to her. He *liked* to think about holding her breasts in his hands, kissing her, running his tongue across her hard nipples, and shoving his face into her cleavage. He absolutely *loved* to think about positions, too – horizontal, vertical, upside down, sideways. He thought about burying himself between her soft thighs all the time, but that didn't mean he would do anything about it. 'Sorry I can't help you out,' he said. He was in control of his body if not of his thoughts. Still, it was best not to let his mind travel that pleasurable path, especially in Hansen's.

She returned her gaze to his and pushed the corners of her mouth up into a halfhearted smile. 'That's okay.'

'Maybe if I . . .' He shrugged. *If he what?* Waited until his son was out of town to skirt around and hope like hell that he got lucky? Sneak around and hope no one in town noticed their sheriff having sex with their favorite topic of gossip since Hiram Donnelly? He might have been able to figure out a way past the gossip, but there was no getting around the huge fact that Hope was a writer. He couldn't sleep with her and all the while pray to God she didn't find out about Adam. And if she did find out, would he read about his life in *People* magazine? Or worse, in the *Enquirer*?

He couldn't risk it, and Hope deserved better. He took a step backward and almost stepped on Adam's foot.

'Dad!'

He'd been so completely focused on Hope that he hadn't even noticed his son had moved up beside him. 'Sorry, buddy. You okay?'

Adam nodded. 'Hi, Hope.'

Hope looked at Adam and her smile grew. 'Hey, what have you got?'

'Snorkel and skivvies.'

She took the package with the mask and snorkel from him and studied it. 'Looks pretty good,' she said, then gave it back. Adam handed her his underwear and she studied them also. 'Who is this guy on your behind?'

'That's Wolverine. He has really big claws and he can claw his enemies.'

'I remember. You drew a picture of him the other night. Is he a good guy?'

'Yep,' he said and took back his underwear.

'Where did you put the hummingbird I gave you?'

'We put him in the kitchen window.' He paused to scratch his elbow. 'Maybe you could come over and see it sometime.'

Hope glanced at Dylan, and the thought of her in his house made his heart beat heavy in his chest.

'Maybe,' she said, then reached out and ruffled Adam's hair. 'You got your hair cut.'

'Yep,' he said without backing away. 'Got it cut today.'

Beyond a very short list that included the females in his family and Shelly, Adam didn't like women to touch or make a fuss over him. And except for that short list, this was the longest conversation Dylan had ever heard Adam have with a woman. Usually he resorted to monosyllabic grunts. He wondered how Hope had managed to pass Adam's test. He knew she would have instantly failed if Adam suspected Dylan had any interest in her at all. And the irony of it was that out of all the women he knew, Hope interested him the most. Hell, the way she filled out her running shorts downright fascinated him, and he had to keep his gaze glued to her face to keep his eyes from wandering to the tight spandex covering her crotch. 'We better get going,' he said and placed his hand on Adam's back.

Hope moved with them to the front of the store and took

her place in line in front of him at the checkout counter. As Eden Hansen rang up the purchases of a couple buying T-shirts, Dylan stared at the back of Hope's head, recalling with perfect clarity the last time he'd stood behind her, watching her somewhat blurred reflection.

'Hey, Hope,' Adam said and tapped her arm to get her attention, 'maybe when I come home, me and Wally can build another tent at your house.'

'Son, you can't invite yourself like that.'

'It's okay.' She looked over her shoulder at Dylan, then answered Adam. 'If you guys come over again, there have to be some rules. Like no wrestling in the house.' She thought for a moment, then added, 'And since you boys like to pull things, maybe you two could come over and help me pull some weeds. I'd pay you.'

'Five bucks!'

'Yep.' They moved forward in line and Hope placed two rolls of film on the counter.

'Is this it for you, then?' Eden asked as she reached for the film. Hope didn't answer right away, and Dylan figured she was stunned into silence by her first good look at Eden Hansen. For as long as he could remember, Eden had dyed her hair purple, worn purple eyeshadow and purple lipstick. She lived in a purple house and drove a purple Dodge Neon. Hell, she even dyed her little yap-yap dogs, too. Her twin sister, Edie, had a preference for blue. It was no wonder both were married to men who had a tendency to hit the bottle before noon.

'Yes, that's all,' Hope finally replied.

Eden rang up the film and reached for a paper sack. 'My brother-in-law is Hayden Dean. He's the one who helped you out at the Buckhorn and ended up getting into that fight with Emmett.'

Hope unzipped her fanny pack. 'I was very grateful he

stepped in when he did. That was very nice of him.'

'Nice, schmice.' She waved a dismissive hand. 'Hayden is a womanizer and likes to fight, no doubt about that. If my sister had the sense God gave a lemming, she'd run his butt off the nearest cliff, and that's a fact. Everyone knows he steps out with Dixie Howe whenever she can't find better. Dixie's as loose as a slipknot, and if it weren't for her talent with hair color, I'd never set foot in her salon.'

'Uh . . . oh, really?' Hope uttered as she handed Eden a twenty.

Dylan chuckled. If Hope was shocked by Eden now, just wait until she was stuck in the same room with her and Edie at the same time. Both women could talk until your ears bled.

'Now, I was thinking,' Eden continued after she took Hope's money. 'If you ever need anyone to die a really painful death in that book you're writing, Hayden would be a good choice. Besides chasin' tail, he's lazy, drinks like a fish, and is as ugly as the mange. Maybe you could have him get that flesh-eating disease.'

Dylan watched Hope's ponytail sway back and forth as she shook her head. 'I don't know who told you I'm writing a book, but I'm not.'

'Iona said Melba told her you're writing a book about Hiram Donnelly.'

'I'm writing an article, not a book.'

Eden pulled her purple lips into a disappointed frown. 'Well, I guess that's not the same, now, is it? Not as interesting, either. A whole book would be interesting.' She handed Hope her change. 'Someone should write about my family. Woo wee, the stories I could tell. Did you know my family owned the first saloon in town? Ran the first brothel, too. You should come in sometime and I'll tell you the story of my great-uncles who killed each other in a fight over a gal named Frenchy.'

'Dad?' Adam whispered. 'What's a brothel?'

'I'll tell you later.'

'Do you know why they called her Frenchy?'

Hope shoved her money into her fanny pack and grabbed her bag. 'Because she was French?' She edged toward the door at the end of the counter, past the polished agates and windup teeth.

'No. On account of her specializing in the ménage à trois.'

'Fascinating,' Hope said as she grabbed the door handle. She gave Dylan one tortured glance and bolted as if demons were on her heels.

'How are you, Sheriff?' Eden asked as he moved forward in line.

'Good,' Dylan said through his smile.

Eden shook her head. 'That gal is an odd one.'

Dylan wisely made no comment and quickly paid for Adam's briefs and his snorkel before Eden could trap him, too. On the way home, he and Adam stopped at the Cozy Corner Café for cheeseburgers and fries. Paris was their waitress, and although no one in town knew *who* Adam's mama was, they all knew he spent the first two weeks in July with her.

When they got home, their neighbor, Hanna Turnbaugh, brought Adam a new coloring book and crayons for 'the trip.' She sat in the kitchen drinking coffee with Dylan until Paris showed up carrying a big white cake with coconut frosting and candied peach slices stuck on it. Adam resorted to his usual grunts and one-shoulder shrugs until both women gave up trying to talk to him.

Neither Dylan nor Adam slept much that night, and both got up early the next morning for the drive to Sun Valley. They ate breakfast at Shorty's and over a stack of pancakes, Adam promised he wouldn't cry this year.

In a small airport where celebrity passengers were the norm, the sight of Juliette Bancroft didn't so much as raise a brow. At the same gate where Demi Moore, Clint Eastwood, and the Kennedys boarded and disembarked from their chartered planes, America's angel waited for her son. Her blond hair subdued into a French braid, Julie rose from a chair, and a smile tilted the corners of her perfect pink lips. Julie had always been gorgeous, with her flawless skin and perfect cheekbones. She was a walking Barbie doll, only better, because she was real – well, except for her breasts; she'd had those done her first season.

Dylan had to give her credit. She'd toned down her Hollywood image and wore a simple pair of Levi's and a summer sweater, but she still managed to look as if she'd just stepped out of a women's magazine. 'Hi, baby,' she said and held out her arms. She went down on one knee and Adam stepped within her embrace. She kissed every inch of his face and didn't seem to notice his lack of response. 'Oh, I've missed you soooo much. Have you missed me?'

'Yes,' Adam whispered.

Julie stood and her smile turned a bit uncertain as she looked at Dylan. 'Hello, how are you?'

'Good. How was your flight?'

'Uneventful.' She let her gaze travel from his hair to the toes of his boots, then back up. 'I swear you get better-looking every time I see you.'

He wasn't flattered. Julie was one of those people who handed out compliments like a Pez dispenser. 'I'm another year older every time you see me, Julie.'

She shrugged. 'You look the same as the day I ran my Toyota into your unmarked car. Remember that?'

How could he possibly forget? 'Of course.'

Julie flashed him her trademark smile, the one that captured America's hearts, the one that used to make his own pulse race. 'Do you have time to grab a bite to eat before you head back home?' she asked. 'I thought the three of us could talk a bit before Adam and I have to go.'

Instantly suspicious, Dylan wondered what she really wanted. It wasn't like her to want to sit around and shoot the shit with him. 'Adam and I just ate. Maybe some other time.'

'We need to talk soon,' she said and reached for Adam's hand. 'Your grandpa is awfully excited to see you. We're going to have lots of fun this year.'

Adam took a step back and leaned into Dylan's thigh. He didn't grab hold, but Dylan could tell that he wanted to.

'I thought you weren't going to make a fuss this time,' he said, as if he weren't dying inside. As if he didn't already feel the loss with every squeeze of his heart.

'I'm not.' But Adam turned his face into Dylan's side. 'But, Dad . . .'

Dylan went down on one knee and took Adam's face in his hands. Adam's eyes were filled with water and his pale cheeks were splotched. The effort not to cry about had him hyperventilating, and Dylan was very proud of his son. 'I can tell you're really trying to be a big boy this year,' Dylan said. 'And that's all I asked, so that's all that counts. If you want to cry, go ahead.' Adam wrapped his arms around Dylan's neck and Dylan rubbed his back. 'Son, there are just some times in a man's life when he has to let it out. If it feels like one of those times to you, then that's what you gotta do.' Dylan hated this; it tore at his aching heart and left him feeling battered and bloody. It clogged his throat and made the backs of his eyes sting. Adam's silent tears soaked the collar of Dylan's oxford cloth shirt. 'I wrote down all the area codes and the phone numbers where I'll likely be, so you can get hold of me any time. I put the list in your suitcase. Whenever you want, you just give me a call, okay?'

Adam nodded.

'But your mom's probably going to keep you too busy to miss me much.' He glanced up at Julie and she had that wide-eyed 'What do I do now?' look he recognized. As always, leaving it up to him to know what to say and do. As much as Dylan wanted the responsibility of his son, there were times when he resented the full weight of it. When he resented *her*. Like now, when he had to pretend he wasn't all torn up inside. When Julie might have stepped in and helped out a little. When she could have at least tried but she didn't, and Dylan tried not to let his irritation show. 'You're going to have lots of fun with your mom and grandpa, and when you come back, we'll go catch that Dolly Varden that got away from you last time, okay?'

Again Adam nodded. 'Okay.'

'I'm proud of you, son.' Dylan removed Adam's arms from around his neck and leaned back to look into his son's face. 'You about under control now?'

Adam wiped the back of his hand across his wet cheeks. 'Yeah.'

'Good.' He wiped a tear from Adam's chin. 'I think that went well. You've behaved like a man this year,' he said as he stood and handed Adam his suitcase. 'Did you remember to pack your crayons?'

'Yeah.'

'Good.' He took a step backward. 'I love you, Adam.'

'I love you, too, Dad.'

Dylan gave an abbreviated wave, then turned away from the sight of Julie taking Adam's hand and walking away.

In less than a minute Dylan was back in the parking lot, where he'd left his truck. He opened the door, climbed inside, and shoved the key into the ignition. The morning sun shone on the blue hood and his vison blurred.

It felt like one of those times. One of those times when a man just had to let it out.

Squirrel is Proven Aphrodisiac

Other than the opening day of hunting season, the Fourth of July celebration was the premiere event in Pearl County. The nation's birthday was kicked off with a parade down Main Street, which continued around the lake to the grange hall. The field around the grange was mowed down and Corvase Amusements turned the area north of the building into a swell of motion and beckoning lights. The whirs of the Scrambler and the Ferris wheel collided with the plummeting screams from the Zipper, all but drowning out the enticing calls of carnies, coaxing the citizens to try their luck at such games as Slam-Dunk, Flip-a-Frog, and the Quarter Toss.

Rows of craft booths owned the area south of the carnival, where the Mountain Mama Crafters proudly displayed their latest accomplishments. Their artistry ranged from traditional quilts and flower wreaths to toilet-paper cozies and crazy-eyed, long-haired, neon-colored owls glued to hunks of driftwood. No one had the heart to tell Melba that her owls were truly ghastly.

The smells of boiled corn, fried onions, grease, and brewer's yeast hovered like smog on the hot summer air. It was ninety-eight degrees in the shade, and the dry heat sucked moisture from the skin and toasted unprotected flesh. Next to the food stands was the first-aid tent, where two paramedics bandaged cuts, handed out Pepto, and alleviated heat exhaustion. Deputies Plummer and Williams kept their eyes on the crowd and tended drunkenness. By 6 P.M., Hayden Dean had passed out behind the Hot Dogs for Jesus booth, and at six-oh-five, one of the Hollier kids was caught trying to steal his wallet.

Across the field from the first-aid tent, Paul Aberdeen stood behind a chalk line, determination on his red face, a toilet bowl on his shoulder.

'Come on, baby, you can do it,' Shelly called out to him. 'You're a lean, mean, toilet-tossing machine!'

Hope glanced across her shoulder at her neighbor. *Toilet-tossing machine?* Shelly held her bandaged hand to her forehead to block out the vicious sun. Her freckles stood out against her pale skin, and her cheeks were flushed. But they were nothing compared to her husband's. Paul's face looked like a tomato.

For reasons Hope would never understand, and despite the heat, both Paul and Shelly wore matching Wranglers, cowboy boots, and frilly shirts with pearl snaps. In fact, almost everyone at the fair had duded up as if they were backup singers in a country-and-western band.

Hope on the other hand, had dressed for comfort in her short khaki skirt, black tank top, and leather flip-flops. 'Do you think he's going to pass out?' she asked.

Shelly shook her head. 'He better not. He only has to gain two inches in this throw to move ahead of everyone else.'

A hush fell over the spectators as Paul spun like a shot-put thrower and heaved the toilet. It flew about ten feet, landed on its base, then fell over onto its side.

'Yes!' Shelly raised her good fist into the air. 'The big-screen TV is mine.'

Unfortunately, Shelly's euphoria lasted only until Burley Morton hoisted the toilet onto his shoulder, moved to the line and hurled it eleven feet four inches. The crowd went wild, Burley moved into first place, and a new toilet-toss record was set.

Paul walked away with a second-place ribbon, a hunting knife, and a sore back.

'Is it over now?' Wally asked. 'I want to get my face painted.'

Shelly ignored her son while she rubbed Paul's back with her good hand. 'Do you need a beer, baby?'

'I think I need some Ben-Gay,' Paul answered as he studied his new knife.

'I'll take Wally,' Hope volunteered, secretly envious of the carnival toys he held in his hands. She'd spent most of the day chasing Wally from one booth to the next. While he had a rubber snake, a plastic tomahawk with fake hair hanging off it, and a crooked pencil, Hope had nothing to show for the appalling amount of money she'd handed over to the carnies. Not even a cheap ashtray. She'd been a failure at all the games she'd played, and after she'd accidentally beaned a young cowboy on the side of the head with a sinker, they'd banned her for life at the Fly Casting Booth. 'We'll meet you two later,' she told Shelly and headed out with Wally.

They waited in line to have a football painted on Wally's cheek, and after some coaxing, Hope agreed to have a dagger painted on her shoulder. She'd never spent all day hanging out with a seven-year-old boy before, and she was surprised that she didn't get bored. She supposed it had something to do with her sudden desire to be around people again. She found that the longer she lived in Gospel, the less she liked to spend time alone.

She'd turned in her second article on aliens and was working on her third. Her first alien article had come out that morning, and she'd rushed to the M & S to buy a copy of the newspaper. She'd been given the center spread, knocking Clive's cow mutilation out of the prime space.

Lately, she'd spent quite a bit of time across the road with Shelly. She helped her neighbor clean house, do laundry, and deadhead the petunias in the window boxes. They talked a lot, about a lot of different things, but Hope still hadn't been able to tell her new friend about the really bad times in her life. She wanted to, but she couldn't.

They talked about Hiram Donnelly and the FBI report that had arrived the day before. Some of the text had been blacked out, and she was no closer to understanding than before. After Hope returned home tonight, she planned to go over the information again.

They talked about Dylan, too. No one had heard from him since he'd taken Adam to the airport. That had been four days ago, yet no one seemed worried. Even though Hope knew better than to expect him, she sometimes found herself walking to her front window, looking for the white-and-brown sheriff's Blazer. Or when she went into town, her gaze would wander, searching for a certain straw cowboy hat or a faded pair of jeans. Of course she never did see him and hated the disappointment that settled on her shoulders and pulled her down.

The last time she'd seen him was that day in Hansen's Emporium when his gaze had burned her everywhere it touched. She hadn't imagined that his voice got a little deeper, and a bit huskier, when he talked to her. She hadn't imagined all that sexual desire directed right at her.

Then again, maybe she had imagined it. If he'd really wanted to spend time with her, he certainly knew where she lived. Yet he hadn't made an effort to contact her, and now, as she and Wally walked toward the game booths, she wondered if whatever she'd felt between herself and Dylan had been all in her head.

Or perhaps he was one of those guys who played with women's emotions. Maybe the thrill for him was in the chase, and God knew she hadn't run very fast. Okay, she hadn't run at all. In fact, she'd stood perfectly still while he'd pulled up her shirt. She'd even moved his hands to cover her breasts.

She and Wally tried their luck at a few games, and Hope finally won a pink plastic ruler after tossing rings on pop bottles. She put her prize in her fanny pack, and by the time she found Paul and Shelly eating hot dogs and drinking beer, the sun hung low in the sky. The carnival lights kicked in and the food booths lit up. Hope's stomach growled, and she and Wally grabbed two corn dogs with extra mustard before joining the small group that had gathered amongst the picnic tables set up behind the food stands. Wally abandoned her to eat with the other children and Shelly introduced Hope to her friends. They all seemed very nice, and while she ate her corn dog, the owner of the Buckhorn filled her in on his secrets to tossing a good toilet.

'It takes pure muscle to toss a toilet that far,' Burley said as laughter a short distance away drew her attention over his left shoulder. Like a magnet, her gaze settled on a tall, lean cowboy in a battered straw hat.

Dylan Taber leaned one shoulder against the Pound of Fries trailer, his arms folded across his chest, absorbed in conversation with several women standing in front of him. His sudden appearance at the fair was as unexpected as the warm flush spreading across Hope's abdomen and up her chest. Her crazy heart pounded in her ears, and she pretended to listen to Burley, but in reality she didn't hear a word.

Dylan lifted his gaze and his eyes locked with Hope's. He looked at her across the distance, his head cocked to one side as he listened to the women speaking to him. At the sight of him, hot pleasure settled low in Hope's stomach, and she couldn't stop the smile that curved her lips. She waited, but Dylan didn't acknowledge her in any way. She couldn't tell by his expression if he felt the same pleasure or warm flush, or if he felt anything at all. He simply looked at her, his handsome face unreadable. Then he looked away.

'Stanley told me you're writing a magazine article about Hiram Donnelly.'

She returned her attention to the man standing in front of her. 'Yes, I am,' she said, her thoughts scattered, her emotions chaotic.

'Hiram and I were third cousins,' Burley told her. 'When he was little, his daddy ran over him with a tractor. So we all pretty much figured he was damaged from an early age, only it took years for it to surface.'

Oh, geez, not again. A few days ago she'd been cornered at the post office by a group of Minnie's friends. They'd wanted to assure her that Minnie had been a God-fearing Christian who would never do anything illegal. When Hope had informed them that kinky sex wasn't necessarily illegal, and that even Christian women enjoyed a bit of kink once in a while, they'd looked at her as if she were speaking the Devil's tongue.

'Anyway, his family would appreciate it if you'd mention that the rest of us are normal,' said the toilet-tossing champion. He sniffed and crossed his big arms over his barrel chest. 'And none of us believe in spanking of any kind.'

'I'll remember that,' Hope assured him and she excused herself. She moved to a trash can to throw away her corn-dog stick. Around her, people talked and joked, filling the tent with the kind of ease and laughter that came from knowing one another all of their lives.

Someone lobbed an empty cup into the trash, and she strolled through the crowd toward Shelly. She felt very alone, but it certainly wasn't the first time in her life she'd felt alone while standing in a crowd of people.

A big, warm hand grabbed her from behind, and she looked at the strong fingers wrapped around her upper arm. She turned and glanced up into Dylan's face. He still didn't appear very happy to see her.

'I didn't expect to see you here,' she said.

'I didn't expect to come.' He dropped his hand and cool air replaced the warmth of his palm. 'I haven't been in town on the Fourth for several years.'

'Did you get called into work?' she asked and watched his lips form the word 'no.'

Like most everyone else at the fair, he'd gone completely native in a blue-and-white striped shirt that snapped down the front and at the cuffs. Instead of his usual Levi's, he wore dark blue Wranglers. His belt was made of tooled leather, and the silver buckle had two T's in the center and must have weighed five pounds. 'Then what brought you to town? Do you have an uncontrollable desire for a corn dog?'

'I have an uncontrollable desire, but not for a corn dog,' he said, then gave her an all-over perusal, starting at her feet. Slowly his gaze traveled up her legs and thighs and rested on the front of her black tank top where the logo *bebe* was written in white. Then his eyes did meet hers, instantly heating her. No longer indifferent, he looked like he would eat her up right where she stood.

He pointed to her shoulder. 'Nice tattoo.'

'Thanks. I thought it made me look like a biker chick.'

One brow lifted and disappeared within the shadow of his hat. 'You don't look anything like a biker chick. First off, you need leather and a bad attitude.' He paused for a moment before he added, 'But come to think of it, you just might have the attitude part.'

Hope didn't have an attitude, she just didn't put up with a lot of crap.

'If you were a biker chick, you'd have to listen to your old man and sit on the back of his hog.' He bent his head over hers. 'And quite frankly, honey, you strike me as a woman who likes to drive.' From ten feet away, someone called his name and he placed his hand on the small of her back. 'Come on,' he said in a low, husky voice that sent shivers up her spine. 'Let's go shoot some squirrels.'

'Squirrels?'

He led her away from the food booths, and at that moment Hope would have followed him anywhere. 'You want to shoot squirrels?'

'Yep.'

She would have followed him to the moon, the end of the earth, or shooting squirrels, but she had to admit that it was weird, and not a typical date. 'I suppose they taste just like chicken,' she reasoned.

'I wouldn't know.'

They moved down the midway, past the crowded food stands to the relatively deserted game booths. Most people had taken a break to eat, and the Shoot a Squirrel game was empty except for the carnival worker. She'd seen the booth earlier but had forgotten about it, because not only didn't she have any desire to shoot a BB gun, each game cost the exorbitant price of two bucks.

She glanced at the five happy squirrel targets, then looked up at Dylan. One side of his face was lit by the light pouring from the booth; the other was covered in shadow. 'When you said you wanted to shoot squirrel, I thought . . .'

'I know what you thought.' He removed his hand from

the small of her back and pulled his wallet from his pocket. He handed the carnival worker, named Neville, ten dollars and was given two BB guns. 'We're going to have a contest,' Dylan said as he shoved his wallet into his back pocket. 'I get two games and you get two. You also get a free practice round.'

She took the gun and held it at arm's length. 'What makes you think I need practice?'

'Just a wild guess.' He smiled, a slow and sensual turn of his mouth. 'We're also going to place a little side bet.'

'You don't think I have a chance of winning, do you?'

'Nope.'

He was probably right. 'What's the side bet?'

Dylan leaned his gun against the booth. Then, without a word, he stepped behind her and positioned her gun against her shoulder. He placed his warm hand over hers and positioned his finger over the trigger. 'Now squeeze the trigger,' he said next to her right ear. She did and the BB hit the tarp behind the first squirrel. He folded her within the warmth of his solid chest, and the hairs on the back of her neck tingled as she fired again. The shot hit a bushy-tailed target happily munching on an acorn. 'The secret to a steady shot is knowing how to handle a loaded weapon,' he said just above a whisper as he cocked the gun for her. 'It takes a smooth motion of the wrist . . . and a slow, firm squeeze of the trigger.' The third shot hit the third squirrel with a loud ping that sent Hope's nerves pinging through her body. 'You look like a girl who'd be good at nice, smooth strokes and a firm squeeze.' The fourth target fell, and then the last. 'Are you, Hope?'

Hope glanced at the carnie standing several feet away. He was watching them, but he couldn't hear anything. She chose to ignore Dylan's question, but that didn't keep her insides from heating up and her nerves getting jumpy.

She looked up into Dylan's face and asked, 'What's the side bet?'

He stared into her eyes for a moment and then lowered his mouth closer to her ear. 'When I win,' he said, 'I get to lick you up like you're ice cream.'

His breath on her ear warmed the side of her throat. 'What happens if I win?'

He didn't answer right away, as if he hadn't considered the possibility. 'You won't.'

'What if I do?'

'Whatever you want.'

She tried to think of something to lighten the sexual tension, but her words came out sounding more sensual than she'd planned. 'Like I could order you to come over and mow my yard?'

'That's the best you can do?'

'Naked,' she added.

'Naked is good. Take out the part about mowing your yard and I just might let you win.' He brushed her arm with his hot palm and thought for a moment. 'Nah, I like mine better. Maybe you should admit defeat right now and save yourself some embarrassment.'

'Do I have a choice?'

He dropped his hands and took a step back. 'Hope, you always have a choice. I'd never make you do anything you don't want to do. What's the fun in that?'

She believed him. 'I get to go first.'

He picked up his BB gun and handed it to her.

She waited until Neville had reset the targets. Under Dylan's watchful eyes, she shot two of the five squirrels. 'That was pretty good,' she said, proud of herself.

Dylan laughed, three low 'huh-huh-huhs.' Then he raised his BB gun, squinted down the barrel, and knocked out all five targets in less than five seconds. He had that smooth squeeze motion down real good, an obvious expert at handling loaded weapons.

'I think I've been set up,' she said.

'You never stood a chance, city girl. I got my first BB gun when I was about four years old.' He lowered the barrel. 'But I'll tell you what I'll do. All or nothing, and in the next round, you only have to hit three, but I have to hit every shot to win.'

'You're on.' As soon as the squirrels were once again standing, she took aim.

'Look down the sights.' Neville stepped forward to advise her.

Dylan turned a narrow gaze on the carnie, and Neville went back to his position at the side of the booth. At the end of the barrel, she noticed what Neville was talking about. She lined it up on a squirrel with a green bow tie. 'Take that,' she said as the target fell. She missed the next two targets, but hit the fourth. She sighted the last squirrel, wearing a pair of pink pumps. 'I'm going to nail her good.'

'Now, there's an interesting choice of words.'

She glanced over at Dylan, then back at the squirrel. 'Don't think you can distract me.'

'I'm not' – he paused to lower his voice a fraction – 'but if I were trying, I'd probably just come right out and tell you I'm wondering about the color of your panties again.'

She shook her head. 'Not even your juvenile attempt to distract me is going to work.' She hit the target, then blew on the end of the barrel as if there were smoke coming out. 'Worried, Sheriff?'

'Honey,' he drawled as he shot and hit the first squirrel, 'you've got me shakin' in my boots.'

Hope decided it was time to do a little distracting of her own. She leaned her behind against the edge of the booth and crossed her legs. Her beige skirt slid up her thighs, and she ran her gaze from his big belt buckle up his chest to his face. 'Why don't you tell me again how to handle a loaded weapon?' She licked her lips and lowered her voice to a seductive whisper. 'Tell me about that smooth stroke and gentle squeeze.'

He shot and the second target fell. 'It was "firm squeeze."' The third squirrel went down and Hope straightened. 'There's a difference.'

'Pink,' she said, loud enough for his ears only.

He cocked the gun and looked across his shoulder at her. 'Pink?'

'My panties are pink.' She raised a seductive brow. 'Silky pink with little red chili peppers and the words "Warning: Hot Stuff" embroidered on the front.'

His gaze dropped to her crotch. 'Really?'

No, not really. 'Yeah.'

Ping. Ping. Ping. The rest of the targets fell and Dylan leaned the gun against the booth. 'Well, look at that. I guess I win.'

Neville offered Dylan his choice of a rubber chicken, an assorted selection of fake vomit, a Corvette mirror, or a plastic hard hat that held a beer on each side. Dylan took the hat and placed it on her head. 'For your next twofer night,' he said.

It was the first time in Hope's life a man had given her a cheap carnival prize. The gesture touched her more than it should have, which she supposed was just one more reflection on her life. It was a pretty sad commentary when a beer helmet could make a woman feel sort of weepy.

'Time to choose,' he said, placing his hand on the small of her back. They stepped away from the light of the booth and were wrapped up in the rapidly falling darkness. 'No more games, Hope,' he said as they walked away from the carnival booths. 'I either take you to your home or take you home with me. If I take you home with me, I'm taking you to my bed.' They moved in the opposite direction of couples heading toward the edge of the lake, where the town would shoot off fireworks. 'I doubt you'll get much sleep,' he added.

'I rode here with Paul and Shelly.'

'I know.' He stopped at the entrance to the parking lot, giving her time to make her decision. 'I already told them I'd take you home.'

'When did you do that?'

'When I first got here.'

She gazed into Dylan's dark face. Could she go through with it? Could she spend a night with him and feel good about herself in the morning? 'Were you that sure of yourself?'

He shook his head. 'No. I was hoping you'd let me sweet-talk you out of your clothes, but I wasn't sure of anything. I'm still not.' His hand moved from her back to her bare shoulder. 'I wasn't planning on coming here today. I wasn't planning on coming back to town for a couple more weeks.'

Could she? Could she get past all the emotions and treat an affair like men did? Could she be a man?

'Remember when you asked me if I have an uncontrollable desire?' he asked, sliding his palm down her arm to squeeze her hand. 'Well, I do. I have an uncontrollable desire for you.'

Yes, she could, and the last of her pitiful restraint melted right there in the middle of the Idaho wilderness. Right there in her fake tattoo and beer helmet. 'Okay,' she whispered. 'I want to go home with you.'

'Thank you, God,' he whispered back.

She thought he might kiss her. A romantic little kiss under the moon and the stars, but he didn't. Instead, he about jerked her out of her sandals. They walked through rows of cars, station wagons, and Jeeps. He pulled her behind him until they reached the passenger side of a dark blue truck. Opening the door, he practically shoved her inside. In under a minute, he had fired up the engine, shoved the truck into drive, and they were heading away from the grange. Complete darkness filled the cab, and only the weak dash lights illuminated the bottom half of Dylan's face. Hope looked across the bench seat at his profile. He stared straight ahead, deadly serious about something. He had a death grip on the steering wheel, and she wondered if he was having second thoughts.

'Dylan, what's wrong?'

'Nothing.'

'Then why are you staring straight ahead?'

'I'm just sitting over here trying to keep the truck on the road, but it's damn difficult because I keep thinking about sliding my hand down your panties.' He glanced at her, then turned his attention back to the black highway. 'I don't want to pull over and jump on you before we make it home.'

She laughed and he shook his head. 'It's not funny,' he said.

'Maybe you should recite something in your head.'

'I've tried that. It never works.'

'I'll help you.' Hope tossed her helmet on the floor and slid across the seat. 'Let's try something that isn't sexual.' She rose to her knees beside him. 'Like, "Fourscore and seven years ago, our fathers brought forth on this continent a new nation." ' She tossed his cowboy hat next to her helmet, then tugged at the front of his shirt, popping the snaps one at a time until the shirt lay open. She slipped her hand inside, and he sucked in a breath. His muscles flexed and turned hard beneath her touch. ' "Conceived in liberty. Dedicated to the proposition that all men are created equal." ' She ran her finger through the short hair on his chest. Abraham Lincoln had been wrong. Not all men were created equal. Some just possessed more. More than charm and good looks, they had that certain elusive something. Whatever *it* was, Dylan had more than his share.

He reached for her hand, flattening it against his chest so she couldn't move. She kissed the side of his neck and slid her open mouth to the hollow of his throat, tasting his aftershave and warm skin.

'Hope, I can barely see.'

'You don't need to see.' She moved his hand from on top of hers and placed his palm on her breast. 'You're a big boy, feel your way,' she breathed right before she sucked his neck.

'Jesus.' His fingers closed over her and the whoosh of air he'd been holding rushed from his lungs.

Hope's breasts grew taut, her nipples puckered, and she pulled the ends of his shirt from his jeans. She looked down at the hair on his chest. The gold light from the dash caught in the short curls and shined across his tight skin. As the truck motored down the highway, she combed her fingers down the thin line of hair to his flat belly. 'Am I helping?' She moved her hand to his zipper and, through the heavy denim, pressed her palm against the impressive length of his rock-hard erection. 'You haven't answered my question,' she said, her insides turning liquid, responding to him.

'When you touch me like that, I can't remember what you asked.'

She kissed her way across his collarbone. 'Are you still having trouble keeping the truck on the road?'

'Hell, yes.'

She had a vague sensation like the truck was turning. Then the next thing she knew, they'd stopped and she was on her back on the bench seat, staring up into Dylan's dark face. And he kissed her. Long and hard, his tongue thrusting into her mouth. The bottom of her skirt was up around her waist and he knelt between her legs. He shoved his pelvis snug against her crotch, and he might have hurt her if she hadn't wanted him so badly. She wrapped her legs around his waist and placed her hands on the sides of his head, kissing him like he kissed her, like neither would ever get enough. Enough mouths or tongues or the hot, liquid juices flowing through their bodies.

Dylan hit the horn with his foot, and he pulled back, gasping for air. His shirt hung open, his gaze wild within the shadowy cab. 'Let's get out of here,' he said and somehow managed to get them both out of the truck. He grabbed a box of condoms from the jockey box before heading across the driveway to the back door.

Hope looked over her shoulder at the truck, parked sideways, like it had skidded to a stop. She couldn't remember if they'd skidded or not. She couldn't remember much beyond the taste of Dylan's skin beneath her tongue.

As they walked into the kitchen, Dylan hit the switch by the back door and his keys and the box of condoms slid across the counter. Hope squinted against the overhead light, catching glimpses of blue walls, white floors, and appliances. Marble counter-tops and a wooden table in the middle of the room. Seeing a white cake with slices of candied peaches on top, sitting on the table, surprised her, but then Dylan tore at his shirt and she forgot all about the cake. He balled the shirt up and tossed it on the electric stove. Without a word, he pulled Hope against him. Her hands landed flat on his bare chest, her palms covering his nipples. She looked up from his golden-brown hair curling about her fingers to the dip in his throat. She placed a kiss on the mark she'd left there earlier, and she lowered her hands to his big belt buckle.

'You could kill someone with this,' she said as she unhooked it and pulled it from his pant loops. She glanced up at him and added, 'It could be considered a lethal weapon in some states.'

His green eyes looked at her from beneath lids heavy with desire. A blatantly sexual smile pushed the corners of his mouth upward. 'You got that right,' he drawled, and she had a feeling he wasn't talking about the buckle. The belt slipped through her fingers and hit the floor with a thud.

Dylan reached for her waist and grasped the edge of her tank top. 'Raise your arms,' he said and slowly pulled the shirt up her stomach. The soft cotton snagged under her breasts and he gathered the material in his hands and drew it over her head. The cool ends of her hair fell about her shoulders, and she dropped her hands to her sides. Dylan tossed her shirt with his, and Hope stood before him in her black stretch bra and khaki skirt.

Suddenly she didn't know if she could go through with it. Not like this. Not in the bright kitchen light where all of her flaws would be magnified. When she took off her panties, he'd see the thin silvery scar on her lower belly. He'd see her scar and he'd ask about it.

She looked up at him, up past the perfection of his corrugated stomach and broad chest with its swirls of fine hair and hard muscle. Up past the strong column of his throat and chin and the finely etched lines of his sensual lips. He was perfect, standing there beneath the bright light, wearing nothing but his jeans and boots. Absolutely perfect, while she had an old scar.

He reached for the button on her skirt and she grabbed his wrist. Maybe he wouldn't notice the scar, but he would notice she wasn't wearing pink silky panties. For a few seconds she couldn't remember if she was wearing her good underwear or getting-close-to-laundry-day underwear.

Then she did remember and relaxed a bit. White. Plain white bikini panties. They were new, but they didn't match her bra. She should have planned better. She should have worn something silky. She should have worn something to knock him off his feet, but she hadn't even known he was in town. 'Maybe we should turn off the lights,' she suggested.

'Why?'

He was going to find out soon enough. 'My panties don't match.'

He looked at her as if she weren't speaking a language he understood. 'Don't match what?'

'My bra.'

He blinked once and his brows lowered. 'You're kidding me.'

'No, my panties are white and . . .'

Dylan lowered his mouth to hers. 'I don't give a goddamn about your underwear,' he whispered against her lips. 'I'm more interested in what's inside.' He kissed a warm trail across her cheek to her ear. 'Inside where you're soft and warm.' The wet tip of his tongue touched the side of her throat, and he slid his fingers between her breasts to the black rose holding the cups together. 'But I'll tell you what I'll do.' With a twist of his wrist the closure sprang free and he pushed the straps from her shoulders. The bra fell to the floor. 'Problem solved.' His hot hands closed over her bare breasts as his mouth once again closed over hers. And suddenly Hope forgot about everything but the touch of his rough palms sliding back and forth across her hard, sensitive nipples. She drove her tongue into his mouth as he walked backward, driving her against the kitchen counter. Lust coiled low in her abdomen, pooled between her thighs, and tightened her breasts. The feelings were almost painful, they were so intense. Wonderful and overwhelming. She moaned deep, deep in her throat and ran her hands over him. His hair, the sides of his face, down his neck to his shoulders. She touched everywhere she could reach, his back, his sides, and his belly.

His hungry mouth slanted hard across her lips, and he gave her hot feeding kisses. He tasted like excited man. Like sex. She arched into him, into the warm wall of his chest and kneading hands, into his erection. Against her lower belly he was fully aroused, hard as stone, and she craved more, needing closer contact. Wanting the one thing he had, the one thing that only he could give her, she moved her hands to the front of his pants. She unsnapped the waistband, and when she pulled down the zipper, she found him naked beneath his jeans. His flesh jutted forward into her palm, and she closed her fist around the hot circumference of his erection.

A groan tore at Dylan's chest, and Hope pulled back to look into his face. His eyes were slits of green and his breath was uneven. She lowered her gaze to her hand, to the dark pubic curls visible between the edges of his zipper and his large penis. She slipped her palm up the smooth shaft and slid her thumb over the velvet head. She spread a bead of clear moisture over the plump cleft, learning the weight and texture of him.

'Hope,' he whispered, his voice rough as if she were torturing him. He took her hand from his body and set it on his shoulder. Then he grasped the backs of her thighs and lifted her until she sat on the counter. He took a step back and within less than a minute he stood before her completely naked. She would have preferred a moment or two to look him over, to appreciate the beauty of his body, the solid muscles and impressive proportions, but he didn't give her the chance. He stepped between her legs and placed a soft kiss on the side of her neck.

'I want you, Hope,' he said as he kissed a trail along her

collarbone. 'You've driven me crazy wanting you.' He kissed the inside slope of her breast. She arched her back and he said, 'Crazy thinking about this.'

He kissed the very tip of her nipple, then rolled it beneath his tongue. Hope's eyes closed as a shudder ran up her spine. Dylan licked her like the ice cream he'd talked about earlier; then he sucked her taut flesh into his hot, moist mouth. He drew on her as his hand moved beneath her skirt and between her thighs. He cupped her there, pushed his palm into her crotch, and softly squeezed. He moved to her other breast and popped her nipple into his mouth. His hand slid to the inside of her thigh, and he slipped his fingers beneath the edge of her panties.

'You're wet,' he whispered as he touched between her legs, feeling her where she wanted it most, where she was slick and where his touch made her greedy for more. 'I want to be inside you.' With each caress, each stroke of his hand, he brought her close to orgasm. He pulled her panties down her legs, and said, 'You're wet, and I'm extremely hard.' He dropped the twisted cotton on the floor. 'I think it's time.'

As Hope wiggled out of her skirt, Dylan grabbed a condom from the box on the counter behind her. She kicked the skirt free of her feet and watched him roll the thin latex down the length of his thick shaft.

'Come here,' he said and she wrapped her arms around his neck and her legs around his waist. He slid her off the counter and onto the warm head of his penis. He glided himself to her opening and shoved up as he pushed down on her thighs. He didn't get far before a stitch of pain penetrated Hope's lustful haze and she cried out in distress.

'Shhh, it's okay,' he whispered, and with her held tight against him, he moved to the kitchen table. 'I'll make it all right. I'll make it good for you.' He laid her on the cool wooden top and her hand landed in the white cake. The cake skidded to the far side of the table, but neither cared. He leaned over her and kissed her neck and breast while he put her feet on the table and pushed her thighs wide. He rocked his hips, slowly thrusting into her, easing his way further and further until he was buried to the hilt. His groan was a deep rumble that came from the pit of his soul.

'Goddamn,' he swore and he tangled his fingers in her hair. 'Are you okay?'

Hope could honestly say she didn't know. She'd never experienced anything quite like Dylan Taber, and then he moved and it was like white-hot lightning danced across her skin. Her gasp turned into a moan as he pulled back and thrust deep. The heat gathered between her legs and spread across her belly and breasts like a flash fire. He filled her completely, touching her so deeply that she felt utterly consumed by him.

She raised her hands to the sides of his head, getting frosting on his jaw and in his hair. She lowered his face to hers. 'I'm better than okay,' she said and kissed his lips.

He kissed her long and deep as he moved over her, slipping in and out with a slow, even rhythm that built up and up until neither could hardly breathe at all. He pulled back far enough to look into her eyes, and his breath became ragged with the punctuating thrust of his hips. Every nerve ending in her body was alive and tingling with warm liquid pleasure, pushing her up, up, up toward release. It built tighter, hotter, the pleasure curling her toes. And then it pulled her completely under. Wave after wave seared her from her head to the bottom of her feet and she cried his name.

She grasped his bare shoulders and clung to him as the walls of her body pulsed around him. It went on and on like nothing she'd ever experienced in her life. He moved faster, harder, pumping into her again and again until the air whooshed from his lungs as if he'd been smashed in the chest and his muscles beneath her hands turned to stone.

In the aftermath, the only sound was that of heavy, spent breathing. Their skin was glued together and neither seemed to have the energy to lift themselves off the table. Dylan's forehead rested next to Hope's right ear and his fingers were still tangled in her hair. A warm, fluttery afterglow settled on her flesh and she turned her head and kissed his temple.

'My God,' he moaned. 'That was amazing.'

Hope smiled. She thought so, too. He'd just given her the most amazing sex of her life. It wasn't love. Hope knew the difference between sex and making love. What he'd given her was the most incredible orgasm of her life. No, it wasn't love, but it had been wonderful. He was wonderful, too.

Lightning Shoots from Man's Fingertips

Dylan leaned a bare shoulder into the doorframe and raised his coffee mug. He took a swallow and shoved his free hand into the pocket of his Levi's. The morning sun spilled through the blinds, striping his bed with light and picking out the gold in Hope's hair. She lay beneath a tangle of sheets, one arm thrown above her head, her face turned slightly into his pillow. Her breath was slow and steady in sleep.

Dylan rubbed the warm mug against his chest and watched her. She'd wanted him to take her home in the wee hours of the morning. Instead, he'd taken her mind off leaving.

It had been a while since he'd had sex. Even longer since he'd slept with a soft woman draped across him, and he didn't know which he had missed most. Waking up with her warm curves pressed against him and her silky hair in his mouth was something he'd forgotten he missed. The other . . . he hadn't forgotten that, he just hadn't remembered it feeling so good.

In his life, Dylan had been with more women than he could remember. He wasn't proud of his past, but he couldn't change it. As a teenager, he'd been wild. In his twenties, he'd slowed down a bit. By the age of thirty, he'd certainly become more choosy, but he'd never really thought about the full ramifications of such an intimate act. It had taken his relationship with Julie to bring it home. It had taken a broken condom and the birth of his son to make him realize the full physical consequences, but beyond that, he'd discovered there were deeper emotional consequences, too.

Hope stirred in his bed and he watched her foot peek out from beneath the sheet.

Until now, he hadn't been willing to risk it, but there was definitely something about Hope Spencer that made him forget about the consequences of becoming involved with her. Something beyond the scent of her skin and the taste of her mouth. Something beyond her beautiful body and how she made him feel.

Dylan liked her dry humor and sarcasm and laughter. He liked that she didn't take a lot of bullshit. He liked her pink toenail polish, too.

He wanted to know more.

They'd made love three times last night. The first time fast and explosive, the second time slow and . . . explosive. The second time he'd taken his time, licking frosting from Hope's nipples and munching peach slices that he'd placed on her breasts but had slid down her body to her thighs. She'd eaten cake from him, too. From his belly and lower. The third time the sex had started in the shower and ended in his bed.

And he'd do it again. He couldn't seem to help it. He didn't want to hurt Hope. He didn't want to hurt himself or Adam, but he knew he'd be with Hope again. He'd thought one night would be enough. It wasn't nearly enough. He'd have to be very careful.

Hope moved her hand and Dylan watched her slowly come awake. She blinked and her brows lowered.

'Good morning,' he said and pushed away from the doorframe.

She sat straight up as if she'd been doused by water. Her hair swung across one side of her face, and the sheet slipped to her waist. 'Where am I?' she asked, her voice husky from sleep and a night spent using her mouth for something other than talking.

'If you don't remember, then I didn't do my job,' he answered as he moved to the side of the bed. Keeping one foot on the floor, he sat next to her and brushed her hair from her face. 'Is it coming back to you now?'

She didn't answer, but her cheeks turned pink.

'Here,' he said and held his coffee mug to her lips. 'This might help.'

Hope took several deep swallows, then pushed the mug away. 'You were supposed to take me home.'

Dylan lowered his gaze to her full breasts, her pink nipples beginning to pucker against the cold. 'I guess I forgot.'

She scooted away from him and raised the sheet to her arm pits. 'I didn't want to wake up here.'

He lifted his gaze to her face. 'Why?'

'Because I always look like crap in the morning. I don't have clean clothes or underwear, and my eyes are puffy.'

He would have laughed, but she appeared to be very serious. To him she looked so good he wanted to pounce on her and bury his face in her neck. He wanted to make her smile and sigh his name. Instead, he stood and walked over to his closet. He took out a terrycloth robe that was too short and which he never wore. Tossing it onto the end of the bed, he moved to his dresser. 'These have never been worn,' he said after he found a pair of boxer shorts. 'My mom bought them for me for Christmas, but I don't wear underwear.' He tossed them by the robe. 'She hasn't given up on trying to reform me.' He slanted her a smile, but she didn't say another word. So much for putting her at ease. 'I'll make you breakfast,' he said as he left the room, giving her a chance to dress by herself.

His bare feet didn't make a sound when he moved down the hall, past Adam's room and the bathroom. In the kitchen, the cake mess was still everywhere. Earlier, while he'd waited for the coffee to perk, he'd picked up the biggest hunks, but a lot of the frosting still smeared the table and floor.

Dylan opened the refrigerator door and looked inside. Since he hadn't expected to come home for a few weeks, he'd cleaned it out and there wasn't much inside. A tub of margarine, a jar of mustard, and some ketchup. In the cupboards he found boxes of macaroni and cheese, instant potatoes, and canned fruit and vegetables.

Down the hall, he heard the bathroom door open and shut, and then the water run in the sink. There was nothing in his house to eat, and he couldn't take her to breakfast. Not when she was wearing his boxer shorts, and not when the news of them together would be served up at lunch.

Dylan took the broom and dustpan from the closet and swept up as much cake as possible. If this were any other town, if he were a man other than the sheriff trying to live down his own past and Hiram Donnelly's, no one would have cared so much, but he wasn't just any man and Hope didn't exactly blend in with the locals.

He threw more cake into the trash and smiled to himself. The next time Paris asked him how he'd liked her cake, and she would, she always did, he could tell her in all honesty that it was the best damn cake he'd ever eaten.

Dylan put the broom and dustpan away, and when he

turned, Hope stood in the doorway. Her hair was brushed, her face scrubbed. The edges of his boxer shorts hung just below the bottom of his robe.

'I'm afraid I don't have anything for breakfast,' he said.

Her gaze slid from his and moved around the kitchen. 'That's okay. I never eat before noon anyway. Have you seen my clothes?'

He pulled out a kitchen chair and pointed to the bundle he'd folded earlier.

'You folded my clothes?'

He shrugged and watched her move to the table. He hadn't known what to expect this morning; he hadn't really thought about it. But even if he had, he wouldn't have expected her to be chilly. She reminded him of the Hope who'd first driven her Porsche into town. Sometime during the night, between the time he'd pulled her against him and the time she'd opened her eyes, something had changed, and he didn't even pretend to know what that something might be.

When she reached for her clothes, he reached for her hand. 'What are your plans today?'

'I have to work. I'm really behind.'

'Did you get the police files yet?'

'Yes.'

'I could help you look them over.'

'Ah, no, thanks.' She looked somewhere over his left shoulder, and he placed the tips of his fingers against her jaw and brought her gaze to his. Her eyes gave nothing away, and in giving nothing, she told him what he needed to know. She was hiding from him, and he would have none of it. He lowered his lips to hers and lightly kissed her. She tried to take a step backward, but he cradled the nape of her neck in his palm. With his mouth poised just above hers, he ran the tip of his tongue across the seam of her lips and felt her relent by degrees. Her shoulders relaxed, her stance softened, then a light puff of a sigh and a silent 'Ahh.' He kissed her more fully. He kissed her until her hands found the back of his head. Until she'd risen on the balls of her feet and pressed her breasts into his bare chest. He drew back and looked into her eyes. 'Sorry about breakfast?'

'Mmm . . . I'm still full from all that cake.'

Dylan smiled. Damn, but he liked her.

Hope chose a photograph of a normal-looking grandmother from her computer files. She gave her purple hair and lipstick. As she made the alien's eyes beneath the purple eyeshadow a little rounder and her fingers a bit too long, she wondered if Walter would think all the purple was too far-fetched and make her change it. In her wildest imagination, she'd never have thought to make up a character like Eden Hansen.

Not even she was that good.

She'd already sent two alien articles to her editor. He liked them both and wanted more. She clicked the SEND icon on her computer screen and shot her third story through cyberspace.

The first article had just hit the stores, and according to Walter, the preliminary reader response was positive. The paper wanted to run with the series as long as possible. Which was fine with Hope. She had enough material to last a while. And when she ran out, she'd just make a trip into town.

She was writing some of the best articles of her career, and she didn't need a psychiatrist to tell her it was because she no longer felt empty, trying to create from a dry well.

By moving to Gospel, she'd inadvertently kickstarted her career and her life. She was sleeping and feeling better than she had in a long time. She'd always known that her life and creativity were so intertwined that when one suffered, they both suffered. She supposed for a while she'd just tried to ignore the truth. She'd focused on something she'd thought she could control, her career, but she'd found herself hanging on by her fingernails.

Now she had a social life, and she had something else entirely different to work on besides her stories for *The Weekly News of the Universe*. When her aliens were giving her a headache, she took out her article on Hiram Donnelly. She didn't know if she'd ever sell it, but writing it gave her another outlet.

She reached for the large envelope she'd received in the mail a few days prior and removed the FBI report inside. From the sections that weren't blacked out, she'd read that the FBI had been tipped off and provided proof of embezzlement by someone inside the sheriff's office. An informant who had access to book-keeping records. Hope wondered if that someone was Hazel Avery. Or perhaps even Dylan.

She leaned back in her chair and her gaze lowered to the telephone next to her computer screen. Dylan said he'd call. When he'd dropped her off that morning, he'd said he had some work to do at the Double T, but that he'd call her tonight. She glanced at the clock on her monitor. Five-fifteen. Officially evening.

Hope pushed back her chair and stood. When she thought of last night, she felt equal parts thrilled and terrified. Like she wanted to laugh one second and hide the next. She felt schizophrenic. Torn in two. Wonderfully alive and scared to death. Looking for meaning in a meaningless affair. Trying to protect herself while running toward a collision with something that was bound to hurt her. Completely out of control.

He'd licked frosting from her body and they'd been as

intimate as two lovers could be, yet before he'd taken her home that morning, he'd given her a baseball cap and helped shove her hair up into it. He'd given her one of his big Levi's jackets to wear so no one in town would recognize her and start rumors. That was what he'd said anyway, and she wondered if that was true, or if he was secretly embarrassed to be seen with her.

He'd asked about her scar. He'd finally noticed it as he'd bathed her in the shower. She'd told him her ex-husband had given her a tummy tuck, because it hadn't been the time or the place for the truth. Then he'd kissed her old hysterectomy scar and made her feel bad for lying.

He'd folded her clothes. Such a small thing for him to do, yet it felt huge. While she'd slept, he'd folded her bra and panties in half and laid them with her skirt and tank top in a neat pile like they'd just come out of the dryer. And as she'd tried to draw away from him, tried to put some distance between them, he'd pulled her close and made her feel as if the sex the night before hadn't been so meaningless after all.

Falling in love with Dylan would be easy. So easy and so stupid. He'd told her once that a girlfriend was the last thing he needed. She believed he meant it. If he'd wanted a woman in his life, he certainly would have had one before she'd shown up in town. There were plenty in Gospel to choose from. He didn't want a relationship. He'd made that clear. He wanted sex, and while she wanted sex, too, she knew she would ultimately want more. She knew she would begin to care about him more than she did already, and she would be hurt when he didn't feel the same. It wasn't his fault. It wasn't anyone's fault. It was just the way things were between them.

It would be best to end it now, before she got hurt.

If and when he called, she would just have to tell him she

couldn't see him any more. She'd have to find the willpower to just say no.

In the end, she didn't talk to him at all. When the telephone rang, she didn't pick up. She didn't trust herself. Since the moment Dylan had kissed her the night of the Buckhorn incident, her willpower had gone into hiding. She didn't trust that it would make an appearance now. Not after the memory of his kiss, and not after the night they'd spent together painting each other with frosting. Not when all she had to do was close her eyes and feel his mouth on her body. Not when she could recall with perfect clarity the seductive timbre of his voice when he'd lowered his face between her legs and said, 'Relax, honey, I'm just going to eat this little peach right here.'

No, her willpower was less than zero.

She would have to avoid him for as long as possible, but complete avoidance would be impossible in such a small town.

The next time she saw him, she'd just act natural. Cool, as if she'd had lots of affairs in the past.

At around midnight, she went to bed and jumped at every sound, wondered if he'd show up at her house, or if it was even Dylan who'd called earlier. It could have been Shelly. Or Walter. Or a telemarketer. It probably hadn't even been him. The jerk.

At a little before ten the next morning, Shelly knocked on Hope's front door. Hope had just gotten dressed and her hair was still wet from her shower.

'Dylan just phoned me,' Shelly said as she followed Hope into the kitchen. 'He wanted me to come over and see if you were okay. He said he tried to call you last night, but you weren't home.'

'I wasn't answering the phone.' Hope reached for the coffeepot and poured two cups. 'I was busy working.'

'He said he called this morning, too.'

Hope raised her mug and blew into it to keep from smiling. She hadn't heard the phone, but maybe she'd been in the shower when he'd called.

'Is something going on between the two of you?'

'Not a thing. Do you want milk and sugar?'

'No.' Shelly raised her own coffee and blew into it. Both women stared at each other through the steam. 'Did you know that an informant inside the sheriff's department gave the FBI information about Hiram Donnelly?'

'I'd figured that out.'

'But have you figured out who is it?'

'Hazel?'

'No.'

'Dylan?'

'Wrong again.'

'Do you know?'

'Yes,' Shelly answered through a smile. 'But I'm not going to tell you. And do you know why?' She didn't wait for Hope to answer. 'Because I can keep a confidence. No one knows but me and the FBI. If someone tells me to keep something a secret, I can. I'm a good friend.' She looked pointedly at Hope as if to say Hope was not.

'Okay.' Hope relented and it all came out in a rush. 'Okay, I spent the Fourth of July night at Dylan's house.'

'I knew it! When Paul told me that Dylan was giving you a ride home, I knew he was going to try his old cheap moves on you.'

Hope was too embarrassed to admit that he hadn't tried very hard. 'You can't talk about this to anyone. I don't know how I feel about what happened, and Dylan doesn't want this to turn into town gossip.'

'Oh, that Dylan,' Shelly scoffed and waved her bad hand. 'He thinks his business is sacred or something. Somehow more off-limits than everyone else's. He thinks everyone is just dying to know what's up with him.' She shrugged. 'Which, of course, we are, but I swear I won't breathe a word.'

Hope blew into her own coffee and took a drink. When she looked up, Shelly was staring a hole into her. 'What? Do you want details?'

'Not if you don't want to give them.'

'I'll just say that I stayed with him all night, and I had a really good time.' She took another sip and added, 'Really good.'

Over their coffee mugs, they smiled at each other. Two completely opposite women who recognized a true friend in the other.

'How's your hand?' Hope asked.

'Good.' Shelly looked at it and remarked, 'This polish makes Paul frisky, but it's staring to chip now.'

'Come on, let's do our nails.' Hope motioned for Shelly to follow. She gathered her supplies and set them on the coffee table in the living room. She chose Rebellious Red polish, while Shelly settled on Mountain Huckleberry.

'Are you going to see him again?'

Hope shook her head. 'No. I don't think that would be a good idea.'

'Why?'

Hope reached for a bottle of remover and a bag of cotton balls. 'Well, it can't go anywhere because I'm leaving in five months.' The thought of leaving sent an unexpected qualm of dread through her. She felt so alive here and had found so much, but this wasn't her home. She just couldn't see herself living here forever, but then she'd never tried to envision it, either. She removed the lid and soaked a cotton ball. 'Dylan doesn't want a girlfriend, and I would end up hurt.'

Shelly thought for a moment, then said, 'Probably. Too

bad you can't just have fun. You know, use and abuse him while you're here.'

Hope thought it was too bad, too.

After Shelly left, Hope fixed her hair in an inverted ponytail and put on a blue summer dress. The top of the dress looked like two bandannas sewn together and tied behind her neck and back, while the skirt hit her about mid-thigh. When her make-up was perfect, her lips a glossy red, she drove into town. She stopped first at the M & S to pick up some fresh produce and a Hershey's big block.

She looked over a small selection of CDs displayed near the postcards and gum. She'd never been a fan of country-and-western music, but since she was living in a town where if it wasn't country it wasn't cool, she grabbed a Dwight Yoakam CD and placed it in her basket. She'd never listened to his music, but she'd seen him in *Sling Blade*. She figured that anyone who could act so good at being so bad had to be talented in other areas also.

Stanley stood behind the counter as always, a copy of *The Weekly News of the Universe* spread out in front of him.

'Are you reading about aliens again?' she asked him as she set her basket next to the cash register.

'Yep, only this time there is a pack of 'em living in the Northwest. Says right here they're masquerading as humans, running around playing tricks on people.'

'Really? Hmm.'

'Says they're responsible for lost backpackers and a few injuries.'

She made her eyes go wide. 'Wow.'

'Says they place bets.'

'That's horrible.'

'It ain't right betting on others' misery.' Stanley spun the paper around and pointed to the center spread. 'Call me crazy, but that looks like Gospel Lake.'

Hope took a closer look at the photograph she'd taken the day she'd met Shelly and the boys on the beach. She hadn't thought anyone would recognize the picture. 'I think it looks like Eugene, Oregon,' she said, to throw him off the track.

'Could be. An alien could blend in real good with all those militant tree huggers they got over there in Eugene.' He shook his head and reached for her basket. 'Sure could be Gospel, though.'

Hope was a fairly good actress when she put her mind to it, and she tried to appear as if she were giving his idea some serious thought. 'Do you really think so?'

'Nah, but it's fun to wonder who in this town might be an alien.'

She glanced up from the paper and smiled. 'Maybe the woman who runs the Sandman Motel.'

'Ada Dover?' He laughed and rang up her oranges. 'Could be you're right. She is an odd one at that.'

'Yeah, kind of spooky.'

'Don't you worry.' He patted her hand, then rang up her items. 'I'll protect you from aliens.'

'Thank you, Stanley,' she said and was still smiling when she left the M & S. She dropped off some film she'd shot of the mountains taken from her backyard, and drove into the self-serve Chevron. The pumps had yet to enter the new century, and after filling her car with gas, she had to go inside to pay with her debit card.

When she walked back outside, Dylan stood on the other side of the pumps, leaning against his dark blue truck, filling it with gas. His black T-shirt was tucked inside his black jeans, and his black Stetson was pulled low on his forehead. He looked like he'd stepped off the silver screen – an irresistible baddie – on a mission to wreak havoc and break the hearts of good women.

Her steps slowed and her heart ground to a halt. She couldn't see his eyes for the shadow of his hat, but she could feel his gaze on her. Like always, it reached across the distance and touched her all over. As she approached her car, he straightened and a slow smile curved his mouth.

'Looks like someone wrapped you up in his hankie,' he said, his smooth voice pulling her to him like an invisible tractor beam, tempting her with the memory of his hands and mouth touching her.

She looked down at her dress and couldn't think of anything intelligent to say. 'Oh' was the only sound she was capable of uttering. She looked back up into his shadowy eyes and seductive smile, and like the coward she was, she ducked her head and dove into her car. She fired up the Porsche and sped off, leaving temptation in her dust.

Oh. That was it? *Oh?* Her knuckles turned white on the steering wheel and her cheeks burned all the way home. *Oh?* He probably thought she was an idiot. So much for acting cool and sophisticated.

She carried her bags into the house and put her groceries away. She wondered what Dylan thought of her now. Now that she'd behaved like a boob.

She didn't have long to wait. She'd listened to only a few songs on her Dwight Yoakam CD when someone pounded on her door. She hit the STOP button on her stereo, then opened the door, and there Dylan stood, over six feet of extremely irritated man. 'What in the hell were you trying to prove?' he asked and stormed into the entry, bringing the scent of his aftershave with him. She looked behind him outside but didn't see his truck.

'Where's your truck?'

'You pulled out of the Chevron and nearly T-boned Alice

Guthrie's station wagon. She had her kids strapped in the back, and you could have seriously hurt someone.'

'That station wagon was a long way from the inter-section.' She shut the door behind him and folded her arms beneath her breasts.

The light from the chandelier bounced prisms about the hall and across Dylan's black T-shirt. Within the small confines, he seemed larger than life. A big, muscular he-man dressed in black. He placed his hands on his hips and studied her beneath the brim of his hat. 'Why are you avoiding me?'

'I'm not.'

'Why won't you answer your phone?'

'I've been working.'

'Uh-huh.'

He wasn't buying it, so she decided to be honest. 'I just don't think we should see each other any more.'

'Why the hell not?'

But not completely honest. 'Because I just can't have you coming over here whenever you want sex.'

His gaze narrowed. 'You think that's why I'm here?'

She didn't know, but she was getting that out-of-control feeling again. The feeling like she was running toward a collision. 'Isn't it?'

'No.' He leaned toward her and said, 'Maybe I wanted to see for myself if you were all right. Maybe you're a sparkling conversationalist. Maybe I just like looking at you.' He leaned in a bit closer. 'And maybe I just like spending time with you.'

Hope's heart pounded in her chest.

'Maybe the reason I'm here has nothing to do with sex.'

'Really?'

'Maybe.' He placed his fingers beneath her chin and raised her face to his. 'Maybe I just want to kiss you. Maybe that's all I want.' He turned his head slightly to the side and said against her lips, 'Maybe I just miss the taste of you in my mouth.'

Her breath caught in her chest next to her pounding heart, and she couldn't remember exactly why she should tell him to go. Well actually, she could remember, but at the moment, what might happen in the future didn't matter so much. She was standing in the present, and it was filled with a tall, seductive cowboy whose touch set her on fire and made her want to run her hands up his chest and lean into him. 'Would you like to come in?' she asked, although, technically, he was already inside.

'Maybe.' He opened his mouth over hers and soul-kissed her, deep down where nothing mattered but him. He was magic, spreading lightning through her body.

He pulled back and looked into her eyes. 'Do you want me to come in?'

If she said yes, she would be saying yes to more than sparkling conversations. Was that what she wanted? To be with him for as long as it lasted, or to be alone and thinking about him? 'Yes,' she said, as much to him as to herself. She turned before she could change her mind, and the thud of his boots echoed on the hardwood floor as he followed behind her. 'Can I get you anything to drink?' she asked over her shoulder, glancing back at him.

'No,' he said and slowly looked up from staring at her behind.

She had very little control over him and herself and the situation between them, and she was losing more with every beat of her pounding heart. But before losing completely, she said, 'We have to set some ground rules.'

'Fine. I'll call before I come over.' He reached for her hand and stopped her by the coffee table. 'But you have to answer your phone.'

'I will, but you have to . . .' She paused as he raised her palm to his mouth and his warm breath tickled her wrist.

'I have to what, honey?' he asked, but the expression in the green eyes looking down into hers told her he knew. He knew he had her right where he wanted her, and he was enjoying himself.

'Uhh . . . call first.'

'I just said I would.' He kissed the little tickles on her wrist and sent them up her arm.

'Oh.'

'What other rules did you have in mind?'

With him staring at her as if he were about to eat her up, she couldn't think. She removed her gaze from his and looked into the dining room at the FBI report sitting on the table. 'I'm not into anything dirty,' she said, which she supposed was true, as far as she knew.

A frown furrowed his brow, and he dropped her hand. 'Okay.' He took off his hat and tossed it on the couch. 'Before we go any further, define dirty.'

'Kinky.'

'You better define kinky.'

She thought for a moment. 'No whips.'

'Are you speaking from experience?'

'No.'

'Then how do you know you won't like whips?'

'I don't like pain. If I get a paper cut, I want morphine.'

'Do you like being tied up?'

Hope had never been tied up before, and the thought of Dylan tying her up made her skin tingle with anticipation. 'Yes.'

'Handcuffed to the bedpost?'

She'd never been handcuffed to a bedpost, either. She nodded. Yeah, she could do that. 'Can I handcuff you?'

'Any time,' he said through a wicked grin, then pulled her into his chest. 'Is that it, or do you have more rules?'

'I think that's it.'

He lowered his face to her ear and whispered, 'So if I were to tie you to my bed and kiss your feet, that'd be okay?'

'Yes.'

He raised a hand to her cheek and kissed the side of her neck. 'And what if I slid my hands up the backs of your thighs to your behind and raised you to my mouth? Is that too dirty?'

'No.' Her eyes closed. 'That would be okay.'

'It's better than okay.' He slid his hand up her arm. 'And, Hope?'

'Hmm.' She opened her eyes and looked up at him.

'I'd never do anything to you that you didn't want me to do. I'd never hurt you or cause you pain.' He reached for the knot at her nape. 'Not unless you asked me real nice.'

Detour on Highway To Hell

The knot beneath Dylan's fingers slipped free, and the straps of her dress slid from her shoulders. Dylan looked deep into Hope's eyes, and saw exactly what he needed. It was there in the slight lowering of her lids and the spark burning like a clear blue flame. He cupped her breast and felt her pucker beneath his touch. She ran the tip of her tongue across her lip, and he kissed her, tasting desire on her mouth. Her desire for him. His desire for her. The same desire that had kept him up last night and had turned him hard as stone.

He pushed down the straps and the dress fell to her waist and stayed there. Then he leaned back to look at what he held in his hand. Perfect. Soft. The shape of a pear, her nipple like a tight little raspberry. Her breast filled his big hand, and he squeezed softly. He felt the intake of her breath; she held it.

How could he have ever thought one night with her would be enough? After one night he wanted her more than before, when she'd been just a fantasy. Now he knew she was better than a fantasy. Better than anything he'd ever held in his hands. And he knew that as long as she was within his reach, he would reach for her.

She grasped the end of his T-shirt and tugged it from his jeans. He took over and pulled it over his head, and before the T-shirt hit the floor, her hands were on him. On his sides and shoulders and moving down his chest. She leaned forward and kissed his throat. Her warm, moist tongue sent shivers throughout his body and made him so hard he throbbed.

Her fingers combed through the hair on his chest, leaving a path of fire to the waistband of his pants. She unbuttoned his fly, reached into his jeans, and took him out. That was one of the things he liked about Hope. She wasn't shy about going after what she wanted.

Dylan looked down between them, between her breasts to his penis resting in her soft white hand. He didn't know how things would work out for them, and at the moment, he didn't care. His blood pounded in his veins, his head, and his groin. Lust pulled his gut into a hard knot. He wrapped his hand over hers and moved it up and down, sliding within the soft velvet of her palm.

He knew there would come a time when he would not be able to touch her. When she wouldn't be here to touch him, but she was here now, and he wanted this. He wanted the ache in his gut and the heavy throb in his belly. He wanted the feeling of being hit by a runaway train. Of being flattened by something he couldn't and didn't want to stop.

He kissed her mouth, the side of her face, and her throat. He untied the back of her dress and it fluttered to her feet. She stood before him in nothing but silky blue panties. She brushed the head of his penis across her smooth stomach, and his knees about buckled under him. Even though he knew better, he wanted this to last forever.

'Make love to me, Dylan,' she whispered.

He placed both her hands on his shoulders. 'You city

girls,' he said as he lifted her from the pool of her dress. 'You're always in a hurry.' Slowly he lowered her, sliding her down his body. The hard points of her breasts grazed his chest, and he held her against him. Nipples to nipples, their groins pressed together, his erection shoved up against her thigh and crotch. 'We have all day. All night, too.'

With her mouth poised just above his, she asked, 'You don't have to be anywhere? No pressing responsibilities?'

'Nope. I already talked to Adam today, and I left his dog at my mom's.' He ground his hips into her. 'The only place I want to be is right here.' He would have stood like that longer, but she wiggled from his grasp. With his body painfully aroused, he watched her walk away.

'What are you doing?'

'Don't go anywhere.' She looked over her shoulder and smiled. 'I'll be right back.'

He glanced down at himself, at his erection jutting from his pants like a piece of driftwood, and wondered just where in the hell she thought he would go. Hadn't she just asked him to make love to her? He reached for his wallet and pitched it onto the coffee table.

'Do something useful,' she called from the dining room. 'Take off your clothes.'

He kicked off his boots and stuffed his socks inside. As he shoved his pants down his thighs, the sounds of a steel guitar and a fiddle filled the house. He tossed his jeans by his boots and looked up. Hope reappeared, walking to him, her breasts bouncing a little with each step. From the other room, Dwight Yoakam sang about a wild ride. Damn, he wasn't going to be able to hear Dwight any more without thinking of Hope moving toward him in nothing but her little panties.

'I've never listened to country-and-western music,' she said. 'I want to broaden my horizons. Experience something new.'

He grabbed her and folded her into his chest. With the length of her pressed against the length of him, he figured it was his duty to give her a new experience. While Dwight sang about a woman rubbing her hand up his thigh, Dylan created a little friction, rubbing against Hope Spencer's thighs and filling his hands with her little behind covered in those thin, silky panties. Her breasts were pressed into his chest and he ground his pelvis into her. He kissed her hard, a long, wet tangle of tongues and smashed mouths gasping for breath. He slid one hand around her side and down into the front of her panties. She was wet, and when he felt her where she was warm and slick, a long, rough moan sounded deep in her throat.

She wiggled from his embrace once more, but this time she didn't leave him. 'Sit down,' she ordered, her voice sounding as drugged as he felt. She didn't wait for him to follow her request. Instead, she shoved her hands on his chest and pushed until he sat on the couch. She stood between his widespread knees and pushed her panties down her thighs. As she kicked them behind her, he ran his gaze up her legs to her bikini line. Just last week, he'd wondered if she was a natural blonde. Now he knew she was, and Jesus H., walking around with that kind of knowledge had nearly killed him already. Just that morning, he'd been picturing her crotch and had driven a tractor into the side of his mother's barn.

Just looking at her now made it hard to breathe. 'I need a party hat,' he said.

'What?'

'There's a condom in my wallet.'

She took his wallet from the table and slid the gold foil-wrapped condom from inside. 'I thought you didn't come over here for sex.'

He smiled. 'Well, a guy can hope, Hope.'

One brow lifted as she unwrapped the condom and slipped it between her lips. Then, before his astonished eyes, she put it on him with her mouth. 'Oh, God,' he groaned as she broadened his horizons and gave him a whole new experience.

By the time she straddled his lap, he was very close to the point of no return. She positioned the head of his penis, then slowly sat until he was buried deep inside her. Through the thin layer of latex, her hot flesh surrounded his erection as if she'd been custom-made for him. She shuddered and he felt every ripple of her tight passage. She grabbed his shoulders and leaned back. Her lips were parted, her breathing shallow, and her head fell to one side. Her cheeks were flushed pink. The hunger in her clear blue eyes focused on him as if he were the only man who had exactly what she needed.

She sighed his name and he placed his hands on her back. He kissed her breasts, and when she squeezed her tight muscles, he had to fight to keep from coming before she did. He tried to think of something else while every cell in his body was focused on her. On the way she felt inside. On the warmth of her contracting muscles. On the sharp pain and dull ache twisting his groin.

She straightened and pressed her forehead to his. He breathed the air from her lungs as she moved up and down, touching him with a slow and steady rhythm that built a fever for more. He grabbed her behind and brought her down hard, moving her faster.

He didn't think anything could feel as good as the inside of Hope, but with the next push, it did. It got a whole lot hotter. And wet, like her mouth, only better. Heat swept across his flesh like a raging fire. Hope moaned and squeezed him tight, pulsing, constricting around him. The strong contractions of her orgasm wrung a release from him that twisted his vital organs and left him without air in his lungs.

He came deep inside where she was hot and slick, and even as he pumped into her one last time, he knew why it suddenly felt so damn good.

The condom broke.

Hope rested her head on Dylan's shoulder while the music from her CD player filled the silence, broken only by their gasps of breath. She hadn't thought sex with Dylan could get better than it had been the other night. She'd been wrong about that. Perhaps it was better now because she was more relaxed. More at ease with her body and his. More comfortable acting like herself.

She waited until her breathing returned to normal before she spoke. 'I think you've ruined me for any other man.' When he didn't say a word, she pulled back and looked into his face. He didn't look like a man basking in afterglow. 'What's wrong?'

'Hop up,' was all he said.

As soon as Hope rose to her knees, he grasped her hips and stood her in front of him. Without a word, he grabbed his jeans and headed to the bathroom.

Hope stared after him until he was out of sight. The bathroom door shut, and her own afterglow bubble popped like a balloon. She stood in the middle of her living room, suddenly feeling very naked and exposed. What had happened? What had gone wrong? What had she done?

She grabbed her dress and slipped it over her head. She didn't know what had happened or what she'd done. Everything had been wonderful until afterward. Until she'd made that crack about him ruining her for other men. Maybe that was it. Maybe that had sounded like a commitment to him.

Hope tied the dress behind her neck and glanced toward

the hall. That had to be it. She'd made him angry. He'd probably leave now. The thought of him walking out her front door left her cold.

The CD stopped and the toilet flushed. Dylan appeared in his black jeans, but he didn't look any happier than when he'd left. 'Are you taking birth control?' he asked.

'What?' Her gaze locked on the grim line of his mouth. She shook her head. 'I mean, no.'

'Shit!'

Hope jumped. 'What?'

'What?' He ran his fingers through the sides of his hair. 'Didn't you feel the condom break?'

She thought for a moment. Thought of the exact second when everything suddenly felt a whole lot better than it had. 'Oh,' she said.

His hands dropped to his sides. 'When are you due for your period?'

He was worried about pregnancy. Something that she hadn't thought about for so long, it never entered her head. 'Not for a long time,' she assured him.

'How long?'

'I'm not pregnant.'

'You can't be sure of that.'

'Take my word for it.'

He moved to the couch and sat with his elbows on his knees. His bare foot landed on her balled-up panties. 'Jesus, what a mess.'

'I'm not pregnant, Dylan.'

'You don't know that, Hope. At this very minute my DNA is swimming upstream, millions of happy little tadpoles gearing up to knock at ground zero.' He scrubbed his face with his hands. 'Fuck!'

Hope tried not to take it all too personally, but she didn't succeed.

'I can't have another illegitimate child whose mama lives in another state. I just can't do that again.' He shook his head and looked up at her. 'I won't do that.'

Hope tried not to let her surprise show on her face. She didn't know if he realized what he'd just told her. 'Trust me. I'm not pregnant.'

'How do you know?'

It was no big deal, she told herself. It didn't matter, but just when she'd begun to feel comfortable with him, telling him would bring up every insecurity she had about her body. 'There is no ground zero.'

His gaze lowered to her stomach, and he drummed his fingers on the back of the couch. 'What do you mean?'

Hope moved to the fireplace and stared at the cold stone mantel. She stood with her back to Dylan, her toes curling in the bearskin covering Hiram's blood-stain. She didn't know exactly how to tell him. It shouldn't matter, but for some men, it did. 'Remember when I told you that the scar on my abdomen was from a tummy tuck? Well, I lied about that. When I was younger, I had a condition that was so bad, I missed a lot of school. Doctors were afraid it might spread to my other organs, so when drug therapy didn't work, I had to have surgery that left me unable to have children.'

'Cancer?'

She looked over her shoulder at him. 'No, endo-metriosis.'

'Jesus.' He sighed. 'Why didn't you just say that? You made it sound like you were one breath away from death.'

'Have you heard of endometriosis?'

'Sure. My mother had it and had to have a hysterectomy when I was about sixteen.'

'I was twenty-one.'

He rose and went toward her. 'That must have been rough.'

She shrugged and looked down at the bobcat on the

hearth. 'I felt so much better afterward, it was worth it to me. I had so much more freedom. I didn't have to spend half a month dreading the other half. I thought that if I ever wanted children, I would adopt. Having my own biological child was never an issue for me. Maybe because I thought it wouldn't matter to a man who loved me.'

'It shouldn't.'

She knew better. 'But it does.' She felt him move behind her.

'I gather it mattered to your ex-husband,' he said, crowding her personal space with his big, solid body and intimate questions.

She'd never talked to anyone about what had happened in her marriage. She really didn't want to talk about it now, but he rested his hands on her shoulders and turned her to face him. She looked up at him and he was looking back through patient green eyes, like he was prepared to wait all day for her answer. 'He thought it wouldn't matter, but it did,' she said.

His thumbs brushed her bare skin. 'Then he's an ass.'

'Yes, for a lot of reasons, but not for that.' Again Hope found herself in the position of defending her ex-husband to Dylan, but if he was to hear the truth, he had to hear everything. 'When we were first married, I really do believe that it didn't matter to him. He was busy with his practice and we traveled a lot. We told each other that our lives were full and our marriage was wonderful because we could just pick up and go and spend the weekend in Carmel if we wanted. We told ourselves our life was better than the lives of our friends who were tied down with children, and that we could make love in every room of our house if we wanted. We could hop on a jet and fly to Scottsdale or Palm Springs to play golf. And we did do all those things, but it wasn't enough. At least not for him.'

'He left you for a nurse, right?'

'No. I lied about that, too.'

His thumbs stopped and his brows rose up his forehead.

'I certainly didn't know you well enough to tell you my husband had an affair with my good friend. It was too embarrassing.' She looked away, but he placed his hand on the side of her face and brought her gaze back to his.

'He's an ass,' Dylan repeated.

'He said the affair was an accident, but I don't think so. He said her pregnancy was an accident, too. I didn't believe that, either. He might not have even known it until it happened, but I think he wanted what I couldn't give him. He wanted his own child.' She lowered her gaze to his bare chest. 'I think it's biology. I think men want their own children.'

'Maybe it's just more important to some men.'

'That's easy for you to say. You have Adam.'

'Yeah, I do, but that doesn't mean I was always sure he was mine.' He slid his palm down her arm and took her hand in his. 'Julie and I weren't even living together at the time Adam was conceived, and I wasn't so sure she didn't have other boyfriends.'

'But Adam has your eyes.'

'He does now. When he was born, they were dark blue and all swollen. He kind of looked like Winston Churchill, to tell you the truth. He had a hard time and was an ugly little spud. But the second I looked into his tiny face, and the second he looked at me, we were buddies. And biology didn't mean squat. He was mine. He was *my* son.'

Hope looked in Dylan's eyes, and her silly heart swelled. She was proud of him and didn't really know why. Maybe for being a real man. Maybe just for being him. She leaned forward a little and laid her head on his bare shoulder. 'You're a good man, Dylan Taber.'

'Why, because I do what I'm supposed to do? Most men are like me. You just happened to marry a guy who was hung up on the wrong things.'

'I think somewhere in our marriage he changed. He looked at me different, I think. At first he thought I was enough for him, but I wasn't.' Everything inside Hope stilled. She hadn't meant to say that. Hadn't meant to confess her soul. Dylan made her feel too comfortable.

'You're kidding me. You're about the most perfect woman I've ever had the pleasure to touch.'

She wanted to believe him. She wanted it more than she could remember wanting anything. But she didn't. Not really. 'No, not quite perfect.'

He was silent for a moment, then said, 'Why, because you don't have a uterus?'

The way he said it sounded so clinical. 'You make it sound like we're discussing an appendix.'

'Just about.' He placed his hands on the sides of her face and raised her gaze to his.

'No, it not the same thing. It's not a reproductive organ.'

'I don't mean to sound insensitive here, but there is a hell of a lot more to being a woman than reproducing. A hell of a lot more to being a man than knocking up women. If you ask me, your ex-husband sounds like a jerk, and he did you a real favor by having that affair with your friend. I know he did me a favor. Otherwise, you'd be in Carmel or playing golf in Palm Springs. Instead, you're standing here with me without your panties on.'

She laughed. 'That's true.'

He slid a hand beneath the back of her dress and grasped her bare behind. 'And I wouldn't have ruined you for other men.'

'You heard that, huh?'

'Of course.' He brushed his nose against hers. 'Anything

else you want to tell me you've lied about before I ruin you some more?'

No, she'd confessed enough for one day. 'That's it.'

Wind whipped Hope's ponytail about her head as she pawed through the cassette tapes in Dylan's truck. More Dwight Yoakam, Aaron Tippin, John Anderson, Garth Brooks . . . and AC/DC. She took the latter out of the case and held it up. 'Highway To Hell?'

He looked over at her through his mirrored sunglasses and grinned like he was sixteen. 'Partied a lot with those boys.'

'I thought cowboys listened to country.'

He shrugged and turned his attention back to the road. 'I used to listen to Blue Oyster Cult, too. And, of course, Waylon Jennings and Willie Nelson.'

'I remember my brother listening to AC/DC.'

'I didn't know you had a brother.'

'Yep.' She plugged in the tape and said, 'Evan lives in Germany with his wife and kids. I don't see him much.'

Suddenly the inside of the truck was assaulted with an electric guitar and screeching vocals. Hope turned the volume down several notches below earsplitting and sat back to enjoy the ride into the Idaho wilderness. Earlier, Dylan had woken her up from a sound sleep with the wild idea of backpacking to a lake he wanted her to see.

Since she needed pictures for her alien stories anyway, she hadn't been opposed to a hike. Until he'd told her they would spend the night and return tomorrow. She'd refused to even consider sleeping in a tent, but then he'd sat on her and kissed her neck and told her he wouldn't let the bears get her. It hadn't been his promise of safety that had swayed her, but she'd discovered days ago that she was a sucker for the way he kissed her neck.

It had been a week since that Wednesday afternoon when he'd barged into her house and assured her he hadn't come over for sex. A week since the condom incident. A week since they'd bothered with one. She'd seen him every day. Slept with him every night. He'd taught her how to do the two-step and taken her night fishing. He'd told her about his life as a homicide detective. How and why he'd come to hate it, and how much he enjoyed his life now. She told him about college and writing obituaries for *The Los Angeles Times*, and how she was trying to enjoy her life again. They discussed the article about Hiram she was working on. She asked him questions and he answered. No, he hadn't been the FBI's informant and he didn't know who it had been. No, he hadn't been first on the scene the night the old sheriff had killed himself, although he'd arrived shortly after the FBI agents. He'd seen the photographs and videos and the dead body of a man out of control.

She'd asked for his perspective.

'He had a sickness that got too big for him. When you cheat and steal and risk everything, you have a problem. The more he got into it, the more he wanted. In California, it's not that difficult to find a place that caters to that sort of thing. But this is Gospel, honey. If you want to get tied up, you have to go to where the talent resides. And that takes money.' He smiled and winked at her. 'Unless you find someone who enjoys that sort of thing as much as you do.'

Hope felt herself blush at the reminder of his tying her to a chair the night before. She'd never mentioned her job with *The Weekly News of the Universe*. He'd reacted somewhat negatively when she mentioned she'd queried *People* magazine about her article. She didn't know if he'd cop a patronizing attitude, but she wasn't sure. It was better for now that he thought she wrote for a Northwest magazine.

Mostly, they watched movies, or just held hands and didn't do anything. She liked that best of all. Just sitting still, being quiet, knowing he was there.

Shelly thought things were getting serious between the two of them. Hope knew better. Whenever he came to her house, he parked behind the Aberdeens'. Sometimes he came across the lake in his boat. When they were at his house, he parked his truck in his barn. His reasons all sounded perfectly logical. If people knew he was home, they'd stop by. They'd want to chat and gossip and bring him food, and he wouldn't have as much time to spend with her. Yeah, it sounded reasonable, but it didn't feel like the whole truth. It felt like there was something he wasn't saying, and Hope wondered again if he was embarrassed to be seen with her. She knew he didn't like to be the subject of gossip, but she wondered if he would mind so much if the gossip weren't about his relationship with *her*.

She looked at him now, at his Stetson resting on his head, fingers tapping the steering wheel to the beat of hard rock, and she wondered exactly how he did feel about her. She knew what she felt for him, and it frightened her. It sneaked inside her chest and gave her heart panicky palpitations. She wasn't in love with him, not yet, but it could happen if she weren't careful. And she planned to be very careful.

Dylan slowed and turned onto a dusty, bumpy road. They quickly rolled up the windows, and Dylan ejected the tape from the player. The rolling meadows gave way to a lodgepole forest and within three miles the road ended at the Iron Creek trailhead. Before they'd left that morning, he'd insisted that she borrow Shelly's hiking boots and down parka. The boots on her feet were made of waterproof mesh and Gore-Tex and were lighter than she would have expected. The puffy coat had been rolled like a sausage and stuffed in her backpack. Presently it was ninety-four degrees beneath a cloudless sky, and Hope wore a pair of camouflage shorts and a green tank top. She'd applied a few swipes of waterproof mascara, and Dylan had given her a tube of SPF 15 Chapstick, which she had in her pocket. She felt a little naked without blusher and lip liner, but Dylan told her he liked the way she looked. She didn't believe him for a second, but he'd certainly seen her in the morning when she looked her worst.

The truck rolled to a stop in a parking area sectioned out of the forest by logs. There was one Jeep and a pickup and camper parked on the far side. Earlier, Dylan had mentioned that the area wouldn't be busy because it was the middle of the week. He'd been right.

Dylan was dressed in his usual Levi's, blue T-shirt, and hat. There were two notable differences: He'd traded in his cowboy boots for hiking boots much like Hope's, and he'd strapped a pistol to his hip.

'What are you going to do with that?'

'Keeps the bugs away,' he said, then took off his sunglasses and sprayed himself down with insect repellent.

There had been a time not too long ago when she would have thought he meant to shoot flies, and he would have had a good laugh at her expense. Now she thought she knew him better than that. 'No. The gun.'

'Cover your face,' he said and sprayed her, too. 'I told you I'd protect you from bears, didn't I?'

'Oh, my God,' she said from behind her hands. 'You didn't tell me you were going to shoot bears.'

'You didn't ask.'

She dropped her hands as he sprayed her stomach and the front of her legs. 'Okay, isn't this the part where you tell me bears taste just like chicken?'

'Bear doesn't taste anything like chicken.' He walked behind her and sprayed. 'It's tough as a boot and real gamey.'

She didn't want to know how he'd come by that information. 'Do you think we'll see bears?'

'Not likely.' He stuck the can of 'bug juice' into his
backpack. 'Chances are they'll smell us and run away long
before we see them. Black bears usually aren't aggressive,
but if we see one, we'll just make some noise, and I'll shoot
my gun in the air to scare it off. Mostly they just want to
know where you are so they can head in the opposite
direction.' He grabbed the backpack that belonged to Adam
out of the bed of his truck and helped her into it. Unlike the
cute little Ralph Lauren backpack she'd bought at Saks last
summer, this one had a metal frame and two sturdy mesh
harnesses that belted across the hips and chest. Dylan
widened the straps for her, then stepped back to eye the fit.
Her breasts were squished together at the top, and he
widened the straps a bit more. His hands lingered at the
task longer than was necessary. His knuckles brushed across
her tank top, and then he gave up all pretense of strap
adjusting and cupped her left breast. When she looked up,
he turned her face to the side and settled into a slow, soft
kiss. His hand moved to her stomach, then slid around her
side. 'I want to show you the most beautiful place I've ever
been,' he whispered lightly against her mouth. His tender
kisses left her wanting more, but when her tongue chased
his, he pulled back. 'I think you'll like it.'

Which meant, she supposed, that it wasn't a great time
to confess to him that she really wasn't into Mother
Nature.

Dylan shrugged on his own pack, a bigger version of
Adam's. Still, she wondered how he'd managed to get a two-
man tent in there.

He reached for her hand. The first hour of the trip was
easy. They walked the Iron Creek trail through thick
lodgepole pines, and he stopped to show her flowers she

might be interested in photographing for her fictional magazine article. Growing near the crystal-clear water of Iron Creek were Mountain Bluebell, Heather, and Alpine Laurel. He picked a wild daisy and and stuck it behind her ear, and he seemed to be having such a good time helping her, she just didn't have the heart to tell him there wouldn't be any wildlife article. She snapped a few photos of the flowers, and she took a few of him, too.

The second and third hours weren't quite as easy as the first. The forest grew thicker and the trail became a series of narrow switchbacks worn into the side the mountain. Dense vegetation carpeted the ground and all but swallowed fallen trees and rocks. Squirrels chattered as they raced across the ground and disappeared into the foliage. Birds called to one another in the trees above Hope's head. Their songs carried on the pine-scented breeze.

Hope's calves ached, and she thought she might be getting a blister on her heel. She had to keep her weight pitched forward as she climbed, afraid she'd tumble backward if she didn't.

Dylan told her the names of different mountain peaks and about the time he'd hunted bighorn sheep in the White Clouds. She broke a fingernail, and he dug out his nail clippers so she could fix it with the little file.

'You're such a girl.' He laughed and made her walk in front of him when the trail narrowed. She missed watching the backs of his legs and his behind, and during lulls in conversation, she again wondered how he felt about her. She tried to picture her life with him and couldn't, but she couldn't picture her life without him, either. They'd made no promises to each other. Never spoke of tomorrow, and she wondered how their relationship would change once Adam returned from visiting his mother. Dylan's son was due to return home that Sunday, and Hope was certain that would change everything. What she wasn't so certain about was *how* things would change.

Dylan helped her balance on rocks and fallen logs as they crossed a stream. They rested on a huge boulder so Hope could catch her breath, and they took off the packs and leaned them against the rock. While she ate peanuts and drank from her canteen, Dylan took his hat off and poured water over his head. It ran down his neck and soaked his shirt, and he shook like a dog, sending clear droplets everywhere. And then he finally mentioned Adam. Hope sat very still, waiting to hear his plans. Whatever they were, she would be okay, she told herself.

'He seems to like you,' Dylan told her as he sat next to her and polished a red apple on his sleeve. A breeze ruffled his damp hair and dried the ends a golden brown. 'But after he's home, I can't spend the night with you any more.' Dylan took a bite of the apple, then held it out for her to take a bite. 'When my son's older, I don't think I can tell him he can't bring girlfriends home for the night if I have. I start back to work next week, too. I want to make time to be with you, but it won't be easy.' He took another bite of the apple. 'And I don't just mean time to have a quickie somewhere.'

She let out a breath she hadn't even known she'd been holding. 'Well, we can plan fun things that include Adam,' she said and meant it. 'He's a funny little kid, and I wouldn't mind hanging out with him.' She looked up into his eyes, the same dark green as the pine trees behind him. 'And you do have a lunch hour, don't you?'

'Yes,' he said through a smile as he tossed the core. 'At least an hour.'

She ran her hands up his wet T-shirt and locked her fingers behind his neck. She leaned into him and her breasts brushed his cool, wet chest. 'And what if I had to come to your office and swear out some sort of complaint? Would I get past your secretary?'

'Depends on what you have to complain about.'

She brought his head down and kissed his lips. 'Maybe that I'm lonely,' she whispered. 'Maybe that I miss a certain cowboy and his big—' She broke off and slid a hand to his button fly. Through the worn denim, she cupped and caressed him until he grew hard.

'Big what?'

'Ego,' she said, then teased him with her mouth and tongue. He carefully laid her back on the boulder and sealed his lips to hers. He created a tight, wet suction and gave her a hot kiss that scorched her skin in a way that had nothing to do with the sun pouring down on their heads. It had her pressing her hips into his and running her fingers through his damp hair. He buried his face in her neck. 'I love the way you feel right here,' he whispered against her throat. 'I love your soft skin and the way you smell, like powder.'

It wasn't exactly a declaration of deep emotion, but it was the closest he'd come to it, and it made her heart ache. 'I like you, too,' she said and shoved her hands beneath his shirt and rubbed his back.

He looked into her face, his breathing a bit labored. 'Sorry, honey. I can't show you my big ego right now.' He removed her hands and kissed her forehead. 'Later. Under the stars.'

Hope's hands stilled. 'Under the stars? You packed a tent, didn't you?'

'Nope, but I brought my big sleeping bag. It'll be a little snug.' The grin curving his lips suggested he'd had the whole evening planned before they'd even packed. 'I think we'll manage somehow.'

Hope sat up. 'What about bugs?'

'You'll only suck in a few.' She clamped a hand to her mouth and he laughed. 'You won't even know it. You'll be asleep. And if you get a beetle, just chew.'

She didn't want to suck bugs and eat beetles in her sleep. She didn't want to be a baby, either, but a little whine of distress escaped from behind her hand.

'I was kidding about the beetle,' he said, which did little to relieve her mind.

They hiked to Alpine Lake ridge and looked down into the tiny green lake nestled hundreds of feet below. Voices carried up to them, but they could see nothing for the dense sea of emerald trees. Hope almost felt as if she were standing on top of the world.

'Listen,' Dylan whispered.

'I don't hear anyone talking now,' she said.

'Not to the voices.' He was silent for a moment and reached for her hand. 'Do you hear it?'

She heard the breeze whistling through the treetops, the call of birds, and maybe the stream they'd crossed. 'What am I listening for?'

'It's hard to explain, but Shelly says it's like listening to God. I think it's more like a pulse, or like hearing beauty instead of seeing it.' He shrugged. 'It's different for everyone, but you'll know when you hear it. You'll feel like you're falling and there is absolutely nothing you can do to stop it.'

They hiked higher, the trail now chiseled out of rock. Hope listened carefully, but she didn't hear God. She didn't hear beauty or anything, but she was feeling increasingly exhausted. She and Dylan crossed outlet streams and walked around tundra ponds. Her ponytail was a snarled mess, she was sure her nose was burned, and she'd had to file one fingernail a lot shorter than the others.

Just when she was about to ask if they could stop and rest

again, they stood on the snow-covered shores of Sawtooth Lake. She looked out at water so crystal blue, she could see the bottom all the way across to the base of the granite mountain towering above them.

'This lake is two hundred and fifty feet deep,' Dylan told her. 'But it's so clean it looks like you could wade across it.'

She was quiet for a few moments, watching the glaciered snow drip into the lake the color of the purest sapphire. While the beauty around her was awesome, she didn't hear God.

'This is what I wanted to show you. This is the most beautiful place I've ever seen.' He took her hand and gave it a squeeze. 'It reminds me of you,' he said.

And that was when Hope heard it, and it was better than anything she'd ever heard in her life. Her heart swelled like a balloon in her chest and her pulse raced. She felt herself fall, just like he'd said she would. She fell head over heels in love with Dylan Taber, and there was absolutely nothing she could do to stop it.

Angels Visit Your Dreams

'There's the Big Dipper.' Dylan grasped Hope's wrist and pointed to the night sky. 'And there's the Little Dipper.'

He'd been right about the sleeping bag. They were somehow managing. Cramped but comfy, the down bag provided just enough room for them to lie side by side. Except for their shoes, they were fully clothed in jeans and sweatshirts. Dylan told her she'd be grateful in the morning when she didn't have to change into cold clothes. Since she'd never camped before, she took his word for it.

She lay with her head on Dylan's shoulder, his body throwing off heat like a human furnace. He'd blown up an air mattress to lie beneath the bag, and although her nose was getting chilled, Hope had absolutely no complaints.

'There's the North Star,' he said and slid their hands to the west. 'And Cassiopeia.'

Hope had never been a constellation buff and had to take his word for that, too.

'She's chained upside down in her throne and has to circle the heavens on her head.' He brought her hand to his lips and kissed her fingertips. 'I'm glad you came here with me.'

'I'm glad you brought me.' Of all the wonderful places she'd been in her life, or could think of being in at the exact moment, none held the appeal of lying in a sleeping bag in the Idaho wilderness with Dylan Taber. The man she loved with her heart and soul.

He rose up onto his elbow, and she gazed into his dark face, outlined against a sky crammed with stars. 'Hope?'

'What?'

'I want to tell you something.' He placed her palm against his cheek, rough with stubble. 'In my life, I've been with women I didn't care about and women I cared a great deal about. But I've never been with a woman who makes me feel the way you do.' He lowered his head and whispered against her lips, 'Sometimes when I look at you, it's hard to breathe. When you touch me, I don't care about breathing.' He kissed her slow and sweet, and with each press of his lips and touch of his tongue, her heart swelled and ached. It was wonderful and awful and brand-new. Then he pulled back to say, 'I don't know how this is all going to work out, but I want to be with you. You are important to me.'

It wasn't exactly a declaration of undying love, but it stung the backs of her eyes. She slid her hands under his sweatshirt and combed her fingers through the short, silky hair that grew on his chest. She felt the sharp intake of his breath and the heavy beat of his heart. 'I want to be with you, too,' she said and her heart swelled yet again.

Then, with her body, she showed him without words how she felt. And through the tangle of their clothes and the cramped confines of the sleeping bag, he touched her as if he felt it, too. He caressed her as if she were fragile and very important to him. Beneath the shooting stars, he made love to her as if they were the only people on the planet. Beneath Cassiopeia, she felt as if she, too, were circling the heavens on her head.

She forgot all about bugs and beetles and lay wrapped up in the arms of the man she loved. And while that was incredibly scary, it was also incredible. For the first time since she'd driven into town, leaving wasn't quite so clear. She wondered what she would do if he asked her to stay. She'd fallen in love with the sheriff of a town without a Nordstrom, a movie theater, or even a 7−11. She wondered how she would live without him if he didn't ask her.

In the morning, he made her a dreadful breakfast of oatmeal and dehydrated eggs, which was only slightly better than the dinner of dehydrated stew he'd made the night before. He laughed and kissed the snarled part in her hair and called her high maintenance.

They repacked their backpacks and made it down the mountain in half the time it had taken them to hike up. When they got back to Dylan's house around noon, they peeled off their clothes and fell into bed without even bothering to shower the trail dust off their skin.

Exhausted, Hope didn't remember falling asleep before her eyes opened again. A bit disoriented at first, she glanced at the bedside table and recognized Dylan's clock. Beneath the sheet, his chest was pressed to her back and his hand rested between her bare breasts. Through her thin, silky underwear, she felt his hot groin shoved against her behind. She figured his grasp must have awakened her. She could still smell the scent of Dylan's cookstove in her hair and on their clothes, which lay in a heap next to his bed.

Her eyes drifted shut, then popped open again. She had a feeling like someone was watching her and raised herself onto her elbow. She glanced down at the end of the bed. Adam Taber's big green eyes stared back at her. His face looked blank, as if he couldn't quite comprehend what he was seeing.

'Dylan,' Hope whispered. 'Wake up.'

His only response was to cup her breast and pull her tighter against his chest.

She took her gaze from Adam and glanced over her shoulder. She nudged his big chest with her elbow. 'Dylan, wake up.'

'Hmm?' His lids fluttered open. 'Honey, I'm too tired,' he said, his voice rough from sleep. But he wasn't too tired to slide his hand down her stomach to her hip and back up again. 'On second thought, I'm never too tired.'

'Dylan!' She grasped his hand through the sheet. 'Adam's home.'

'What?' The hair on his chest tickled her back as he lifted himself up and glanced toward the end of the bed. A prolonged silence filled the room as father and son stared at each other. 'Adam,' he began slowly, then cleared his throat. 'How did you get here?'

'Mom brung me.' Adam pointed to his left, and both Hope and Dylan shifted their gazes to the tall blonde leaning against the doorjamb. She wore leather pants the color of buttermilk and a silk blouse of the same color. She looked vaguely familiar, but Hope didn't believe they'd ever met.

'I guess we should have called,' she said as she straightened. 'I'll just wait in the living room for you two to get dressed.' She held out her hand to Adam. 'Come on. Let's go wait for your daddy out here.'

Adam stared at his father and Hope for several seconds, then walked out of the room.

'Jeez-us,' Dylan swore as he fell back onto his pillow. He plowed his fingers through the sides of his hair and stared up at the ceiling. 'What in the hell is he doing home? It's not Sunday, and what is Julie doing here? This is messed up. This is a goddamn nightmare.'

Hope sat up and held the sheet to her chest. 'What do you want me to do?'

'Did you see Adam's face?' He sighed and covered his own face with his hands. 'Hell if I know. Maybe he'll think you came over and got so tired you just had to take a nap or something. Maybe you fell and hurt yourself and had to lie down.'

'Yeah, and you were just helping me out with a breast exam.'

He looked at her from between his fingers.

'Adam saw your hand moving around beneath the sheet. He's not stupid. I don't think he'll fall for some lame story. Just tell him the truth.'

He lowered his hands. 'Please don't tell me how to talk to my son. I really hate it when people who don't have children tell me what to do. I'll decide what's best for him, and I don't think explaining my sex life with you is best for him right now.'

'Fine.' She threw off the sheet and rose from the bed. 'Tell him whatever you want.' She shut the bedroom door, then picked up her clothes.

'Hope.'

She turned her back on him, stepped into her shorts, and buttoned them around her waist.

'Hope.' He came up behind her and placed his hands on her shoulders. 'I shouldn't have said that about you not having children. I'm sorry.'

She grabbed her bra and turned to look up at him. He was sorry about the wrong thing. 'I respect your moral position and raising your son by example. I really do.' She hooked her bra behind her back and adjusted the straps. 'It must be very difficult, but I will not be your nasty secret.' She thought about the times he'd come to her house and parked his truck at Shelly's. 'I will not be something you lie or won't talk about. I don't want to live like that.'

'Okay.'

She reached for her shirt and he grabbed it from her hands. 'We'll work through this,' he said. 'Somehow. But I'm warning you, Adam isn't going to like what he saw today. He won't make it easy for me or for you.' He lifted her chin and looked into her eyes. 'That woman out there is his mama, and he has dreams of the three of us moving in together and living like a happy family. He's been working on it—'

'Oh, my God,' Hope interrupted and grabbed his wrist. 'Juliette Bancroft!'

'I wondered how long it would take you to recognize her.'

'Crap!' She patted her dusty hair. 'I look like complete crap.'

Dylan handed her her shirt. 'On your worst day, you're prettier than Julie.'

Which was an outrageous lie but suddenly wasn't her biggest worry. Now she remembered why the woman in the doorway had looked so familiar, and it wasn't because of her television show, either. Hope had to get out of the house fast before Juliette remembered they'd met in Blaine's office a few weeks before he'd served her with divorce papers. During the divorce, Hope had done a few things to get back at her ex-husband. One of them had involved a certain starlet and her secret breast implants.

While Dylan pulled on a pair of clean Levi's and a T-shirt, Hope stuck her feet in her dirty socks and tied the laces of Shelly's hiking boots. 'I think it would be best if I just hurried up and left so the three of you can talk.'

'Probably, but I'll take you home.'

'I can walk. It's only about three miles and I jog more than that every day.'

'I'll take you.'

'I want to walk. It'll give me time to think. Really.'

'Are you sure?'

'Yep.'

She walked slightly behind Dylan as they moved down the hall to the living room. Adam sat in a recliner, rocking so hard the springs squeaked and the back of the chair hit the wall, bam, squeak, bam. He leveled his angry eyes on Hope, and seeing all that pain directed at her bothered her more than she would have thought possible. It slid right next to her heart and lay there like a cold lump, and she wondered if they would ever be friends again. She switched her gaze to Juliette, who stood with her back to the room as if she didn't hear a thing, looking at framed pictures of Adam and Dylan that were sitting on the television.

'Adam, stop that,' Dylan told his son. The chair crashed into the wall harder.

Juliette turned and looked at Dylan. 'I always wondered what your house would look like. It reminds me of the house we used to live in when Adam was a baby.'

'You never liked that house,' he said and pointed a finger at his son. 'Stop now.'

'That's not really true.' Juliette's gaze moved to Hope, and under normal circumstances, she would have been mortified by her appearance, especially compared to the perfect and beautiful Juliette Bancroft. Today, she just hoped the dirt in her hair and the spots on her shirt concealed her identity. 'Adam didn't mention that you had a girlfriend.'

'I'll just be going now.' With a quick exit out the back door in mind, Hope sort of slid sideways across the room. 'I'm sure you all have tons to talk about.'

The recliner slammed into the wall one last time and Dylan pulled his son out of the chair. 'I'll call you later. Say good-bye to Ms Spencer, Adam,' he said.

Adam didn't utter a sound, and Hope made it as far as the doorway to the kitchen when Juliette's voice stopped her.

'Wait! I know who you are. You're Dr Spencer's ex-wife.'

Hope closed her eyes. Crap!

'You work for *The National Enquirer*,' Juliette added.

Hope looked from the angry face of America's favorite angel to Dylan. A frown furrowed his brow, and he stood frozen, holding Adam by one arm.

'No, I don't work for the *Enquirer*,' she said.

'You were the unnamed source who leaked confidential and privileged information about Dr Spencer's patients.' Juliette's voice rose and she pointed an accusing finger at Hope. 'You told them about my goddamn boob job!' Hope was taken aback by the woman's language. America certainly had never heard foul words pour from her perfect angelic lips. 'He told me he couldn't prove it, but he was certain it was you.'

Under the circumstances, Hope figured Juliette was justified in her anger, but not in front of Adam. 'In my own defense,' she began, 'Blaine was a pig, and I wanted to hurt him. I didn't think about who might get hurt, but I've always felt really bad that I hurt other people as well. I'm sorry about what happened.'

Dylan finally let go of his son. 'You're a reporter for *The National Enquirer*?'

'No. About four years ago I was their unnamed source for a few inside stories, and then I did a few freelance articles on fashion blunders. That sort of thing, but I don't do that now.'

'You write flora-and-fauna articles. Right?'

She didn't want to tell him. Not like this. 'Well, not exactly.'

'What do you write? Exactly.'

But she couldn't lie any more, either. Hope took a deep breath and said, 'I'm a staff writer for *The Weekly News of the Universe*. I write Bigfoot and alien stories.'

He leaned his head back and looked at her through a

narrowed gaze. 'Adam, go to your room,' he ordered without taking his eyes from Hope.

'I don't wanna go to my room.'

'I didn't ask if you wanted to. I told you to go.'

As if his feet were made of lead, the boy slowly left the room. No one spoke until the door had shut behind him.

'So,' Dylan began, 'the whole flora-and-fauna thing was complete bullshit. You write for a tabloid.'

'I don't write gossip. I write alien stories,' she said and spread her arms wide. 'That's what I do.'

'And I'm supposed to believe you? After you've done nothing but lie about it since you drove into town? Christ! You must have had yourself a good old laugh yesterday when I was showing you all those flowers for your "article."'

'I wasn't laughing.'

'And the whole thing about Hiram Donnelly was bullshit, too, wasn't it?'

'No, I plan to write that article. I never—'

'How did you find out about Adam?' he interrupted.

She didn't know what he was asking.

'And how long before I get to read about my son in your paper?'

It took Hope a moment more before she understood exactly what he meant. The secret love child of America's favorite angel would be big news. Huge. 'I would never do that to Adam. I would never do that to you, and as hard as it might be for you to believe, I wouldn't do that to Juliette, either.'

'You're right, that's hard for me to believe,' Juliette said.

Hope looked at the faces before her. Juliette didn't even bother hiding her anger, and Dylan was becoming more remote as the seconds ticked past. 'Who sent you here, Hope?'

'My paper, but not for the reason you're thinking. They sent me here to take pictures and write articles. Right now I'm writing a series about a town filled with aliens.' She shook her head as her heart squeezed within her chest. 'Just last week I used Eden Hansen. Her purple hair and eyeshadow, but I swear I didn't know Juliette was Adam's mother until two minutes ago. You have to believe me.'

'I don't think I even know you.'

Hope covered her heart with her hand, as if she could protect herself from his cold gaze. As if she could protect her breaking heart. 'When I first met you, I didn't tell you what I do for a living because it was none of your business. After I got to know you, I didn't know how to tell you I'd lied about it, and the time never seemed right.'

'I can think of a few times when you could have said something. Like any time between the Fourth and today would have been good.'

There was nothing she could say except, 'You're right, maybe I should have told you.'

'Yeah, maybe. The very first day you drove into town, I wondered what would bring a big-city girl to a wilderness town like Gospel. I guess I finally know, and it has nothing to do with Bigfoot or aliens or corrupt sheriffs. You found out about Adam and came here to snoop into our lives.'

'Do you really believe that?'

His mouth settled into a grim line and he didn't say anything. He didn't have to.

'I told you I wouldn't do that to you, and I won't, but I guess you'll believe me when you don't read about it in the papers.' She looked at him one last time and walked out the door, past the backpacks they'd leaned against the house before they'd raced inside and fallen into bed.

The Idaho sun burned her corneas and she shaded her eyes as she headed down Dylan's driveway, past a car she didn't recognize, and went out into the street. She'd tried so hard not to fall in love with him. Deep down she'd known he would break her heart. And she'd been right.

From the moment Dylan had opened his eyes and glanced at Adam at the foot of his bed, his life had gone straight to hell.

'What do you think she'll do?' Julie asked him.

'I don't know what she'll do,' he answered truthfully. He wanted to believe Hope. He wanted it real damn bad, but he didn't. 'We have to tell Adam we were never married. Before he hears about it from someone else.' He pinched the bridge of his nose as if that could suppress the sudden pounding behind his eyes. He'd told Hope so much about his life. A *tabloid reporter* who'd lied to him. 'He needs to be told before he walks into the M & S to buy a pack of gum and reads about it off a tabloid at the checkout counter.'

'Yes, I guess it's time you told him. Do you suppose there is any chance your girlfriend won't report this?'

He lowered his hand and looked at Julie. She was worried about her career. 'What are you doing here?'

'I brought Adam home.'

'I know. Why?'

She folded her arms beneath her breasts and took a deep breath. 'Well, remember when we were in the airport and I told you I needed to talk to you?'

He didn't remember, but that didn't mean she hadn't mentioned it.

'You probably know I've been spending a lot of time with Gerard LaFollete,' she began, assuming he kept up with her business.

'No, I didn't. Isn't he a French actor?'

'Yes, and he asked me to marry him. I said yes.'

'What does Adam think of all this?'

'Well, I thought you could tell him.'

Of course she did. Dylan sat on the edge of the couch with his elbows on his knees and his head in his hands. Under normal circumstances, he might not have minded the responsibility of telling Adam about his mama marrying the French dude. That would have made it easier for him to talk to Adam about Hope, but now he didn't know if he had or wanted a relationship with her. He knew only two things for certain about Hope: one, she worked for a tabloid, and two, he loved being with her. The two shouldn't have been mutually exclusive, but they were.

He looked up at Julie, standing there as if she expected that he would just naturally handle Adam for her. 'No,' he said. 'You'll have to tell him.'

'I tried. Gerard met us last week so Adam could get to know him before I told Adam my plans. Well, Adam behaved so horribly I didn't get the chance to talk to him about it. I tried to call you, but you were never home.' She sat in the rocker-recliner and shoved her hands between her knees. 'He called Gerard the f-word.'

'Whoa! He called your boyfriend a fucker?'

'No. A fag.'

'Oh.' From what Dylan had seen of him on television, the guy did look like he had the potential to swing either way. The few times Dylan had spoken with Adam on the telephone, he'd sounded like he always did.

'I'll talk to Adam about that, but you're going to tell him about your marriage plans. Sounds to me, though, like he has a pretty good idea and that's why he's acting up.' He leaned back against the couch. 'We'll both tell him that we were never married. If we handle it right, I doubt it will be a traumatic deal for him. The timing could be better, but I don't see that we have a choice.'

He shrugged; how much worse could it get? His son had

been home less than an hour, he'd seen Dylan in bed with Hope, and he'd been yanked out of a chair and sent to his room. Things could only get better. 'I'll go get Adam from his room,' he said, but stopped by the bathroom first to down four aspirins.

Two hours later, he figured he should have just run his head through a wall, for all the good those aspirins did him.

From the back door he watched Julie's rental car pull out of his driveway and head toward town. She hadn't been able to get a flight out of Sun Valley until the next afternoon, and she'd just assumed she would be staying with him and Adam. After the past hours he'd spent with her, there wasn't a chance in hell he'd agree to let her stay with him. He'd called the Sandman and got her a room for the night. By morning, the whole town would know his business, but for once he didn't care. If he had to spend any more time with Julie, he couldn't promise that he wouldn't strangle her.

She'd totally crapped out on him, making it sound as if she would have married him if he'd ever asked her. He'd never asked her, because they'd talked about it and decided that a baby wasn't a good enough reason to get married. They'd both decided that, not just him, because the truth was, if she'd felt strongly about it, he would have married her even knowing it would be a mistake.

He shut the back door and went in search of his son. He found him lying on his bed, crying into his pillow. One of his sneakers had disappeared, his socks were scrunched down around his ankles, and his shorts were twisted around his waist. He was a pitiful lump of misery.

'Are you hungry?' Dylan asked from the doorway.

'No.' Adam rolled onto his back, and his face was splotched from crying. 'Why's my backpack outside?'

'Hope and I hiked up to Sawtooth Lake.'

Adam looked across the room at his father. 'She used *my* backpack?'

'Yes, she did.'

'I don't want her to touch my stuff. I hate her.'

Dylan moved toward the bed. 'Just a few weeks ago you liked her.'

'That was before.'

'Before what?'

Adam turned his face to the wall. 'Before you guys were doing sex!'

About a year ago Dylan had explained most of the birds and the bees to Adam, but not the real embarrassing stuff. He thought about his response and chose his words carefully. 'There is nothing wrong with what Hope and I were doing. We're both adults and you weren't even supposed to be here until Sunday.'

Adam sat up and his eyes got squinty. 'You don't have to do that any more 'cause you got me. Let her find someone else to make her a baby.'

'What?' Dylan sat on the edge of the bed. 'People don't have sex just to make babies, Adam.'

'Uh-huh. That's what you said. You said men put their penis in women to make babies.'

Okay, maybe he'd screwed up the whole birds-and-the-bees thing more than he thought. 'Men want to make love to women even when they don't want to make babies.'

'Why?'

'Because . . . well . . .' He didn't know what to say, but he'd already messed up, so he figured he'd just muddle through with the truth. 'Well, because it feels really good.'

'Like how?'

How did you explain sex to a seven-year-old kid? 'Hmm . . . like when you finally scratch an itch that you've waited all day to scratch. Or when your feet are really cold and you slide into a warm tub and get all shivery,' he said and watched himself fall in his son's eyes.

'Sick!'

'You'll feel different about it in a few years.'

Adam shook his head. 'No way.'

Dylan figured it was time to change the subject. 'Why don't you tell me about your trip?'

Adam looked as if he wasn't going to let the subject drop, but he did. 'It was okay.'

'Your mom said you met her boyfriend, Gerard.'

'He talked funny.'

'Your mom also said you called him a fag. That wasn't very nice.'

'Why couldn't Mom stay here?' Adam asked, obviously figuring it was time to change that subject, too. Dylan would let him, for now.

'There was no place for her to sleep.'

'She could sleep with you. Hope did.'

Yes, Hope certainly had, but truth be told, there had been very little sleeping. 'That's different. Your mom's marrying that French dude.'

'Maybe you could marry her instead,' Adam suggested as he picked at the Band-Aid on his knee. 'She said she would have married you if you'd asked her. So go ask her now.'

'Too late. She loves Gerard LaFollete.' Dylan patted his thigh and Adam crawled into his lap. 'There are a lot of different reasons why people don't get married, but just because your mom and I never got married doesn't mean we don't love you. Or,' he added, stretching the truth a bit, 'that we don't care about each other. I'll always love your momma because she gave me you. And if I didn't have you, I'd be real sad all the time.'

'Yeah.' Adam laid his head on Dylan's shoulder. 'I'm your little buddy.'

'Yep.' He wrapped his arms around his son and squeezed. 'I'm glad you're home.'

'Me, too. Where's Mandy?'

'The last time I saw your puppy, she was chasing your grandmother's peacocks, and your grandmother was chasing her.'

Adam pulled back, his eyes bright. No one loved naughty-dog stories more than Adam. 'Did Grandma catch her?'

'Nope, but maybe we should go get her.'

Adam nodded and laid his head again on Dylan's shoulder.

'When Mom gets married, will my name be Adam LaFollete?'

'No, you'll always be Adam Taber.'

'Good.'

Yeah, good. For the first time since Adam had walked in the door, things were looking better. The fact that he'd mentioned Julie's marriage was a step in the right direction. Perhaps Adam was letting go of his dream of them all living together. Julie was free to live her life, and Dylan suddenly felt a lot freer to live his. Yeah, now that it was too late.

'And you're not going to be doing sex any more with Hope, right?'

Maybe not so free after all. He didn't know how to answer. He knew what Adam wanted to hear, but he couldn't say it. It would be like taking a step back when he was finally moving forward. And the funny thing was, he hadn't known how badly he wanted to move forward until he'd met Hope.

Sitting on his son's bed, holding him tight, he felt more alone than he could ever remember feeling. Before Hope, he'd known he was lonely, but now he felt it more keenly than ever. Somehow she'd crawled inside him, and it was like she'd breathed new life into his lungs, made his blood and his juices flow again. And now that she was probably gone from his life, he just felt hollow.

'Let's go get that dog of yours,' he said, because he just couldn't tell Adam what he wanted to hear. Not yet. Not until he knew what he was going to do. Not until he figured out exactly what he felt about Hope and the whole screwed-up mess.

Hope wasn't going to hide like she'd done something wrong. She wasn't going to hide in her house, pacing the old wooden floors and running to the window every few minutes. At seven forty-five that evening, she changed into her peach sundress, put on her make-up and took herself to dinner. Unfortunately, the fanciest establishment in town was the Cozy Corner Café.

Honky-tonk played on the jukebox, and the diner smelled exactly how it had the first time Hope had set foot inside. The dinner rush had died down and a couple with a baby occupied one booth, while three teenage girls sat at the counter laughing and smoking cigarettes.

Apparently, the Cozy Corner hadn't heard of providing a smoke-free environment and wasn't too concerned about underage smoking. But at least the girls didn't have pink hair and safety pins in their faces.

Hope took a booth near the back and ordered a cheeseburger, no onions and extra mayo on the side, a large order of fries, no salt, and a chocolate shake. Maybe she could find comfort in comfort food.

Work had been out of the question, and she'd spent most of the day trying not to cry and wondering if it was really over between her and Dylan, wondering if she should call him and waiting for him to call her. She'd spent the day reliving all the time they'd spent together, especially the closeness of the night before. He cared about her; she'd heard it in his voice and felt it in the way he'd touched her.

She'd spent hours thinking she should go back to his house and make him listen to her, make him believe that she would never betray him. He had to believe her, but she supposed the only way he would know for certain was when no stories appeared about him or Adam or Julie.

She'd mopped her floors, done her laundry, and scrubbed the bathrooms. She'd taken a long bath, given herself a facial and a manicure, all in an effort to take her mind off Dylan. To take her mind off the cold, closed-up expression on his face as he'd told her he didn't think he even knew her. Nothing had worked.

Paris Fernwood set Hope's milkshake in front of her. As the waitress placed a long spoon and a straw on a napkin, Hope remembered her first day in town and her second encounter with Paris. She remembered the way Paris had looked at Dylan, her brown eyes melting and her harsh features softening. He'd lit her up from the inside out, and Hope wondered if *she* looked at him the same way, and if he noticed.

'Thank you,' Hope said, sliding the straw from its wrapper.

Without looking up, Paris muttered, 'You're welcome,' and walked away.

Pathetic, Hope thought as she watched the waitress move behind the counter and empty ashtrays. That was how she'd thought of Paris that first day. Now she understood a little bit better. Loving Dylan Taber wasn't an easy thing to get over. Especially when she didn't know if it was really over. She was in limbo, her heart not quite broken. Not yet. She felt as if she were teetering on the edge of a cliff and Dylan was the only one who could pull her back.

She stuck her straw into the shake and sucked up a big

dose of chocolate ice cream. She'd placed her heart in his hands, and it was up to him to decide what he would do with it now.

Paris returned with Hope's meal and tore the ticket from the little green book she kept in her apron pocket.

'Is there anything else you're needin'?' she asked as she plunked the ticket on the table.

'I don't think so.' Everything appeared just as she'd ordered it. 'Thanks.'

'Uh-huh.' Again Paris didn't even look at Hope before she walked away.

Hope didn't know what she'd ever done to the waitress, but it must have been a major offense. She poured ketchup onto her plate and dipped a few fries. They were hot and greasy and not quite as wonderful as she'd expected. She smeared extra mayonnaise on her cheeseburger. It wasn't as wonderful, either, but she suspected it wasn't the fault of the food. It was her mood. She wanted comfort, but food wasn't going to be the answer.

Out of the corner of her eye a glimpse of red caught her attention and she glanced up at the woman standing by her table. She lifted her gaze up Ralph Lauren jeans and a red silk tank, but even with the brown chin-length wig and dark sunglasses, Hope immediately recognized Juliette Bancroft.

'If you don't want to draw attention,' Hope said, 'lose the sunglasses.'

Without asking if she wanted company, Juliette slid into the seat across from Hope. 'Have you called Mike Walker?' she asked, referring to *The National Enquirer*'s infamous reporter. She reached for her sunglasses and tucked them into her purse.

'I told you, I don't work for *The National Enquirer*.'

'I know. You work for *The Weekly News of the Universe*, which, the last time I checked, had a gossip section.'

'True.' Hope paused and ate a few more fries. 'But we don't pay reporters to look through your trash. Everything you read in our Hollywood gossip section is pretty much old news.'

Juliette grabbed a menu. 'I've already talked to my agent,' she said as she looked it over. 'He's spoken with my publicist, who will issue a standard "No comment" to the press until we feel the time is right for a statement.' She flipped the menu to the back.

'No one will hear a word from me.'

Juliette glanced up. 'Because of Dylan?'

'Of course,' she answered without hesitation. 'But even if I felt nothing for Dylan, I would never hurt Adam.'

'Dylan and I have talked to Adam, and I think he'll be okay. I'm the one who will be hurt the most if the story gets out,' Juliette said.

'And me,' Hope added. 'Dylan would never forgive me if he read the story in a tabloid.'

Paris set a glass of water on the table. 'What can I get for you?' she asked.

'Is this bottled water?' Juliette wanted to know.

'Straight from the tap.'

Juliette pushed it aside. 'Do you have anything low-cal?'

'Salad,' Paris answered.

'Fine. I'll have a chicken salad with vinaigrette dressing.'

'Don't have vinaigrette.'

'Then give me Thousand Island, but put it on the side. And I'll have a Diet Coke, lots of ice.'

'Do you want that ice on the side?'

Surprised that Paris might actually be making a joke, Hope looked up at her, but by the extremely irritated expression on her face, it was very clear she wasn't kidding.

'In the glass will be fine.' Juliette shook her head as Paris walked away. 'I don't know how anyone can stand to live here.'

'Actually, it grows on you,' Hope said and was surprised as much as Juliette by her statement.

'How long have you known Dylan?'

'Long enough.'

'It was a real shock to walk into his house today and find you in his bed.'

'It was a shock to wake up and find you in his house.' A reluctant smile tilted the corners of Juliette's red lips. 'He must care about you.'

Hope took a drink of her milkshake. She didn't know for certain how Dylan felt about her. Beyond telling her she was important to him, he'd never actually said. Now she might never know.

A local couple sat down in the booth behind Juliette and wanted a booster seat for their toddler. Paris brought it, and Hope was struck by how nice and chatty she was to them.

'You don't look like the sort of woman I always pictured with Dylan,' Juliette said, drawing Hope's attention away from the change in Paris.

'Why's that?'

'I always knew he'd end up with a pretty woman, but I figured he'd want someone more . . . homespun, I guess.' Juliette tucked the brown wig hairs behind her ears, then laid her hands on the table. For the first time, Hope noticed the impressive diamond on her finger. 'How much has Dylan told you about me?' she wanted to know.

'Not a lot. Just that you and he were never married and when he left, he took Adam with him,' Hope answered and figured she didn't owe Juliette anything more.

'When Dylan left L.A., he took Adam because he is a wonderful father.' Juliette lowered her gaze to her hands. 'People look at a woman differently if she gives up custody of her child, even if it is best for the child, like there is something wrong with her, like she has no heart. That's just not true. I love my son, and I never meant to keep him a secret.'

Hope didn't know what to say about that. She didn't have children, would never have children, but she didn't think she could give up custody no matter how wonderful the father.

'I'm only telling you this in case you go ahead with a story. I'm telling you so you know my side. I gave Dylan custody of Adam because Dylan is a good father and a good man. I gave him custody because I love them both.'

As Hope looked into the heavenly blue eyes of America's favorite angel, she believed her. It didn't matter if she understood Juliette Bancroft or even liked her. She was right. Dylan was a good father and a good man.

Even before she'd fallen in love, she'd made a connection, and for the first time in a very long time, she'd shared her life and dark, painful secrets. She'd shared with Dylan because she felt safe with him. She trusted him, and he'd trusted her enough to share his life with her, too.

But only to a certain point. She hadn't told him the truth about what she really did for a living, and he'd lied to her about the woman sitting across the table. He'd told her Adam's mom was a waitress. He hadn't trusted her that far. She'd lied to him, and he'd lied to her. Perhaps not the best beginning for any relationship, but they could work through it.

Dylan was being a big hypocrite about it all now, but that would shortly change. When he realized she wasn't a gossip reporter, he'd have to apologize. She'd forgive him, but she just hoped he didn't wait too long. She wasn't a patient woman.

And Adam. During the short time she'd been in Gospel, she'd come to care for him, and his anger hurt almost as much as his father's.

Microphone Detects Sound of Breaking Heart

The cord to Hope's Discman bumped against the front of her gray sweatshirt as she jogged toward Main Street. Her sunglasses shaded her eyes from the morning sun, and through her earphones Jewel provided commiseration for her breaking heart. She sucked cool mountain air into her lungs as her ponytail bobbed and swayed on her head.

Dylan hadn't called. He hadn't called the night before, and he hadn't called that morning. Hope wasn't good at waiting. Not when it felt as if her whole life were at stake. She'd given him until nine-thirty that morning before she'd pulled on her jogging shorts and set out for his house.

She was in love with him, and she was certain he cared about her, too. It had taken three years and more than a thousand miles to find him. They could work through their problems because she wasn't going to give up now, but the closer she got to his house, the more her stomach twisted into a knot. As she entered town, she wasn't so certain showing up at his door was the wisest move, but she'd had enough of waiting around for him. She had to know for certain what he was thinking and feeling. And exactly *how* important she was to him.

She rounded the corner at Hansen's Emporium and slowed. A crowd had gathered outside the Cozy Corner Café half a block away, and it appeared to be a film crew, photographers, and a chaotic mess of spectators.

Immediately she recognized the back of Dylan's battered cowboy hat in the crowd. She pushed her headphones down around her neck, and the knot in her stomach tightened. The closer she got, the tighter it got.

Dylan's voice rose above the chaos. 'Ms Bancroft has no comment,' he said.

The throng moved as one down the street, past Jim's Hardware, as reporters shouted questions that were never answered, photographers snapped pictures, and film footage rolled. Above it all, Hope heard Adam's cries and his pitiful pleas to go away and leave his mother alone. The mob circled Dylan's truck, and Hope squeezed her way through the shifting wall of reporters. Over the shoulder of one of the photographers, she saw Dylan shove Juliette and Adam into the cab of his truck and shut the door. She pressed forward and broke free of the melee.

'I didn't do this,' she yelled as she grabbed his forearm.

His jaws were clenched and his eyes burned as he glared at her. 'Stay the hell away from me,' he said and shook off her grasp. 'And stay away from my son.' He fought his way through the crowd to the driver's side of his truck. He fired up the engine, and if the reporters hadn't quickly moved aside, Hope wasn't so sure he wouldn't have mowed them down.

As they pulled away from the curb, Hope looked into the cab at Juliette's pale complexion, bleached so white no amount of make-up could hide her shock. She caught a glimpse of Adam's face, of the tears rolling down his cheeks, and her heart hurt for him. For herself, too. It was over. She'd lost Dylan. He would never believe her now.

Numb disbelief settled over her as she glanced at the photographers snapping photos of Dylan's fleeing truck. She held her hands up as if she could stop it all, the cameras clicking, the film rolling, Dylan leaving. Then suddenly it did stop. The crowd dispersed and she was left standing on the sidewalk alone, rooted to the spot where Dylan had told her to stay away from him. Where her life had fallen apart.

She turned to the people standing behind her, in the doorways of shops and spilling from the Cozy Corner. She recognized the faces of those who lived in Gospel, and she also recognized the stunned confusion in their eyes.

Hope didn't know how long she stood there, staring down the street, nor did she know how long it took her to walk to Timberline Road. Her feet felt leaded, her hands cold, and her heart so battered it hurt her to breathe too deep.

Instead of entering her house, she walked to Shelly's back door and knocked. She didn't know what her friend had heard or what she believed, but the second Shelly opened the door, Hope burst into tears.

'What's wrong?' she asked and herded Hope into the kitchen.

'Have you talked to Dylan?'

'Not since the two of you borrowed my hiking boots.'

Hope threw her sunglasses on Shelly's counter and wiped her moist cheeks. 'He thinks I told the tabloids about him and Adam,' she began. Shelly handed her a Kleenex and Hope told her the whole story, starting with waking up in Dylan's house and finding Adam staring at her. When she was finished, Shelly didn't even look surprised.

'Well, I'm glad it's all out in the open now,' Shelly said as she took two wineglasses from the cupboard. 'A little boy shouldn't have to live with that kind of secret.'

'You've always known?'

'Yep.' She opened the refrigerator and poured zinfandel from a box. She held out a glass for Hope. 'Dylan is a great father, especially considering he has no help, but sometimes he is so protective of that child that he is bound to hurt him.'

Hope took the glass and looked down into the wine. It wasn't even noon, but she didn't care. 'I think Dylan hates me now.' She thought of the way he'd looked at her. 'No, I *know* he hates me now. He believes I moved here to report the story for a tabloid.' She looked up. 'Do you believe me?'

'Of course I believe you. I know how you feel about Dylan, and besides, I doubt you would have told me you worked for *The Weekly News of the Universe* if you were here secretly digging up dirt on Adam.'

'Thank you.' Hope took a long drink of her wine.

'Don't thank me. I'm your friend.'

She looked over the top of her glass at Shelly's curly red hair and freckles, her 'Garth Rules' T-shirt, huge belt buckle, and tight Wranglers. 'I'm glad,' she said. It had taken her three years and more than a thousand miles to find not only Dylan, but Shelly, too. Together they moved to the small dining room off the kitchen, and Hope opened up to Shelly about her feelings for Dylan.

'I didn't mean to fall in love with him,' she said, 'but I couldn't stop it. I knew he would hurt me, and he has.' She told Shelly about her marriage to Blaine and why it had really ended, and when she was through, she thought she should feel better, somehow purged, but she didn't. She just felt more hurt and broken.

Wally came in for lunch, then took off on his bike for Dylan's, once Shelly had called to make sure it was okay for him to be there. While Shelly had stood with the phone at her ear, Hope had sat frozen in her chair, her ears straining to hear the sound of his voice coming from the receiver. Her heart had been lodged in her throat, and when she realized what she was doing, she stood and went into the living room.

Over the course of the next few hours, she and Shelly polished off several more glasses of wine and a box of doughnuts.

'I think you're really tanked,' Shelly told her when she couldn't stop crying.

'I'm usually a very happy drunk,' Hope sobbed. 'But I'm emotionally distraught!'

'I'm impressed you can still say "emotionally distraught." '

By the time Hope stumbled home, she was having a hard time putting thoughts together. Everything in her head collided and churned into an undecipherable mush. She managed to crawl to her bedroom, where she found her beer helmet and the boxer shorts Dylan had given her to wear the morning after the first time they'd made love. She put on the helmet and the boxers; then she did herself a favor and passed out. When she woke up her head felt as if someone had hit her with a concrete block.

She sat up, her stomach heaved, and she ran into the bathroom. As she sat on the cool tile floor, wearing Dylan's boxers and praying at the porcelain altar, she got angry. Angry at herself and angry at Dylan. Sure, she probably shouldn't have lied to him for so long, but hers hadn't been a big lie. Not like his. He should have trusted her and believed in her, but he hadn't, and she never should have fallen in love with him. She felt like she had the day Blaine had served her with divorce papers. Like she'd been kicked in the chest, only this time it was worse. This time it was her fault, because this time she could have prevented it.

From the start, she'd known there was no future with him, and yet she'd let it happen. Well, maybe 'let' wasn't the right word, but she could have prevented it. She could have run the other way and told him no the night of the Fourth of July. She should have protected her heart from his smiles and the sound of his deep voice melting her and calling her honey. She should have backed away from his touch that tingled her skin and made her heart beat faster. She should have avoided his gaze that seemed to reach out and caress her like the touch of his hand. She should have put up some sort of resistance, but she hadn't. She'd run toward him even as she'd known to run the other way. Now she was paying with a shattered heart.

'What am I going to do?' she whispered. A part of her wanted to go. Just pack up and leave. Run away from this place. Gospel wasn't her home.

She lay down and pressed her cheek against the cool, clean tile. Yet there was another part of her that rebelled at the thought of running away. She'd been knocked flat before, but this time she wasn't going to hide from life. She wasn't going to let the pain get the best of her again. She wasn't the same woman she'd been before she'd driven into Gospel. She wasn't going to stay down. Her heart was broken and it hurt like a bitch, but she was going to live her life on her feet.

She raised her head, the room spun, and she lay back down. Yeah, she was going to live life on her feet. Just as soon as she could pick herself up off the bathroom floor.

Dylan looked across the table at his son. Adam rolled his corn on the cob across his plate for about the five-hundredth time in the past five minutes. It bumped into the bites of steak Dylan had cut up for him, then rolled into a biscuit. 'Why don't you eat that instead of playing with it?'

'I hate corn.'

'That's funny. Last time we had corn on the cob, you ate four or five pieces.'

'I hate it now.'

Yesterday they'd taken one step forward. After the ordeal in town that morning, they'd taken two steps back. Seeing Juliette so upset, Adam blamed himself. He blamed Dylan, too. In his seven-year-old mind, he figured if he hadn't acted naughty, his mom wouldn't have brought him home early. She wouldn't have been in Gospel, and the reporters wouldn't have found her. She wouldn't have cried.

'Your mom's going to be okay,' Dylan tried to reassure his son.

Adam looked up. 'She said they were going to cancel her angel show.'

She'd said a lot of things during the hour-long drive to the Sun Valley airport. 'She was just upset. No one will cancel her show.' In all the time he'd known Julie, he'd known she could be very dramatic, but he'd never seen her *that dramatic*. She'd cried and ranted that her life was over, and when he'd tried to reassure her, she'd accused him of being insensitive. She'd also accused him of bringing a tabloid reporter into all their lives. She'd made it quite clear that she blamed him as much as she blamed Hope.

Hope. Even if Hope hadn't known about Adam and Juliette before she'd moved to Gospel, she'd run with the story the moment she'd discovered the juicy details. He didn't believe for one second that she wasn't responsible for that scene outside the Cozy Corner. And even though she'd denied involvement, even as she'd stood there surrounded by other tabloid journalists and paparazzi, looking into his eyes and telling him, 'I didn't do this,' it was just too big a coincidence for him not to think she wasn't involved up to her little blond ponytail.

He'd gone into the relationship with Hope thinking he would end it when Adam returned home. He'd thought he could spend a couple of weeks enjoying her company and then go back to the way things had always been. He'd quickly discovered that he didn't want to go back. When she was around, she made him laugh. She made him happy, and she made his life better. He hadn't wanted to give that up. To give her up. He hadn't wanted it to end, but it had. It was over, and it was ironic as hell that it had ended according to the original plan.

'Why aren't you eating?' Dylan asked Adam.

'I told you, I don't like corn.'

'What about your steak?'

'Hate that, too.'

'Your biscuit?'

'Can I put jelly on it?'

Since nothing had gone Adam's way since he'd been home, Dylan decided to give in about dinner. 'I don't care.' He bit into his corn and watched his son open the refrigerator.

'Where's the grape jelly?'

'I guess we're out. Try the strawberry.'

'I hate strawberry.'

Dylan knew that wasn't true. In a pinch, Adam would eat it.

'Why didn't you get some?' his son asked, like he'd committed a heinous crime.

Dylan set his corn on his plate and wiped his hands on his napkin. 'I guess I forgot.'

'Probably too busy.'

And they both knew what Adam meant. Hope. He'd been too busy with Hope. Ever since they'd returned from the airport, Adam had been spoiling for a fight. Dylan recognized what was happening and tried not to let it get the best of him. 'Are you going to eat any of your dinner?'

Adam shook his head. 'I want grape jelly.'

'Too bad.'

'You're not going to get me jelly?'

'Not tonight.'

'I won't be able to eat breakfast without jelly.' Adam stuck his chin in the air. 'Lunch, either. I guess I won't ever eat again.'

Dylan stood. 'That will save me the trouble of fixing you anything to eat.' He pointed to Adam's plate. 'Now, you're sure you're finished?'

'Yes.'

'Then go brush your teeth and get your pajamas on.' For a few tense moments, Adam looked like he was going to fight about that, too, but he stuck out his lower lip and left the room. Dylan grabbed Adam's plate and put it on the floor. 'Here, dog,' he said, and Mandy crawled from beneath the kitchen table and devoured the steak and biscuit in seconds. She licked the corn, then turned away.

He should have saved himself some trouble and just fixed Wheaties for dinner, he thought as he picked up the plate from the floor. A little over twenty-four hours ago, he'd thought his life had gone straight to hell. He'd been wrong about that. It hadn't quite hit bottom yet. Now. *Now* it was hell.

Before dinner, he'd spoken to his mother on the telephone, and in her most optimistic voice, she'd reminded him that 'things could always be worse.'

Yeah, he supposed she was right. He could get kicked in the nuts or Adam could get sick, but barring physical abuse or illness, he didn't see that things could get much worse.

Dylan left the dishes on the table and the pans on the stove and relaxed in front of the television. He reached for the remote and started to flip channels. *Jeopardy! Wheel of Fortune*, and *Inside Hollywood*. Just as he was about to flip to the next channel, a picture of Julie flashed across the screen.

'*Heaven on Earth* star, Juliette Bancroft, has a seven-year-old son that she has kept secret from the world,' the report began as film footage rolled of him and Julie and Adam leaving the Cozy Corner. 'An unnamed source informs us that Juliette's son lives with his father in the small town of Gospel, Idaho, about fifty miles west of . . .'

Dylan watched himself shove Julie and Adam into his truck. A few seconds elapsed and Hope burst from the crowd and grabbed his arm. She appeared pale and as beautiful as ever. He watched her lips move, but the microphones didn't pick up what she said. But then, he didn't need to hear it. He knew. He knew she pleaded her innocence. It was a lie, of course, but even as he watched her image fade from his television, even though he knew she'd lied, there was a part of him that wanted to believe her. She twisted him inside out and had the power to make him want her even after what she'd done. Even after what he knew about her. She made him want to grab her and shake her and hold her and bury his face in the side of her neck. Wanting her was a constant ache in the pit of his stomach, like he was standing on the edge of a cliff, swallowing air.

Disgusted with himself, he switched the television station to *Cops* and tossed the remote onto the couch.

He was absolutely going to stop thinking that things could not get worse. Because the minute he thought it, they sure as hell did.

When he went to bed that night, his thoughts returned to Hope. He figured that if he'd run a check on her before they'd become involved, he could have saved himself a lot of trouble. It was too late now, but he figured he should probably do it first thing in the morning. Just in case.

But the next morning, he found paparazzi camped at the end of his driveway. He and Adam jumped into the truck and headed for the Double T. They spent the weekend riding horses and doing the little things his brother-in-law hadn't gotten around to doing yet, like fixing the chicken wire around his mother's henhouse and regrating the gravel road. Julie called to let him know that she and Gerard were hiding out at his family's vineyards in Bordeaux and that she planed to do an interview with *People* magazine in a few days.

By the time Dylan went to work early Monday, most of the reporters were gone. He was brought up to speed during roll call, and he had Hazel bring him the accident reports and booking actions for the past two weeks. He skimmed the DUI arrests, and read a complaint filed by Ada Dover which charged Wilbur McCaffrey with purposely letting his dog out in the morning to 'do his duty' in the motel's flower beds.

He waited until he'd read through the stack of reports before he contacted the California Department of Motor Vehicles. Within a few minutes, he received Hope's address in Los Angeles and her social security number. Once he had that, finding out information about her was incredibly easy.

He found out that she really was employed by *The Weekly News of the Universe* and that she had three pseudonyms. Before the Porsche, she'd owned a Mercedes, and right out of college, she'd worked for *The San Francisco Chronicle* and later *The Los Angeles Times*. And he dug into her court records and read the date she'd been married and the date her divorce had been final.

He dug deeper and read about the civil-harassment restraining order she'd won against a wrestler named Myron Lambardo, a.k.a. Myron the Masher. She'd won it three months prior to her arrival in Gospel, and in his defense, Mr Lambardo had argued that he was angry and only wanted Ms Spencer to continue with the Micky the

Magical Leprechaun series and turn him back into a 'stud muffin' so people wouldn't think he was a 'homo.'

The court not only found in Hope's favor, but ordered 'that the defendant not threaten, strike, or make physical contact with the plaintiff, not telephone plaintiff, not block plaintiff's movements in public places or thoroughfares, and stay at least one hundred yards away from the plaintiff while at work, home, or any other place the plaintiff may request.'

Dylan shook his head and leaned back in his chair. He guessed he shouldn't be surprised by what he read. She hadn't mentioned the restraining order, of course, but there were several important things she hadn't mentioned. Being stalked by an angry dwarf was just one of them. He wondered what else he didn't know.

Over the course of the next week, Hope refused to keep herself locked up in her house. She drove to Sun Valley to shop in the trendy boutiques and spent a lot of time with Shelly. She learned how to can pickles and hunt for huckleberries and she worked on her stories. She finished several for *The Weekly News of the Universe* and had most of the rough draft down for her article on Hiram. After writing fiction for so long, nonfiction was proving more difficult than she expected, but she was enjoying the challenge.

From Shelly, Hope learned that the Donnellys had been a picture-perfect family. The three children were older than Shelly, but she remembered that they never got into trouble and kept mostly to themselves. Two boys and a girl, raised by the county sheriff and his God-fearing wife. Together, Hiram and Minnie had been the moral compass of the community. Holding themselves up as the perfect family, yet their children had never come back to visit once they were out of the house. Something had been horribly wrong with the picture. But what?

It had taken Hope a few days of digging to find out more information on the Donnelly children. Although none of them would speak to her directly, what she discovered was enough to answer her questions and add a new dimension to her article.

She learned that the older son had died of alcoholism, the younger was in prison for domestic abuse, and the daughter was a crisis counselor. Hope didn't need to hear the particulars to figure out that behind closed doors, the picture-perfect family was dysfunctional as hell. What Hope found particularly amazing was that they'd managed the facade in a town that fed off everyone else's business.

Most of the time Hope spent trying to forget about Dylan, but she never succeeded for very long. He appeared in her sleep and in her daydreams as well. He'd even made an appearance in her work, too. In her latest alien feature, she'd added a bit of a new slant. A new character in the form of a cross-dressing alien sheriff. She'd named him Dennis Taylor.

The morning the story was due to hit the stands, she drove to the M & S and grabbed the most recent issue of *The Weekly News of the Universe* from the magazine rack. She flipped it open to the center spread. Once again, her article was the featured story. This was the first article featuring Dennis, and it showed him as a muscle-neck cross-dresser with a gold star pinned to his marabou teddy. While that should have made her feel vindicated, it didn't.

She chatted with Stanley as she paid for her paper, then left. Walking to her car, she thumbed to the gossip section. Her gaze skimmed the columns, but there was no mention of Juliette and Adam. It would appear, though. Probably in next week's edition.

Hope folded the paper and took her car keys from the pocket of her jeans. Her stories were doing better than she'd ever imagined, yet she felt nothing. Not happy. Not sad. Just blah. There was more to life than successful alien articles. Like living. Like opening yourself up and falling in love and getting your heart stomped on by a size-twelve cowboy boot.

She thought she heard someone yell her name, and she glanced up from the keys in her hand to the far end of the parking lot. A big cardboard sign caught her attention. It said: MAKE MICKY A STUD MUFFIN. She couldn't see who held the sign, just a pair of little sneakers peeking out from beneath the cardboard. That was all she needed. She knew, and it shoved her heart into her throat.

Myron had found her.

She jumped into her car and peeled out of the parking lot, startling a family riding bicycles. As she drove down Main, her hands shook and her heart pounded in her ears.

She didn't know if her restraining order was in effect in Idaho, or if Myron was free to harass her here. She really didn't know what to do until she pulled into a space behind the sheriff's office. She needed answers and she needed help, but she really didn't want to involve Dylan. Maybe she could just talk to one of the deputies. She was sure someone besides Dylan could tell her what she wanted to know.

She looked for the sheriff's Blazer and spotted it by the back door. He was in his office. Her pounding heart skipped a few painful beats. She didn't want to involve him in her problem. The last time she'd seen him, he'd told her to stay out of his life. He'd meant it. And as much as that hurt, and as much as she thought of him every minute of every hour of every day, she meant to get over it. To get over him, but she couldn't if she had to see and talk to him. Then she remembered his guard dog of a secretary and relaxed. Even if she *wanted* to see him, she didn't believe Hazel would let her past. Not even if her hair was on fire and Dylan held the only extinguisher.

Hope took a deep breath and glanced in her rearview mirror. She reapplied her red lipstick and wished she'd worn something nicer than her white cotton shirt that buttoned up the front, jeans, and black leather belt. Not that what she wore wasn't nice. It just wasn't going to make anyone kick himself in the ass for dumping her.

Proof: Head Banging Causes Brain Damage

Hope approached the information desk and waited for the female deputy to look up. 'I need some information on a restraining order,' she began.

'Is this an emergency?'

'I think so.'

'Have you been assaulted?'

'Not yet.'

The officer picked up the telephone receiver and punched a button. 'Hazel, I have a woman out here who needs to obtain a TRO.'

'No.' Hope shook her head, stopping the deputy before she made the mistake of involving Dylan and his secretary. 'I already have a restraining order. When I lived in California, I had to take Myron Lambardo to court. I won, but I just saw him at the M and S Market.'

'Just a minute, Hazel.' The woman pressed the hold button. 'And you're positive it was him?'

'Yes. You can't miss Myron. He looks a little like Patrick Swayze, only shorter.'

'How short?'

'He's a dwarf.'

The officer blinked twice, then lifted her finger. 'Hazel,' she began again, 'the woman here says she's being stalked by a dwarf from California. She wants to know about a restraining order.'

Hope groaned. 'Oh, my God.'

'Just a sec. I'll ask her.' The deputy looked Hope up and down. 'Are you the woman with the peacock boots?'

'Yes.'

'Yep.' The woman pointed to the double glass doors that led to Dylan's office. 'Go right in there and Hazel will help you.'

Hope looked at the big gold star painted on the doors, and her dread of seeing Dylan replaced any lingering fear of Myron. 'I just want some information. Can't you help me?'

The deputy shook her head. 'If a stalker has followed you here from California, the sheriff needs to be informed.'

Hope figured she had two choices. She could be an adult and brave it out, or she could run and hide like a coward. She stood frozen for several indecisive moments. Maybe it wasn't Myron. Maybe it was some other dwarf who wanted her to make Micky the Magical Leprechaun a stud muffin. If she left, she could always return on a day when Dylan was out of the office. Maybe if she just ignored Myron, he'd get tired and go away. Problem was, she'd tried that and it hadn't worked.

Hazel swung open one of the glass doors and settled the issue for her. 'Sheriff Taber said to come on back.'

Hope's stomach got a bit queasy as she moved toward Hazel and followed her past her desk and down the short hallway. The closer she got, the worse she felt. And then there he was, standing as she entered his office, looking better than she remembered. Tall and handsome, his hair rumpled as if he'd combed it with his fingers. Her footsteps faltered and she stopped just inside the doorway.

'Shall I hold your calls, Sheriff?' Hazel asked.

'Yes,' he said, and the sound of his voice after so many days without it poured through Hope like warm sunshine on a December day. 'Unless it's the prosecutor's office.'

Hazel shifted her gaze to Hope as if she were a scanner, trying to detect the true nature behind Hope's visit. 'I'll be at my desk if you need me, Sheriff,' she said, then left, and Hope was alone with the man she loved, her broken heart, and her queasy stomach.

'Why don't you sit?' Dylan offered.

'No, really. I know you're busy, and I don't want to disturb you. I just have a quick question that I thought one of the deputies could answer for me. I guess no one knew the answer and just assumed you'd want to see me. I know that you don't, and I wouldn't have come if I'd known—'

'What's your question?' he asked, interrupting her.

She placed a hand on her abdomen and took a deep breath. 'Is a restraining order obtained in California enforceable in Idaho?'

'Yes.'

'Okay.' She let out her breath and took a step backward. 'Thanks.'

'Why?'

She stood close enough to see his green eyes, close enough to see him looking back at her as if she were just any ordinary citizen stopping by to fill out a complaint. As if he'd never shown her Sawtooth Lake and Cassiopeia spinning around on her head.

In his gaze, there was no spark of hunger nor even the interest that had been there from the first moment she'd met him. There was nothing, and she hadn't realized until it was gone how much she'd delighted in it and how desired he'd made her feel. The backs of her eyes stung and she slid her palm over her stomach as if she could hold in the pain of seeing him.

'Why?' he asked again.

Looking at him made it hard to think of anything beyond how much she still loved him and how little he felt for her now. She lowered her gaze to the clutter of paper on his desk.

'A few months ago I was granted a restraining order against a man named Myron Lambardo.' She paused and her fingers nervously rubbed the smooth leather of her belt as she told herself not to cry. 'He was part of the reason I came to Gospel. I needed to get away from the whole mess and stress of the court hearing.' She glanced up. 'I saw him when I was coming out of the M and S.'

'Today?'

'Just a few minutes ago.'

'What did he say?'

'I think he called my name.'

'What else?'

'He held a big sign that said, "Make Micky a stud muffin." '

'Are you sure it was him?'

'Who else could it be?' Dylan was so professional. So impersonal, and although she wouldn't have thought it possible, he broke her heart just a little bit more.

'How close was he to you?' he asked.

'A parking lot away.'

He pointed to the chair opposite his desk. 'Have a seat, Hope.'

Finally he said her name, and she wished he hadn't. It made everything so much worse, reminding her of all the other times he'd said it, or whispered it against her neck or into her mouth.

'I'm okay,' she said but took a step further into the room.

He looked at her for several long moments; then he sat in his chair and typed something into his computer. 'Are you afraid he'll physically assault you?'

'Not really. He's never touched me, but he used to threaten me with a tombstone.'

He glanced up.

'It's a wrestling move.'

'I know.' He read something off the screen, then lifted his gaze to her once again. 'By following you to Gospel, he has violated the terms of the restraining order,' he explained. 'Of course, he can always say he's here for some other reason, but I doubt a judge will believe him.'

'What happens now?'

'I'll bring him in, and depending on what time he's actually booked into jail, he'll go before the magistrate either today or in the morning. Bail will be set as well as a court date.'

'I'll have to go to court again?' Hope didn't want to go through another hearing.

'That depends on his plea. He might plead guilty, pay his fine, and leave town.'

Hope doubted it. 'Can't you just talk to him? He's easy to spot in a crowd. He's not even four feet tall and he looks a bit like Patrick Swayze. Maybe you could just scare him into leaving?' But she doubted fear of Dylan would send Myron running. Dealing with him had never been that easy.

Dylan leaned back in his chair and folded his arms across his chest. 'If that's what you want, but you still need to swear out a complaint. Just in case we need something to take to the prosecutor.'

Hope raised her hands to her face and rubbed her forehead. She was sorry she'd come here. Myron would pay a fine, and then be free to hassle her by morning. She'd accomplished nothing by talking to Dylan, and ultimately, she would pay for it more than Myron. Myron would pay in cash, but looking at Dylan, hearing his voice, and loving him cost Hope another chunk of her heart.

She dropped her hands and shook her head. 'Just forget it,' she said. 'I guess that little weasel is free to harass me.' The tears which had stung the backs of her eyes since she'd walked into the room collected on her bottom lids and blurred her vision. She wasn't sure if she was crying out of frustration with Myron or because the man she desperately loved didn't feel anything for her. 'The restraining order means nothing to him, so just forget it.'

As if he could no longer stand the sight of her, Dylan turned his attention to his computer monitor and seemed to become instantly absorbed in whatever he read there. One appalling tear slid over her lower lashes and down her cheek.

'Just forget I was here,' she said and practically ran from the room before she embarrassed herself further.

Dylan watched Hope leave his office and rose from his chair. He started to go after her but stopped. If he caught up with her, he wasn't certain what he'd do. He wasn't certain he wouldn't pull her against his chest and bury his nose in her hair. The second he'd heard she was in the building, his body had responded to her. His chest got tight and that was before she'd even walked into his office, looking incredible in a simple white shirt and jeans just tight enough to hug the curve of her sweet behind.

Thankfully, he'd been able to ignore his body. He'd been in control and handling the situation as if she were just another citizen off the street. Until she cried. Seeing her tears, he'd about jumped out of his chair and gone to her. Even after everything, she still tore him up inside. He still wanted her.

He leaned his behind against his desk and stared at the framed accommodations and service awards hanging on the wall. He remembered the day he and Hope had hiked to Sawtooth Lake and she'd joked about coming to his office and filing a complaint just in case she got lonely for him.

Ten minutes ago, when Hazel had buzzed to say Hope was in the reception area, the memory of that day had popped into his head with the subtlety of a lightning bolt. The memory of her hand on the zipper of his Levi's and her tongue in his mouth had had him holding his breath, wondering if she'd made up an excuse just to see him. When he realized she hadn't, there was a part of him that was disappointed as hell.

He missed Hope, or rather the Hope he thought he knew. He missed talking to her. He missed the sound of her voice and the scent of her skin. He missed making love to her and waking up seeing her head on the next pillow. But perhaps most of all, he missed looking across his dinner table and seeing her face.

He crossed one foot over the other and studied the razor crease running down the leg of his pants. As much as he missed her, and as much as he wanted her, he distrusted her that much more. Although he couldn't reconcile the Hope he knew with the Hope who worked for a sleazy tabloid, he knew she was one and the same person. She'd put her loyalty to her job over him. She'd had two choices: her desire to report a big juicy story, or her desire for him. She hadn't chosen him.

Dylan walked to the corner of the room and grabbed his hat from the coatrack. Now he had no choice but to forget about her. And he would. Just as soon as he took care of her problem with Myron the Masher.

*

At three o'clock that afternoon, Myron Lambardo sat on a stool at the Cozy Corner, munching on French fries and polishing off a BLT. He'd eaten in worse dives, he supposed. Wrestled in them, too.

Some kind of shitty country-and-western music poured from an old jukebox, and he wondered if they had any head-banging music, like Metallica. The place was deserted except for the cook, who'd gone on a break in the back, and a waitress with a long braid. Paris; he'd read her name off her tag and thought it sounded exotic. She had big hands, big bones, and big breasts. Just the sort of woman he loved to wrestle. There was a lot to grab. She brought him a refill on his Coke and didn't stare at him like he was a freak.

'Thanks, Paris,' he said and decided to strike up a conversation and maybe get information. 'Are you named after Paris, France, or Paris, Texas?'

'Neither. My mom just liked the name.'

'So do I. It sounds exotic.' He took a drink of his Coke, then asked, 'How long have you lived here?'

'All of my life. Where are you from?'

'Everywhere and nowhere. I'm a professional wrestler, so I move around a lot.'

'You're a wrestler?' Her eyes got wide, and her cheeks flushed red with excitement. 'Do you know The Rock?' she asked.

'Sure,' he lied. 'We're tight.'

'Really! He's my favorite wrestler.'

He was every woman's favorite wrestler. The Rock was famous, and for a short time, Myron had touched a bit of fame himself. While he'd been Micky the Magical Leprechaun, people had wanted to talk to him. He'd even swung a few matches in higher-ranking venues and wrangled a few dates with normal-sized chicks. Then that bitch of a reporter, Hope Spencer, had turned him into RuPaul, and poof, it was all over.

At twenty-six, he was a has-been. He wanted the fame back. One article. All Hope had to do was write one article and restore his reputation. Give him everything he wanted, and then he'd leave her alone.

'Do you wrestle in the WWF?'

'Nah, but it's my dream,' he confessed and polished off his BLT. The current wave of political correctness riding the country had killed the sport of midget wrestling. The WWF was too afraid of the backlash to sponsor matches, like somehow what he did was less dignified than regular-sized men. Lately, he'd been thinking of going to Mexico, where mini wrestling was big. 'Have you ever thought of wrestling?'

'Me?' Paris laughed and placed a hand over her heart. 'I could never wrestle.'

Myron focused on her hand and large breasts. 'Sure you could, sweet thing. I bet you'd look great in spandex.' He gazed into her flushed face. 'I'd love to wrestle you sometime.'

'Oh, I don't think so.' She glanced over the top of his head, and a worried wrinkle appeared between her brows. 'Oh, no, here comes Dylan,' she said.

Myron looked over his shoulder at the tall cowboy getting out of a sheriff's Blazer. 'Holy frijole,' he said. 'You've got to hide me.' He jumped up onto the stool and vaulted over the counter like it was a pommel horse, landing on the other side. 'If he asks about me, don't tell him I'm here.

'I think he's here because of something I did.'

Myron squatted down and pressed his back against the shelving behind the counter. He hoped Paris was right. He hoped the sheriff wasn't after him. He'd heard plenty about people rotting in small-town jails, and the network of wrestlers he knew had all heard the story of the time Tiny Ted had been arrested in Oklahoma and forced to dance around like a Munchkin while singing 'The Lollipop Guild' for a bunch of drunk deputies. He figured something like that had to be twice as degrading as being morphed into a drag queen.

Myron heard the door swing open, then shut, and the heavy thud of bootheels on the linoleum.

'Hey there, Paris,' said a man no more than a few feet from where Myron hid. 'How are you doin'?'

'Good. What can I get for you, Dylan?'

'Nothing. There's a mini Winnebago outside with Las Vegas tags, and I'm looking for the owner. His name is Myron Lambardo and he's about three-feet-six. Have you seen him?'

'Why, is he dangerous?'

'I just want to talk to him.'

There was a pause and Myron held his breath. 'He was here earlier, but he left,' she finally said, and if Myron hadn't been hiding, he would have kissed her.

'How long ago did he leave?'

'About an hour.'

'Did you see which way he went?'

'No,' she answered. And since Myron couldn't kiss her, he ran his hand up her calf, under the jean skirt she wore, to her knee and gave it a pat.

'Well, if you see him again, be sure and call the sheriff's Dispatch.'

She didn't say anything for another long moment and he wondered if she was going to kick him or turn him in. 'Why, what's he done?'

'He's in violation of a restraining order.'

'From who?'

'Ms Spencer.'

'Oh.' This time she did kick him.

'What's the matter?' the sheriff asked.

'Nothing. Just squishing a bug.' Myron wrapped his arm around her thigh and hung on so she couldn't kick him again. She got real still, and he waited for her to squeal on him.

'If you see him near the Winnebago, give us a call.'

'I'll do that.'

The bootheels faded and the door opened and shut. 'Is he gone?' Myron whispered.

'Get your hand out from under my skirt!'

Slowly Myron slipped his palm down her soft thigh to her knee. 'You have great skin.'

She took a step back and stared down at him as if he really were a bug. 'You're here to chase after Hope Spencer.'

' "Chase" is an awfully strong word.' He stood, then hoisted himself up onto the counter. He sat on the edge facing Paris, which nearly brought him to her height. 'I just need her to do one little thing for me.'

'What's that? Have your baby?'

'Hell, no. I hate that woman.'

The frown wrinkling Paris's brow lifted. 'You do?'

'Yes. She ruined my life.'

'Mine, too. Ever since she drove into town, all the men have been chasing after her.'

'Hope? She's too scrawny.'

'Oh, you're just saying that.'

'No. I like full-figured gals.' He looked her up and down. 'Gals like you.'

Hope shoved her hands into a pair of sturdy work gloves and tackled the weeds growing in the old rose garden in front of the Donnelly house. The late-afternoon sun beat down on her head, covered with her Gap hat, while insects buzzed around her. She wore a pair of beige shorts and a red tank top, and she'd protected her exposed skin with sunscreen and bug juice. On the porch sat her big covered tankard of iced tea, and Bonnie Raitt sang from the CD player.

It had been three days since she'd first seen Myron outside the M & S. She hadn't seen him again, but she'd heard from him. She didn't know how he'd gotten her unlisted phone number, but he had, and although he never said anything, she knew it was him. She recognized his breathing. He'd done the same thing when he'd followed her to L.A.

When she'd told Shelly about it, her friend had waved aside Hope's fear as nothing to be concerned about, but after the creepy phone calls kept coming, Shelly volunteered Paul to kick Myron's ass. If only it were that simple. Hope knew from prior experience with Myron that he was very good at hiding.

'What're ya doin'?'

Hope looked over her shoulder at the two little boys walking into her yard wearing nothing but their swimming suits and cowboy boots. Wally's gaze quickly moved to the big sickle leaning against the house, while Adam kept his eyes glued to the ground.

At the sight of Adam, Hope felt a warm little glow in her heart. She was surprised at how glad she was to see him. At how much she'd come to care for him in such a short time. A little boy who had a passion for rocks and anything gross.

'Do you boys have sunscreen on?'

Wally nodded and asked again, 'What're you doin'?'

'I'm trying to clear this rose bed.'

'Need help?' he asked.

Under normal circumstance, she would have welcomed help from anyone who offered. 'No, thanks.'

'You could pay us,' Wally continued as if she hadn't refused the offer. 'And we'd do a good job, too.'

Hope looked at Adam and he finally took his gaze off his shoes and his eyes met hers. His cheeks flushed; then he looked away, as if he were embarrassed and uncertain. 'I would, but I don't think Adam's father would be too happy if he saw him here.'

'He won't care. Will he, Adam?'

Adam shook his head. 'No, he won't care if I pull your weeds.'

She knew better. 'I'll tell you what,' she said, rather than argue. 'You go get hold of your dad and ask him. If he says it's okay, I'll hire you both.'

'Okay,' they said at the same time and darted across the street.

Hope watched them disappear and didn't believe there was even a slim chance that the boys would come back. Her thoughts returned to Myron as she got busy pulling the fireweeds choking the garden under the front window. Earlier, someone from the sheriff's office had called to say that Myron's Winnebago had disappeared and they thought he'd left town. Hope knew better, but she hadn't said anything. The last time she'd gone for help, she'd been sent into Dylan's office. She'd rather face harassment by Myron than gaze across a room and see Dylan's blank face looking back at her.

Myron drove her insane, but at least he didn't hurt her. She tugged a big weed from the ground and tossed it on a pile. She would rather be driven crazy by a demented dwarf than have her heart continually crushed by Dylan's disinterest.

She glanced up as the boys returned.

'Adam's dad said it was okay.'

Hope couldn't believe Dylan would allow his son around

her. Not after he'd told her to stay away from him. 'Did he really say that?' she asked Adam.

He looked her right in the eyes and said, 'Yeah, he did.'

'And he said you could work for me? You mentioned *my* name?'

'Yes.'

Surprised and perhaps a tiny bit relieved that maybe Dylan didn't think she was such a horrible person after all, she took off her gloves and dropped them on the ground. 'Well, okay. Follow me.' She led them into the house and gave them each a pair of pink rubber gloves she used to wash dishes. She poured them iced tea with lots of sugar; then they went back outside and got to work. Wally talked almost nonstop, but Adam was much more quiet than usual.

'Hope, I have a question,' Wally announced as he tackled a weed almost as tall as he was.

She looked up. 'Go ahead, but I don't have to answer if I don't feel like it.'

'Okay.' He tossed the weed onto the pile. 'Can I drive your car sometime?'

She glanced at her Porsche parked in the driveway. 'Yes.' Wally's face broke into a big smile, until she added, 'When you're sixteen and have your license.'

He sighed. 'Oh, man.' Then, together, he and Adam worked on a weed that took both of them to pull it from the ground.

As Hope knelt in a different bed a few feet away, she watched Adam out of the corner of her eye. She watched him closely, and over the course of the next hour, he looked at her whenever he thought she wasn't looking at him, his brows lowered over his green eyes as if he were seriously trying to figure something out.

'Hope?'

'Yes, Wally?'

'How come you don't have kids?'

She placed her gloved hands on her thighs and gazed at the boys from beneath the brim of her hat. Like always when she was around these two, she didn't know exactly how to answer their questions.

'Is it 'cause you're not married?' Wally wanted to know.

Adam finally spoke. 'You dope. You don't have to be married to have kids.'

'Uh-huh.'

'Nuh-huh. My mom and dad had me and they weren't married,' Adam announced, and Hope was glad to hear he knew now and that he seemed okay.

Wally looked his friend over. 'Really?'

'Yep.'

'Oh.' Both boys turned their attention back to Hope and waited for her to answer.

'Well,' she began, deciding to wing it, 'when I was a lot younger, I had to have an operation. When it was over, I couldn't have children.'

Adam's eyes got big. 'You had an operation? Where?'

Hope stood and placed her hand on her abdomen. 'Right here.'

'Does it hurt?' he wanted to know.

'Not any more.'

Adam walked toward her, keeping his gaze pinned to her abdomen as if he could see beneath her shirt. 'Do you got a scar?'

'Yep.'

'Wow!' He looked up and a lock of hair fell into his eyes. He needed it cut again. 'Can I see?'

Hope raised her hand and combed his hair from his forehead. The hot sun heated his scalp, and Hope felt the warmth of it beneath her palm and travel to her heart. Adam didn't flinch or move away and she smiled down at him. 'I don't think so.'

'Oh, man.'

Dylan's truck pulled off the highway onto Timberline Road, and Hope dusted the dirt from her knees. She wondered how much longer her heart would react when she saw him. She walked to the porch and picked up her tea, purposely turning her back on him. She didn't want to see him and know he was looking at her and feeling nothing. Someday it wouldn't matter and she wouldn't feel anything for him, either. Just as she felt nothing for her ex-husband, but it would take time, and that someday was not today.

'Bye,' the boys said in unison and tossed their rubber gloves on the ground.

'Wait, guys. You forgot your money,' she called after them as she glanced over her shoulder.

'Later,' Wally yelled, and the two of them barely waited until the truck had passed before they tore out of her yard and headed for the Aberdeens'.

Hope had a sneaky suspicion that she'd been had. That they'd looked her right in the eyes and lied their little buns off. She suspected Dylan wouldn't be pleased, and she fully expected him to say something about it. Something along the lines of 'I told you to stay away from my son,' like he thought she would pump Adam for information for a story.

Hope went back to work in the flower bed beneath the front window and waited for him. She waited no more than ten minutes until he strolled up her drive and into the yard. Except for his service belt, he still wore his sheriff's uniform, complete with mirrored sunglasses.

She stood and held out one hand as if to stop him. 'Before you yell at me, I asked Adam to make sure it was okay with you before I hired him to pull weeds. He and Wally left to call you, and when they came back, Adam told me that you'd said he could work in my yard.' She took off her gloves and held them in one hand. 'And in case you're wondering if I tried to wheedle Adam for information about you and Juliette, I didn't. Frankly, I don't care what you think.' The last was an absolute lie, but she figured it would be true enough someday.

Dylan shifted his weight to one foot and looked at her through his sunglasses. 'Are you through?'

'I think that's about it.'

'I came over here to ask if Deputy Mullins called you today.'

'Someone did, yes.'

'So you know that we think Myron has left town.'

'Yes. I know that's what you think.'

He raised one brow. 'You don't think so?'

'I know he hasn't. He's been calling me.'

'What does he say?'

'Nothing. He just breathes heavy.'

A frown curved his lips, and with two fingers he pushed the brim of his hat up his forehead. 'You recognized his breathing?'

'He's done this before. Unless there is another phone breather in town, it's Myron.'

'Could be he's calling from out of town.'

Hope shrugged. 'Maybe.' But she doubted it. 'Wait here while I get my purse. Adam ran off before I could pay him.'

'Forget it. Adam lied about calling me and asking permission to work in your yard. He doesn't get rewarded for lying. His punishment will be that he pulled your weeds for free.'

That sounded harsh to Hope. 'Are you sure? He worked pretty hard.'

'I'm sure, but in the future, he doesn't need my permission to work for you.'

'Are you saying it's all right?'

'Yes. Whatever happened between us, and despite what

you've done, I don't believe you would interrogate Adam for your paper.'

She supposed he meant that as a compliment. He probably was under the mistaken assumption that he was being nice – the big jerk. She threw her gloves to the ground and walked toward him, stopping just inches away. 'What *I've* done? I've done nothing, and someday you're going to realize you're a . . . you're a . . .' She was so angry and frustrated, she couldn't think of the right word.

One corner of his mouth twitched. 'A what?'

He was laughing at her. He'd broken her heart, and now he was laughing at her. She folded her arms beneath her breasts and said, 'A redneck sheriff who can't even find one dwarf. I could understand it if there was a Little People of America convention in town, but there's not.' His lips flattened and she pressed her luck. 'How hard could it be to find a man who isn't even four feet tall? It isn't like he blends.'

'I'll tell ya what, honey. If you didn't have such a unique way of making friends, you wouldn't be stalked by a dwarf in the first place.'

He'd called her honey, which only enraged her more. 'Get out of my yard.'

'Or you're going to do what? Call the sheriff? Get a pen and take down the number. It's nine-one-one.'

Hope stuck her hands on his chest and shoved. He didn't budge and she tried again, pushing hard enough to lift her heels off the ground. The momentum of her body carried her forward, and her hands slid up the creases of his work shirt. She slammed into the solid wall of his chest, knocking the air out of her lungs.

Dylan's hands grasped her waist, and for several prolonged seconds he held her as if he meant to shove her away. She saw herself in the reflection of his glasses, caught a glimpse of her shock and surprise, and then he wrapped his arms around her and pulled her onto her toes. He said something about leaving, but he lowered his mouth instead and kissed her. As always, he made her skin tingle and sent warm little shivers along her nerves. His hands swept her back as he pressed her into the warmth of his body. It had been so long and she missed him so much. She missed the scent of his skin and his touch on her. His tongue stroked hers, and the kiss caught fire.

Dylan groaned deep and in his throat, a sound of pure lust and frustration. It called to the deepest, basest part of her, and before she could answer, she did something she'd never done before. She found the strength to step away from his embrace before he sucked her in again.

She licked her moist lips and sucked air into her lungs. She felt dizzy and confused. He wanted her no matter how much he'd pretended he didn't. 'You're a liar, Dylan Taber.'

'Me? I'm the liar?'

It wasn't fair. It wasn't fair that she had finally found a man to love and he didn't love her back. 'You're a hypocrite, too.'

He took off his sunglasses and shoved them in his pocket. 'What the hell are you talking about?'

'You're angry because I lied about who I really work for. It was one little lie that just kept getting bigger and bigger and gained more importance than it deserved. And you're right, I should have told you before you found out, but you lied to me, too, Dylan. You lied when you told me Adam's mother was a waitress.'

'I had a good reason for that.'

'Yes, you never trusted me.'

'I was obviously right not to trust you.'

Hope grabbed her gloves from the ground. 'I'm tired of defending myself to you for something I didn't do. For the last time, I didn't call the tabloids.'

He looked at her as if he could stare a true confession out of her. 'I'll never know that for sure, will I?'

'No.' She shook her head. 'You never will, because that means you'd have to believe in me, without proof. It means you'd have to have faith in me, but you'll never do that, because you never really cared for me.'

'You're wrong.' He raised his gaze to a point over her head, then said, 'I cared.'

'Not enough.' She took one last look at the man she loved with all her broken heart. 'And I deserve better than a man who doesn't care enough for me.'

Myron Lambardo grabbed his Swisher Sweet between his stubby fingers and pulled it from the corner of his mouth. He blew a fog of cigar smoke and smoke rings toward the ceiling. If he had to spend one more day hiding out in his Winnebago in Paris's barn, he was going to go freakin' nuts. Maybe go medieval on someone.

He rose on his elbow and looked down into Paris's face. Beneath the sheet on his bed, her bare body was pressed to his. She was a nice woman, and he cared about her more than he'd cared about any woman, except for his mama, of course.

Paris could cook like nobody's business, and until two days ago she'd been a virgin. The first night she'd come to the Winnebago, they'd had sex, and it was still a bit unbelievable to him that he was her first. *She'd* chosen *him*, and that knowledge puffed out his chest and put a swagger in his step. It was just too bad he wasn't the type of guy to settle in one place for very long, because if he were, he could see himself settled with her.

'I wish you could go to the dance tomorrow night,' she said, all dreamy as she looked at him. 'They get colored streamers and decorate the grange for the Founder's Day

Ball. Everyone dresses up real nice, and they even hire a band. I could teach you the two-step.'

She already knew he couldn't be seen anywhere in town, but he thought it was real sweet of her to want to go dancing with him. Even if it was to crappy country-and-western music.

'I'm afraid I'm going to have to be leaving here soon.'

A frown settled between her brows. 'I don't want you to go.'

'Do you think I can hide here in your barn forever?'

She smiled. 'I've enjoyed having you here. It's been fun sneaking out.'

'Yeah, but I can't stay much longer. The thing is, I've been thinking of going to Mexico. Since the WWF won't sponsor midget wrestling, and Hope Spencer made everyone think I'm a pansy, I don't know that I have a future in this country. I've been thinking of making a name for myself in Mexico. It's always been a dream of mine to be one of the top wrestlers. Those guys get respect.'

She turned her face into his chest and he felt her tears. 'I'll miss you, Myron.'

He stuck his cigar in his mouth and rubbed her shoulder. 'I'll miss you. You're a good woman, Paris.'

'Not so good. I'm not proud that I got angry and called all those reporters up here.'

'If you hadn't, we wouldn't have met.'

'That's true,' she sobbed. 'And you're the best thing that has ever happened to me.'

Lost Woman Found in Wilderness

Dylan pulled the sheriff's Blazer off the side of the highway and parked in the shadow of a dense crop of pine. It was close to eight in the morning, and he positioned his radar to pick up speeders. Not that he thought he would get many. The highway was usually quiet this time of morning, but there were always a few stragglers late for work and pushing the posted limit. He radioed his location to dispatch, then sat back with copies of *People* magazine and *The Weekly News of the Universe*. He'd picked up both at the M & S this morning and flipped open *People* to the interview Julie had given them. He read about half before he became so disgusted he lobbed it into the back. She'd all but come right out and said he'd kidnapped Adam and brought him to Gospel to live. She'd made Dylan look like a jerk, while she'd come off smelling like a rose. He wondered how many people would believe her bullshit.

He reached for *The Weekly News of the Universe* and thumbed past a 'Bloodsucking Vampire' story to Hope's alien article. He chuckled a few times, thinking it was all pretty amusing, until he read on and discovered Dennis Taylor, the cross-dressing sheriff of the small wilderness town.

'Jesus,' he swore as he read about himself dressed up in a pink marabou teddy. The story reported that the sheriff always placed bets on how many unsuspecting female tourists he could lure up into the mountains under the guise of 'wanting to show them the most beautiful place on earth.' The sheriff in the piece didn't bet on broken bones, but on broken hearts.

He folded the paper and tossed it on the seat beside him. He was obsessed with Hope, there was no other explanation. Especially after he'd kissed her yesterday. He'd thought of little else but the texture of her tongue and the taste of her lips. His heart had pounded in his chest, draining the blood from his head and sending it to his groin, and in those short moments while he'd held her again, he'd felt an almost overwhelming . . . rightness. A feeling like every cell in his body whispered yes, and his hair stood on end.

He'd thought with each passing day he'd miss her less, but the opposite was true. He missed the tangle of her hair in his fingers, and he missed looking across his pillow and seeing her sleeping beside him. The other day in the M & S, he'd picked up a peach and smelled it before he even realized he'd been searching for the scent of her skin. Just this morning, as he'd reached into the freezer for a box of Eggos, he'd thought of her naked on his kitchen table, him buried deep within her body, her eyes filled with lust shining up at him. Remembering had gripped his belly and flushed his face, and he'd stuck his head in the freezer to cool down. Adam had walked into the room and asked what he was doing. He'd lied and said he was inspecting the ice cubes.

You really never cared for me, she'd told him, but she was wrong. He was in love with her. He'd been in love before, but not like this. For the first time in his life, the love he felt for a woman was total and consuming and he ached for the touch of her hand in his. Heart and soul, it went to a place so deep, he couldn't imagine living without her. It filled him up and left him longing for a glimpse of her smile and the sound of her voice. Something had to be done. Each day without her was worse than the day before, and as he sat in the sheriff's Blazer, morning light spilling through the windshield, he knew what he had to do. He had to believe her. Not just for himself, but for Hope also. He had to believe her without proof or witnesses. He had to listen to his heart, and to the deep-down part of his soul that knew about unconditional love and faith in another person. And in the end, he believed her simply because he loved her.

The radar's digital display flashed, and Dylan straightened as a small Winnebago with Las Vegas plates sped past. He pushed his hat down on his forehead and shoved the four-by-four into gear. His foot hit the gas pedal, and the Blazer shot onto the highway as he radioed the code. He flipped the switch to his grille lights, and within less than half a minute he came up behind the Winnebago.

He didn't know what to expect from Myron Lambardo. He hoped he didn't have a long chase ahead of him, and he hoped Myron didn't resist arrest. Dylan just didn't feel right about wrestling a dwarf to the ground. Especially a dwarf who knew how to tombstone.

The Winnebago slowed and coasted to the side of the road. Dylan parked behind the recreational vehicle and turned on the video camera mounted overhead. As he approached the driver's side, the window rolled down, and he got his first good look at Myron the Masher. He had to admit that the wrestler really did look a bit like Patrick Swayze, just more compact.

'May I see your license, please?' he asked as he took in the cab; then his gaze suddenly stopped on the woman sitting in the passenger seat. 'Paris?'

'Hello, Dylan.'

He stared at the woman he'd known for as long as he could remember. 'What are you doing in there?'

'I'm leaving town with Myron.'

Paris had never had much of a sense of humor, but she had to be pulling his leg. Myron shoved his license at him, and Dylan took it. He'd seen the same picture of the man when he'd searched the NCIC.

'Myron's going to teach me to wrestle. My wrestling name will be Sweet Thing,' she gushed.

Dylan glanced up from the license. 'Now I know you're kidding.'

Her pursed lips got all puffed up. 'Is it really that hard for you to believe that a man could want me?'

He felt as if he'd been transported into the twilight zone. Or one of Hope's stories. This could not be happening. 'I didn't say that, Paris.'

'Myron appreciates me. We're in love and going to get married as soon as we get to Vegas.'

She sounded serious, but really, how serious could she be? 'That might be a while. Your fiancé here has violated a restraining order.'

'But I'm leaving the country for good.' Myron spoke for the first time. 'I don't ever want to lay my eyes on Hope Spencer again. That broad ruined my life. Until I met Paris, I had no direction. I'm a new man now.'

'Sure you are.' Dylan studied the woman who looked like Paris but sure as hell wasn't acting like her. 'Do you realize you're involved with a stalker?'

'He's not a stalker.' She smiled at her fiancé and reached for his hand. She looked all soft. Like a woman in love. 'He's just persistent.'

'Well, his persistence is going to land him in jail.'

Paris's bushy brows lowered over her narrowed eyes, and

Dylan was exposed to a whole new side of the easy-tempered girl he'd known since first grade. 'Don't you dare ruin this for me, Dylan Taber. I've waited all of my life for someone like Myron. Someone who could love me. God knows I wasted enough time waiting for you.'

'Me?' Dylan took a step back.

'Do you think I baked all those cakes and pies for you for the heck of it? Didn't you ever notice that you were the only man in town I baked for?' She laughed, but it came out sounding very bitter. 'I bet you didn't notice. Especially ever since Hope Spencer drove into town. You're obsessed with her. Her with her blond hair and skinny behind.'

'Now, Paris,' he began, but stopped because he didn't know what to say. He'd always thought she baked because it was her hobby, and he wasn't altogether certain she was wrong about Hope. 'Do your parents know about this?'

'I plan to call them from Vegas.'

'I'll tell you what,' Myron interjected. 'If you give me back my license, I'll get the hell out of this state.'

As much as Dylan hated the thought of letting Myron off the hook, he listened while the man talked.

'As far as I'm concerned, Hope Spencer and I are square,' Myron continued. 'She ruined my life, but if it weren't for her, I never would have met Paris. By this time next week, I'll be in Mexico starting a new life with her, and you won't ever see me again.'

The alternative was hauling him back into town, booking him into custody, another court date and hearing that Hope had said she didn't want. Dylan handed back the license. 'You better make sure I don't see you. And you better not even think about bothering Ms Spencer.' He looked at Paris. 'Are you sure about this?'

'Oh, yes.' She went back to gushing, and her face softened once more as she looked at Myron. 'I've never been more happy in my life. I finally have a chance for a life outside of my parents' diner, and for a family of my own.'

Dylan thought he'd probably heard crazier, but he couldn't remember it if he had.

Paris reached for her big purse and set it on her lap. 'I was going to mail this to you,' she said and removed a stack of sealed envelopes and handed him one. 'But since you're here . . .'

He took it and stepped back. 'Good luck, Paris.'

'She doesn't need luck as long as she's got me,' Myron said as he shoved his Winnebego into gear and pulled out onto the highway.

Dylan stood on the side of the road until he completely lost sight of the vehicle. Damn, what a crazy morning. He walked back to the Blazer and climbed inside. Paris Fernwood marrying Myron Lambardo, a.k.a., Myron the Masher, a.k.a., Micky the Magical Leprechaun, and becoming a wrestler herself. He just couldn't picture her wrestling anyone.

He turned off the grille lights and opened the envelope Paris had addressed to him. He expected a membership to the dessert of the month club. Instead, it was a rambling, mushy note about how much she loved Myron Lambardo. Christ, all the *i*'s had little hearts above them instead of dots. At the end, she included a quick 'by the way . . .'

I never meant to hurt you or Adam. And I wish I could say I was sorry for placing a few calls to the tabloids, but how can I be sorry when that is what brought my true love to me.

Paris Fernwood – soon to be Mrs Myron Lambardo

Dylan reread the last paragraph three times before he crumpled the note and dropped it on the next seat. For a few moments he let rage tighten his fists on the steering wheel, but then he let it go. Knowing it was Paris and not Hope didn't matter now. Not since he believed Hope without proof, but last week it would have mattered. If he'd known last week, he could have saved himself a lot of misery.

When he thought of the nights he'd lain awake torturing himself about his troubles with Adam and Hope, anger again welled up in his chest, and he was extremely glad Paris was on her way to Mexico and no longer living in the same town. He didn't wish Paris harm, nor did he wish her happiness. In fact, he hoped some big Mexican señorita got her into the wrestling ring and tied her into a pretzel.

The Founder's Day committee worked long hours to come up with the perfect theme for this year's Founder's Day Ball. They fought and argued and finally drew straws. The winner, Boot Scootin' into the Millennium, was Iona Osborn's idea.

The outside of the grange had been given a fresh coat of green paint, and the inside had been decorated to reflect the wilderness outside. Thousands of foil stars hung from the ceiling and the air was scented with the freshly cut pines stuck in Stanley Caldwell's papier-mâché and wire masterpiece. It towered in the far corner, an impressive rendering of the Sawtooth Mountains.

Pete Yarrow and his band, The Wild Boys, provided the night's music. Pete's one claim to fame was his two guest appearances on *Star Search*, which was enough to make him a local favorite and all-around celebrity. The music was a raucous mix of country, bluegrass, and rockabilly. If Pete occasionally missed a note, the citizens filling the dance floor didn't seem to mind.

Beers were a buck fifty, a glass of wine two dollars, and a can of soda a dollar. Water was free from the fountain. The people of Gospel were decked out in their finest. The women in yards of tulle and lace, the men in suits, a few opting for the cowboy leisure kind.

Stanley Caldwell's monument of the Sawtooth Mountains stood in one corner of the grange, lit by a soft white light.

Hope stood in front of Stanley's monument, paying particular interest to the splash of blue glitter that represented Sawtooth Lake. Never big on tulle, she wore a basic black dress she'd bought in Sun Valley on one of her shopping trips. The dress was sleeveless, with a scoop neck, and fit tight against her body. Twin seams ran up the backs of her legs, and she'd shoved her feet into a pair of four-inch pumps. She'd curled and pumped up the volume of her hair and wore diamond studs in her ears. She looked good and she knew it.

According to Shelly, Dylan never showed up at the Founder's Day Ball, and since he'd been in such a bad mood when he'd picked up Adam from her house, she didn't think he intended for this year to be any different. Which was okay with Hope – she hadn't dressed with him in mind. Well, maybe just a little bit in mind. A little – just in case he showed – bit.

Even though she knew she looked good, she did feel somewhat out of place amongst the other women who'd decked themselves out in vivid color and foofaraw. Even Shelly, who usually dressed strictly for comfort, had squeezed herself into satin and sequins like she was a prom queen. She and Paul were out on the dance floor two-stepping their hearts out.

'Excuse me.' Someone spoke above the music. 'I don't think we've met.'

Hope glanced over her shoulder at an old lady clouded in blue net and gave a long, mental groan. The light from the mountain display shone through the woman's baby-blue hair and lit up her blue eyeshadow and lashes. Just like that day in Hansen's Emporium, Hope found herself staring in horrified wonder. It was like staring at a bad traffic accident. She didn't want to look, but she couldn't look away.

'We met in your emporium last week,' Hope reminded her.

'No, that was my sister, Eden. I'm her twin sister, Edie Dean.'

Egad! 'There are two of you?'

'Yep, but my sister prefers purple.'

Hope forced herself to look past all that blue and into Edie's eyes. 'I remember.'

'Iona Osborn over at the Cozy Corner told me you write those articles for that *News of the World.*'

'*News of the Universe,*' Hope corrected. 'How did Iona know about the articles?'

'Iona Osborn works with Paris, and last night Paris told her all about it.'

She supposed it was bound to get out sometime.

'Since you haven't been in town long, you've never met my brother-in-law, Melvin.'

'No, I don't think I've had the pleasure.'

'Pleasure, schmeasure. Melvin is a rat-faced, sheep-lovin' two-timer, and that's a fact. If my sister had the sense God gave a goat, she'd ram him with her Buick.'

Lord, not again.

'Now, I was thinking. If you needed those aliens in your stories to abduct someone, Melvin would be a good one. And when they beam him up into one of them spaceships, they should attach electrodes to his privates.' Edie held up a fist and shook it in the air. 'And give him a good zap!'

'Ahh . . . okay.' Hope took several steps sideways until she was lost in the crowd. She'd always figured there was a possibility that someone in Gospel would discover what she really wrote for a living; she just hadn't figured that it would be Paris Fernwood. And since Paris and Edie knew, Hope assumed everyone in town knew by now. She didn't really know how she felt about everyone finding out. Maybe a mixture of apprehension and relief. No more lies. No more secrets. Of course, she'd have to listen to everyone's ideas for her next article with a few life stories thrown in. But if a few of them cast disdaining glances at her for her articles, why should she care? They bet on broken legs and tossed toilets, and ate testicles, for goodness' sake.

Hope walked around the edge of the large hall, casting her gaze through the crowd as she made her way to the bar. Even though she knew better, she still caught herself looking for Dylan.

She ordered a glass of zinfandel and dug into her little black bag for her money. 'I heard about your articles,' Burley said over the music as he handed her the glass. 'I've never known anyone who's met Bigfoot before.'

Hope looked closely at his face and saw the humor in his eyes. 'I've never met Bigfoot.' She passed him the money. 'But I have interviewed several aliens and one possessed dog.'

He laughed and Hope turned away. She took a drink of her wine and scanned the dusky dance floor. The overhead disco ball shot sparks off Shelly's green sequins and Paul's emerald tie as he spun her around like a top. The song was one that Hope had never heard before, something about a cowboy and his pickup truck. She spotted Hazel Avery dressed in pink satin and dancing with a man Hope assumed was her husband.

Hope took another drink of wine and remembered the day Dylan had taught her to two-step. They'd been completely dressed at the beginning of the lesson but naked by the end. They'd made love on the bearskin in front of her fireplace, and now she wondered how many other women he'd stripped while he'd danced with them.

A tall, lean cowboy she'd never seen before asked her to dance, but just as she placed her glass on an empty table, Dylan stepped in front of the younger man.

'Take a hike,' he said and gave the cowboy a hard look. Then he added for good measure, 'Buddy.' Before she could say anything, Dylan grabbed her hand and pulled her along to the middle of the dance floor.

Once she recovered from the shock of seeing him there, of his touch and the sound of his voice scattering little shivers across her flesh, she looked up into his dark face, lit only by the disco ball hanging above his head. Slivers of mirrored light slipped through his hair and across his shoulders, which were covered in a nice navy wool blazer. He wore a white dress shirt and burgundy tie, and through the darkened shadows of the dance floor, she recognized the desire in his eyes. She'd seen it directed at her many times. She lowered her gaze to the knot in his tie. 'That wasn't very nice,' she said in a tight voice as he slid his palm to the small of her back. 'He asked me very politely. You didn't have to call him buddy like that.'

'That's his name. Buddy Duncan. He lives in Challis.'

'Oh.' She looked up again, up into his face and at the outline of his mouth. 'What are you doing here? Shelly told me you never come to the Founder's Day Ball.'

'Shelly talks way too much.' He tried to pull her against his chest, but she resisted. He wanted her. She could read it in his eyes and feel it in the restless way his hand caressed the small of her back, but desire wasn't love. And she wanted more from him.

'What are you doing here?' she repeated.

'Relax and I'll tell you.' He tugged harder and she lost

the battle. 'That's better,' he said and settled her against his chest. He bent his head over hers and spoke next to her ear. 'I'm here because you're here. When a man loves a woman, he wants to spend time with her. Even if that means he has to put on a suit and tie. He wants to hold her tight and smell her hair.'

His words pinched her heart, and she stopped trying to put distance between them. She was afraid to breathe. Afraid she hadn't heard him right.

'I've been thinking about what you said yesterday,' he said as they slowly moved across the dance floor. 'About me caring enough to believe you, and you're right. I should have believed you all along.'

She looked past his chin to his eyes. She had to know why he believed her now, although she feared the answer. 'Did you find out who really contacted the tabloids?'

In the few seconds it took him to answer, her hopes plummeted. He hadn't believed her. Someone had confessed. Nothing had really changed and they had no future.

'Yes,' he said, and she again struggled to put distance between them. 'Be still or I'll have to tie you up again.'

'Let me go, Dylan.' The backs of her eyes stung and she was afraid she would cry right there in the grange in front of the whole town.

'Honey, that's not likely to happen ever again.' His grasp on her tightened and held her so close she could hardly breathe. 'I found out it was Paris who called the tabloids, but by then it didn't matter any more. When you discover you love someone, you have to believe in them or you just cause yourself a lot of unnecessary misery.' His warm breath whispered across her temple when he said, 'I love you, Hope. My life has been miserable without you.'

She'd been so unhappy without him, she had to know. 'Have you really been miserable?'

'Yes.'

She smiled for the first time since he'd taken her into his arms. She felt like laughing and crying and curling up into his chest all at once. 'How miserable?'

He rested his forehead against hers. 'Every morning when I wake up, I get a real cold feeling in my gut, like something is missing in my house, like oxygen or sunlight. Something I need. Then I look over at the empty pillow and realize it's you I'm missing. And when I go to bed, I lay awake and wonder if you're thinking about me, too. Wondering if you miss me as much as I miss you.'

'Dylan?'

'Hmm.'

'I've missed you, too.'

The song ended and before another began, Thomas Aberdeen tapped Dylan on the shoulder and asked if he could cut in.

'Hell, no,' Dylan answered, his voice loud and clear, his eyes narrowed at Thomas. 'Go find your own damn woman. This one is mine!'

Well, she guessed their relationship was out in the open now. She placed her hand on Dylan's cheek and brought his gaze to hers. 'He didn't know I'm your damn woman.'

'Then I guess I better show him,' he said, then lowered his mouth and kissed the breath from her lungs. He bent her over his arm like he was Rhett Butler, and right there in front of anyone who cared to watch, the kiss turned hot and wet and so good. When he straightened, he placed his palms on the sides of her head and looked deep into her eyes. 'I want everyone to know I love you, Hope.'

'I want everyone to know I love you, too.'

A smile crinkled the corners of his eyes. 'I am glad you just said that, because I was thinking that I might have to take you home and handcuff you to a chair until you did.'

'You don't have to handcuff me. I love you. I've loved you since the day you showed me Sawtooth Lake. Probably even before that.'

He brushed his nose against hers. 'I know I messed things up between us, but if you'll let me, I'll spend the rest of my life making you happy.'

Hope blinked but couldn't stop the tears in her eyes. 'Then what are we doing here? Take me home.'

'Honey, I've been waiting for you to say that since I walked in.'

On the drive to the Donnelly house, Hope sat beside Dylan in the cab of his truck. She had her hand on his thigh and her head on his shoulder. The last time she'd ridden in his truck at night, she'd torn at his clothes, but for now, she was content to sit within the glow of the dashboard lights and listen to the sound of his voice. Later, there would be plenty of time for tearing clothes. She had the rest of her life. Right now they had something important they had to do. They had to talk to Adam.

She kissed Dylan's shoulder through his jacket and shirt, and he put his arm around her. Within the dark confines of the truck's cab, she felt as if they were the only people on the planet. Like the night she'd fallen in love with him at Sawtooth Lake. Her heart swelled and her head spun like poor upside-down Cassiopeia.

She listened while Dylan told her about Myron and Paris leaving town together and their plans to start a wrestling career in Mexico. Personally, she couldn't see it happening, but she certainly wished them success so that neither returned to darken her life again.

'I love you,' she whispered.

'I love you, too, but you know I'm a package deal. How do you feel about Adam?'

She didn't even have to think about it. 'He's a great kid, Dylan. He's smart and funny, and I like being around him.'

'Then stay with us,' he said and kissed the top of her head. 'Stay with us forever. I know it's asking a lot of you, but I'm asking anyway. I'm asking you to give up your life in L.A. for me, a man with a young son. I don't know how you feel about being a mama, and I know it's a lot to think about.'

It wasn't a lot to ask, and she didn't have to think about that, either. Not at all. She would be whatever Adam wanted her to be, a mother or a friend or both. 'Have you told Adam how you feel about me?'

'Yes, and while he wasn't jumping up and down, he did say he was going to find you a special rock. That means he likes you.' He picked up her hand from his thigh and kissed her fingers. 'I guess I need to find you a special rock, too. A big, sparkly one.'

'I don't need a special rock. I just need you.' She straightened and turned to his dark profile. 'Are you asking me to marry you?'

'Not right now.'

She supposed it was better to wait a few months. She wondered if he would want to wait a year.

'After we talk to Adam, I'm going to take you to your house and make love to you, and when you're all soft and happy and satisfied, that's when I'll ask.'

She laughed, vastly relieved. 'Why wait?'

'Well, I discovered that when you have an afterglow, you'll say yes to anything. Eating cake off your body, being tied up, marriage.'

She shrugged. 'Okay.'

She'd come to Gospel to find Bigfoot and aliens, but she'd found something else. Something better. She'd found where her heart belonged. The future was in front of her and beside her. She had Dylan and Adam and Shelly. She had her career, and just that morning she'd received an e-mail from *Time* magazine. She'd sent them a query letter, and they were interested in seeing her article on Hiram Donnelly. It wasn't a guarantee, but then, guarantees came only with toaster ovens. The rest was hard work and luck. Since moving to Gospel, she'd found herself and a man who loved her. She didn't need a guarantee.

Maybe next she'd write a book. A book about a small town where the people ate Rocky Mountain oysters and tossed toilets. Where two elderly twins dyed their hair and plotted the painful death of the other's husband.

Nah, Hope thought as the truck turned into Dylan's driveway. Fiction had to be truer than real life, or no one would believe it. No one would believe a town like Gospel existed outside of her writer's imagination.

Not even she was that good.